ZOMBIE BOYZ

LOVE NEVER DIES

GEOFFREY KNIGHT
ETHAN DAY
ETHAN STONE
DANIEL A KAINE
TJ KLUNE
ERIC ARVIN

Praise for
ZOMBIE BOYZ

★★★★★

"An incredible collection of brilliant stories by some of the finest authors today." *Reviews by Jessewave*

★★★★★

"A biting thriller that will tear your heart out and slay you with laughter." *Madison Reviews*

★★★★★

"This is the first anthology I've ever read (and I've read quite a few) where each story was an easy 5 stars for me."
On Top Down Under Book Reviews

★★★★½

"A really great collection and each story is quite distinct in the style from the rest - the whole thing was fabulous and the stories work together really well." *Joyfully Jay Reviews*

ZOMBIE BOYZ

LOVE NEVER DIES

GEOFFREY KNIGHT
ETHAN DAY
ETHAN STONE
DANIEL A KAINE
TJ KLUNE
ERIC ARVIN

WILDE CITY PRESS

WILDE CITY PRESS

www.theempirepress.com

Published in the US and Australia by Wilde City Press 2013

Published by Wilde City Press

ISBN: 978-1-925031-42-3

CONTENTS

Guess Who's Coming At Dinner

Zombie Boyz

Geoffrey Knight
Ethan Day

CHAPTER ONE
BEEFCAKE BOB'S BURGERS

"Is that what I think it is?" Grammy Gabby shrieked, her eyes bulging so big that her gigantic, tinted 70s-style specs slipped an inch down the bridge of her nose.

And all my studly zombie boyfriend Zane could do was grin that big, stupid, handsome, kinda-undead smile of his while he pawed and tugged at the raging tentpole erection in his ripped jeans and announced to the whole table in that animalistic tone of his, "Me haaaaaawny."

My mother dropped her fork. Clang!

My father started choking on his beans. "Blarrrk!"

My sister, Sister Mary Abigail, crossed herself several times and started talking in tongues. "Muhl-sun-lun-acka-clacka-yada-zirka-blirka!"

Grumpy Grampy cupped his hand around his ear to hear better and shouted, "What that little sonna-bitch just say?"

My drunken Aunt Tilly just chuckled calmly with a "he-he-he" and said, "He's a real tiger, ain't he!"

Zane took it upon himself to confirm Tilly's suspicions by growling at me as if he were an actual tiger before announcing loudly again, "Me horny, Chand-lerrrr!"

But wait, I'm getting ahead of myself. This story doesn't start with me wanting to curl up and die of embarrassment at my grandfather's ninetieth birthday dinner party. It began the day a boy named Zane Addison seemingly took notice of me the first time. Before the zombie apocalypse and all the hoo-ha that followed. He was human back then, and I was in love.

I still am, actually. Even more so than before.

Some things even a heinous, zombie-making-virus plague can't change.

Love is love, you know?

Of course, coming out to my family at my grandfather's birthday dinner with the shocking news that I was in love with a zombie…well…that was practically an apocalypse unto itself. You'd think it was the End of the World, Part Two…or hell… maybe it was actually like Three or Four at this point?

Who the hell can keep track these days?

But I digress into my own mini-existential crisis.

So yeah, this night was not going so well, and Grumpy Grampy's ninetieth was sure to go down in history as the night Chandler Cox died from embarrassment—

—or saw the first glimmer of hope for humanity's survival.

But perhaps I should start at the beginning.

I'm Chandler, nineteen years old and should be living in a college dorm at Harvard. But instead, I still live at home or did up until a few days ago. Why? Because like most other people on the planet, any plans I had for the future totally imploded after the Pandemic Transviral Apocalypse of 2013, which was swiftly shortened to PTA for tweeting purposes.

Trust me when I tell you, the parents and teachers were no longer using it anymore. My engineering dreams had vanished faster than a pallet of flatscreens from a looted local electronics store.

So cliché, right?

The world as we know it is under siege but hey, don't screw with our God-given right to life, liberty and our ability to access streaming content…bitches.

Along with the end of the global economy, public safety, and any chance of ever having a room to myself again – life as I'd once known it had evaporated before my very eyes.

I'd sat through all the motivational speeches about how we're all still human—at least some of us still were—and all the BS about how we can like, totally adapt and stuff…but holy hell, as selfish as it may sound, a teenage boy has needs, damn it!

While it's true that those needs don't technically suck up that much time, considering your typical nineteen-year-old guy can rub one out in a matter of mere minutes, the fact is I now sleep on the floor of my own bedroom while Grumpy Grampy snores his way through the night in my bed, dribbling on my once stain-free pillow. Let's just say that even though he can barely hear, his wheezing is a total mood killer.

He's so noisy!

Even Grammy Gabby refuses to sleep in the same room with him, preferring the tiny-ass cupboard under the stairs over sharing space with the cranky old coot. Not that she's a whole lot better with her constant complaining about her aches and pains. We put up with it because I guess we'd rather have them with us than out on the streets, all infected and begging for brains and shit.

Most days, anyway.

But this is what people had to do post-PTA. They started mending relationships, putting aside petty squabbles, and living in larger groups, because everybody knows that the family who hoards and boards together remains uninfected by the undead together.

To say that the PTA came out of nowhere is an understatement. Apart from Charlie Sheen, everyone else was leading a fairly normal life up until that point in modern history. I was starting my senior year in high school.

I hung out with my best friend, Dong.

I went to the movies.

I even worked my shitty part-time job, trying to save up enough money for my first year in college.

And I suffered the sling and arrows from assholes who hated my guts simply because I was gay.

Eighteen months earlier...

Pulling at the itchy gold and brown polyester Beefcake Bob's uniform, I pressed the intercom button with my free hand and spoke into the microphone.

"Would you like fries with that?" I asked.

"Are they free if I let you choke on my ten inch cock, Cox?" Laughter echoed through the speaker as the muscle car full of jocks tire-squealed its way around to the drive-thru service window. I rolled my eyes as I slid open the glass window, but I fully admit I couldn't completely look away as Brett 'Bruiser' Hayes rubbed at his crotch. "You probably like to swallow, huh Jack-hole?"

No comment.

"So that's a no to the fries, then?" I asked with a deadpan expression.

Let's press pause on this charming walk down memory lane for a second.

Being toe-tally honest, I think we all recognize the sexual tension at play here, am I right? Fucking meat-headed, teen age cock-jocks are the worst. I mean, really, get over yourselves already.

The DL is soooo nineteen nineties.

Call me crazy if you will, but that cheeseball machismo lingo Brett was forever spouting off at me sounded like total gay porn plagiarization.

Not that I'm a porn ho or anything, and my apologies to O. Henry and my English teacher for the bastardization, but the guy totally screamed Gift of the Tragi—closet queen to me.

This twisted little scenario was the sort of thing that happened on a regular basis, working the nightshift at the drive-thru of Beefcake Bob's. However, that particular night was different. For one, it was the first night that I really ever spoke to Zane, the high school quarterback I had watched out of the corner of my eye between classes and had breathlessly fantasized about while alone—night after blissfully hot masturbating night—over the past three years. You know, back in the good old days before Grampy moved into my room.

The second reason that night was memorable was because it had all begun that night. Yep, just my luck to have officially fallen heels over head in love the very same night that a zombie apocalypse kicked off.

Totally f'in rude, right?

That's the way the universe likes to fuck with poor tortured me, but I'm used to it now, I guess.

But for posterity's sake or whatever, I should get back to the point, back to the night I fell in love. Back to the drive-thru.

Eighteen months earlier...again...

"So whaddaya say, Cox?" Bruiser asked. "You wanna suck each of us off, you little jizz monkey?"

Brett was the captain of the football team, as well as a grade-A asshole.

From where I stood in my little booth, I could see Bruiser's bestie, Mike 'Mad Dog' Morgan, laughing so hard he could hardly catch his breath.

Clearly this meathead never tired of hearing the same lame-ass jokes.

I rolled my eyes, already feeling the boredom of defeat and humiliation setting in, which is when I glanced toward the backseat and saw him—Zane 'No Stupid Nickname' Addison. The junk inside my Jockeys totally twitched, and my heart went all aflutter; moreso when I saw he wasn't laughing like the other two in the car.

Nor did he look particularly impressed with Bruiser. In fact....

"Why don't you leave the guy alone?" Zane said from the backseat. "Let him do his job."

"I'll let him do a blowjob!" Bruiser kept on laughing. "Ain't that want you want, Cox? You wanna suck my dick?"

"Not particularly," I said matter-of-factly. "I'm sure your mom's a great person and all, but why would I wanna suck on what she had for breakfast?"

I was trying to act all cool and snarky in front of Zane, but all I managed to do was incur the wrath of the biggest asshole in town. Bruiser's stupid grin instantly morphed into a twisted barbwire snarl, and his face went beet-red.

Without warning, he pushed the car door open so hard that it slammed into the life-sized plastic statue of Beefcake Bob, knocking the caricature flat on its back.

"You little faggot, I'm gonna fuck you up."

Holy roid-rage, Batman!

I gasped as poor Beefcake Bob buzzed and zapped outside the drive-thru window, flickering for a moment before his light blew completely out.

I realized too late that my mouth had just issued a check it could, in no way, cash. Not even the cooler, hipper version of me that existed in a much happier alternate universe, where I was the most popular kid attending Shawnee Mills High, could've survived Brett the Bruiser wrapping his meaty paws around my scrawny neck.

But before I could slide the service window shut, Zane kicked open his door, launched himself from the backseat and seized Bruiser mere moments before the stupid thug could grab me.

"Let it go!" Zane ordered sternly in Bruiser's ear, his teeth clenched.

For a second, I thought I was going to faint, unsure whether it was the sudden jolt of fear or a lack of blood flowing to my brain, given that most of it had just rushed to my cock due to Zane's mega-sexy bout of heroics.

Bruiser let out a growl that kinda slurred into a furied, "One of these days, Cox."

I watched, near drunkenly, as Zane forced Brett back into the driver's seat—an added bonus for me, considering Zane's biceps flexed and rippled impressively in the process. After slamming Bruiser's door shut, Zane turned back to me while retrieving his wallet from his back pocket.

"Sorry about that, Chandler. Let me just pay for the burgers, and we'll get the hell outta your hair."

He tried handing me some cash, but I shoved their bag full of Beefcake Bob's Burgers into his big, muscly arms, all the while staring at him mildly dumbfounded.

"On the house."

Zane grinned sheepishly, which made him appear even sexier. I mean, I don't have a photo or anything, but you can totally take my word for it.

"Can't believe you know my name," I said—more like breathed it—the expression on my face no doubt stunned and stupid in that Looney Tunes, hit-with-a-mallet kinda way.

Zane laughed, visibly curious as he tossed the bag of food through the driver side window onto Brett's lap. "You look shocked by that fact."

"I just.... I wasn't...." I shook my head attempting to rid myself of any last remaining pretense that I might manage coming off cool or collected. "Of course you know my name. We've been in the same class since...."

"2009," Zane said, shoving the bills back into his wallet. "When I first moved to town with my folks. You were the hall monitor back then. Everyone knows the hall monitor."

"Yeah, everyone knows the hall monitor," I agreed. And everyone gives the hall monitor a good punch on the arm when they pass by for being such a nerd.

Except Zane.

He never once punched me.

Suddenly the blare of a horn combined with the buzzer from the drive-thru menu made me jump. Zane, of course, barely flinched.

"Come on, Zane, you fuckin' faggot-lover." Bruiser barked. "Get back in the car, and let's get the hell outta here. We got a party to go to!"

The man of my dreams winked at me then and said, "Gotta go. Maybe I'll see you around sometime."

"That'd be great," I said, way too shocked and quiet as I watched him climb into the back of Bruiser's car.

I pressed the intercom button so it would finally stop bleeping at me as Bruiser's car jolted forward with a screech of tires, then harshly braked before backing up to the window, almost running into the next car in the queue.

Bruiser leaned out the driver's window shouting, "Hey, loser. You can keep these."

With astounding accuracy, he hurled two slices of warm pickle, each smacking me in the face, splattering bits of ketchup and mustard all over me. I stood there completely stunned for several moments as Bruiser and Mad Dog Mike cackled while their muscle car peeled off into the night.

The pickles slowly slid down my chin and cheeks as a BMW, filled with skanks I may or may not have recognized from school, pulled up to the window.

They all started laughing at me as well.

"Does anybody actually work in this dump?" asked the pretty blonde driver, sounding exceedingly put out.

"What are we even doing here, Wendy?" one girl whined. "This place is like a fatty's paradise."

"We can't drink on an empty, Val, unless you wanna skank out like you did last weekend, Gang-bang-Becky."

The Val chick slumped back into the seat with a scowl as the second pickle slid off my chin and landed on the dirty tiled floor with a plop.

"Welcome to Beefcake Bob's Burgers," I muttered in a flat, well-practiced tone of humiliation. "May I take your order?"

* Z * Z * Z *

Nobody knows for sure exactly how it happened since it's been one of those re-active apocalypses instead of the pro-active variety showcased in fine films such as Armageddon and Deep

Impact.

The most popular theory on Facebook—which is now reportedly run from a bunker six miles underground that Mark Zuckerberg built in the event things ever got really nasty with those hot twin nemeses of his—revolved around a diseased bat, run out of its natural habitat due to deforestation, that ended up biting a feral cat which, in turn, puked up the grass it had eaten to try to cure itself. The pukey grass slow baked in the ridiculously hot global-warming-zero-ozone-layer-gamma-ray sunlight, where it was eventually eaten by an overly hormoned, genetically-mutated cow which incubated the deadly virus that some scientist subsequently named: ZD7HY_L*8-djgfkagse.

It's a tricky name to remember, I know, but that's because the scientist naming the virus accidently contracted the disease and died while in the process of lodging his findings. The name was the apparent result of a face-plant onto his keyboard, followed by his head rolling over the Enter Key, which officially logged the name for the virus with the World Health Organization.

But none of that really matters, because if the media and online world has one talent, it's giving things a catchy name so we mere mortals can remember them.

And the name that caught on after the virus began wreaking havoc on humankind was none other than Beefcake Fever.

Why, you may be wondering?

Well, it probably had something to do with the fact that the spread in the US began that fateful night at Beefcake Bob's.

Eighteen months earlier...again...only the very next day after that whole drive-thru drama we covered before...

"Have you seen the fucked-up-ness happening in China, dude?"

Dong rushed toward me, waving his feather boa and weaving so dexterously through the crowded school corridor that I thought he was going to break into song and dance, which was something he actually did. Often.

Thankfully, Dong was entirely too distracted for any musical-montages today, retro or otherwise. At least for the time being. However, when it came to Dong, songs were like weeds. One could pop up at any moment.

"What are you about to post on Tumblr now?" I asked, already in a bad mood after someone—aka Bruiser—decided to carve the word Sux into my locker door between the words Chandler and Cox, which I had so carefully penned in marker one day against all school rules and regulations in an attempt to claim my territory. It was my 'killing Tristan Ludlow' moment, just like when Brad Pitt cut off his beautiful locks after Legends of the Fall and decided to go cross-eyed for Twelve Monkeys. It's called finding your voice and being true to thineself. I wanted the world to know that this locker belonged to Chandler Cox…rebel without so much as a pause!

Unfortunately, the locker now belonged to Chandler Sux Cox.

Not completely inaccurate, mind you, but the atrocious spelling and grammar was probably the more heinous crime committed on this day in our world history. But it inspired my furthering the dialog by whipping out my Sharpie in order to clarify that, Chandler Sux Cox, except when they're attached to illiterate, ignorant assholes who are unable to spell sucks correctly.

A little wordy, I admit, but I was having a moment, okay?

"Way to take back your power, bitch," Dong said dismissively.

Sometimes surviving high school revolved solely around maintaining control over the content. I was gay, yes, but I had standards, damn it.

I smiled at my bestie, who'd already gone back to fretting over whatever was loaded onto his iPhone.

"Cows!" Dong suddenly shouted in my ear. "Killer cows!"

"What the F are you talking about, dude?" That was my normal bad mood response when trapped within the hallowed high school halls of Shawnee Mills High, where using your grown-up words was apparently still a no-no. Lesson learned after receiving two weeks of detention when my Chemistry teacher, Mrs. Venable, overheard me telling her to go fuck herself.

Dong held up his mobile phone for me to inspect something on the screen.

At that moment, Bernie Brewster cruised past and hollered loud enough for everyone around us to hear, "Stop watching porn, you homos, and get a room. We all know you wanna slip your kong into Dong and have a gay ole time."

Giggles filled the corridor before Dong shouted, "Shut up, Brewster. You're the biggest queer-bait ho-bag I know."

"Don't judge me." Bernie snapped back with a finger shake. "I was born this way."

"Do not use Goddess Gaga for your defense, Slutster."

Nose in the air, Bernie turned, only to come face to face with the BMW blonde skank from the drive-thru last night.

"Watch where you're going," Bernie snapped, throwing in a head-bob for good measure. At which point, blondie's cheeks suddenly puffed like a blowfish before she projectile vomited all down Bernie's face and chest.

Bernie gasped in horror.

Kids eeeeeewwwww-ed and gagged in unison as they scattered like rats.

The barf bitch—who would forever, from this day forward be known only as Vomie-blonde—raced for the nearest bathroom, mortified.

I muttered, "Gross," before Dong spun me around and pointed to his phone once more.

"Not as gross as this. Look."

I flicked through images he'd hacked aka 'downloaded' from the net. "What is that in the cow's mouth?"

"Only a human foot," Dong said, eyes widened.

"This little piggy didn't make it to market," I said flatly, cracking a smile.

"It's a massacre. The cows have turned on their farmers. Ate them all. One minute they were regurgitating cud from their second stomach—"

"TMI, dude."

"—the next they were eating people's faces."

I squinted, attempting to determine if this was merely another in a very long line of photoshopped National Enquirer specials, but I had to admit the blood-stained, entrail-covered mouth and crazed eyes of the cow looked real.

"An entire herd of them turned into rabid beasts. It was like that scene with the double-decker bus in An American Werewolf in London. Except these were cows, not werewolves. And they weren't in London but otherwise? Nearly identical!"

"Where was this?"

"A village in Qinzhou Province in China. Very remote. But this could spread, dude. Trust me. I know pop culture, and pop culture has been prophesying this for years. Pop culture always prophesizes the future."

"Um, Exhibit A would be...?"

"The Truman Show. That movie pre-dates reality TV. Absurd at the time; now it's all we watch."

"Correction, all you watch. Is there an Exhibit B?"

"Glee! Who knew that being a singing, dancing geek could make you popular?" To demonstrate, Dong did his best prima donna twirl through the air, at which point someone passing by threw their drink all over him.

"See?" he said, shaking the water off his feather boa.

"Not cool, asshole!" I yelled after them.

"Thank God they banned soda from campus," Dong said.

"That Michelle Obama is one determined woman."

Dong nodded. "Militant anti-fatty, right?"

I nodded. "I'm afraid to ask, but is there an Exhibit C?"

Dong broke into his best zombie walk and let the words, "The Walking Dead," fall out of his mouth like broken teeth.

I shook my head and grabbed the books I needed for my next class from the locker. "Pop culture does not prophesize the future, Dong."

"Of course it does. What rock have you been living under?"

"That would be my mother's."

"My advice to you would be to buy a shovel and start building a shelter in your backyard before it's too late."

"Oh, we've already got one of those," I said, a little too excited by the knowledge I might actually be ahead of the curve for once. "Our house used to belong to Grammy and Grampy. We have this real-life bunker left over from the Cuban Missile Crisis. There's even fourteen crates of baked beans still down there. Although why someone would wanna feed people beans in a sealed, airtight bunker is beyond me."

"But that's a good thing. I mean about the bunker, not the beans. You've got somewhere to go when the apocalypse arrives."

"And when are these killer cows expected to be here to exact their revenge against humanity? I mean, when was this footage taken? Yesterday? Last week?"

"According to the Chinese press, it's recent. But these pictures could have been taken months ago for all we know. The killer cow virus could already be spreading, and we wouldn't even know it. I don't trust the Chinese. These are my own people. I know what they're like, though you can't trust any government."

"Dude, you're Korean, not Chinese."

Dong glared at me angrily for raining on his paranoia-parade. "Why are you the only American who knows the difference?"

"Because I'm your bestie, my fine feathered friend." I reached out and tugged on his boa, regrettably so, considering it was still wet. "And best friends are full of good advice. And my advice to you is to stop worrying about the end of the world, go dry off your shirt and get to class before you wind up joining me in detention."

Suddenly someone else puked in the corridor, sending another excited, grossed-out wave of squeals down the hall.

I looked up and saw who it was.

My dreamboy, Zane.

I wanted to rush to his side to help him, to see if he was okay. But as he raised his head, wiping those thick, full lips of his with the back of his hand, our eyes connected, and I could see the look of embarrassment on his face. I stayed where I was, knowing he didn't want my help.

At least that's what I tell myself now; I'm so not good with the vomit.

Looking back, I will always wonder how differently things might have been if the PTA hadn't ruined my life.

* Z * Z * Z *

I didn't see Zane at school again the rest of that day, not surprising considering everything had completely gone to hell by fourth period. More and more kids had begun vomiting during the day throughout classes. The nurse's office got so full they had to set up stretchers in the cafeteria in order to house all the sick kids. Not exactly a decision made by geniuses, mind you. Anyone who's ever eaten cafeteria food would know it's a horrible place to take anyone with a weak stomach.

By 2 p.m., the principal shut the entire school down and ordered everyone home, casting us all out of a frying pan and into a raging fire.

Parents with crazed looks in their eyes came to pick up their kids, but a lot of them didn't make it. Their cars ran off the road and slammed into trees.

Somewhere in the northern part of Shawnee Mills, an airliner came crashing to the ground, sending up a pillar of smoke that blotted out the afternoon sun.

Dong and I ran home together. I dropped him off at his place first, and we hugged on his front lawn. It was something we had never done before, but we were frightened.

I suddenly realized that our bond had been built on late night phone calls about Say Yes to the Dress and confused questions about Lost, about being picked on and teased and taunted, and about sharing the pain we so vehemently denied. I figured out then that some of the strongest bonds in human history had been built on these things.

Well, maybe not that whole Lost thing, but you know what I mean.

Suddenly I didn't feel as scared.

We pulled out of our embrace awkwardly, neither of us wanting to part.

"Will you be okay getting home?" he asked.

I nodded. "I think you might have been right. About the killer cow thing," I said apologetically. Freaked, but also totally annoyed that he'd been right.

Dong's bottom lip began to quiver. "We may not see each other again. I think I should sing something—"

I held up my finger to stop him. "If you break into Lana Del Rey right now, I swear I'll kamikaze myself with a rock from your parent's garden."

"Okay," Dong said, obviously re-thinking his initial plan, "What about Maureen McGovern? There's got to be a 'Morning After'? Right?"

I shook my fists. "We are not in an upside-down ship! We are in a world that is going to hell!"

"ABBA then?" Dong nodded with a smile. "Best happy-goodbye-songwriters ever!"

I smiled, my way of letting him know that I could deal with that. I squeezed his hand and he said, without singing, "Hasta mañana, Chandler."

I teared up before I could stop myself, letting go of his hand and once again hugging him as fiercely as I could manage. "Till we meet again, Dong."

"Don't know where," Dong whispered. "Don't know when."

I wanted to continue squeezing him, terrified that if I let go now I truly never would see him again. Before I had a chance, my best friend since third grade broke away and went running toward his front porch, crying as he rushed into the arms of his panicked parents.

They shuffled Dong inside and the door closed.

I heard multiple bolts sliding and locks clicking.

While Dong had been born in the USA, his parents had grown up in South Korea before relocating to Indiana. But once you've had North Korea for a next door neighbor, I suppose you get used to precautions.

I looked at Dong's door one moment more, wondering when mañana might come.

An explosion down the street ripped my thoughts back to the survival of my very own hide. My entire world had changed in a matter of hours.

So I ran.

* Z * Z * Z *

You know things are bad when the air becomes filled with sirens.

Police sirens.

Ambulance sirens.

Fire truck sirens.

Car alarms.

Burglar alarms.

And finally, nature itself sounding its own alarm in the form of barking dogs, shrieking flocks of birds, and the screams of your fellow man, who were already saying "fuck you" to their neighbors and fending for themselves.

That's when I heard another sound.

"Chand… Chandler?"

I'd been sprinting home as fast as I could, sneakers pounding the pavement as my backpack swung left-right-left-right across my shoulders, when I passed a tree and heard the strained voice calling out my name.

I turned sharply and stopped at the sight of Zane leaning against the trunk, barely able to stand. Dark circles had formed under his eyes, and his normally tan skin was pale.

And yet, he still looked kinda hot.

So not fair how some people manage to pull off sexy no matter how shitty they look.

"Zane, you okay?"

He shook his head in response to my first stupid question.

"Can you walk?"

He collapsed to the ground in response to my second stupid question.

"Should I call an ambulance?"

As if on cue, an ambulance tore down the street, wailing with urgency. And swerving precariously. I stared at it wide-eyed, so surprised that my body failed to react when the vehicle began to veer straight toward me.

That's when Zane somehow found his feet long enough to make a desperate lunge for me, like the football star he was, tackling me to the ground and knocking me out of the ambulance's path mere seconds before it would have plowed into me.

With a metal-crunching crash, the ambulance nosed right into the tree that had been holding up Zane only moments before.

The driver's door swung open, and the ambulance driver leapt from the vehicle, its siren still howling like a cat in heat. Without so much as a backward glance, the driver bolted, abandoning his vehicle and running as fast as he could down the street.

The back doors of the ambulance also exploded open, and a second screaming EMT took off in the opposite direction, blood trailing from his ear. Seconds later, a crazed woman who looked like the offspring created by the unholy union of the Creature from the Black Lagoon and Mrs. Epstein, our math teacher, sprang from the vehicle in hot pursuit of the bloodied EMT.

I blinked in shock, then heard another pained cry from Zane on the ground beside me.

Having saved my live twice in the last twenty-four hours, I felt I owed it to Zane to rescue him from whatever was going on. Even though he was now foaming at the mouth.

God, he even made that look sexy!

I quickly shook away any and all completely inappropriate thoughts about self-lubrication—

—so not the time, asshole!

A blood curdling scream somewhere off in the distance was all it took for the adrenaline to kick in. I jumped to my feet, wrapped my arms around Zane, and hoisted him up over my shoulder.

Okay, so, that was the intention at any rate.

I grunted, attempting to keep myself upright. To my puny credit, I managed to stumble about for a moment. Unfortunately, with Zane being all muscle and almost twice my weight, I weaved and I bobbed before we toppled over onto the grass. He fell back and smacked his head on the ground, letting out a loud "Arrrgh!"

Through the bubbles he managed a guttural, "What…are…you…doing?"

"I'm saving your totally hot ass."

I gasped, clutching my shirt for the briefest of moments, unable to fathom what sort of mental breakdown could've caused me to refer to his ass as hot outside of my own head.

Apocalypse be damned—teen angst knows no bounds, people.

"Chandler," Zane wheezed, staring up at me, visibly frightened despite being so sick.

"Plan B," I said, grabbing him by the ankles.

Minds out of the gutter, slut-bags. Honestly.

We both grunted and gasped as I hauled him one inch at a time toward the ambulance. As I did so, his jeans bunched up around his crotch and the bulge was more than impressive, not to mention slightly distracting. However, in his current state, I figured he wouldn't even notice me taking a nice long look while I dragged his sick, sorry, sexy ass along the ground.

Surely my totally selfless, Good Samaritan-like efforts deserved some sort of reward, for crying out loud.

Once we made it to the ambulance, I tried to sit him up again, though I was fairly certain he'd gained weight during the drag. I fumbled awkwardly with his limp, yet totally muscular arms. His sweaty, sexy armpits smelled like heaven and, that tightly-toned torso of his was hard as a rock.

But it was no use. Apart from a good fondle—hey, my intentions were noble—I couldn't get him up into the back of the ambulance.

With a floppy finger, Zane pointed into the ambulance and groaned, "Gurney."

"Right," I said excitedly.

Der, way to impress the man, dumbass.

I pulled the gurney out of the ambulance, trying not to focus on the bloodstains and chewed-through straps. Rolling Zane on the gurney was way easier than trying to lift him up, even if he did end up face-down. I didn't have time to roll him over, not when I noticed the horde of people, all screaming and growling as they turned the nearest corner.

They spotted me in no time and started staggering our direction like a bunch of angry drunks.

I pulled and yanked every lever I could find on the gurney till it finally sprang to waist height, nearly catapulting Zane into the air. I held him in place as I shoved the gurney into the back of the ambulance. With a glance over my shoulder at the blundering, stumbling mob getting closer by the second, I slammed the back doors shut and jumped into the driver's seat, quickly locking both doors.

The keys dangled in the ignition.

The mob of moaners appeared large and scary in the side mirrors.

I heard several loud thumps as they reached the ambulance and pounded on the back doors, frantically trying to get inside and attack my Zane.

I said a quick prayer as I turned the key, grateful once the engine roared to life. I punched the gas pedal and gunned the engine—a macho choice of words, I know, but I was suddenly feeling so butch and brave that I heard myself shout, "Get away from my man, you bitches!"

With that, I rammed the vehicle into reverse, stepped on the gas and backed into the crowd of crazies as hard and as fast as I could. We bounced over several of them, like a 4WD you see on a camping trip in one of those exceedingly manly beer commercials.

If I hadn't been terrified for my life, I'd have totally sprouted some serious wood over my newly discovered masculinity.

I changed gears again and turned the wheel hard, screeching through the horde as they threw themselves in front of the ambulance.

One or two slid down the windshield as I slammed the accelerator all the way to the floor. Bounce-thump-bounce. Hands like twisted branches snapped off the side mirrors as though it might slow me down. But nothing could stop me from plowing through that bunch of lunatics and getting the hell out of there.

Sadly, that wasn't the only mob I had to cut through to get Zane to the hospital. Even though I took every back street I knew, the number of zombified freaks only seemed to multiply with every mile.

When I finally screeched to a halt on the street just outside the road that led to the hospital's emergency entrance, my mouth fell open. I wasn't able to physically turn into the drive due to the gridlock of cars and stretchers and panicked people blocking the road.

It finally sunk in that we were living in a war zone.

Staying up all night to finish my physics assignment? Yeah,

screw that, I thought, officially chalking it up to a complete waste of my time.

I took a deep breath, more determined than ever to get Zane all the way up to the front of the line. Gunning the fragile engine one last time, the entire cab rocked side to side as I jumped the curb and drove straight through the landscaping and across the well-manicured lawn. The 'little ambulance that could' slowly crept just under the awning in front of the emergency room before it gasped and sputtered its final breath. Between the tree and all the zombies I'd run over, she'd certainly seen better days.

Exiting the cab, I ran around back and unloaded the gurney like a pro. Wheeling Zane around the people suffering from shock, the capsized wheelchairs and in between the nose-to-tail abandoned cars, we made it to the sliding doors of the emergency room entrance.

The automatic doors had turned lunatic like everything else, opening and closing in random spasms, so I did my best Jason and the Argonauts maneuver, sailing through as fast as I could without getting us squished.

The hospital was even more crazed inside than out.

People were running, shouting, crying, and collapsing everywhere I looked.

I grabbed at random strangers. "Are you a doctor? Are you a nurse? I need help here."

I was frantic until I looked down and saw that Zane was awake again. We stopped long enough for me to finally help roll him onto his back. He took my hand for a moment, his way of letting me know he was grateful.

Before I knew it, an exhausted looking woman in a green gown descended upon us, shining a small flashlight into Zane's eyes.

"Is he okay?" I asked.

"We'll take him from here," the woman said without so much as looking at me. "Another one! Here!" she shouted over the chaos to a manic orderly trying to round up a group of hysterical patients.

"Another one? What does that mean?" I demanded.

But the doctor had vanished back into the crowd as quickly and quietly as she'd appeared.

From his gurney, Zane grabbed my hand once again, holding it tight. He looked me in the eye and faked a smile, his teeth perfect and white... and frothy. "I'll be okay. You need to get... to your...family."

Oh God, my family! He was right. My mom would be completely terrified and freaking out by now, while my father would no doubt be puttering about, calmly trying to find the right-sized nails in his toolbox to board up all the doors and windows.

"But I can't leave you," I told him. "I refuse to leave you alone."

He squeezed my hand, and for one moment the entire world fell away. I couldn't hear or see a thing apart from him as he said, "I'll be fine."

Suddenly, the moment was gone as an orderly shoved me aside, announcing, "We have to take him now."

My hand began to slip from Zane's so I tried going with them.

He squeezed my fingers even tighter, holding on to the last touch.

"Chandler!" he called out, sounding scared for the very first time.

"Will you stop, damn it!" I pleaded, trying to walk faster as people bumped into me like obstacles attempting to rip us apart.

"Always wanted to tell you," Zane began, using what little strength he had left to sit up slightly. "When you were the hall monitor, I never needed any of those hall passes."

"What do you mean?"

"Just an excuse...to see you."

Then suddenly the gurney jerked, whipping around a corner faster than I'd anticipated.

His fingers slipped from mine.

And before I knew it—

—Zane was gone.

* Z * Z * Z *

"The Cubans are coming!" Grumpy Grampy shrieked. "Duck and cover! Duck and cover! And hide my goddamn cigars, they'll wanna loot those first!"

This was the cry of panic that met me as I rushed through the door of my house.

Followed quickly by the blast of a gun and my mother screaming, "Eat lead, you zombie-freak!"

An actual shotgun!

Fired at me!

By my own mother!

As the door behind me partially exploded, I covered my head and screamed, "It's me! Don't shoot!"

Splinters from wooden door rained upon the ground as my mother, gun in hand, gushed apologetically. "Oh, I'm so sorry, dear! I've never used one of these before and I thought you were one of those things out there! I'm just terrified at the thought of one of them breaking in here and killing us all!"

My head cocked to the side as I brushed several pieces of wooden door shrapnel off my shoulders.

"I may have gotten a smidge carried away, there. My goodness that was exhilarating." Mom put the gun down and apologized again for nearly killing me. "I'm sorry, Chandler, dear. I hope I didn't startle you."

I stared at her blankly, more frightened now than I had been when the gun was going off.

"Let me fix you a snack. You must be starving. How was school, dear? Tell me all about your day. Have you asked that darling Deidre May out yet? She's sweet on you, dear, and it's not nice for you to string a sweet girl like that along, you know."

I was fairly certain she'd rattled all of that out without taking so much as a breath in between. I rolled my eyes and sighed my frustration over my mother's fascination with the girl who lived next door. "Let it go Mother. Deidre and I are classmates and will never be anything more."

She huffed, scowling at me. "Step away from the door, dear, your father's about to board it up."

As if our speaking her name had conjured her out of thin air like the infamous Bloody Mary, my mother and I both shrieked in horror as Deidre May began clawing and scratching at the hole my mother had just blown through the front door.

I bumbled several steps backward till I was standing next to my mother, each of us looking on in horror.

Deidre's eyes were crazed, and she hissed my name over and over like some love-sick undead freak straight from hetero-hell. Flashes of a prom gone horribly wrong filtered through the back of my mind, and we both jumped slightly when she ripped a small chunk of wood off the door and began chewing on it, momentarily distracted.

"Still think we'd make a great couple?" I asked, as we stepped away from the front door.

"Nobody likes a smart ass, dear," Mom said.

"I found just the right sized nails," my father announced proudly, coming around the corner. He held several of them up as proof just as Deidre kicked open the door.

She howled like a zombie freak straight from the bowels of hell, and my parents and I all screamed simultaneously, completely frozen in fear.

Deidre made a beeline straight for me as I fumbled blindly along the wall; finally grabbing hold of the shotgun Mom had nearly killed me with only moments before. I frantically pointed and pulled the trigger without a second to spare, which sent both me and Deidre flying backwards in opposite directions.

I landed on the living room floor with a thud and a grunt, accidentally pulling the trigger once more, sending my entire family into screams and wails as I put a hole into the ceiling.

Deidre sailed back out the front door, screeching in a pained groan that curdled my blood as she landed in a heap on the front lawn.

The world seemed to go dead quiet as I got up off the floor, eyes still wide as saucers. My parents and I slowly crept down the hall toward the open doorway.

Dad began clamping the nails between his lips like a tradesman while juggling the hammer and several planks of wood. I could hear all three of us breathing heavily as we stared out toward the lifeless corpse in the yard, still smoking slightly from the bullet wound.

"Let me help," I said, offering to take a plank from my father with a renewed sense of urgency.

"No, no, no, son. I can do it. Although you might like to watch how I do it. There's a particular way that will ensure—"

We all jumped slightly, seeing Deidre's body twitch back to life.

"Dad!" I screamed, slamming what was left of the front door shut in a panic. "The streets are full of murderous zombies! Just hammer the fucking wood across the door already!"

Mom and Dad both stiffened with shock at my outburst, making a point to pass judgment over me.

"Language, darling," my mother said after a moment's pause. "I realize things aren't exactly normal outside, but can we try to keep them normal inside."

"The little sonna-bitch got a point though," Grampy said, tapping his hearing aid so hard we could all hear the feedback. "So shut your pie-holes and secure that door 'fore that she-hag comes back to life and kills us all!"

"She used to be such a sweet girl," Mom declared as she grabbed the stack of wood planks from my father.

Grampy grumbled something under his breath as I took the pieces of wood from her one at a time and held them up while Dad hammered in the nails with impressive speed and precision.

We were humming right along with only two more pieces to go when Mom muttered, "At least all the supplies we purchased two years ago for the extra room that never got built won't completely go to waste."

I sighed, listening to my father groan his disgust, while praying he didn't turn the hammer on her. I'd seen enough gore for one day.

Grampy snorted. "At least I didn't let you two drag me out of that retirement home for nothing. Tonight's poker night, goddammit. I was gonna bootleg two bottles of my own homebrew when the nurses weren't lookin'."

"Homebrew?" I asked.

Dad just shook his head, indicating that I didn't wanna know.

"Where's Grammy Gabby, anyway?" seemed like an appropriate question to change the subject.

"Oh she's up in your room, dear," Mom answered. "Grampy will be bunking with you until all this nonsense blows over. She's doing a little re-arranging so all of Grampy's things fit. You know…." My mother made a strange, awkward gesture at that point, as though she was patting a large, invisible fanny on her behind while mouthing the word diapers.

I wasn't sure which hit me first, panic or nausea, but I didn't wait to analyze it. I charged straight upstairs to my room, leaving Dad to fend for himself with my Mom.

I had to push my bedroom door open twice, since the first time I burst in so hard that the door hit the wall and bounced back to slam me in the face. My second, more wary attempt, revealed my pint-sized, giant-spectacled grandmother sitting on my bed with one of my gay porn magazines in hand.

"Oh, Chandler, you're home, good. I could use your help. I was trying to get your grandfather's suitcase under the bed but a whole pile of these magazines were in the way."

Kill.

Me.

Now.

"I'm so glad to see you're getting more into fitness these days. You could do with a few muscles." My heart stopped when she began peeling back the cover to take a peek inside. "Your grandfather and I are always saying how scrawny you—"

I sailed through the air and dive-bombed my very own grandmother in an attempt to knock the magazine out of her hand.

Grammy squawked as I bounced off the corner of the mattress and hit the floor with a thud. We both scrambled to our feet in time to see that my mission had epic-failed. The magazine had naturally fallen open revealing the smoking hot Charlie Harding centerfold, a glaring indictment to the fact I'd apparently over-appreciated that particular photo so often that the mag was now conditioned to automatically open to that page.

Grammy Gabby shrieked as she glared at Charlie's amazingly huge boner staring back up at her from the floor.

I gasped, trying to knock the glasses off Grammy's face so she couldn't see.

As if I couldn't make things worse, I misfired and ended up slapping my own grandmother in the face.

If I wanted to distract her from an eyeful of the hunky Mr. Harding and his hard-on, I had officially achieved my goal.

"What are you doing?" she shrieked.

I didn't know what to say except, "Grammy, the streets are filled with zombies. We all need to toughen up and start accepting reality."

She violently shoved me away from her, apparently still irritated by that accidental slap. "I'm 87 years old, Chandler. Not blind and stupid."

I heard the distinct Birkenstock stomp of my emo sister coming down the hallway. She pushed open the door to my bedroom and glared at me like the bride of freakin' Frankenfurter that she was.

"Chandler, what the hell are you doing to Grammy?" She glanced down and added, "With your gay porn on the floor?"

"Jesus, Abby! How many times do I have to tell you to knock first? And don't you know there's a zombie apocalypse happening outside? God, why is everyone in this house determined to focus on all the wrong things?"

"Chandler, you're the queen of denial," my sister said with a black lipstick sneer, crossing her lace-gloved forearms like some sixteen-year-old Rocky Horror dominatrix. "Always staring at Zane Addison like some sort of stalker-freak. He's way out of your league, loser."

Considering I was still worried about Zane and what might have happened to him, all I could come up with was, "Shut up, freak. You don't know."

Effective, huh?

"Perv," Abby said, rolling her eyes, which were so coated in eyeliner and mascara they looked like a charcoal painting that had been smudged into oblivion, before storming off.

I slumped onto my bed, defeated and humiliated.

Grammy Gabby sighed, clearly disgusted as she pushed her enormous specs up her nose before shaking her finger in my face. With one badly drawn eyebrow crooked to the heavens, she made an "A" sign with her fingers and said, "Awkward!"

"How do you even know what that means?" I said, making the "A" gesture too as my grandmother stormed out after my sister, her little shoulders shrugging as she departed my room.

Indignantly, I scooped up the porn and hurled it into my closet, wishing I could crawl back inside there with it and hide until I was dead. I could already hear Grammy Gabby screaming from downstairs announcing that I was one of them big, giant perverted queers.

I closed my eyes and took a breath to calm myself, but all I could see was that frightened look in Zane's eyes as they wheeled his gurney away from me earlier at the hospital.

I had two choices in that moment: anger or tears.

In an indignant huff, I hurried downstairs after my grandmother and sister, choosing distraction over fear.

Mom was peeking out through the curtain and calling to Dad who was carrying larger boards of wood in from the garage and stacking them against the wall in the hall. "Dear, you might want to hurry it along with the boarding up the house plan. I just saw a crazed horde chasing Mr. Berkowitz down the street."

Grammy Gabby was visibly irritated that no one seemed to be affected by the news that I was a sicko penis puffer.

"I never realized those motorized wheelchairs could move that fast," Mom continued, sounding impressed. "Perhaps we should think about one of those for Grampy?"

"I'm right here in the damn room," said Grumpy Grampy. "Why don't you ask me if I want one first?"

"Grampy, would you like—?"

"Not on your damn life. Those things are for old people, and I ain't dead yet, you know." He paused for a moment, probably so he could catch his breath before screaming, "Arrrrrggghh!! Zombie!!!!!!"

Grampy stared wide-eyed, pointing out toward the patio where one of the hideous creatures had appeared, her hair all knotted and twisted, feet stumbling and shuffling, her boney hands reaching out for my father.

Dad fell backward in fright and started spider-walking across the floor, scrambling toward the shotgun.

Mom and my sister both screamed.

Grampy did a slow, awkward duck-and-cover maneuver, hiding under the dining table.

I actually winced at the sound of his bones cracking.

Grammy waved her hand casually in the air. "Don't panic. It's only Aunt Tilly." She turned to my aunt, now shuffling clumsily through the open sliding glass door and asked, "What, did you run out of vodka or something?"

Aunt Tilly hacked up something that looked like a hairball, which made a rather disgusting splat as it landed on the floor, before flipping Grammy off and heading toward the kitchen. All she said in response was, "Yes."

She followed it up with a loud humph for greater effect.

Grammy shouted at my father, "Board up that damn door, before anyone else gets in. We don't have enough beans for the whole neighborhood."

"I'm your sister," Tilly huffed, the fumes of alcohol sweeping through the house like a blastwave.

"Dammit, Chuck, you're way too slow," Grammy told Dad. "Gimme that hammer, and I'll do it myself."

Abby and I seemed to be the only ones concerned by the fact Aunt Tilly appeared to be infected. Of course, I wasn't a hundred percent sure either considering she was a raging alcoholic. She did appear to be slightly green, and she had a bite mark on her arm, but that wasn't exactly the first time I'd seen something like that on Tilly either. She was a bit of a slut, even at seventy-six.

The sounds of nails being pounded into wood echoed through the house. I looked around at the rest of my family—the people I was about to be sealed inside with—and couldn't help but think that this was what it must feel like to be hammered into your own coffin.

"Would someone help me up?" groaned Grampy from under the table.

"You got yourself there, help your own damn self up," Grammy shouted back.

"Dear, once you're done boarding up the house, you might wanna look at that leak under the bathroom sink," Mom said, pulling out the vacuum to clean up the debris from the blasted door.

"Will do, dear. I'll add it to my list of chores on the fridge."

"If anyone needs me I'll be in my room," my sister grumbled, "for like, all of eternity. Or whatever."

"Do we have any cranberry juice for this vodka?" Aunt Tilly asked, leaning against the kitchen door frame with a bottle in hand.

I sighed, wondering if I might have been better off taking my chances out on the street.

CHAPTER TWO
BEEFCAKE FEVER

My father pulled the generator out of the basement and tinkered with it till he got it working. We raided the old bomb shelter in the backyard when all was quiet in the neighborhood and filled the kitchen cupboards with tins of beans. And over the next few months, we pretty much hunkered down in the house as the PTA ran its strange and frightening course.

For the first few days, we watched the chaos unfold on live TV as MSNBC and CNN went into a ratings war, trying to get the best footage possible of towns under siege and cities on fire and middle-class families running from marauding mobs.

"Mommy, my feet hurt in these shoes," a little girl tearily complained in one piece of footage.

"They'll hurt even more when a zombie's chewing them off," her mother snapped back. "Now move it, young lady!"

A lot of investigations were also launched—some classified, some wiki-leaked—all concentrating on what caused the virus which, as Dong had suspected, originated months ago in the Qinzhou Province of China. Somehow, the media pieced together enough sketchy reports to confirm that the disease came from mosquitoes that were hatched in stagnant pools of nuclear waste found outside the old reactors of Qinzhou. The mosquitoes transferred the virus to cows in a nearby field, many of which were unknowingly sold over a period of months as part of the beef trade. Eventually, they were turned into beef patties, frozen, and exported to thousands of fast food chains around the world.

First stop: Beefcake Bob's Burgers!

Which is when the zombie virus named ZD7HY_L*8-djgfkagse quickly became known as Beefcake Fever.

Overnight, the entire planet became vegetarian, except the zombies, of course. Meanwhile, the world's top scientists quickly began trying to figure out exactly how Beefcake Fever affected the human brain, turning its victims into moaning, drooling, lumbering, cannibalistic monsters eager to eat their own friends and family. They rounded up countless zombies and conducted thousands of experiments, releasing findings that made headlines using words like: Groundbreaking! Astonishing! and Hopeful!

One of the first revelations was that zombies and cows were somehow able to communicate. Endless footage was released across the web showing zombies and cows together in the same laboratory mooing at one another. Zombies imitated the way cows moved, the way they chewed food, and even took to defecating on the floor simultaneously.

One female zombie the science community named Daisy even learned how to milk herself. Needless to say, I was scarred for life after watching that one.

Other findings were far more shocking, however, like the fact that some zombies could apparently access their human memories. It seemed to occur in varying stages as evidenced by a video of one zombie child who was filmed cuddling a doll from her human childhood before biting its head off.

To be fair, the zombie child did appear remorseful for a few moments after the dolly decapitation, but rumors circulated about zombies who were able to reject the symptoms of the disease, if not the disease itself. Apparently, it occurred most frequently in individuals who were desperately in love at the time they were infected.

The phenomenon became known as the Aberration-amoureux.

According to scientists, a couple of important things happen to human beings when lost in love: a dramatically heightened production of dopamine and norepinephrine coupled with a highly active caudate nucleus, which is part of the primitive reptilian section of the brain. Our brains become drenched in chemicals that give us laser-sharp focus, stamina, and determination when we're in love. It's that whole Romeo and Juliet effect that drives people to risk personal peril, willing to kill and die for one another, moving mountains and crossing continents the world over just to be with the one they love.

Individuals suffering from the effects of that particular emotion managed to counteract the innate savagery created when the human brain is attacked by the virus. The human side of the host is able to cling to the memory of that connection to its life pre-PTA.

"That could explain Aunt Tilly," I said under my breath, as I continued to read the news article aloud to myself from the computer monitor.

"The slut," Grammy Gabby muttered as she passed by my bedroom.

"Awkward," I said, reviving the already-overused "A" formation with my hands.

Seriously, once the grandparents start doing it, you know it's no longer cool.

I suppressed my urge to choke and gag over the completely unhealthy relationship of the so-called older and wiser elders in my life, concentrating on the next passage from the online news article instead.

Zombies had a blatant affinity for fornication, which apparently took hold regardless of age, gender, or any touchy-feely emotional connections to their previous lives. They were an undeniably horny bunch, often seen blundering out of dirty magazine shops with armfuls of pornos or filmed participating in these throbbing, massive zombie orgies, which often took place right in the middle of the damn street.

One video showing a middle-aged, naked zombie dude taking a massive shit while diddling his Oscar-Mayer was definitely the most disturbing thing I'd ever laid eyes on.

Of course, we learned these things from the media until the major networks and news outlets stopped broadcasting altogether, probably due to ever-dwindling staff numbers. After that, we were left with social media for updates on the crisis. YouTube, who according to rumors had the forethought to lease some bunker space from Mark Zuckerberg, carried new footage daily.

This was, of course, filmed by amateurs and proved to be the start of the turnaround in some people's attitudes towards the zombies.

Why?

Because this was when the unprofessional Jerry Springer-watching 'real people' started in with practical jokes and zombie bashing.

The first craze was called blanking. Much like planking, it involved a certain pose, this one being a zombie pose. Friends would film each other in an apparent state of zombification, as though they had been turned, and watch their loved ones scream and howl and run in fright as they laughed hysterically. Of course, occasionally, blanking resulted in tragedy, like the poor kid who was shot in the head by an uncle who had served in Afghanistan.

The lesson the world learned that day was that imitation had its price.

The second craze was targeted at the zombies themselves. Because of their slow and stupid state of being, kids would douse everything from old gym socks to home-made bombs in pig's blood before hurling them into the path of a staggering, stumbling horde. Drawn by the scent of blood and the promise of food, the zombies would devour whatever was thrown their way, chewing on old footballs and swallowing explosive devices. A few teens occasionally became overly cocky, getting too close with their lures and ended up losing a finger or a hand or a face.

That's when the craze morphed into what became known as zombie-fishing. Pranksters would hook their bait on a fishing line and dangle it out a second story window. Many found this hilarious since, after consuming the bait, zombies couldn't figure out how to get the hooks out of their mouths. That got old pretty quick though. I mean, really, if you've seen one zombie filmed wandering the streets dragging along entire rods on the ground behind them, you've seen 'em all.

As I watched those videos, I couldn't help but look for Zane, scanning the jumpy badly-filmed footage for his face, wondering if he was still out there. Was he still human or was he one of them now?

The guilt was eating me up. All I had was time and each time I closed my eyes at night, trying to sleep through Grampy's hacking and wheezing, all I saw staring back at me through the dark was that same frightened look in Zane's eyes as they wheeled him away on that gurney.

I never should have left him there to begin with, and the thought that he might be out there somewhere, frightened and alone, tore me up on the inside. Mom could tell that something was up with me, but I had the perfect excuse lying in wait just outside our boarded up house – the PTA.

I never once laughed while watching the videos. In fact, I found them kinda sad. Apparently, I wasn't alone. A lot of other people weren't very happy with the zombie bashing either, considering a movement to protect the zombies began. It was the subject of much debate.

"I can't believe my own granddaughter is a zombie lover!" Grammy Gabby shrieked, bringing her wrinkled fists down on the dining table and making all the cutlery clink on our plates.

"Grammy, I'm not a zombie lover. I just think it's cruel the way they're being treated."

"But Abby dear," my Mom said. "They're monsters. We saw them eat Mrs. Hodgens across the street, remember? "

"Was the damned zombie equivalent of an all-you-can-eat buffet. Those undead assholes chomped on her for days," Grumpy Grampy piped up. "I always said that woman needed to go on a diet. All that unpleasantness coulda been over in a few hours if she'd have lain off the damn Fluffernutters!"

"But don't you see?" Abby argued. "That's just who they are now. They're not eating because they're monsters. They're eating to survive."

"I agree with Abby," I chimed in. "Zombies are no different from tigers or lions or sharks, most of which are now protected species. The zombies are simply feeding themselves, doing the only thing they know how to do. None of this is their fault. They didn't ask to be zombies."

"Poppycock!" Grammy snapped. "People these days need to take more responsibility for their actions. You youngsters got no idea what it means to stand up and fight, you're all too busy sexting on your damn phones and complainin' that us old folk messed up the environment. You think we littered? Take a look at all the crap out on the streets now. It ain't my generation takin' the rap for that shit, little miss sunshine."

"But those zombies used to be people," I said. "Some of them could be my friends."

For a moment, the whole table fell silent and stared at me in shock before they burst into laughter. Even my sister, who I thought was on my side.

"You never had any friends, you dork," Abby said, nearly choking on her beans.

"Except Dong," my Mom said, her defense a subtle mask for mockery as she wiped her tears of laughter away with her napkin. "But dear, he's not out there. We know he's okay."

This was true. A week or so ago, while surfing the net, we stumbled across a hijacked episode of Korean Idol on You Tube, featuring Dong doing his best "Bad Romance." Personally, I was thrilled for several reasons, most importantly because someone needed to take up the Gaga mantle after she'd been unfortunately eaten by a rabid group of her 'little monsters.' Nepotism kinda bit her in the ass, literally and figuratively.

But all in all, I was pretty proud of Dong, and happy he and his family somehow made it out of the country.

"Chandler, you've got your family," my Dad said, chuckling and scruffing up my hair as though I were still seven years old. "That's all you need."

My sister grinned deviously across the table and did a frighteningly good Freddy Krueger impression. "We're your boyfriend now, Nancy boy."

"I was just defending your stance to protect zombies," I said indignantly.

"What's going on?" Grampy demanded, jiggling his hearing aid. "Has Chandler got a boyfriend?"

"No! I don't have a boyfriend!"

"Why the hell not?" Grampy demanded.

I shrugged my shoulders in disbelief. "Oh, I don't know, maybe the zombie apocalypse has something to do with it."

"You know, when I was fighting in the Bay of Pigs, I met me several young Havana hunks, if you know what I mean." Grampy winked at me.

I nearly threw up in my mouth.

Mom began humming as she glanced upward toward the ceiling, as if refusing to have heard a single word.

Grammy slammed her hand down on the table. "Grampy, you were never in Cuba! You're dreaming these things."

"Really?" Grampy looked confused, then rather happy. "That was a good dream."

"Keep it in your pants," Grammy growled before turning to the rest of us. "He's gonna turn ninety in a few weeks. After all these years together, you would think I'd heard everything from this man, but the surprises keep on comin'."

"Then it's probably a good time to tell you I slept with him. Twice."

We all turned to see Aunt Tilly standing in the kitchen doorway with a bottle of vodka in her hand. To be honest, I wasn't completely sure whether she'd ever left the kitchen since we'd first boarded up the house all those months ago. Tilly had been carrying a torch for Grampy for as far back as I could remember, we all knew that. The adultery, however, was a bit of a news flash.

"You what?" Grammy breathed in fury, her eyes darting from her sister Tilly to Grampy and back again. "Is this true?"

Grampy promptly took his hearing aide out of his ear, dropped it on the table and smashed it repeatedly with his fist until it lay there dead. He then turned to his wife and shouted at the top of his voice, "What was that dear? I can't hear a thing."

He wasn't lying, because he didn't flinch a muscle as the night outside suddenly filled with the most God-awful moan any of us had ever heard. It was a low and loud, sad and mournful.

A bellow.

A cry.

A moo?!

It grew louder and louder until it was so deafening it even stopped Grammy from launching at Tilly with every claw the old cat had left.

Of course, it wasn't so deafening that it disturbed the deaf. So as Grampy sat there oblivious to the noise outside, the rest of us rushed to the boarded-up windows and peered through the cracks in the planks.

We saw flashing lights outside, something we hadn't seen for some time. They were coming from several large military trucks crawling down the street. On the back of the trucks were numerous Marines armed with assault rifles, and mounted on the roof of the lead vehicle was an enormous speaker blaring a recording of a cow mooing.

And behind the vehicles, hobbling and teetering along in a trance-like state, was a gigantic horde of zombies that was growing by the minute. As the trucks made their way slowly down the street, more and more zombies climbed out of Dumpsters and the burnt-out shells of cars and joined the parade.

"Just like the Pied Piper," my Dad said.

"Except with zombies instead of rats," Grammy added.

"And a cow recording instead of a flute," I said, rounding off our obvious but somewhat stunned statements.

A moment later, we all jumped at the sound of heavy pounding on the boards that used to be our front door. It was followed by a loud, stern voice.

"Is there anybody in there? This is the US Marine Corps."

We all started shouting and clamoring at the door at once.

"Hello!"

"Yes, we're here."

"What's happening?"

"Have you come to save us?"

"Is it over?"

"Do you have any vodka?"

The marine shut us all down with, "Please be advised this is not a rescue mission. Are there any zombies in your house?"

"No," we all answered, with the exception of Grammy who bluntly asked, "Does my drunken whore of a sister count?"

"What's going on?" my father asked, all of us ignoring Grammy's question, including the marine.

"Sir, we're rounding up all the zombies to test a new vaccine."

"Vaccine?" My voice suddenly full of hope for the first time in a long time. "You mean they've found a cure?"

"Scientists believe they may have something, yes sir."

We all jumped up and down excitedly.

"There will be an announcement made shortly so if you have a radio keep it on at all times," the marine continued to shout through the boards. "We're working on setting up a new infrastructure and getting power completely restored to all of Shawnee Mills. In the meantime, stay in your house. Listen out for any new broadcasts. And God bless America!"

"God bless America!" Grumpy Grampy suddenly hollered from his seat back at the dining table.

Apparently his deafness was more what you'd call selective hearing, but no one seemed to care, not even Grammy.

I rushed straight up to my bedroom and shut the door, collapsing into a heap on my mattress on the floor. It was the first inkling of real hope we'd had in all the horrible months that had dragged slowly by since this nightmare had begun. All I could think about was Zane. I closed my eyes and prayed to anyone who might be listening that Zane was okay and out there somewhere. Waiting for me.

CHAPTER THREE
SANE WITH ZANE

The television stations started broadcasting again in the weeks after the Marines came through the area rounding up all the zombies. The sound from the news broadcasts was intermittent, and the flickering picture was often covered by a blizzard of interference, but at least we weren't stuck having to watch only You Tube anymore. The first reports on the vaccine hailed it as the miracle cure we had all been praying for. Indeed, many people starting thanking God for saving us all, and many found their faith for the first time, including my own sister.

Yes, the bitter, twisted, sarcastic teenager I had somehow learned to grow and love after having been locked in a house with her for well over a year, suddenly saw the light in Jesus Christ.

I supposed she was already halfway there with all the crucifixes in her drawer of emo jewels and treasures, most of which had originally been part of some sort of fanatic infatuation with all things Victorian and vampire. She just lost the heavy eye make-up and black lipstick. With all the black clothing already part of her wardrobe, she was able to easily repurpose her look into something I called nun-pimp chic.

Of course, my sister had never been big on church life before, and didn't really know what finding God entailed until Grammy started giving her flack at the dinner table one night.

"I'm hungry. Can't we eat now?" Grammy was getting twitchy. A hungry Grammy was never a good thing.

"Just a moment longer, Grammy," my mother said, trying to keep the peace. "Abby has—"

"Sister Mary Abigail," my sister interrupted passive-aggressively.

My mother paused long enough to sigh her frustrations before continuing, "Sister Mary Abigail has discovered her devotion to the Lord. We should all join her in prayer to thank Him for His blessings."

"We joined her ten minutes ago, and all she's done is bow her head and mumble. Next thing you know she'll be speakin' in tongues!"

Abby looked up at Grammy. "What do you mean, speaking in tongues?"

"You know, power of the Holy Spirit talking through you and all that palooha!" Grammy then went into her own impression of speaking in tongues, which was really quite scary. "Mulli-arga-dohinra-tala-yabba-dabba-do!"

If my sister hadn't received her calling by this point, she certainly had now. And that calling was to the most annoying, attention-getting, born-again Christian imaginable.

Within moments of Grammy's mock possession, Abby's eyes rolled back, her shoulders began to shake, and her head swayed around on her neck like a stack of dishes on a juggling pole. She then capped off her 'rapture' by launching into a non-stop, nonsensical monologue of complete and utter babble.

"Oh for Pete's sake," Grammy mumbled, rolling her eyes and digging into her dinner.

My mother looked at Abby curiously. "Dear? Sister Mary Abigail? Are you okay, hun?"

"What's the matter with her?" Grampy pointed at my convulsing sister with his fork. "I can't hear a word she's sayin'."

"I think she wants to go dancin'," Aunt Tilly offered groggily. She'd been passed out at the table with her head lying next to her plate of beans, and was only now coming to, what with all the commotion going on. "You wanna go dancin', baby girl? Aunt Tilly will take you to the hottest club in town, pick us up a couple of young studs. What do you say, girlfriend?"

"Tilly, you're seventy-seven years old," Grammy told her. "The only stud you could pick up at this point is the kind that's being hammered into a frame to hold up the wall." With a poke of her finger she pointed at Grampy and added, "Or him."

"That reminds me," my father muttered to himself. "I must

fix the stud in the wall joist beneath the stairs. Have you noticed there's a slight crack there, dear?"

"No dear, I hadn't," Mom replied politely. "Make sure you add it to your list of chores on the fridge. Don't forget, now."

"I won't, dear. I'll add it to my list of things to remind myself to add to the list on the fridge."

Sister Mary Abigail slammed her palms down on the table, her head on the verge of spinning. "Blaka-blirdaka-tanagrisda-falaka-din-mahza-birumpfa-soldana!"

All I could do was sigh and ask, "May I be excused?"

"Why of course, dear," Mom said. "You're not hungry? Are you feeling okay? I hope you're not coming down with what your sister's got."

"God, I hope not," I said, and with that I headed up to mine and Grampy's room. I flicked on the old-timey TV set on the floor beside my mattress, toying with the rabbit ears in an attempt to stop the picture from jerking to the left of the screen.

There was a new report on the round-up of the zombies and the latest news on the vaccine.

The trials had been a success.

The drug was working.

I turned the volume up as the footage showed a compound filled with thousands of zombies, all queued up obediently awaiting their next round of vaccine shots. A reporter, flanked by military guards, stood in the foreground.

"Calm, controlled, almost human again," the reporter said to the camera. "That's how authorities are describing the zombies following the success of the first round of trials from this ground-breaking new vaccine. The Viral Antidote—discovered by Dr. Julius Johansson and now dubbed VA-JJ or, as it's more commonly known, VAJ—"

I liked that the reporter on screen had trouble keeping a straight face as he uttered the tag-word aloud, which despite the spelling, totally sounded like vag-ina.

"What every homo in the world is looking for, a vag vaccine."

I snickered over my own funnies as the reporter continued, "—the vaccine suppresses the impulses in the brain that trigger violence along with curbing and controlling appetite. Zombies have been responding positively to the drug, with reports that one patient actually starting playing with a kitten after just one treatment. It's not all good news, however. The vaccine has no effect on the libido of the zombies, creating fears of a zombie population explosion."

"Awesome," I muttered, rolling my eyes. "So, no end in sight for those 3 a.m. scream and howl-fests that accompany the mindless zombie orgies."

I could see the reflection of my sneer in the screen of the television. I was actually just jealous. I mean, aside from that whole disgusting raw, people-sushi cannibalistic thing, zombies got to roam free instead of being under house arrest and they got to party like it was 1979.

"Great," I said, dry humping the mattress. "Now I have a hard-on just from thinking about it."

I did my best to force all the inappropriately hot zombie gang-bang fantasies starring Zane out of my head so I could try concentrating on the news cast.

"The other downside of the drug is that it wears off quickly in the beginning and must be constantly re-administered every twenty-four hours for the first month, giving the drugs ample time to break down the virus so its effects can begin to be reversed. This hands-on process places a huge strain on our already depleted medical and military resources. As a result, the government is asking for your help. It's a step considered by many to be bold and risky but for now, completely voluntary."

At that moment, as the camera panned over the crowd of zombies, I saw him. Zane. His eyes blank. His mouth agape. His body swaying slowly from one foot to the other as he stood in line waiting to be injected.

"I could inject him!" I declared courageously to television. "Let me be the one to take care of him. I want to volunteer!"

* Z * Z * Z *

Getting out of the house was no mean feat. Mom flustered about, packing too many canned beans in my backpack and pulling at the tags on my shirt and jacket to write my name on them in case I got lost or zombified. "How about your underpants, dear? Do they have your name on them?"

"Mom!" I went about swatting her hands off me. "I'll be fine."

"Where's that little bastard going?" Grampy was grumbling.

"He's off to volunteer for some new zombie vaccine program," Grammy shouted in Grampy's ear. "God knows why."

"He'll get eaten out there." Grampy said, before embracing the bright side, "Does that mean I get my own room now?"

Dad pulled away enough planks for me to squeeze through the boarded door, and I hugged him and Mom goodbye before heading out into the night. Behind me, I heard the planks being hammered back into place, followed by the sound of my mother's tears, along with some crazed Christian jibber-jabber from my sister.

I walked by moonlight along the footpath I used to take to school. Once upon a time, I used to pass by Mr. Drayson on a jog with his happy Golden Retriever on a leash. I would wave to Mrs. Plimpton pruning her roses and run to catch the bus before it left without me.

Now there was not a soul in sight. It was like those end-of-the-world docu-dramas that used to be on The Discovery Channel. It was both easy and frightening to imagine myself the last person left on the planet.

Cars littered the street, left where their drivers abandoned them. I passed by the house where I'd stumbled across Zane that afternoon—the very same tree the ambulance had plowed into—chest aching unlike anything I'd ever experienced before.

I felt the spring night air on my face and remembered how much I had once loved that breeze, filled with the scent of orange blossom and backyard barbecues. Now it was heavy with the stench of distant buildings ablaze and the rotting flesh of the unfortunate, still decomposing victims of Team Zombie. I sighed, watching the trash blowing down the street like tumbleweeds.

Seeing it all firsthand was very disheartening and a sadness fell over me, heavy and oppressive.

I wondered what I was doing out here.

What exactly was I trying to prove?

Was this some sort of atonement?

Was I trying to absolve myself of the guilt of handing Zane a contaminated burger that night? Or leaving him at the hospital the next day?

Or was this something different?

Something new?

Something I had never truly felt before.

Perhaps the fear and hope for a love I'd once thought to have lost forever?

The fear of hoping for a love I may never find again?

At that moment, I heard galloping behind me, the long stride of large hooves. I turned, terrified, to see two giraffes galloping down the street. Zoo escapees, I guessed, now trying to figure out what to make of their future, just like the rest of us. When they saw me on the street they slowed cautiously, and for a moment, as if to reassure themselves that they still had one another, they wrapped their necks around each other, the moon full and bright behind them.

It was a moment I'll never forget.

Surreal.

Perfect.

Crazy.

This whole situation was crazy. Everything was insane now—my family, this whole, infected world, and most of all me for walking these streets in the un-dead of night with no real idea what the hell I was doing. I looked around and saw nothing left of the world we once knew.

We'd lost it all.

I understood in that moment that I truly had nothing to lose aside from my own life, and the world had already been schooled in how fleeting life could be. But a life without Zane would be impossible now that I knew he was out here, somewhere.

That's when you strap on a backpack and go out into the night, hopeful for what you might find.

* Z * Z * Z *

The compound was so bleak, it looked like something out of a grim World War II movie or contemporary Russian rom-com. The entire grounds were flood-lit by blinding industrial lights. Coils of barbed wire lined the high walls of the buildings. Guards were everywhere, their rifles at the ready and belts full of grenades wrapped around their waists.

Hundreds were crowded around the entrance to the facility, desperate to get in. I was surprised. More people were here than I ever imagined might have braved the night, but it didn't take long to figure out why.

I stood on the edge of the throng of people, not wanting to linger too long, but an armed guard eyed me suspiciously, obviously trying to weigh up whether I was a zombie or not.

As he raised his rifle, I wasn't sure how to prove I wasn't infected. I panicked. I didn't know what to do.

So I started doing the dance to "Single Ladies."

My put-a-ring-on-it moves weren't exactly Beyonce' standard, but the guard lowered his weapon so I guess they were remotely recognizable. That or I displayed enough coordination to be deemed human.

Relieved, I wasted no more time before pushing my way into the crowd to avoid any further suspicion. That's when I noticed them. My hands. They were empty. The rest of the crowd were all holding pictures. Some still had working smartphones they raised high into the air, hoping one of the officers might recognize their loved ones. Others were holding framed pictures or, in some cases, photos half crumpled in their anxious hands. Everyone was looking for someone.

With each photo came the cries and the pleas.

"Have you seen our son? Is he in there?"

"Our daughter was only seven. We dropped her off at school and haven't seen her since."

"His name is Ricky. He needs his medication. I have it here."

"My mother suffered from dementia. She wandered off. I'm so frightened, please help me."

"I'm all alone now. Can you please let me in to see if my family is there?"

It was a heart-wrenching scene, and I understood why they'd chosen not to show any of this on the news.

I looked at the man standing next to me, rubbing his bald head with fear and hope and concern. He looked at me and said, "If you get inside before I do, if you see my little girl, please grab her. Please get her out of there. She's only six. Her name's Zoe." He shoved a picture at me of the cutest little girl with red curls. Suddenly I thought of Abby. You'd never know it now, and I'd almost forgotten it myself—but before my little sister started dying her hair black and dressing like Morticia Adams as her way of telling the world 'Hey, look at me,' she too had red curls and a smile that could make a buttery-yellow sun melt.

Suddenly it dawned on me that it wasn't attention she wanted. It was acceptance. For being a little different. For not being the norm.

Just like me.

At that moment, the crowd started to push and sway, and the crush to get through the massive iron doors began.

I lost sight of the bald man and felt myself being pushed and shoved with the current of the crowd. We flowed through an entrance that remained open long enough to fill a large waiting room—crammed in shoulder to shoulder and chest to back—before the guards closed the doors and sealed out the vast majority of the crowd, who screamed and wailed over not having made it inside. I quickly pushed aside any guilt I experienced over getting through when many left on the other side had been waiting much longer.

At the head of the room a man stood with a megaphone and began shouting instructions at us.

"Ladies and gentlemen, welcome to the Volunteer Vaccine Program. Please listen carefully. The VVP was designed to act like a buddy system. Each of you will be able to claim one patient and one only, as your responsibility. We need each of you to get a registration form, then we will open the doors to the main courtyard of the compound. We know that many of you are here looking for loved ones, but we need you to act in a calm and restrained manner so as not to frighten or unnecessarily agitate the patients. Once you have claimed someone, proceed to the registration room where your form will be collected. From there, your new assignee will be tagged for monitoring purposes. You will be given a medipack containing a three-month supply of the vaccine and instructions on how to administer it. If you have any questions, please proceed to the information room on your right. Otherwise, please collect your registration form and enter the compound courtyard now."

A siren blared, a flashing red light blinded us, and several large automatic doors opened at the front of the room.

Clipboards with a form and pen were thrust at us from guards on either side as the throng surged into the courtyard with an obedient and eerie silence.

The air remained quiet with tense anticipation until a woman somewhere at the front of the crowd cried out, "Ellie! Ellie, it's me. Your mother!" She began sobbing with joy, after which everyone else in the crowd started calling out names. The noise grew quickly into a deafening outpouring of excitement and shock and a fear of all that had changed and all that was about to change even more.

I pushed my way through this crowd, apologizing to people

both infected and uninfected as I shouldered past them, searching for one thing.

"Zane?" I called, my eyes scanning the faces all around me. "Zane! Zane, are you here?"

That's when I saw him, standing still and alone, his face blank, his eyes dark, staring numbly as he slowly backed away from all the commotion going on around him.

I rushed toward him, calling even louder, fearing that any second he might disappear into the crowd, and I'd lose him forever. He didn't seem to notice me, but he must have heard his name because he stopped moving.

I pushed through the small grouping of people now standing between me and my zombie, not bothering to issue an apology when they screamed in protest over my rudeness.

I stopped when I finally stood face to chiseled chest, afraid to even breathe. Would he recognize me? Would he turn away, unable to look at me after I'd abandoned him at the hospital and poisoned him in the first place?

He barely moved a muscle, even when my hand tentatively grabbed his forearm.

It took a moment, but Zane finally glanced down at me, his head cocking slightly to the side. That's when I heard the words he'd been muttering absent-mindedly under his breath the entire time.

"Love Chandler."

My heart stopped for a moment, and I instantly felt the burning behind my eyes. Dozens of emotions washed over me, leaving me momentarily unable to maintain control over my own faculties. I was deliriously happy that he actually remembered who I was, but he also loved me—so much so that no virus, no amount of time had been able to beat it out of him.

The skin on his face was washed out, grey and gashed and bruised in places.

"Chandler here for Zane," I said, my voice shaky. "Chandler love Zane."

He wore the same shirt he'd been wearing that day at school, but it was shredded and frayed, threadbare in places and splattered with dried blood. Through my tears I could see his torso—his chest, his stomach, that football-star body of his. It was covered in scratches, no doubt the scars from fights he'd had, perhaps with other zombies. Perhaps with victims he had killed.

I tried not to think about that as I placed my now-shaking hand gently over his heart.

"Lost Chandler," Zane said, still staring blankly down at me.

"Chandler very sorry. Zane will never lose Chandler again. Chandler promise."

His eyes were now a pale reflection of the blue they once were, yet I could still see the old Zane in them.

And he could obviously see me.

For a moment, his brow creased with recognition.

His pupils studied my face.

And he simply uttered, "Hall… pass?"

A laugh of joy escaped me, and I resisted the urge to hug the life out of him choosing to wipe any remnants of tears from my face as I nodded and said, "Yes. Hall pass. I'm here to give you a hall pass."

I took his hand firmly in mine.

Zane squeezed tight, the kind of grip that told me he never wanted to let me go.

I pushed my way back through the heaving, confused crowd, pulling Zane along behind me. He was heavy and sluggish, and it took all my strength to get us to the registration checkpoint near the guarded exits where an extremely intimidating female officer barked more instructions at us.

"Form! You haven't filled out the form, civilian."

I fumbled clumsily with the pen, scribbling away as she shoved a small medikit into my chest.

"This is the three-month supply of the anti-viral. You administer it like so."

From the registration desk, she snatched up one of those scary sci-fi-looking syringe pistols, jabbed it against Zane's jugular vein and triggered it. Zane jolted. I gasped and thought I was going to faint for a moment, but the woman's loud, stern voice kept me conscious and alert.

"Do you have a secure location to house you and your new assignee?" she snapped.

"Duh, yeah," I lied, "like I'd be here if I didn't."

She looked at me suspiciously and I tried on my best attempt at an innocent grin.

"The patient must wear this at all times." She grabbed Zane's wrist—my hand still holding his—and snapped a tight-fitting metal bracelet on him. A small red light on the bracelet instantly began flashing. "This is a monitoring device and alarm. It'll beep every twenty-four hours to remind you to re-administer the drug. It also acts as a tracking device so we know where he is at all times. If your zombie escapes or you feel that you can no longer supervise him, notify us immediately and we'll have the situation dealt with."

This time I gasped and gulped.

"Do you have any questions?"

Was she kidding? I had a million questions. I just couldn't think what to ask first. Before I had a chance to open my mouth, she screamed, "Next!"

I turned, holding Zane's hand tighter than ever, and that's when I saw the little, red-haired girl in the crowd of people shoving and pushing. She was all alone, her blank eyes staring into space.

Frantically I tried to look over the heads of the crowd to try and spot the bald man, but I couldn't see him in the chaos. I called the girl's name instead.

"Zoe! Zoe!"

She did not respond until I heaved my way over to her, grabbing her arm.

"Zoe. Come with me."

Slowly she turned.

She lifted her arms as if to be picked up.

I hauled her off the ground with one arm while still clinging to Zane with my other hand. I fought my way back to the registration and interrupted the female officer. "I need to take this one too."

"Sir, step back."

"I need to take her. Her name's Zoe. I'll find her father, I promise."

"Sir, only one patient per registered human."

"But I can't leave her here. God knows what'll happen to her if her father doesn't find her."

"Sir! Step back now!"

I didn't know what to do. I thought about running. I thought about pushing through the guards at the exit. I thought about doing the best damn Jedi mind trick I could and say, 'These aren't the zombies you're looking for.'

Then suddenly, I felt a hand on my shoulder.

I spun about and there was the bald man, crying with joy, wrapping his arms about the small red-haired girl and holding her tight. "Thank you," was all he could say. "Thank you. Thank you."

With another lurch of the crowd, Zane and I shoved toward the exit. I lost sight of Zoe and her father, but I could have sworn I caught a glimpse of that female officer smiling briefly before yelling at the next person in line.

The stench of the zombie crowd was replaced by that lingering smell of smoke from far away as we were pushed from the building and out into the night once more.

Our hands were still locked in their unbreakable grip, our fingers entwined, my palm sweaty, his cold.

I didn't know what to do.

Where to go.

I thought about taking him back to my house, since I knew

I had to return at some point, but how was I going to introduce Zane to my family?

If worse came to worst, I could always take him to the bunker, though the thought of having my family hovering that close by wasn't jiving with the romantic notions running rampant through my mind.

"Wanna go to Mexico?" I asked in all sincerity.

Zane turned to me slowly and simply said, "Home. Want… go…home."

He looked so cute, I just wanted to chew him up. In a non-people-sushi cannibalistic sort of way, of course. Unfortunately, I was ashamed to admit that I had no idea where he used to live.

"Want…go…home," he said again.

"Okay, okay, settle down E.T. I just need to figure out where home is."

Zane pointed off to the west, toward the suburbs. "Home."

"Wait? You know the way home?" I asked.

Zane tugged gently on my arm, still pointing. "Home, Chandler love."

"Oh sure. Turn on the charm, and you think I'll follow you anywhere, huh?"

He cracked what I assumed was a sorry-assed attempt at a smile, which unfortunately made him look like he had gas, but I nodded, giving his hand a squeeze before following alongside him as we slowly lumbered off into the horizon.

* Z * Z * Z *

Sunrise spilled down the street where Zane used to live, revealing a house with partially smashed windows, broken shutters, and a battered front door that now dangled precariously from its frame. I wanted to tell Zane that his parents were probably already gone. If they were lucky, they had fled. If not, then chances were they were dead. But I could tell by the solemn expression on his face that he was already aware of that. It dawned on me that he'd just displayed his first real hint of emotion. Sadness or perhaps regret. I took it as a sign that the anti-viral was beginning to work.

He walked slowly up the steps to the front porch and through the open doorway with me behind him, our hands still clasped together.

Inside, the furniture had been overturned and wrecked. Shards of glass and ceramic from the broken knickknacks lay scattered across the carpet. Broken spindles barely held up the hand railing of the staircase.

I slipped the backpack off my shoulders, allowing it to fall to the floor. We both stood silent for a long time.

Eventually he said, "Why you come for me?"

His language was getting better. He was starting to sound like himself again, just a little. Less like a caveman. More like a football player, though, realistically, was there that much of a difference?

I shrugged. "I was worried about you."

"Why?"

I hesitated, then answered. "Because I like you." When the world goes to shit, honesty seems to be the best policy.

He didn't respond straight away. After a few moments he lifted his hand, the one holding mine, the metal bracelet on his wrist. "Does this mean…we together?"

I didn't know if he was talking about the monitoring device or the fact that we still couldn't let go of each other.

For that I didn't have an honest answer. I had no idea what was going to become of us.

As I stood in silence, the sun rose higher and streamed in through the torn, gently-blowing curtains. Sunlight touched my arm and it was warm, and I realized I hadn't felt it on my skin for such a long time. I was almost as pale as Zane, but without all the nasty cuts and scratches.

I saw that he noticed me looking at his filthy, ravaged skin.

And he said in a quiet, almost pleading tone, "Wash me clean? Please?"

* Z * Z * Z *

My hand shook as I turned on the taps which thankfully still worked. Sorta. It dawned on me that I hadn't trembled this much the day the apocalypse started. No amount of killer zombies can strike terror into the heart of a geek like the thought of standing in a bathroom with the boy of your dreams, about to undress and bathe him.

The water spluttered loudly from the tap, and I jumped nervously.

The pipes groaned and the flow coughed and spewed out brown, rusty water for a few seconds, evidence that nobody had been here for some time. Slowly the water became clear and fresh. The city had made keeping the water running and free of contamination a priority to prevent further deaths or spread of disease.

When I turned from the tub back to Zane, the sight of him already shirtless took my breath away for a moment. The shirt was on the floor beside the tattered sneakers and socks he had heeled off, and Zane's scratched and scathed muscles now bulged and flexed as he waged a slow and somewhat apathetic war with his belt buckle.

"Can't… "

His fingertips were rough and swollen, and I could see the frustration behind his eyes.

My heart launched from my chest into my throat, pounding so hard I thought I was going to choke on my own convulsing ticker. I found it even harder to breathe when I noticed the enormous bulge in Zane's jeans just below his belt.

"Chandler help mmme?"

I felt my own cock swell and writhe in my pants, pushing the denim of my jeans this way and that to announce itself.

Like a baby staring at a lollipop, Zane couldn't take his eyes off it.

He dropped his hands away from his belt and continued gazing at my crotch as I took hold of his buckle in my still-trembling hands. I managed to unbuckle the belt and quivered even more as I twisted the top button of his jeans in my fingers. It popped open.

I sucked in a breath of air.

"Why so…" Zane forced a swallow, "…scared? It's just me."

I laughed—embarrassed at my nerves and how absurd and honest and real everything became in that moment. "That's the thing. You were never 'just you'… at least not to me. We never knew each other. We'd barely even talked to one another. And I was an idiot because I was okay with that, at least in the old world. You were far away. Untouchable. Made it easy for me to picture you up on a pedestal. I was never close enough to see anything other than perfection. It was easy. Safe. I didn't have to risk my...."

I could feel Zane watching me as I'd trailed off, unable to finish that sentence.

"That's exactly…." The second button of his jeans popped open and he didn't finish his sentence.

I had to know.

"Exactly what?"

Gently he touched the side of my face with his rough fingertips. I thought I might flinch, but I didn't. It wasn't as cold as it was before. He was getting warmer and surprisingly I found the scratch of his skin reassuring.

"That's how I felt too…" he said, "…about you."

My head spun. Everything seemed so damn surreal. I had to shut my eyes to try to steady myself. At the same time my shaking fingers unfastened the third button on Zane's jeans.

I could feel the denim shift, the strain on the material give way, as his pants released Zane's cock.

My eyes opened before I could stop them.

And there I saw all my teenage fantasies come true.

Zane Addison's cock pulsed and throbbed before me, hard and huge and perfect, its veins thick, its head big and bulbous, its slit shimmering with pre-cum.

Pre-cum that was tinged with the slightest hint of greyish-green, but hey, nobody's perfect. And in that instant I didn't give a damn, I simply wanted to live out years of wet dreams by dropping to my knees and taking that glorious cock in my mouth.

But I was too afraid.

Afraid yet again that the one thing I wanted might not want me.

Instead I stepped back.

Zane's loosened jeans fell to his ankles.

He stepped out of them awkwardly.

At one point, he almost lost his balance and fell.

I caught his hand and held him upright, after which I helped him into the tub and turned on the shower.

Zane held onto the shower wall to balance himself with my help. Instantly the dust and dirt and dried blood ran down the taut hills and valleys of Zane's hardened body, sending brown and red swirls into the water at his feet before disappearing down the drain. I took a sponge and soap from the shower recess and held them out for him.

Zane shook his head. "Need help, too weak, please?"

I was completely embarrassed, but I couldn't deny him, those sad eyes gazing longingly into mine. I set the contents of my hands on the side of the tub and quickly went about removing my own clothes, realizing for the first time how filthy I was as well. I was aware he was staring, but I swallowed my own discomfort and embarrassment over my own raging hard-on as I quickly shucked off my pants and briefs, slipping into the shower stall behind him.

He moaned softly from my touch, and I nearly blew my load as a result. I tried to concentrate on the task at hand, retrieving the soap and sponge.

I squeezed the sponge beneath the stream of running water and let it grow heavy and wet in my hand, then tenderly, I moved around his big, hulking body, rinsing and washing Zane's shoulders, his back, his chest, letting any evidence of his horrific past wash away.

His erection still hung throbbing in the air and he looked at me and said, "Me… horny…."

"Me horny too… I mean, I'm horny too, as you can no doubt see for yourself. But let's just get clean first, huh?"

He raised his arms one at a time as I washed his forearms, his biceps, his beautiful armpits, rinsing away days, weeks, months of sweat and savagery. It seemed odd watching the soapy water wash over his cuts, both old ones and new, without so much as a twitch or wince from him.

"Do they hurt? Your wounds?"

He nodded and said nothing more.

"How did you get them?" Part of me didn't want to know, but the other part wanted the complete truth, no matter what he'd done, no matter what he'd been through.

"Bruiser and Mad Dog," he grunted, and I heard disdain in his voice. His emotions were definitely returning.

I stiffened at the sound of their names. "Those assholes are still alive? Is there no justice in this apocalypse? Did they get rounded up with everyone else?"

"No," he said. "They still out there. They cause trouble. I tried to stop them. Sometimes they kill for fun, not food."

I took a deep breath. His words had more gravity than I could bear to think about. I leaned in close to him and gazed into his eyes, which appeared to be growing bluer by the hour. "Well, you don't have to worry about them anymore, you're safe with me. And you never have to kill anything or anyone for food ever again."

That's when Zane attempted to smile again, a little more successfully I might add.

Then without any warning at all, he leaned forward and kissed me.

His tongue shot straight into my mouth, licking my gums and teeth, savoring the taste of me. To be honest, I wasn't sure if he was actually kissing me or if he just liked the taste of my saliva, which was borderline creepy considering he used to eat people, but I went with it.

When I pulled away, surprised and confused, I just about kicked myself for prematurely ending my first kiss-thing with the boyfriend I'd always dreamed of having. But it wasn't really much of a surprise when I started to freak a bit.

"Wait. We can't…I need to...I don't know what I'm doing here. This is all new to me."

"No, it's not."

"You're right. It's not new to me. I've been in love with you longer than I can even admit to myself. But taking everything I've always wanted and turning it into reality? That's a whole new ballgame, and I've never been very good at sports, if you catch my drift. Yes I'd love to kiss you. And hold you. And you have no idea how much I want to touch that hard, throbbing, totally hot cock-rocket of yours. And hell, one day maybe we'll even sit next to one another in matching rocking chairs on a front porch somewhere when we're ninety years old, but till then—"

Suddenly my jaw dropped, my eyes bugged wide open and I practically screeched, "Grampy! It's Grampy's birthday! Holy crap, Grammy'll kill me if I miss it!"

I killed the faucet, hopping out of the tub. "Quick! We gotta go!"

"Where we going?"

I hauled him and his erection out of the bath. "You're coming to dinner!"

As his naked body dripped water in puddles on the dust-covered floor at his feet, I wrapped a towel tightly around him. "We need to get you dressed in some clean clothes," I said.

"Something nice," Zane smiled again. "If I'm going to

meet…your family."

He caught me off-guard with that one, and for a second I thought I was going to start bawling with joy. I held it in, just, especially when he grabbed my hand and asked—

"If I couldn't be your boyfriend before…now I be your boyfriend?"

Weird how it took the entire world turning upside down to make something that felt nearly impossible before the PTA struck seem so right in the aftermath.

"I'd love that," I smiled back.

CHAPTER FOUR

GUESS WHO'S COMING AT DINNER

There are some things you think through quite strategically in a zombie apocalypse. How will we generate power to know what's going on in the outside world? How long will our food supply last? Where should we stash the spare shotgun pellets where Grammy can reach them in case of an emergency? Or perhaps where she can't reach them in case of a non-emergency?

Then there are other things that you know you're just gonna have to wing, like: family, I'd like you to meet my zombie boyfriend Zane. Zane, I'd like you to meet my crazy, cooped-up family. Yes, I could see it now; tonight was going to go swimmingly.

We reached my house just as the sun was setting. I stopped to inspect Zane on the porch steps, convincing myself that maybe he could pass as human till I worked my way up to telling my family the truth about him. He looked presentable enough in a clean black shirt and jeans that he'd picked out himself; in fact, he looked downright sexy as ever. Then I caught sight of dried blood in his hair.

"Shit," I whispered before licking my fingers like a mother cat and wetting his hair, trying to smooth things out.

Instantly Zane licked his own fingers and mimicked me, patting down my hair. He was a tad rougher than I was, but I couldn't exactly blame him for that. "You don't have to do that, my hair's fine. It doesn't have the matted remnants of blood in it."

"But I like to," he said innocently.

He said it so sweetly, who was I to deny him?

I waited long enough for yet another erection to subside before knocking on the boards nailed across the doorway. "Mom? Dad? It's me. I'm back."

"Oh, thank God." I could hear Mom's voice almost melt with relief.

With a groan of wood being pried away, my father began pulling the planks off with a crowbar.

As the light began to pour out of the house in shafts, I nudged Zane back a little, praying to God or Buddha or whoever was doing such a bang-up job of looking after humankind at the moment that my family wouldn't pick up on Zane's zombieness straight away.

My mother reached through the doorway to hug me awkwardly while my father continued pulling boards away.

"Are you alright? We've been so worried? Did anyone try to hurt you? Did you see any other survivors?"

"Lots of them," I said, answering the last question first, speaking as quickly as I could to try and distract my parents with good news. "Mom, there's people everywhere. And now that the anti-virus treatment is being handed out, things should start to return to normal. And look, I even found a friend of mine while I was out there."

I grabbed Zane's wrist and pulled him into the light beaming through the door.

Mom and Dad both stepped back in surprise before my mother said with a kinda polite cautiousness. "Oh. Hello there."

"This is my friend Zane. We go to school together, or at least we used to. He plays quarterback. He's very normal."

My Dad raised one eyebrow in shock, perhaps even pride. "You have a friend who's on the football team?"

"Was," I said quickly before saying to Zane, "Zane, this is my Mom and Dad."

I could see Zane concentrating as hard as he could, straining so much a vein began to pulse on his forehead. I thought for a second it was going to pop and spurt blood, but then he managed to blurt out, "Pleased to meeeeet you, Mrs. Cox, Mr. Cox. I've heard sooooooo muuuuuch about you." His voice dipped precariously mid-sentence, but I thought he did an okay job at introductions.

"Well, lovely to meet you too, Zane," my mother nodded.

She held her hand through the opening in the boards and shook Zane's hand. "My goodness, you're freezing. Please come inside and meet our family. Do watch the splinters on the boards as you climb through."

I clambered through the opening, first dumping my backpack by the entrance while Zane's muscled frame squeezed through after me.

My family hurriedly gathered around, their faces a mixture of excitement, suspicion and apprehension.

My sister came running up to me first and hugged me. "I prayed to the Almighty that you'd come back to us safely. I will now send him my eternal gratitude for hearing my prayers."

"You do that," I said and introduced her to Zane. "Sister Mary Abigail, this is my friend, Zane Addison."

"Zane Addison!?" she stared at him, stunned. Then back at me. Then back at him. "As in quarterback-Zane-Addison? As in the-most-popular-hunk-in-school-Zane-Addison? As in every-teenage-girl-in-town-wants-to-get-knocked-up-and-have-his-babies-Zane-Addison?"

When nuns swoon, do their eyes roll back into the heads as they start speaking in tongues? I'm not sure, but that's what Sister Mary Abigail began doing at that point.

"Runca-jingo-taraha-singahana-kha-baka…!"

Zane evidently panicked at this stage and, obviously having no idea how to respond appropriately, he mimicked my sister right down to the convulsing limb movements. "Runca-jingo-taraha-singahana-kha-baka…!"

I grabbed his forearm, and it stopped him instantly. "You don't have to do that, trust me," I said to him quietly. "She's apparently got the Holy Spirit inside her."

My mother was already continuing with the introductions. "Zane, this is Aunt Tilly. Aunt Tilly, this is Chandler's friend—"

"I heard his name," Aunt Tilly said, her right hand nursing a vodka martini while her left primped her hair. When she was done fixing her birds nest as best she could, she held her hand out for Zane to kiss it. "Please to meet ya, handsome!"

Zane looked at my aunt's hand in his, lowered his head and began licking her fingers.

My mother's eyes widened, and I could see the look of concern spreading across my family's faces faster than the initial outbreak of the ZD7HY_L*8-djgfkagse virus.

Both my parents appeared slightly uncomfortable, gazes flitting nervously back and forth unsure exactly where to look as Zane continued to tongue-rape Aunt Tilly's hand.

I grabbed Zane by the back of the collar and pulled him back, laughing nervously. "A real prankster, this one."

Aunt Tilly gasped with excitement. "Oh my! I certainly don't mind in the least." Tilly wiggled her fingers at him as if encouraging him to do it again. "You sure ain't backward in coming forward, are you Zzzzzaa—"

Before Zane's name could leave Aunt Tilly's lips, Grammy grabbed her by the arm and spun her across the room.

"Get your filthy paws off him, you tramp!" she snapped. "Can't you see he's young enough to be your egg? Not that you have anything left down there aside from some dust mites and a few cracked shells held together by cobwebs." Grammy turned to Zane and said, "That's my sister. She's a goddamn whore. Just ignore her. I'm Grammy Gabby."

Zane chuckled, looking a teensy bit loopy as Tilly muttered a few choice words between clenched teeth.

Suddenly Grammy Gabby eyed Zane skeptically. "Say, there's somethin' not quite right about you, isn't there?"

I stepped in quickly. "Zane's not been feeling well, lately. Old football injury, you know."

Grammy leaned in close and whispered, "I hate to tell you this, but I don't think your friend is all there in a One Flew Over the Cuckoo's Nest kind of way."

I nodded quickly and whispered back, "Mild concussion, that all."

"Who's this?" Grampy shouted, blundering over to meet

Zane, cupping his ear to better hear. "He looks pale as a ghost. And what are all those scratches on him. You been in a catfight or somethin', boy?"

"Grampy," I shouted so he could hear. "This is my friend, Zane. Zane, it's Grampy's ninetieth birthday today."

Again with the forehead vein! This time Zane clamped his eyes shut, he had to concentrate so damn much. "M-m-merrrrry biiiiirthday."

Grammy shouted in Grampy's ear, "Football injury," by way of explanation.

I tried to divert the attention away from Zane by shaking Grampy's hand, "Happy ninetieth, Grampy. I wish I had a present for you."

"Oh Grampy doesn't want anything," Mom said. "He's just happy that we're all together safe and sound."

"A new TV might have been nice," Grampy grumbled. "You coulda looted one of those stores while you were out there having fun with your friend."

"Now, now," my mother said, "why don't we all just take a seat at the table? You boys are just in time for dinner. Your father made party hats out of some old newspapers to cheer us all up. He's very clever, your father."

Aunt Tilly already had hers on... with the headline ZOMBIES ATTACK! on her newspaper hat. Mom and Dad both donned a hat, oblivious to the headlines they so proudly wore—PLAGUE OF DEATH and DOOMSDAY IS HERE! Grammy's hat declared UNDEAD SWARM NEW YORK. Grampy's read END OF THE WORLD! While my sister's hat warned of APOCALYPSE WOW!

I glanced down at my place setting and read the headline printed diagonally across the hat my father had so carefully folded for me: 2 IN 3 NOT HUMAN, with a sub-heading that read, There Could Be A Zombie Standing Right Next To You!

I glanced disconcertingly at Zane before saying, "I think I'll pass on the hat if that's okay. Since Zane doesn't have one. I don't want him to feel left out or anything."

"Oh, of course dear. Why don't you go get another place setting for Zane."

As I turned quickly I heard my Mom whisper to Dad, "I think he's a bit old for party hats now. Looks like our little boy is growing up. Perhaps he'll stop with all that silly gay nonsense and settle down with some sweet gal so we can finally get some grandbabies."

I stopped and turned, taking a deep breath of courage so I could break the news once and for all that my addiction to dick was not just a phase. "Mom, Dad, there's something I need to tell you."

"What's that, dear?"

"I'm…" I'm a chicken is what I am. "I'm afraid I've forgotten where the place settings are kept."

Mom got up from her chair, all concerned. "Oh dear, did you bump your head as well while you were out there? They're right here in the buffet and hutch where they've always been."

She held her hand against my forehead to feel for a temperature and inspect for bumps. "Mom, I'm fine. I just had a mental blank, that's all."

"Speaking of mental blanks," called Grammy from the table, "your friend here is eating your party hat."

As Mom took care of the extra setting, I hurried back to the table and pulled the shredded newspaper out of Zane's mouth. "Oh, this is just a joke we share. 'I'm so hungry I could eat a hat!' Haha!" My first laugh wasn't very convincing.

"Meee…huuungry…"

My second laugh was downright nervous as I saw Zane staring at Aunt Tilly, his gaze kinda ravenous and unblinking like a dog under a table trying to stare the food off your fork, while all Aunt Tilly could do was smile back and wink, lapping up the attention.

I quickly took Zane's chin in my hand and turned his head to face me, shaking my head as a clear signal that it was not okay to eat Aunt Tilly.

"I won't keep you waiting another minute. Dinner's coming right up, Zane," Mom said with the perfect hostess smile. "Of course, you're hungry, dear. You're a growing boy."

Mom wasn't wrong there. With a glance down at Zane's lap, I saw he was growing in more ways than one. His eyes had turned from hungry puppy dog eyes to adoring puppy dog eyes, accompanied by a stupid, loving grin on his big, dumb handsome face.

"Not right now, please," I whispered to him. "Later, I promise."

"Here we are," Mom announced proudly, placing a large casserole dish in the middle of the table and lifting the lid. "Bean stew!"

"Oh, my damn favorite," Grampy offered sarcastically.

Mom started serving everyone a plate. "Now, now, Grampy. We make do with what we have. Besides, you heard Chandler. Things are changing in the outside world. Isn't that right, Zane? I bet you've seen some progress happening out on the streets."

Mom's effort to bring Zane into the conversation would have been appreciated any other time, but not tonight.

"Me huungry… and hornyyy."

"Oh," Mom said, wide-eyed. "Well, everyone, please start before your dinner gets cold."

"Grace, first," Sister Mary Abigail insisted.

"Not tonight, dear," Mom said firmly through her cemented-on smile. "Let's just eat before—"

"Is that what I think it is?" Grammy Gabby shrieked, her eyes bulging so big that her gigantic, tinted 70s-style specs slipped an inch down the bridge of her nose.

And all my studly zombie boyfriend Zane could do was grin that big, stupid, handsome, kinda-undead smile of his while he pawed and tugged at the raging tentpole erection in his ripped jeans and announced to the whole table in that animalistic tone of his, "Me haaaaaawny."

My mother dropped her fork. Clang!

My father started choking on his beans. "Blarrrk!"

My sister, Sister Mary Abigail, crossed herself several times and started talking in tongues. "Muhl-sun-lun-acka-clacka-yada-zirka-blirka!"

Grumpy Grampy cupped his hand around his ear to hear better and shouted, "What that little sonna-bitch just say?"

While my drunken Aunt Tilly just chuckled calmly with a "he-he-he" and turned to me to say, "He's a real tiger, ain't he!"

Zane took it upon himself to confirm Tilly's suspicions by growling at me as if he were an actual tiger before announcing loudly again, "Me horny, Chand-lerrrr!"

That's when it dawned on me: the increasingly slurred speech, the lingering gaze at my aunt like she was a pork chop, the uninhibited declarations of horniness, all zombie signs.

"My backpack," I breathed in panic. As though the thought somehow triggered it, the metal bracelet on Zane's wrist began to beep loudly, the red light flashing brightly.

"What in tarnation's that?" Grampy shouted, startling everyone even more.

I was already running for my backpack by the door. I scooped it up.

"Chandler, dear, is everything alright?"

"Yes Mom. Zane and I just need to be excused for a minute."

I yanked him up from his chair, and my entire family gasped as he tipped his plate up with his erection. I didn't stay to clean up the mess for fear of an even bigger mess about to take place. With Zane in one hand and my backpack in the other, I raced upstairs to my bedroom and shut the door behind us.

I watched as Zane's eyes took in his surroundings, in particular the bed, and a big grin spread across his face.

"No," I said sternly. "We're not here for that. We're here for this!"

I pulled the medikit from my backpack, placed it on the bed, opened the lid and pulled out the syringe-gun-thing.

Zane already had me from behind, grasping my hips in both hands while dry-humping my ass through our pants.

"Zane, I said no." He ignored me as I fumbled with the vials, my body jerking back and forth as I jammed one of the cylinders into the chamber of the syringe. Something clicked in place and I straightened up, twisted around and jabbed the gun against Zane's neck. I squeezed the trigger, releasing a dose of the anti-virus shot into his jugular.

Zane froze, then slowly his body began to relax.

His eyes blinked as though his brain was trying to process the concoction flooding his veins.

A sigh escaped him, and I could have sworn it was one of relief.

The erection, however, remained. As did mine, I realized, noticing that shot or not, Zane had never stopped humping.

"Thank…you," he said to me. There was a pause between words, but no stammering or slurring or syllables excruciatingly strung out for seconds at a time. "That…feels…better."

"Oh good." This time I was the one who sighed with relief. "Are you okay to go back downstairs before anyone gets, you know, ideas?"

Zane nodded, but as I turned to leave he took my hand and pulled me gently back. His head hung slightly, and he gazed at the floor. His humanity had returned, courtesy of the drugs, and brought its sister-in-law, shame, with it.

"I…embarrassed you? At the…dinner table?" His voice was quiet and very still.

I felt for my sad, sorry, beautiful boy so much I thought my fucking heart was going to break, right then and there. I touched his cheek and said, "No… it wasn't you. That wasn't you who embarrassed me."

"I'm sorry," he said. "I used to be able to hide how I feel for you. But I can't seem to do that anymore."

I took a deep breath and smiled. "You know something? Neither can I."

I held my head high as we descended the stairs together, returning to the dinner table downstairs. That is, until I heard my family whispering to each other with the exception of Grampy who shouted, "He's a what?"

It was followed by a lot of shushing as everybody caught sight of us coming down the stairs.

As Zane and I took our seats, I felt the weird, uncomfortable vibe straight away, something that was confirmed moments later as Mom said in her most sympathetic, understanding tone, "Chandler, dear. Perhaps there's something you'd like to tell us?"

My first reaction—the one I'd always had when I felt backed into a corner—was to immediately issue blanket denials or set off with vague arguments and misdirection. Or run and try to hide.

But things were different now, and I was no longer the same person I was before. I could barely remember who he was any more. Zane needed me, was relying on me for so much, and I'd be damned if I ever let him down the way I had that fateful day at the hospital. In a world like this, there was no place left for the truth to hide. And with Zane by my side, I knew we could face anything together.

Sitting there at the dinner table, in front of my entire family, I placed my hand on Zane's and squeezed it tight.

"There is something I'd like say," I told everyone, gathering all the courage I had. "Mom, Dad, everyone. I'm gay…" Drumroll please… "and Zane is my boyfriend!"

For a moment, there was a stunned silence around the table.

Stunned because apparently this was not news at all.

"Yes dear," Mom smiled, "we know that. I've been vacuuming around the pile of gentlemen's magazines under your bed for years now."

I looked at her in disbelief. Then at everyone else at the table, who shrugged indifferently at my announcement. Then back at my mom. "If you knew, then why have you been trying to set me up with Deidre and Nancy and every other girl in the neighborhood?"

Mom tilted her head in empathy and smiled even more. "Oh darling, while I must confess that a part of me secretly hoped you fall in love with a girl, any girl, I always knew that was a bit of a pipe dream. Besides, a woman needs her dreams, darn it, and I dream of grandchildren. Deep down, I understood setting you up with a girl would help you figure out for yourself how much you really liked boys. I'm your mother. I had to do something to get you off your ass and find out which way you swing."

As I sat there in shock, Dad joined in with another condescendingly sympathetic smile. "Son, the fact is we all love you and want you to be happy, gay or straight. It doesn't matter to us. We're family."

"You know how much I always loved that Ellen," Mom exclaimed. "Before she was attacked and eaten by that heinous, dancing zombie mob of an audience on national television, of course."

I looked at the nodding faces of my family all around the table.

"But," Dad continued, "is there something else you'd like to tell us?"

With bombshell number one fizzling out like a dud firecracker on the Fourth of July, I was filled with confidence I could tell them of Zane's condition without too much fuss.

"There is one other thing," I said, squeezing Zane's hand tighter. He squeezed back and I knew I had his permission to announce—

"Zane's a zombie." Chaos instantly descended upon the dinner table.

Mom covered her mouth with her hand as the tears welled up in her eyes.

Dad shook his head and pinched the bridge of his nose with his fingers as though a doctor had just told him the worst.

Aunt Tilly ejected herself from her seat to undoubtedly find a bottle of vodka.

Grammy shrieked, "Oh my God, I never thought there'd be

one sitting at my table!"

Grampy shouted, "No grandson of mine is gonna sit there and tell me he's a zombie-lover!"

"Officially considered a Zombie-Humanoid life form by the Joint Military Commission of the PTA," I added, praying that might help. "They're hopeful the drugs will eventually completely reverse the effects of the virus."

Silence hung in the air, and I could've heard a pin drop as they all stared back at Zane and myself before everyone at the table once again erupted in protest.

My sister Abby liberated herself from the crucifixes hanging around her neck and declared, "Cool! I'm not the biggest freak at this table anymore!"

I was momentarily insulted, but I shrugged. Any acceptance at this point was better than none.

That realization sent me over the deep end. Why should I have to settle for better-than-nothing from my own family? I jumped to my brave new feet and screamed, "What's the problem here? What's everyone so afraid of?"

Everybody immediately fell silent once more, each one looking briefly to one another for an answer until Grammy admitted, "I dunno. But all I know is this is dangerous. It could end to the downfall of all we know. First you're going out with a zombie. The next thing we know, you're gonna wanna marry him."

"And maybe I will. What's so wrong with that?"

"He's a zombie." Grampy pointed out.

"That's not his fault," I argued back. "Do you think he chose to be a zombie? No! He didn't! He just ate the wrong Beefcake burger!"

At the other end of the table, I heard Mom sob.

I turned, angry and heartbroken. "Mom! Why are you even crying over this?"

She wiped her tears with her napkin. "It's just that I wanted so much for you. But now I'm afraid for your future. People will laugh. They'll mock you."

"Let them! Who cares? I love this man. I just wanna be happy."

"Maybe this is just a phase he's going through," Mom brightened hopefully. "Maybe once you get this zombie-sexuality out of your system, you'll be okay?" She turned to my Dad and said hopefully, "Perhaps Deidre's cute younger brother, Tommy is still alive? Wouldn't they make a lovely—"

"Mom, I love you, but enough with the phases already. Zane and I have been in love for years. It just took a goddamn zombie apocalypse for us both to admit it. We're meant to be. Fate. Kismet. This is my destiny."

Zane squeezed my hand hard at that moment.

I looked down at him, brushing the blood-saliva-matted hair off his forehead and smiled. "I know this to be true. I can feel it with every fiber of my being."

"But when..." Grammy said, stumbling over her words to find the right question. "When exactly did you decide to be...I can't bear to say the word...a...zombie-lover?"

"Grammy, this wasn't a decision. We didn't choose this. It just happened. Blame nature. Who knows?"

"I don't know what to say," Dad said in a new wave of shock and, I could hear it, disappointment. "I'm just not sure the world is ready for this. And I hate to think my son won't be accepted. I hate to think that people will see you as anything but normal. Just because of whose hand you hold."

"It's not just about whose hand I hold," I said bravely. "It's about who I love. And I love Zane Addison. I always have."

Zane didn't need to say a word to voice his opinion. He just stood beside me, leaned in and kissed me.

Suddenly a loud guttural groan filled the air.

"Hoooooooww... fuuuuuucking... sweeeeeeeeet..." There was a pause for breath before the voice finished its announcement with, "MEEEEEAAATT!"

My entire family turned and looked at the doorway to see two huge zombies starting to claw their way through the door that we had forgotten to board back up. With an explosion of splintered wood, they busted through into our downstairs living room and sized up the house—and their prey—with blood dripping from their jaws.

I gasped as I realized who they were. "Oh shit, Bruiser and Mad Dog!"

But Zane had recognized them immediately, either by sight or scent or some super-zombie-power. With one leap, he launched himself across the room, putting himself in the path between our intruders and my family. As Bruiser and Mad Dog crouched low, like predators ready to attack, Zane stood tall with his arms stretched wide, like the protector of his clan.

"Nobody hurts this family," he declared in a voice I had never heard before. Given that he'd just received a shot of the anti-virus, I was confused as to where the rage in his voice, his eyes, had come from. Then it dawned on me. He was about to fight for me. He was about to fight for love. And the need to defend the ones you love is more powerful than any drug on earth.

Bruiser just laughed and scowled, "Meeeee....huuuungry!"

In the next second, Bruiser launched himself at Zane, his mouth wide open and his teeth all chipped and razor sharp undoubtedly from ripping open countless bones and skulls. At the same time Mad Dog leapt across the sofa and came for everyone at the dinner table.

Terrified screams and ferocious roars filled the house.

Bruiser slammed into Zane hard, and the two hit the floor and began tearing at each other like rabid beasts.

Instinctively, I grabbed my chair and hurled it at Mad Dog. It hit his shoulder and splintered, slowing him just long enough to give my family time to scatter.

"Run!" I shouted before Mad Dog thumped into me, knocking me backward onto the table. He snarled, ready to tear open my throat, when Mom picked up the casserole dish and brought it down over Mad Dog's head.

"Nobody hurts my son!" Mom declared, before throwing the ladle at him for good measure.

Mad Dog growled and shook his bean-splattered head in a daze.

I quickly rolled off the table and hit the floor.

Across the room, Zane managed to get to his feet just as Bruiser tackled him once more. They crashed into the sofa, at which point Grammy shrieked like a banshee and threw herself onto Bruiser's back, clinging to him like a crab, hitting him repeatedly on the head. "Leave my grandson's zombie-boyfriend alone," she screamed furiously, "you undead douchebag!"

Bruiser spun about, trying to throw my grandmother off him, and turned just in time to receive a right hook to the chin from Zane.

Meanwhile Mad Dog had regained his balance and set his sights on my Mom. He lunged and Mom reeled back, just as my Dad came rushing in from the side, knocking Mad Dog to the ground. My sister grabbed my Mom and pulled her out of the way before grabbing a fork off the table and stabbing Mad Dog in the ass with it while my Dad tried to hold him down. I jumped into the fray, trying to help my Dad wrestle the zombie, but with an eruption of brute force, Mad Dog threw us all off him, sending my Dad, my sister, and me flying across the room.

I hit the foot of the stairs with a grunt.

At the same time, Bruiser managed to hurl Grammy off his back and onto the floor. Grampy hurried to help her and Zane slammed his knee into Bruiser's chest as he lunged for both Grammy and Grampy, sending the zombie staggering backward before coming at Zane once more.

I realized then we were no match for Bruiser and Mad Dog.

I had to do something fast, before these killer zombies tore my family and Zane from limb to limb.

A lightbulb snapped on. "The drug."

As fast as I could, I sprinted up the staircase and burst into my bedroom. The medi-kit was there on the bed. I scooped up the syringe gun and an armful of vials and charged back down the hallway.

But before I could reach the top of the stairs, my feet tangled and I hit the floor.

Somehow I managed to keep hold of the syringe-gun, but the vials flew from my arms and went bouncing and rolling down the stairs.

Amid the chaos below, I saw Grampy watch the runaway cylindrical vials in horror and howl, "My Cuban cigars! Don't let the bastards get my cigars!"

He scrambled frantically to gather them all up as one by one they reached the bottom of the stairs. Behind him, Mad Dog suddenly lunged.

"Grampy!" I shouted. "Duck and cover! Duck and cover!"

Without a moment's hesitation, Grampy did exactly as he was told and dropped into a roll under the table, still clutching the precious vials. Mad Dog missed him by an inch and came face to face with a screaming Aunt Tilly who finally joined the fight armed with an empty vodka bottle that she brought down on Mad Dog's skull again and again till it smashed.

I hurried down the stairs so fast my legs almost gave way under me. When I reached the bottom, I ducked and covered too, somersaulting under the table and crashing into Grampy.

"I need a cigar," I told him, taking one of the vials and ramming it into the chamber of the syringe-gun.

As Mad Dog seized Aunt Tilly, I leapt from under the table, wrapped one arm around Mad Dog's neck and shoved the nuzzle of the syringe-gun against his jugular as hard as I could.

Mad Dog jolted as the first shot flooded his system.

I turned and shouted, "Grampy! Another cigar!"

Like a groundhog poking its head up from the dirt, Grampy emerged just long enough to toss me a vial. I caught it, jammed it into the gun and fired another dose into Mad Dog.

This time his body started to slump a little. His limbs relaxed, and he released Aunt Tilly before turning to me and grumbling in at me, "Would you get your faggot arm off me and stop trying to hug me, you fuckin' queer!"

Yep, Mad Dog was back to normal.

I let him go and turned back to see Bruiser punch Zane so hard that the blow knocked my boyfriend into the air. When he hit the ground, Zane wasn't moving.

I gasped in fear.

My heart sank even faster as I saw Bruiser grab both my Mom and my sister in one arm, pulling them against him and opening his mouth wide, hungry for whatever flesh he could plunge his teeth into.

Grampy saw too, already throwing me another vial which I caught before sprinting across the room.

I hurdled the sofa.

I rammed the vial into the chamber.

I raised my syringe-gun and with a mighty sweep of his free arm, Bruiser knocked the gun clean out of my hand.

The syringe-gun sailed across the room and straight through the open doorway, clattering across the ground somewhere in the dark outside.

Bruiser grinned and gave a guttural laugh.

He bent his head low to rip open my mother's throat.

I tried to grab at him, but he hurled me across the room.

That's when, out of nowhere, my father came charging across the room with an almighty roar, his nail-gun gripped in his fist.

Bruiser looked up just as Dad raised his handyman's tool and pulled the trigger.

Bang! Bang! Bang!

Bruiser's head snapped back with three short sharp jerks as three shiny nine-inch nails thudded into his forehead.

For a moment he just stood there, wide-eyed, staring at my Dad. Slowly his arms went slack, allowing my mother and sister to slide free. With one last zombie groan Bruiser fell backward, thumping against the floorboards, as dead as the undead can get.

"That's one thing I can cross off my list," Dad said, standing over Bruiser's body still valiantly white-knuckling the nail gun. "Kill any zombies that try to hurt my family."

Mom rushed toward him and hugged him, as did my sister. Grammy and Aunt Tilly both helped Grampy out from under the table. Meanwhile, I rushed to Zane's side.

"Zane! Can you hear me?"

He wasn't moving.

I didn't know what to do.

So I kissed him.

Softly, he moaned.

I felt air against my lips.

I sat up, holding my breath for fear I had just imagined it until slowly, Zane opened his eyes.

"Meeeee… sore," was all he could mumble.

CHAPTER FIVE
A MOO BEGINNING

My family helped patch Zane up. Aunt Tilly brought him a glass of water, my Dad fetched the First Aid kit, and my sister dabbed his cuts with antiseptic while my mother bandaged his wounds. Grammy counted his bite marks and raised her drawn-on eyebrows, somewhat impressed, as Grampy recalled old war stories in hopes of making Zane feel better.

Once they were done, my mother said, "We judged you harshly, Zane. I'm sorry. I suppose we were just scared of something we didn't really know anything about."

"You were just worried...for Chandler. That's okay...it's nice to know his family loves him."

"Please know, you're welcome in our house anytime," my father added, shaking Zane's hand.

"Now we've all kissed and made up," Grammy said in her usual frank way, "What the hell are we supposed to do with him?"

We all turned to see Mad Dog sitting at the dinner table, looking sad and sorry for himself.

"Zane and I will take him to the compound. He needs treatment. And who knows, maybe there's someone out there looking for him."

* Z * Z * Z *

It turned out there was. As Zane and I arrived at the zombie compound with a much subdued Mad Dog, a man came racing up to the three of us. He looked like a typical redneck, except tears ran down his face. "Son?" he said. "Is that you?"

"Dad?" Mad Dog said, his bottom lips quivering.

The two embraced, and a guard came to escort them over to the registration zone.

After an exceedingly lengthy explanation of all the whys, whos, and hows, we were finally issued a new medi-kit by one of the officers. Zane and I started on our way home, deciding to take a detour to the hill overlooking town for a little alone time.

We sat on the grass in the dark and looked out at the fires burning in the far west. Without warning, the electricity returned to a blackened section of town, and we could hear the distant cheers from where we were. It seemed light—and life—were returning.

It filled me with hope, and I smiled at Zane, but all I saw was sadness on his face.

"What's the matter?"

"My trophies were gone," he said without looking at me.

I shook my head, not quite understanding. "What do you mean?"

"In my house…There were no trophies on the mantle… My parents left me behind. They took my trophies…and left me behind. They never really loved me. They only ever cared about what I achieved…not who I was."

I didn't know what to say.

A tear ran down his cheek. "Even Mad Dog's father loves him."

I grabbed his hand and squeezed it tight. "It's okay. You've got me now. And my crazy family if you think you can put up with them. You've got us. And you and me, we've got each other. That's all that matters now."

A smile slowly spread across his lips, and I brushed his tear streak away.

At that moment a stray cow strolled slowly by, stopping for a moment to munch on some grass before lifting its head, looking at us and mooing.

As strange and random as the moment was, Zane mooed back, after which the cow continued on its way.

"What did she say?" Crazy as it sounded, I couldn't help but ask.

"She said we looked like we're in love."

"Really? What did you say back?"

Zane smiled. "I told her we are."

THE END

Surviving Sin City

Zombie Boyz

Ethan Stone
Daniel A Kaine

CHAPTER ONE
KALEB

Counting his tips before leaving for the last delivery of the night, Kaleb Pierce grinned and pumped his fist. "Yes!"

With the money he'd made, he could afford a night at his favorite bar on the Las Vegas Strip, Krave, though he'd never tell his family that's where he was going. He could always find plenty of guys to dance with, and if someone caught his eye, he wasn't opposed to doing more. A night of grinding and rubbing against sweaty bodies as the music thumped was exactly what he needed. Just for those few hours, he could feel young and sexy again; something that didn't happen often since he was always delivering greasy pizzas or covering shifts at the 7-Eleven down the street from where he lived.

Kaleb pulled up in front of the customer's house, parking on the wrong side of the street so the driver's side was on the curb. He grabbed his cell phone and dialed the phone number on the order slip.

"Arnie's Pizza. I'm right outside."

Having worked and lived in some of the worst neighborhoods in Vegas, he was extra careful not to leave the car unless absolutely necessary, and he always kept his Glock nearby just in case.

The customer stepped out of the house, and Kaleb squinted to make out the man's face in the dim light.

"Harlan!"

"How are you doing, K?" They shook hands through the car window.

"Doing good," Kaleb replied. "When did you and Rachel move here?"

"Last month," he answered. "She's been sick for a week or so. I don't know if it's a cold or what, but she just can't seem to shake it. How much do I owe you?"

"Twenty seventy-five." Kaleb pulled the pizza out of the heated bag.

Harlan fished twenty-five from his wallet and handed it to Kaleb. The front door of Harlan's house opened, and a brunette woman stepped out. She was frail with a sunken face and empty-looking eyes, and Kaleb barely recognized her. He motioned for Harlan to turn around as she walked stiffly toward them.

Harlan turned around. "Rachel, what are you doing outside?"

She growled at Harlan. Kaleb was sure he'd heard wrong, until she did it again. Rachel stumbled forward, and Harlan dropped the pizza, reaching out to grab her.

Rachel leaned forward like she was going to kiss him, and he dodged her. Couldn't blame the guy for getting out of the way; she looked like shit. Her lips landed on his neck for what appeared to be a gentle display of affection, but Harlan screamed and pushed her away when she made contact. Blood gushed out of the wound, and a flap of flesh dangled from Rachel's lips.

"Ohfuckinghell!" Bile rose in the back of Kaleb's throat, and he fought the urge to gag. He reached for his phone with one hand and the Glock with the other.

"Fucking hell!" Harlan took his hand off his neck and stared at the blood. Rachel snarled and lunged at him. He tried to push her away, but she bit his arm and pulled away with skin and blood in her mouth. Harlan fell backward, jumped back up and ran into the house, slamming the door behind him.

Rachel turned toward Kaleb, reached through the car window and grabbed his arm. He yanked it away before she could sink her teeth in, aimed the gun and shot her in the shoulder. She fell backward and landed on her ass but was back on her feet quicker than should've been possible. He slammed the car into drive and hit the gas pedal while calling 911 on his phone.

"What's the nature of your emergency?" a deep, male voice asked.

"A woman just attacked her husband."

"What's the address?"

"4375 Sadie Street. Rachel and Harlan Barrett."

"What's your name?"

"Kaleb Pierce."

"Are you at the residence as we speak?"

"Hell, no. And I ain't going back."

"The police will need a report, sir."

"There's an empty lot on the corner of Sadie and Lana," Kaleb said. "I'll meet them there."

He pulled over at the empty lot, got out of his car and leaned against it for twenty minutes until a patrol car arrived.

A tall, black woman stepped out of the driver's seat and walked up to Kaleb. "Mr. Pierce?"

"Yes."

"I'm Officer Moss, and this is Officer Gonsalvo." She motioned to her partner. "Will you spell your name for us?"

"K-A-L-E-B."

"Caleb with a C?" Officer Gosalvo asked.

Kaleb sighed and rolled his eyes. "No, with a K, as in key."

"Key-Leb?"

"No!" he snapped.

"There is no need to raise your voice, Mr. Peirce," Officer Moss said.

Kaleb sighed again, pinched the bridge of his nose and slowly spelled his first and last name before finally giving his report.

"I was delivering a pizza to a friend of mine, Harlan Barrett, and his wife came out of their place. She was walking all funny like she couldn't bend her arms or something." Kaleb demonstrated the stiff-arm movement.

"Like Frankenstein?" Officer Gonsalvo asked.

Kaleb shook his head. "No, Frankenstein walks with his arms straight out in front of him. Her arms were at her side."

The cops nodded for him to continue.

"Rachel was gonna kiss Harlan, well I thought she was gonna

kiss him, but instead she bit him. Not a sexy bite, though. She took a fucking chunk out of his neck. I'm talking blood and skin hanging off her lips."

Officer Moss looked at Kaleb under half-closed eyelids. "Mr. Pierce, prank 911 calls can be prosecuted."

"I'm telling the truth, Officer," Kaleb swore.

There was a crackle over their radio, and Officer Gonsalvo stepped aside so he could hear it.

"So what you're telling me is a woman bit her husband?" Officer Moss asked.

"And came away with flesh. In her mouth. Yes. That is exactly what I'm saying."

"Hey, Moss," Officer Gonsalvo waved her over. They talked for a moment before turning their attention back to Kaleb.

"Well, Mr. Pierce, I guess you really aren't full of shit. The officers who responded to the scene had to physically subdue a woman as she was… growling and biting at them."

Kaleb bit back the urge to crow I told you so.

"Moss, we gotta roll," Gonsalvo called out. "We got another one."

"Another what?"

"A guy just reported his boyfriend biting his…."

"His what?" Moss asked.

"Biting his dick. Bit it off, in fact."

"What the fuck is going on in this town tonight?" Moss turned to Kaleb. "I have your phone number from when you called 911. If I have any further questions, I will get back to you."

"Thank God," Kaleb murmured. After everything that had happened, he really needed a few drinks.

Kaleb pulled into the alley behind the two story house he shared with his mother and brother, Pat. He shut off his car and grabbed the Glock, putting it and his keys in his pants pocket. He never left the pistol in the car, preferring to keep it near him even when he was at home.

"Mama!" Kaleb hollered as he stepped through the front door. "You ain't gonna believe what happened to me." No response.

"Mama?" She always answered when he got home, but she might be asleep. His brother might not have heard him if he was in his room playing World of Warcraft.

"Mama? Pat?" he called out again. Still no response. He walked into the living room and found his mother in her recliner, with her feet up and her eyes closed.

Kaleb walked up to the armchair and shook his mother's arm. "Mama!" He shook her again, and her blood red eyes popped open. She was slobbering, too. Not the usual amount of saliva some people have when they drool in their sleep, but serious amounts of slick spit running off her lips.

"KKaaaaallllllleeeeeebbbbbb," she moaned.

"Oh, fuck!" He backed into the wall and grabbed onto it like it was a life support. She said his name again, even more exaggerated than the first time. Her eyes, the way she breathed, her entire presence was foreign to him. She tried to push the footrest down but couldn't. Instead, she thrashed around in the chair until it flipped onto its side.

His mother flopped on the floor like a dying cockroach for a few moments before she rolled to her stomach. She stood slowly and was motionless for a moment before she stepped toward Kaleb, ambling clumsily like the Stay Puft Marshmallow Man on Prozac. Her eyes stared blankly at him the same way Rachel had looked at her husband as she continued to stumble forward.

"Mama?" He felt the acid in his stomach rising, and he knew he should run. What if he ended up like Harlan? He wasn't going to stick around long enough to find out.

Shifting slowly to the left, Kaleb found the doorway and took off. Thankfully, he hadn't emptied his pockets; he still had his keys, cell phone, and Glock. He ran out the front door and down the street.

The neighborhood where he lived had been named number four on the top twenty-five worst places to live in America. People usually stayed inside once it got dark unless they were dealing or buying drugs. But that night, at least a dozen people were outside.

Kaleb dialed 911 for the second time that day, but he got a recorded message. "Voice mail! Since when does fucking 911 have voice mail?" He walked in the direction of the 7-Eleven on the corner, hoping someone there might be able to help him.

"Pat!" Kaleb shouted. He'd forgotten to check to see if his brother was home. Their mother might go after him like she had done to Kaleb. He dialed Pat's cell phone, but it went straight to voice mail. "Pat, something weird is going on. If you're home, get the hell out. If you're not there, don't go back. Trust me on this."

Arriving at the 7-Eleven, Kaleb pushed the door open and stepped inside.

"Something is wrong with my mother. Can anyone help me?"

Of the half dozen people in the store, only one met Kaleb in the eye. The one who did make eye contact, a guy in his mid-to-late twenties with spiked dark blond hair, looked at him like he was an idiot, shook his head and turned away.

Kaleb headed back to his place. He had to go back and check if his brother was there, even if it meant facing his mother again. He and Pat hadn't always gotten along, but there had been a time when all they had was each other.

Kaleb had just gotten back to his car when his cell rang.

He breathed a sigh of relief. "Pat!" Are you okay? Where are you? You're not home, are you?"

"No, I'm at Chelsea's place."

His girlfriend. Why hadn't he thought of that?

"Something weird is going on, K," Pat said. "Chelsea's dad is sick. He's been making these weird gurgling noises. We took him to the ER, and the place is packed, bro. People are coughing and sneezing and even puking all over the place. One guy threw up blood in the waiting room. Another dude came in with fingers missing. It's hella nasty and freaking me out."

"Pat, something happened to Mama."

"What?" There was a commotion in the background. "I can't

hear you, K."

"Something happened to Mama!" Kaleb yelled into the phone.

"Holy fuck!" Pat shouted. "Oh, my mother fucking God, Kaleb. The blood vomit dude just turned to the guy with the missing digits and bit his face. The man's nose is gone, Kaleb."

"Pat, stay somewhere close by. I'm gonna come find you."

"What? I can't...."

The line went dead. "Pat! Pat! Hello, Pat!" He immediately tried calling back, but it went straight to voice mail. He left a message in case Pat hadn't heard what he said.

"Stay somewhere near the hospital. I'm driving up there right now."

CHAPTER TWO
COOPER

A glass clinked against the wooden bar. Cooper glanced up at the barman and gave a weak smile. If there was anything to be happy about it was the ready supply of Jack Daniel's. Nothing else seemed to be going his way. He lifted the drink in a silent toast before downing it in one mouthful, the liquid burning a path straight to his stomach.

"So, what's the deal?" asked the barman, a tall glass in one hand and a towel in the other.

Cooper raised an eyebrow. Since when did his life become the staff's business? "What makes you think something's up?"

"Well, you walked in here like someone killed your puppy, and that there's your third in five minutes." He placed the glass to one side and picked up the bottle of JD. "Another?"

Cooper nodded, pushing his empty tumbler toward the other man. "It's just relationship troubles, that's all."

"Ah, I hear you. Here, keep the freebie a secret, okay?" The bartender winked and filled the glass with a double. "So what happened?"

Lifting the glass to his mouth, Cooper intended on downing the drink. He paused as the alcohol hit his lips, and he took a small sip instead. All the alcohol in the world wasn't going to fix the problem. No point suffering the next day for it. "My... partner and I have been having a disagreement for a while. I thought we were moving past it, but then last week it all blew out of proportion. We were supposed to be coming here together...."

For a moment there was silence. "So you're here on your own?"

"It was too late to cancel. Nonrefundable, the agency said. Figured I could do with some time away."

"Well, if there's anywhere you can forget your troubles, it's

Vegas, buddy. Holler if you need anything, okay?"

"Yeah, sure," Cooper replied, lowering his gaze to his drink as the barman turned to serve a new set of customers at the other end of the bar. Coming to Vegas had seemed like a good idea at the time, putting some distance between himself and his ex. And you couldn't get much farther from England than Vegas. He clenched his fingers around the glass and lifted it to his mouth, gulping it in one go. He let out a long sigh. Fuck the hangover; he needed to get extremely drunk.

Cooper turned his head in the direction of the bartender. A television set behind the bar caught his eye. A woman in a black suit jacket and white shirt stood on a dark street outside a house surrounded by flashing blue lights. The headline crawled across the bottom of the screen:

"Love Bites—Woman tears a chunk out of her husband's throat."

Cooper arched an eyebrow. He lifted his hand, signaling for the barman to return.

"Don't you think you'd better start slowing down a bit?" he asked. "Night's still young."

"Can you turn that up?" Cooper replied, pointing to the screen.

"Yeah, sure." The barman reached beneath the counter to pick up a remote and aimed it at the television set, increasing the volume.

"It appears as though the victim's wife tore a huge chunk of flesh from his throat with her teeth. Police are still investigating but have yet to come up with any clues as to what prompted the attack." The woman paused as the cameras turned to one side. A young female struggled with two cops, who had her by the arms. Her face and clothes were coated brown and red. "This must be the wife now. We'll return with more details later."

The screen flashed back to the newsroom where a middle-aged man sat behind a desk. "In other news, the UNLV football team is celebrating their fifth victory in a row, this time against...."

The reporter paused, holding one hand against his earpiece. Seconds later, he nodded and turned his attention once more to the camera. A "Breaking News" crawl scrolled across the bottom of the screen.

"This just in. Police have responded to a call in Spring Valley, where a young man has been rushed to hospital following a vicious attack. Officers have refused to comment. We go now to our reporter live at the scene, Carmen DeLosa."

Blue and red lights flashed behind the woman as police kept back a crowd of onlookers. "Thank you, Bruce. I have with me here Mr. Foss who was walking his dog when the event transpired. Sir, could you tell us in your own words what you saw here today?"

"Well, I never seen anything like it," the elderly gentleman replied. "One moment everything was quiet, and then suddenly there was this man screaming. People across the street were coming out of their houses to see what was going on."

"Could you tell what he was saying?" the reporter asked.

"Oh, yes. He was yelling that someone had bit his… well, they'd…." The man paused and pulled at his collar. "Made him a eunuch with their teeth."

"You say the man was screaming because someone had bitten his penis off. Is that right?"

"Yes. Wouldn't have believed it myself if he hadn't come barging out the front door in hysterics. There was blood all down his legs, and he collapsed right over there on the lawn."

"Thank you, Mr. Foss." The camera zoomed in for a one-shot on the reporter. "Police have recently apprehended a man believed to be the attacker. He was found wandering the streets with blood all over his face and chest. Two officers confronted the individual, who turned hostile when they attempted to restrain him. Officer Moss, who attended the call, was sent to the ER for stitches after the man bit her hand."

"That's some crazy shit," the barman said. "Something similar happened the other day too. Makes you wonder what this world is coming to."

"Zombies," Cooper muttered under his breath. Was this really happening? Of all the times, it would be when he was halfway around the world from home.

"What happened the first time?"

"Guy took a chunk out of his brother's arm."

"They say why he did it?"

The barman shook his head. "Reckon it's some kinda drug causing people to hallucinate and go psycho."

Cooper stood and placed two twenty-dollar bills on the counter. If the zombie apocalypse was coming, then it would be best to get back home. Wouldn't be long before the whole place was quarantined. At least in England he'd have his secret stash of supplies and weapons at hand. In Vegas, he was totally unprepared. "Thanks. Keep the change."

He left in a hurry, his eyes darting left and right as he passed others on the sidewalk. No sign of anyone lumbering through the streets yet. Hopefully, it wasn't too late to get out of the city. A man to his left coughed. Cooper flinched as though a gun had gone off next to him. His heart pounded in his chest. What if the man was infected? Could it travel from person to person just from a cough? How many people were already ticking time bombs waiting to go off and chomp on the nearest person? Shit, he needed to get the hell out of Vegas and fast.

Cooper reached the hotel and went back to his room. He shoved everything into his rucksack and looked around, making sure nothing was left behind before heading out onto the corridor toward the elevator. The doors slid open. A woman lifted her hand to her mouth and coughed. Cooper froze, his left foot already inside. He took a step back.

"Sorry, I uh, just remembered I forgot something in my room," he said.

The woman glanced at him before the doors closed again. Last thing he needed was to be stuck in a confined space with someone who could already be infected. He hauled his luggage down the stairs instead.

The lobby was packed with groups of people rushing to and from the hotel bar and casino, heading out for a night on The Strip. Coop kept to one side, avoiding close contact with as many people as possible as he made his way to reception. The man at the front desk lifted his head as Cooper approached.

"Your room is still booked for another three days, sir," he said, taking the cardkey from him.

"Family emergency," Cooper said. "Need to get back home as soon as possible. Could you call a cab to take me to the airport?"

"Of course. Was everything to your satisfaction?"

Could have done without housekeeping walking in on him while he was in the shower. "Yeah, everything was great. Thanks."

Cooper tapped his foot, turning his head to give the lobby a once over. No zombies pounding against the glass doors. That was a good sign. But what if the infection had already spread to England? Well, at least there he'd have everything he needed to survive. Those idiots who called him paranoid and crazy wouldn't be laughing anymore.

"Okay, sir. Your cab should be here in the next fifteen minutes."

"Thank you," Cooper replied, heading for a quiet corner near the exit. He turned his back to the wall, giving him a good view of the large hall. No damn walking corpse was going to get the jump on Cooper Lockwood.

The minutes crawled by until the receptionist waved a hand at him. "Mr. Lockwood? Your cab is outside waiting for you."

Cooper nodded and found the cab was parked against the footpath. The driver stepped out and opened the trunk before extending a hand toward the luggage.

"It's okay, I got it," Cooper said, jerking his case away from the man. No one could be trusted. He'd walk to the airport if it wasn't some distance away. With his luggage safely stowed away, he climbed into the back seat. "Airport, please."

"Sure thing," the cabbie replied in a hoarse voice.

The cab pulled out of the hotel car park and onto the main road, joining the rush of traffic. Cooper drummed his fingers against his knees. Wouldn't be long now. Next flight, and he was out of there. Didn't matter which part of England it took him to, as long as Vegas was safely behind him. Changing flights would cost him a small fortune, not that money was much of a concern to him. Getting home was the important thing.

Lights whizzed by on both sides, flashing signs that lit up the night. The place was one giant gambling advertisement. It wasn't even his idea to come here; it was Ewan's. Cooper clenched his jaw and fists. Fuck, why'd he have to think of him? He let out a long breath and relaxed his muscles. Just like every other time, he'd probably go crawling back to Ewan. Never learned from his mistakes. Still, he couldn't just leave him to die or worse, become a mindless flesh-eater.

A cough from the front of the car jerked Cooper from his thoughts. Thank God for the partition between them. The driver continued his hoarse coughing. Definitely a smoker. The cab pulled to one side of the road and came to a stop outside a small neighborhood. The cabbie threw his door open and stepped out onto the pavement, his body doubled over as he hacked and wheezed. Not good at all.

Cooper opened his door and moved around the back of the cab, keeping some distance between them. "Are you all right?"

The driver spat on the ground. A black-red glob landed on the gravel with a splat, highlighted by a nearby street light.

"Fuck. What is that?" Cooper asked. He took a step closer. It was almost like a chunk of rotten meat. He paused, his blood running cold. The man straightened himself up and stared at him blankly. Zombie? Nah, it couldn't be. He was fine not too long ago.

A deep groan rumbled through the cabbie's chest. He lurched forward, his arms outstretched. Cooper's mouth dropped open as he turned and ran. Blood drummed through his skull. Fuck the luggage. A few clothes weren't worth his life, and he could always return. He raced through the streets, a warm breeze blowing against him. Sweat trickled down his back, his black shirt sticking to his skin.

He ducked into an alleyway and peered out again. No sign of Zombie Cabbie. His heart hammered against his chest as he struggled to regain his breath. He'd need to find some other way to the airport. If only he could drive. Why had he never learned? Twenty-six, and he was the only one of his friends who couldn't. Probably because it cost too much, and he didn't really need a car. Would have come in useful now, though.

He took a long, steadying breath before glancing around the corner once more. The street was empty. What now? He'd need supplies first. Food and drink mainly. He patted the left pocket of his jeans. Thank fuck he still had his wallet. There had to be a convenience store around somewhere. After that, he'd need to find someplace safe, at least until the morning.

CHAPTER THREE
KALEB

Kaleb pulled onto the street and checked out the increasing mayhem. One man stumbled blindly around before he bent over and hurled red vomit. Kaleb's gag reflex kicked in, and he opened the door and threw up. When he sat back up, the man was walking slowly toward him, his lips pulled back in a vicious looking snarl. His eyes were bright red.

Pulling the door shut, Kaleb put the car in drive and edged forward. He stopped when the man was right in front of him. Kaleb honked the horn, thinking it would make the man move, but he looked directly at Kaleb and snarled. "What the fuck is going on?"

Not even bumping the guy made him move. "Get out of the way!" Kaleb yelled, though he knew it would accomplish nothing. He accelerated again, and all it did was force the man to step backward.

"Fuck this," Kaleb muttered. "I don't got time for this shit." He put one foot on the brake, one foot on the gas and revved the engine. "Last chance to move, you son of a bitch."

When the man didn't budge, Kaleb took his foot off the brake and slammed into the guy, who fell forward on the hood, his face pressed against the windshield. Kaleb's mouth gaped as the man continued to growl and even pounded the window with a hand. Kaleb turned a corner quickly, tossing the man off the car. He glanced in the rear view mirror, and saw the man stand up. "No fucking way!"

Kaleb turned his eyes back to the street just in time to avoid a Geo Metro, its doors wide open, parked in the middle of the street. Immediately past the Metro was a small group of people all looking as healthy as his mother had. He yanked hard to the right, clipping a woman before T-boning a lifted Ford F-250 with huge tires. His car got wedged under the elevated truck. The hood crumpled like an accordion and the windshield cracked, but he was okay thanks to his seat belt.

Putting the car in reverse, he tried to free his vehicle. The tires screeched and smoke from the burning rubber filled the air, but the car didn't budge. He grabbed his keys, cell, and Glock and tried to open the door, but it was jammed. Leaning back, he put his feet up in the air and kicked the windshield, busting it into small pieces.

He grabbed the top of the window frame and pulled himself onto the hood. Remaining in a crouched position, he looked around before sitting down and sliding off.

"Son of a bitch!" Pain sliced through his left calf, and his leg buckled when he came off the car. He grabbed his leg and felt torn jeans and wet warmth. A crumpled piece of the fender had cut him badly, and blood oozed out. He grabbed a work shirt he had in his car, tore a strip off and tied it around his leg to stop the bleeding.

The woman he'd clipped swayed as her left arm dangled from her shoulder, obviously dislocated. Skin had been torn off her face, but she moved forward with effort, her knee jutting out at an odd angle. The people she had been with were far ahead of her, but two people, an elderly woman and a teenage boy, came up behind her and stepped on either side. The young man looked at the open face wound and growled to the old woman. They stepped in front of the slowly moving woman and faced her so she had to stop. The boy reached both hands out, grabbed the limp appendage and yanked so hard, it detached from her body.

She studied the blood gushing from her shoulder then turned back and roared at the boy. He and his companion bellowed louder as he raised the disconnected appendage to his mouth and took an enormous bite out of it. Kaleb buried his mouth in the crook of his elbow to stop from getting sick but lost it when the old woman leapt on the other female, knocked her to the ground and bit her cheek. Retching as quietly as he could, Kaleb fought to maintain control so he didn't end up as the creature's second course.

He crawled under the truck and took off running when it was clear. A man and woman blocked the other side of the street, so he hid behind a car until they were gone. Neither one appeared sick, but he didn't want to take any chances.

Kaleb hated the idea of walking all the way to Chelsea's place, but not having a better plan, he moved slowly in that direction. He kept pulling out his cell, checking for a signal and dialing Pat's number. It rang a single time and Kaleb heard an automated response saying that all circuits were busy before the signal disappeared.

He peeked around a corner and froze when he saw an obviously sick black man. Kaleb was debating which direction to head when a growl startled him, and he spun toward the source of the noise. Three people stepped out of the front door of the apartment building behind Kaleb. They all had red eyes and their skin had taken on an odd greenish pallor, as if rotting from the inside out.

Kaleb turned and ran up the street away from both groups of sick people—if they could still be called people. Whatever had happened to them, and Rachel, and his mother, and who knows who else, had changed them into cannibals. Killers. Monsters. Though he was running from the creatures, he was also going in the opposite direction from where he'd wanted to go. Survival had to be his highest priority, even above finding Pat.

Kaleb turned down a dark alley but halfway down, he saw a couple creatures on the other side and came to a halt. He glanced back from where he'd come and saw he was trapped with monsters at each entrance. Looking from one end of the alley to the other, Kaleb tried to gauge which set he could dispatch most easily. He pulled the Glock and aimed first at one group of monsters and then the other.

The gang on one side suddenly tore off after something, or, more likely, someone. The other two creatures eyed Kaleb like he was a tasty piece of meat. He aimed the Glock and fired twice, hitting one square in the chest and the other right between his eyes. The second one dropped to the ground, but the first stumbled a bit then kept moving.

Still moving? How the hell was that even possible? The creatures were like Frankenstein's monster or… zombies? It made sense in a weird, nonsensical sort of way. But that wasn't possible. Zombies weren't real. The monster coming after Kaleb, however, was real. He fired a bullet into the creature's head, stopping him for good. Kaleb ran to the far side of the alley and saw at least a dozen monsters tearing apart a man and his dog.

A female flesh-eater wearing a pink dress with butterflies on it gnawed on one of the dog's legs—most likely a black Lab based on the dark fur she spit out. She saw Kaleb and began to amble his way. He aimed the Glock before thinking, but he only had six more bullets in the gun, and the rest of his ammo was back at his house. Conserving bullets was a necessity because he wasn't sure when—or if—he'd be able to get more.

Kaleb waited until the butterfly dress lady was a few feet away from him, then sprinted around her. He dodged the herd she'd been sharing her meal with and ran as fast as possible up a block, jumped over a low fence and cut through a back yard. He stopped when he noticed a basement entrance secured with nothing but a cheap padlock. Kaleb kicked at the lock several times before it busted loose. He flipped open the door, thankful the homeowner had left the lights on. The basement was small with just enough room for a washer and dryer. Another set of stairs were straight ahead, and he walked cautiously up them and into the kitchen after a quick look convinced him it was empty.

Kaleb removed the strip of fabric from his calf, turned on the tap water, and wet a hand towel. Busy cleaning up the wound, he suddenly felt a sharp pain on the back of his knees and collapsed. He rolled onto his back and looked up at a guy holding a lead pipe—the man he'd seen at 7-Eleven earlier.

"What the fuck?"

"Who are you?" the guy asked. He had a British accent, which Kaleb usually found sexy. In this situation, not so much.

"Who the fuck are you?" Kaleb shot back. "This ain't your place."

"It isn't yours either, Red. You been sick?" the man asked.

"Huh?"

"It's a fairly simple question. Have. You. Been. Sick? Coughing. Fever. Anything like that?"

Kaleb shook his head, and the Brit took a deep breath, lowering the lead pipe. "That doesn't mean anything. You could still be infected," he muttered.

"Infected?" Kaleb asked. "Rachel, Mama, all those other people were sick with something?"

He waved off the question off like it wasn't important.

"Can I stand up?"

The British man nodded. Kaleb extended his hand so the other guy could help him, but the Brit ignored him. Grabbing onto the edge of the counter, he hoisted himself up. He almost went back down as his vision blurred and his head pounded, but he gripped the counter until it cleared.

The guy scrutinized Kaleb. "Where did the blood come from?"

"Chill, dude. I wasn't having a human snack. I was in a car accident. Scratched my leg."

He nodded. "You were bleeding pretty badly, right?"

"Yeah. So what if I was?"

"You created a perfect trail for the zombies."

"Zombies?" Kaleb asked incredulously. "Are you batshit crazy?"

"You have seen the sick people, right?"

Kaleb nodded.

"So you've probably seen them chowing down on other people."

"Yeah, I've seen weird shit today. But that doesn't mean they're zombies."

"Believe what you want to," the Brit said. "I don't give a fuck either way."

The sound of banging coming from the front of the house startled Kaleb, but he noticed the other man didn't jump at all.

"What's happening?" Kaleb asked.

The man grabbed Kaleb's arm and dragged him to the living room. At the front door and the large picture window was a group of creatures, including Butterfly Dress.

"You led them right here."

CHAPTER FOUR
COOPER

Cooper's lip curled. He turned away from the redhead and picked up a plastic carrier bag from the floor, filled with bottled water, snacks, and a few odds and ends that might come in handy. With the lead pipe in one hand and his supplies in the other, he marched to the back door and slowly opened it. He popped his head out, glancing left and right. No sign of the undead.

A thud and a groan came from behind. No doubt the zombie in the butterfly dress had finally managed to clamber in through the window. He'd have to get moving quickly. But where to?

Cooper stepped outside into the garden and around the side of the house. More zombies had arrived, seemingly drawn to the sounds of the hungry rabble attempting to break into the house, like a pack of wild animals. Looking to his left, the road was clear. He started down the street as quickly as he could without making much noise, keeping to the shadows and pausing at every corner.

Before him lay a crossroad. Cars filled the streets, though none were moving. Most were abandoned, their alarms blaring and doors left wide open. Many had broken windows and crumpled bodywork. The infection must have hit the area hard. Coop went to take a step forward when a grunt and a crash came from behind. Raising the lead pipe, he spun round to meet his assailant.

"Whoa," the redhead yelled. "Once was enough."

Cooper let out a low groan. The young man picked himself up from the ground where he had fallen. "What the fuck are you doing?"

"Same thing you are. Trying to survive."

"Yeah? Well, I give you twenty-four hours max," Cooper replied. "Now stop following me."

"But we'd be safer together," the younger man protested.

Cooper snorted. "For all I know, you could be infected. I can't risk taking you along."

"I'm clean, really. And how do I know you're not the infected one?"

"You don't, and that's why you should get away from me. Find some place secure and barricade yourself in. Maybe then you'll survive the night. Only this time, make sure you don't have a pack of zombies on your tail."

Cooper turned back to the roads. Damn, if only he knew the area. Maybe the walking-zombie-chow could be of some use after all.

"How familiar are you with this place?"

"Lived here all my life," the redhead replied.

"Much as I hate to admit it, I'm lost here. I need to find somewhere safe. You have any ideas?"

The redhead scratched his chin and sucked in his lower lip. "Well, there's a grocery store not too far from here. Place has metal shutters, and there'll be plenty of food there."

Cooper shook his head. "Too big. Needs to be fairly small with only a few exits. Otherwise it'll be too hard to defend."

"Oh, I know. There used to be an old bookstore on Kenyon Place. Shut down about a week ago, and it's all been boarded up since."

"Sounds great. Lead the way, but I'll be keeping an eye on you. You so much as cough, and I'll kill you. Understand?"

The man nodded and inched out onto the pavement, his gaze going left and right. "It's this way," he said, pointing straight ahead.

Cooper followed behind, keeping a short distance between them. The other man had shown no signs of infection yet, but that didn't mean much. Maybe the virus, or whatever it was turning people into lumbering corpses, was still incubating inside of him. Who knew how long it took for the change to happen? If they could just survive the night, then he'd be able to make a break for it in the morning… alone.

Ten minutes passed before they came to an old brick building. Securely padlocked metal shutters protected the windows and doors. The zombies would have enough trouble breaking in that it would at least give them a chance to escape. Only problem was they had no way of getting inside either,

"Well, this is just great," Cooper said, smacking his forehead with the palm of his hand. "How exactly are we supposed to get in without making enough noise to alert every zombie in the area?"

"Over here," Red replied, motioning to a narrow alleyway with a wire fence blocking it.

Cooper started down the passage and climbed over the fence. The yard out back was littered with black bags of rubbish, giving off a rotten stench. He scrunched his nose and surveyed the area. A fire escape led to a single window. The boards covering it were cracked and splintered, leaving a big enough gap to climb through. He scaled the ladder and peered inside. No sign of life or the undead.

Once inside, he set the bag of supplies down on an old desk and scouted the dark halls, where he found several small rooms, each empty save for a few pieces of furniture. Must have been where the owner of the store below lived, he thought. A set of stairs led down to a door. Cooper descended slowly, gripping the pipe tight in his right hand. With his free hand, he reached for the doorknob and gave it a quick turn. Locked.

He turned around and went back to the first room with the window he had climbed through. A shaft of light spilled into the corridor. He groaned and stormed into the room where Red sat on a wooden chair with one leg raised up. A nearby lamp had been switched on, highlighting the large gash of crimson down his calf. He pulled back the torn jeans, hissing as he exposed the raw flesh.

"Fuck's sake," Cooper said, restraining the urge to shout. Did this man have no survival instinct at all?

Red's head shot up. "What?"

"Where do I start? You could be infected, and you're gonna

get blood everywhere. Real smart move there. And are you trying to advertise our location?" Cooper walked forward and yanked the lamp's plug from the wall. "I take back my previous comment. You're not gonna make it twelve hours at this rate."

"Hey," Red yelled. "How am I supposed to see now?"

"Better blind than dead." Cooper reached for the plastic bag and fished around inside for a roll of bandages. He unwound the roll and tore off a long strip, which he tossed to him, followed by one of the bottles of water. "There, get yourself cleaned and bandaged. We can't have you bleeding all over the damn place."

"Ummm, thanks."

He walked across the room and took a seat by the window. "What's your name?"

"Kaleb Pierce."

"Name's Cooper, but you can call me Coop. Just don't be getting the wrong idea, okay? Once it's daylight, I'm out of here. You'll have to fend for yourself."

Kaleb nodded and opened the bottle of water. He poured a small amount onto his leg, his jaw clenching. That he'd survived this long already was a miracle.

CHAPTER FIVE
KALEB

Kaleb wasn't sure what to think of Cooper. He seemed pretty on the ball and sure of himself, but his self-confidence bordered on arrogance, and his comments about Kaleb not being able to survive for long pissed him off.

Coop looked out the window. "I don't see any zombies nearby."

Kaleb's raised his head. "That's the second time you used that word."

"What word?"

"Zombies."

He rolled his eyes. "What else should I call them? After all, this is the zombie apocalypse."

"Zombie apocalypse," Kaleb repeated. "You can't be serious. That's just fiction like Superman or the Transformers."

"Bloody Americans," he muttered. "How can you be so ignorant?"

"How can you be so sure about what's going on? You act like you knew this was going to happen?"

"I did."

"How could you possibly have known?"

Coop gave a dismissive wave, and Kaleb knew he wasn't going to answer his question. Not right away anyway. But he'd get the information out of him sooner or later.

"What's the plan for tonight?" Kaleb asked.

Coop gave Kaleb the same look he'd already given him more than once. That arrogant glance combined with a roll of his eyes.

"Find the best room to sleep for the night," he finally answered.

"You don't think we need to stay up in shifts or whatever?"

Cooper's sigh told Kaleb what he thought of the question. "The place is pretty secure with the fence and metal shutters."

They sat there quietly for what felt like hours to Kaleb, but was probably just a few minutes.

"So, you're British?"

"Wow, you're a sharp one aren't you?"

"Why do you have to be such an asshole all the time?" Kaleb asked. "I'm just trying to make conversation."

"I don't feel like talking."

Kaleb slammed his hand on the table and walked out of the room. He found the bathroom and fought the urge to slam the door behind him. He really wanted to take a shower but wasn't sure what I'm Too Cool for School Coop would say about that. Probably that the hot water would attract the zombies or some crazy bullshit.

Kaleb splashed some water on his face, leaned against the counter and breathed deeply. Jesus Christ, it was all so unreal. Zombies? Stuck with a snobby Brit who didn't like to talk. Could things get worse? After giving himself a minute to relax, Kaleb rejoined Coop in the living room.

"Why are you in Vegas?" Kaleb asked.

Coop gave him the exasperated look again.

"Look," Kaleb said. "I am stressed the fuck out. My nerves are shot. I just want to make the time pass quicker by talking."

Coop sighed and rubbed the bridge of his nose like he had a headache coming on. "The trip was supposed to be fun. We were going to relax and enjoy ourselves after… well, things hadn't been good for a while."

"I got it," Kaleb replied. "Women problems, huh?"

Coop looked at the young man for a second before answering. "Something like that."

"Where's your girlfriend? Back at the motel?"

Coop shook his head. "I came alone. Thought I could make the best of it, but that wasn't a good idea. The zombie apocalypse had to hit while I was here. All the preparations I made are useless if I can't find a way home as soon as possible."

"How do you plan on doing that?"

"If I can get to the airport, I'll find a way to get a flight."

Kaleb grunted. "Yeah, because getting on a plane with a zombie is a great idea. And you question my ability to survive."

"What I do is my business, not yours," Coop snapped. "I can take care of myself, and I'll do whatever is needed to get home."

"I don't think the chances of you hopping on a plane are very good. You'd be better off finding a place to hide out here in Vegas. I'm going to find my brother then lay low until the worst is over."

"Look, no offense, but I don't care what you want to do, or what you think I should do. Like I said, come morning we're going our separate ways. You do what you think is best, and I'll do what I need to do."

"No offense taken, arrogant prick," Kaleb mumbled. Coop looked at Kaleb, but he didn't say anything.

Neither man talked for twenty minutes, so the room was as quiet as a graveyard when Kaleb's cell phone buzzed. They both jumped at the noise, and Kaleb fished the phone out of his pocket as quickly as he could. He had been sporadically checking for a signal but hadn't had anything for more than a couple hours.

"Who is it?" Coop demanded.

"It's a text from Pat. My brother."

K, this shit is crazy! Hope you've made it so far. I hope this message gets through 'cuz I'm not sure how long cell phones are gonna work. I'm heading to Black Mountain Country Club. Good place to hang out for a while I think. Get there if you can.

Pat had been working at the Black Mountain Golf and Country Club for just under a year. It was a posh resort in Henderson, just outside of Vegas. Knowing Pat was alive and had a goal made Kaleb feel a hundred times better.

"What did he have to say?"

"Just wanted to let me know he's alive and tell me where he's going," he replied.

"To hell, like the rest of us."

Kaleb didn't let Coop's rudeness get him down. Pat was alive, and that was all that really mattered.

The adrenaline finally wore off, and Kaleb could barely hold his eyes open.

"You ready for bed?" Coop stood up and stretched.

"Is that an invitation?" Kaleb smiled, letting Coop know it was a joke, but the perma-scowl on his face didn't go away.

"The only invitation there was for you to go to sleep so I can get some peace and quiet," Coop scoffed. "One of the rooms I saw had a couch and a mattress on the floor. Should be okay for the night."

Kaleb nodded and followed him down the hallway. The couch had to have been from the 70s with a truly ugly floral green pattern. The mattress didn't look much better, but wasn't as dirty as the couch. No wonder the owners had left them.

"I'll take the mattress if you don't mind," Kaleb said.

Coop shrugged and lay down on the couch. Kaleb stretched out on the mattress and was asleep a few moments later.

CHAPTER SIX
COOPER

The next morning Coop woke up first. He'd spent the first part of the night tossing and turning, listening for every little sound. He had finally jammed a chair under the door handle so he could get some sleep. He stood and rolled his shoulders, working out the dull ache before removing the chair and slowly opening the door. After checking to see if the corridor was safe, he went into the bathroom and turned on the shower. Within three minutes, he had dried himself off, pulled on his creased shirt and jeans, and assessed his reflection in the mirror. God, he looked a state. And was that mud on his clothes?

Coop shook his head and headed toward the only open window. The sun had already risen above the rooftops of Vegas, and he squinted his eyes. Everything seemed quiet. No better time to make his escape. He went back to the room where he had slept, inching the door open and peering inside. Kaleb was still fast asleep, mumbling something incoherent. Poor guy. Probably wouldn't last long, but maybe he'd manage if he could make it to his brother.

Shutting the door again, Coop went back to the window and climbed out the fire escape. He paused, his gaze darting back inside. No, it was best this way. Having Kaleb tag along would only slow him down. Coop ignored the churning in his gut and climbed down the ladder. He walked down the narrow passage onto the street and looked both ways. Not a living creature to be seen, or an undead one for that matter. Perfect.

Hours later, Coop stopped at an intersection. He tilted his head back to read the sign and let out a long sigh. Maybe it would have helped if he knew which direction he was supposed to head. After leaving the house, he'd found his way back to the cab from the previous night, so he was able to pick up his rucksack filled with clean clothes. Sweat plastered the black shirt to his back from carrying it. He opened up a bottle of water and swallowed a mouthful before replacing the lid.

"Now where?" he asked out loud.

If only there'd been someone to answer him. He'd been following the same road for an hour at least, and the only cars he'd seen had sped past without even slowing down. Selfish Yanks. Didn't even have the courtesy to offer help. Directions to the airport would have been nice for starters.

Coop fished around in his bag for a map of the city. He'd planned on taking a tour of Vegas and seeing the sights, but that wasn't going to happen now. Running his finger over the map, he found the airport and looked for any major roads that might lead him there. The 515 would take him close to two major airports. McCarran International was probably already packed. No point heading there. He glanced back up at the sign. Finally, some luck. The interstate wasn't far. He crammed the map back into his bag and turned left. The next airport was going to be a long haul, but maybe once he hit the main road, he'd find more people about.

He walked for another fifteen minutes in the sweltering heat. Wiping the sweat from his brow, he found shade at a gas station that hadn't bothered opening for the day. The metal shutters were still locked down. Coop wandered around the side of the building and came to an open door. A red streak decorated the handle, continuing down the frame and along the floor inside.

Coop took a step inside, taking the lead pipe in both hands and tightening his grip around it. He inched forward, stopping to peer inside another door. The stockroom was filled with cardboard boxes piled on top of each other, but no zombies. The next door was locked. He pressed his ear to the wood, listening for any movement. Nothing. He continued to the store and checked each of the three aisles for anything human before finally relaxing his hold on the pipe.

He slipped out of the rucksack's shoulder straps and rested it against the counter. Kneeling down, he opened up the main compartment and pulled out the first T-shirt he could find, a black V-neck. One last glance around him and he unbuttoned his shirt, using the already damp material to wipe most of the sweat from his skin before slipping into the clean top. No doubt he'd be soaked again in no time at all, but it was better than almost drowning in it.

He pulled out his mobile and swiped his finger across the touch screen to unlock it, navigating through the menu to his contacts. The first name that popped up was Ewan. Coop swallowed the lump in his throat and placed his phone down on the counter. He picked up the store's phone and punched the numbers in to dial internationally. The dial tone rang a few times before there was a click, and then the automated message.

Coop took a long breath as the deep voice asked him to leave a message. He hesitated, not sure what to say.

"Hey," he started, running his left hand through his short hair. "It's Coop. Look, ummm... Well, I guess I was right about the zombies. Dunno if you guys back home have heard about it yet, but Vegas is overrun with the living dead. I'm coming home as soon as I can, okay?" He paused, and then glanced down at his mobile on the counter. No signal. Shit!

"I'm not sure when I'll be able to contact you again. Not sure if you're even still alive, but if you get this message, there's a spare key in the top drawer of my desk. The shelter out back has food and weapons. Use it until I return. Just stay safe."

Coop was going to hang up but stopped and added, "One more thing. I'm sorry about the way we left things. Let's talk when I get back, okay?"

He slowly put down the phone and let out a long breath, his heart thudding against his ribs. And there it was, the inevitable attempt at reconciliation. True, things had been going steadily downhill for months with Ewan, but that could all be remedied. Couldn't it? Maybe a nice long chat was just what they needed rather than the drunken arguments and shouting matches that had become so commonplace. And what better time than the apocalypse? Wasn't as though there would be much to do except batten down the hatches and wait it out.

Coop went to one of the refrigerated units and pulled out

a bottle of water. He left the door open, delighting in the cold chill that seeped out. Unscrewing the cap, he downed the bottle in seconds before taking several more and stuffing them into his pack. He moved to the next shelf, picked up a protein bar and tore into the foil wrapper. He took a few large bites before grabbing another handful and placing them into the side pocket of his backpack. It would be enough to get him to the airport at least. Anymore, and he'd have trouble carrying it.

He lifted the backpack, letting out a grunt as it settled on his shoulders. The extra bottles of water alone were like a ton of bricks added to his luggage. He huffed and pulled the straps tight before setting off once more with his pipe in hand.

As he exited the station there was a groan, followed by the sound of soft footsteps. Coop froze, the sound of blood pounding through his skull almost deafening. He took a step back but found his backpack caught on something. The shuffling of feet grew louder and then stopped. His gaze travelled in the direction of the noise, meeting a set of red puffy eyes. The man stared back at him, his jaw slack and saliva dripping from his lips. Patches of black marred his pale skin and torn clothes. He took a step forward and sniffed at the air.

"Shit," Coop muttered. He tried to move again, only to find his rucksack caught on the door handle. The zombie lurched forward with a speed that seemed unreal for a corpse. Coop gave one last yank, freeing the strap from the door and quickly moved to one side, turning to swing the pipe at the zombie's head. It collided with a smack and a crunch, the man collapsing forward into the door. Coop took a few steps back, keeping his gaze on his attacker. Its arms twitched, and the zombie clambered to its feet, a gargled choking coming from low in its throat.

Coop ran toward the road. Another moan sounded from out front. A pair of lumbering corpses stepped from behind a gas tanker, instantly setting their sights on him and blocking his path. He turned to head in the opposite direction but stopped before he could take a single step. The first zombie was already back in action, ambling toward him.

"Three against one," Coop said, gripping the lead pipe like a baseball bat. "Wish I had my crossbow."

He swallowed hard, fighting back the sickly feeling rising up from his stomach. Surely he could handle three of the walking dead on his own. He was faster than they were and probably stronger, too. They lurched toward him, and then stopped. There was a collective groan between them as the humming of an engine grew louder and wheels skidded against the tarmac.

CHAPTER SEVEN
KALEB

Kaleb was furious when he woke and found Coop gone, but he wasn't at all surprised. Coop had said they would be going their separate ways. Kaleb figured he'd have a chance to get Coop to change his mind, but if that was how the jerk wanted it, Kaleb had no problem.

Kaleb wasn't helpless, despite what Coop thought. He didn't need Coop. He didn't need anyone, but he liked human companionship. Kaleb wasn't convinced Cooper was entirely human, but being with him would be better than being alone.

"Fuck him," Kaleb mumbled. "I'll protect myself, and he can take care of his own selfish skin."

Kaleb checked out the bookstore to make sure the British bastard really had gone, not that Kaleb had any doubt Cooper would abandon his own mother if it meant he had a better shot at surviving.

After a quick shower, Kaleb checked his cell phone to see if there was a signal. Nothing, but maybe there were still spotty signals if Pat had been able to contact him.

He needed a vehicle and some weapons if he was going to stand a chance of hooking up with Pat. The gun stores would've already been looted. Well, the legal ones anyway. But there were other places, such as where he'd bought his Glock. Kaleb had purchased his gun from a childhood friend named Emilio who lived about six blocks away. Hopefully, he'd make it there alive with the few bullets he had left.

Kaleb went out the back door, made sure the area was clear of zombies and climbed over the metal fence. He cut down to a street he knew wasn't usually busy and looked for a vehicle he could use. He should've paid attention when Pat tried to teach him how to hot-wire a vehicle. Without that particular talent, he had to rely on some naïve idiot leaving keys in the car. The first block had four cars parked in front of houses; the doors of the first three were locked, and the fourth had the doors open but no keys anywhere.

He continued checking all the cars on the next block and was ready to consider the effort futile when he came to a blue Econoline van with dozens of bumper stickers, like "Shaggin' Wagon" and the old standard, "If this van's a rockin,' don't come a knockin,'" on the back door. Hunching down as he walked up the side of the van, he opened the door without looking in the window.

"Oh, shit!" he said, louder than he wished. A dead body rolled out and landed at his feet. It was a young woman with what looked like a gunshot wound in her right temple. Kaleb stepped over the corpse, trying not to feel callous for doing so, and pulled himself into the van. The keys were in the ignition. He kicked something with his foot, reached down and picked it up—a Smith and Wesson pistol. He tucked the gun next to his Glock in the back of his pants.

He was about to start the van when a tall black man ran down the street, screaming at the top of his lungs. Behind him shambled a few almost fully decayed zombies. What remained of their skin was a moldy green color, and they had lost most of their hair. They weren't moving quickly. The black man could have gotten away safely if he hadn't been constantly turning back to see how far the creatures were behind him. He tripped on a hole in the street and planted his face into the cement. Another monster came out of nowhere, biting into the side of the man's face and pulling away an ear. The beast chomped on the ear while holding the man down.

The other two creatures caught up, fell to the ground and began eating the man's legs. Ear Eater, however, looked around, picked up a brick and slammed it against the victim's head until the skull broke. He then reached into the skull, pulled out a handful of brains and took a bite. He let out a shout and began digging in. When the other two tried to grab some of the meal from his hands, the zombie punched one and kicked the other.

"Dude don't like to share. Time to get the hell out of here." He turned the ignition, and the engine sputtered but didn't turn over. "Fuck!" Kaleb tried again with no luck.

The zombie sniffed the air, looked directly at Kaleb and ran toward him as he turned the key, pumped the gas and prayed to God. He gave a shout of victory when the engine turned over. Putting it in gear, he stepped on the gas and aimed for the zombies. The brain-muncher jumped out of the way, but the other two didn't even attempt to move. They crunched beneath the tires as he ran them over.

Arriving at Emilio's place, Kaleb parked a block away so he could make sure the place was safe and still be able to run to the van if it wasn't. Emilio had a three story home with a two-car garage, nicer than most of the houses in the neighborhood, but not so nice it drew attention.

He climbed a set of stairs to a wooden deck and rang the bell on a side door. When there wasn't an answer, he rang it again. After the third try, it was clear no one was home, or if they were home they weren't planning on answering the door. Emilio had never invested in a conventional alarm system because he or someone who worked for him had always been protecting their assets with the same guns they sold.

He stepped in and checked the rooms one at a time. In the master bedroom were two dead bodies—Emilio and his wife. Both corpses had holes in their heads, but the woman had greenish skin and appeared to have been infected. "Probably shot her then himself," he said aloud.

Patting down Emilio's carcass, he found a set of keys, went downstairs and opened a steel door. In the room were dozens of different types of weapons. He grabbed a shotgun, because all the movies showed zombies getting their head blown off, as well as a couple of rifles and ammunition for both pistols. He also grabbed what food he could from the cupboards: cupcakes, bread, peanut butter, chocolate bars, and several bags of chips. Emilio hadn't been a healthy eater.

He carried everything back to the van and took off, getting

on Flamingo Road toward Interstate15 a few blocks later. There were a few other cars on the road and almost all were going the same way as Kaleb. He wondered how far Coop had made it toward the airport.

"McCarran has to be a mess," Kaleb muttered. "He could be walking into a massacre."

Kaleb pulled off to the side of the road despite the fact the exit to the freeway was just ahead. He pounded his fist against the steering wheel as he tried to make a decision. Coop may have abandoned Kaleb thinking he wouldn't survive long, but Kaleb couldn't do the same thing. He should get on the freeway, find Pat and forget about Cooper, but Kaleb couldn't just leave him. Chances of finding Coop would be slim if he'd managed to get a ride, but Kaleb had to try.

Flipping a U-turn, Kaleb drove on Flamingo for two miles and turned right on Paradise Road. Except for a few cars headed the other way, the road was clear for Kaleb. There were a few full-on monsters and others in the beginning stages. Some walked down the middle of the road, stepping around abandoned vehicles while others kept to the side.

A mile down Paradise Road, Kaleb saw movement near a gas station. At first it seemed like four creatures, but upon closer look, it was actually three zombies and an arrogant prick.

The living dead surrounded Coop while he gripped the lead pipe like a baseball bat. Kaleb didn't give him a high chance of survival and considered leaving him for a second or two. He sped toward the scene, turned the wheel, and skidded to a stop. He jumped out of the van with his Glock aimed at the monsters.

"Get down," Kaleb screamed at Coop, who dropped to the ground. He fired, but the bullet went over the monster's head. Shooting again, this time he blew its ear off. The zombie fell backward and flopped around until Coop slammed its head with the pipe. Another of the beasts reached for Coop's ankle. "Behind you!"

After slamming his foot into the monster's face, Coop knocked the other one away with his lead pipe and ran up to

Kaleb.

"You didn't have to help me," he said. "I would have been fine."

Kaleb glowered at him. "Yeah? Well, unlike you, I'm not completely heartless. Now, do you want a ride or not?"

Coop didn't say a word, but he did climb into the passenger side of the car. Kaleb got in the van, turned back onto Paradise and drove north.

"You're welcome, by the way," Kaleb said a mile down the road.

"I would've been fine," he mumbled. His insistence made Kaleb laugh. Coop looked out the window. "We should be going the other way."

"Chillax, Coop. I have a better plan."

"Oh, yeah? And what would that be?"

Kaleb rolled his eyes at Coop's attitude. "There's a private airport in Henderson, which is where a lot of wealthy people live. They fly in and out of the airport in big, private planes. Maybe there'll be a pilot around who can help you get home."

Coop was quiet for a moment, but the fact that he didn't argue told Kaleb Coop agreed with him, albeit reluctantly.

"Why didn't you just steal a car?" Kaleb asked. "Why walk all that way?"

Coop mumbled something under his breath.

"What was that?"

He muttered unintelligibly again.

"Still didn't catch that."

"I can't bloody drive," he yelled. "Okay? I can't drive."

"I'm not so useless after all, am I?" Kaleb laughed.

"I guess I underestimated you," he admitted.

"Well, thanks."

"Did you have that gun the whole time?"

Kaleb nodded.

"Why didn't you say something?"

"Oh, I don't know. Maybe because you said I was nothing more than zombie food and wouldn't survive for long on my own."

"Guess I cocked that one up."

If Kaleb had been drinking, he would've done a spit take. "What? You did what with your cock?"

Coop rolled his eyes. "Filthy minded bugger. I didn't say anything about my dick. I said I cocked up. Means I made a mistake."

Kaleb nodded and felt a little silly about his own cock-up. Kaleb suddenly couldn't stop thinking about his cock. Coop's dick, specifically. Was Coop uncut like he'd heard most British guys were? He'd never been with a man who wasn't cut.

"Why is it so important for you to get home?" Kaleb asked.

"I've got things to take care of. Need to try and patch things up with Ewan too."

"Ewan? I thought you said you had a girlfriend. Isn't Ewan a man's name?"

Kaleb knew the answer as soon as their eyes met. Yes, it was a man's name, but he hadn't meant to reveal that particular bit of information.

CHAPTER EIGHT
COOPER

Coop met Kaleb's eyes, judging his reaction. Fuck, he hadn't meant to let Ewan's name slip like that. What if Kaleb was homophobic? America wasn't exactly known for its tolerance. If only he could take back that last sentence.

"He's… my brother," he said, turning to gaze out at the road.

"Brother? Yeah, whatever," Kaleb replied.

Coop let out a long breath. So much for that excuse. The silence between them grew heavier and thicker, or maybe that was just the heat. He reached for the radio, twiddling one of the knobs until a male voice broke through the crackling static. The word "virus" rang clear through the cab, and Coop sat up straight. Maybe they had some news on what was happening.

"Official reports now confirm that the epidemic spreading rapidly through Las Vegas is the result of experimental cures for degenerative brain conditions, such as Parkinson's and Huntington's. The virus being used in the studies at the Groom Lake Test Facility was designed to regenerate inactive brain cells. Scientists are struggling to explain what caused the sudden change in the virus's behavior; however, it is thought that a rapid mutation of the virus DNA has caused it to become virulent."

Coop smirked. He knew it. He fucking knew it. Science was always going to come back and bite everyone in the arse eventually. The voice paused for a second before continuing.

"What we do know is that the infected may exhibit a chesty cough, similar to that of a heavy smoker, for a day or two before other symptoms appear. Later signs of infection include increased hostility, bloodshot eyes, and…." A few seconds of silence hung in the air. An audible gulp could be heard over the radio. "There are reports that the infected are engaging in cannibalism. Officials are advising that you stay at home and lock your doors. I repeat, citizens are advised not to leave their homes or to let anyone in. Do not attempt to head to your nearest hospital as they are currently inundated with patients and will be unable to help. Reports so far suggest that the virus is only transmissible by direct contact. If you know of anyone displaying symptoms, you should maintain a distance of at least fifty feet at all times and contact The National Guard immediately. We'll be back with regular updates on the situation."

The radio cut to a second voice. "If I didn't know any better, I'd say the zombie apocalypse has started," said a woman.

"Told you," Coop muttered.

Kaleb glared at him and turned the radio off. "Are you really that worried if I know you're gay?"

Coop grated his teeth. "Who said I was gay?"

"You did, pretty much. So who's this Ewan?"

Nosy little prick. Coop clenched his fists against his knees. He gave Kaleb one little bit of information and now the idiot wanted his life story. "Told you, he's my brother."

"You expect me to believe that?" Kaleb replied. "Look, for what it's worth, I'm gay too."

"I said I'm not gay," Coop snapped. Liar. He spent most his time lying to his family, his friends, and his colleagues. Even though Kaleb had just come out to him, the lie was easier than being truthful.

"Okay, fine," Kaleb said, keeping his eyes on the road. He tapped his hands against the steering wheel. Coop relaxed his fists, thankful that the inquisition had stopped. "So do you top or bottom?"

"What?"

"Give or take?"

Coop clenched his jaw as heat rose up from his stomach and into his cheeks. "I told you already, I'm—"

"Catcher or pitcher?"

Coop closed his mouth and folded his arms. He focused his gaze straight ahead. Maybe if he ignored the annoying git, Kaleb would give up on asking more questions. More and more cars joined them on the interstate, speeding along past the van. Every single one was heading in the same direction, trying to get as far away from the city as possible.

"I'm a top," Kaleb said. "I bottom too, but I prefer to be the one doing the fucking."

"Will you just shut the hell up?" Coop said, digging his fingers into his knees. His previous estimate of Kaleb's life expectancy seemed more and more likely to be true. Forget the zombies though. He was going to be the victim of a lead pipe to the head if he didn't keep his trap shut.

"I'll stop once you admit it," he replied, a grin forming across his face.

Coop's shoulder sagged. As much as he would have liked to bash Kaleb's face in, having someone around who could drive was certainly a big advantage. And anyway, as soon as he got the flight out of Vegas they'd never see each other again. Couldn't do any harm to say those few little words. And if it kept Kaleb quiet for a while, it would be worth it.

He took a deep breath and relaxed his body. "I'm gay."

"Wasn't so hard, was it?"

"Harder than you'd think," Coop replied, averting his eyes from Kaleb's. "Only ever told a handful of people before."

"And this Ewan? He your boyfriend?"

"Well, he was. I dunno anymore."

"Right, you said you came here alone. You guys have a big fight or something?"

"Yeah. Caught him with another guy," Coop said and then stopped himself. Why was he blurting this out all of a sudden? Sure felt like a weight lifting off his shoulders though. Maybe because he had no one to talk to back home in England. Still, he wasn't about to share why Ewan had cheated on him. No, that was too much.

"Damn, that sucks," Kaleb said. "Well, fuck him. If he's gonna cheat on you then he ain't worth shit. I mean, you'd be a definite keeper if you weren't such an ass."

"Apparently my arse is one my best features."

Kaleb was silent for a moment before letting out a loud laugh.

"What's so funny?" Coop asked, arching an eyebrow.

"Nothing. Just the way you said arse."

Coop shook his head and laughed. God, how long had it been since he'd done that? And now he was laughing in the middle of the damned apocalypse. Surely, he was losing it.

"See, you're not so bad once you remove the stick from your arse."

Coop scowled at him. "You do an awful British accent."

"Bite me, Brit boy," Kaleb replied. "And you never did answer my question."

"What question would that be?"

"Top or bottom?"

Damn, that boy was persistent. Coop scoffed and gazed out of the window. More cars surrounded them, the traffic slowing until they were almost crawling along. "Bottom," he said quietly. Not that he'd had any for a while. The arguments with Ewan had seen an end to his sex life for what seemed like an eternity. Hadn't even jerked off for at least a fortnight. Any longer and he was going to go insane. Not like he had any decent options though. Well, unless….

He glanced at Kaleb. Younger guys weren't really his type, but the redhead had a certain boyish charm. Coop blinked and shook his head. No, he wasn't going to be a dick and start sleeping around like Ewan. Better to wait until he got home so they could sit down and actually talk about their problems. After all, it was sort of his fault.

CHAPTER NINE
KALEB

Coop being gay didn't matter one way or the other to Kaleb. It was just funny to get him riled up. But once Coop admitted to being a bottom, an image of him on his hands and knees with his bare ass pointed up popped into Kaleb's head.

How he could even think about sex at such a time? Coop wasn't his type at all.

"How did you know it was the zombie apocalypse?" Kaleb asked. "You seemed to accept it as if it was no big deal."

"I saw a story on the telly about a lady chewing her husband's face off. There aren't many conclusions one could jump to besides the zombie apocalypse. I knew something big was going to happen soon. I may not have known it was going to be cannibalistic monsters, but it was one option I had prepared for."

"Prepared? You one of those conspiracy theory nuts? Do you think aliens killed JFK?"

Coop sighed. "That would be ridiculous. However, aliens did kill Princess Diana."

He noticed a slight smile on Coop's face. Damn, the snooty bastard had a sense of humor.

It was almost pure desert on either side of Interstate 515, no view at all. Further up on the right was Mount Charleston and behind them was Red Rock Canyon. Henderson was only twenty miles from Las Vegas but it always took upwards of forty-five minutes because of the constant traffic.

Kaleb stepped on the brake when he noticed the brake lights of the cars in front of him. "Lots of people trying to get out of town, and it's going to get worse."

The freeway led out of Nevada and into Arizona, which apparently seemed like the best choice to lots of people. Kaleb figured they were expecting the surrounding states were monster free. He didn't have the same hope.

A few zombies wandered on the side of the road, but they weren't attacking each other and didn't seem aggressive. On the right, two Hispanic zombies walked slowly without looking around at all. One tripped in a hole in the ground and didn't even attempt to stop the fall. He just stood up and continued, not bothered by his severe facial wounds. Kaleb wondered if the zombies had a destination in mind or if they were just walking aimlessly. Cars started moving forward. Kaleb eased his foot off the brake but had to quickly stop again. A red RAV4 swerved for a minute, then pulled off to the side of the road. The driver's side door opened and a woman jumped out. Kaleb could hear the woman cursing like a sailor even with his windows shut.

In his rear view mirror, Kaleb saw a tough looking woman carrying a shotgun get out of an SUV. She walked up to the RAV4 and looked in the passenger side window. Opening the door, she stepped back and aimed the shotgun. An older man practically fell out of the car but quickly stood up. He was obviously sick, but it didn't look like he had been so for long. His skin was still a normal color, but he glared angrily at the woman with the shotgun. Suddenly, he lunged toward the woman, but she pulled the trigger and his head exploded.

The driver of the RAV4 screamed, but the woman with the shotgun didn't even look at her and walked back to her own vehicle. Kaleb almost stopped to invite the RAV4 driver to join them, but he knew he couldn't save everyone. Plus, he didn't know if she was infected, and he had to take care of himself, helping Coop in the process.

Half a mile later, traffic was gridlocked. He noticed Coop shifting in his seat. "You okay?"

"I don't do very well sitting for long periods of time. Especially if the traffic stays at a standstill."

"How did you survive the flight here?"

"Sleeping pills."

"That won't work now, will it?" Kaleb braked to a stop then slowly moved forward.

"If this keeps up, it might be quicker for us to walk." Coop rolled the window down and poked his head out, as if seeing how much traffic was ahead would change anything.

"Walking leaves us vulnerable," Kaleb pointed out. "We're in the desert. On the highway, there are no trees or shade. Nowhere to hide. The zombies would get us for sure."

"I don't know how much longer I can sit here." Coop's leg twitched nervously.

"Not to mention if we set out on foot, we'd have to carry the food and weapons. That will slow us down even more."

"Look, Red," he snapped. "I will go off my trolley sitting here. I feel like we're sitting targets."

"Simmer down, chief. I don't want you to go off your trolley or whatever the fuck you said, but we can't just go off willy-nilly. Walking could be just as dangerous as sitting here. I'm just saying we should have a plan." He turned the radio back on.

"Authorities have issued reports announcing the immediate closure of all major highways out of Las Vegas. Interstate 515 is now closed at the Nevada/Arizona border."

"Damn it!" Kaleb didn't need to get as far as Arizona, but if the border was shut down, the gridlock would get so bad they wouldn't even make it to Henderson.

The report listed all the highways that had been closed. "The military has set up road blocks and is also watching the smaller roads out of town. This is an effort to contain the virus before it spreads too far. Everyone is urged to stay in their homes."

"A lot of people are trying to get out of the city, but the CDC urges you to stay put. Please help us contain this virus. Return to your homes. Lock your doors and await further instructions. The Las Vegas Convention Center has been turned into an emergency shelter. The CDC has doctors in place to test for the virus. Anyone who has had contact with any of the creatures is urged to come and be tested. There are precautions in place for infected people to be quarantined until an antidote arrives."

"Bollocks!" Coop slammed his fist on the dashboard and

shut off the radio. "Antidote? I doubt it. Those motherfucking scientists might as well have dropped an atom bomb on us."

"At least we're alive," Kaleb said. "We should focus on staying that way."

"Have you always been an optimist?"

He nodded.

"Optimists piss me off. Trying to see everything positively doesn't always work."

"I like staying positive as well as seeing the best in everybody. That's why I came after you and saved your life."

"I would've been just fine if you hadn't showed up."

Kaleb snorted. "I am just so glad I can help you." Kaleb didn't expect everyone to like him, but, hell, it was the zombie fucking apocalypse, and he had saved the man's life. A little gratitude wouldn't have killed him.

"No need to get your knickers in a twist, Kaleb. Meant no offense."

One of Kaleb's pet peeves was when someone apologized without actually saying the words "I'm sorry." Kaleb didn't bother responding to Coop. Kaleb's gut told him he should leave the egotistical jerk behind and worry about himself. But he didn't have it in him to do such a thing.

The cars in front of him slowed, then came to a complete standstill once again. The occasional honking amped up and was now non-stop. One car pulled off to the side and drove past everyone else like a little kid cutting in the lunch line. Several cars had been abandoned, their owners walking down the middle of the highway. The deserted vehicles would just add to the gridlock.

While most people seemed intent on going forward, some took the closest off ramp and turned onto Interstate 215, the Las Vegas Beltway. Kaleb wondered if they were heading back into Vegas, or if they thought other highways would be easier to get through. More and more people got out of their cars and started walking. Some carried guns, others had food or babies in their arms.

"Idiots," Kaleb murmured.

Coop didn't say anything, but his twitching increased to an annoying level and Kaleb had two choices: cut off Coop's damn leg and feed it to the zombies or get off the freeway and try something different.

Kaleb took the off ramp onto the beltway.

"What are you doing? I thought we had to go that way."

"You did see all the cars, right? We're going to get stuck sooner or later, and we'd end up zombie bait."

"You'd better have a good plan."

Kaleb turned to Coop for a second. "If you have a plan, I'd love to hear it."

Coop didn't reply.

"I realize I'm not as smart and well prepared as the mighty Cooper, survivalist extraordinaire, but I do have a few brain cells. I did manage to get my hands on some guns and saved your ass."

"Fine. So what's your grand plan, Red?"

"Don't call me Red!" Kaleb snapped.

Coop sighed. "Okay, Kaleb. What's your idea?"

Kaleb held up a hand with his forefinger extended, telling Coop to wait. The traffic on the beltway was nearly nonexistent, but there was an occasional empty vehicle as well as lots of zombies walking, fighting, and eating. He didn't need to know what they were munching on; he'd seen enough of that. He turned off the beltway and onto Gibson Road. He drove quickly, ignoring the commotion around him, swerving to avoid two creatures sharing a meal in the center of the road.

Coop coughed to get Kaleb's attention.

"Amargosa Trail cuts through Mt. Charleston, Red Rock and other mountains. The trail is a tourist attraction run by the Bureau of Land Management and is maintained pretty well. If we follow the trail all the way, it'll lead us to the airport. There's an old town at the top of the mountain, but a few miles past that, it's a lot of rough land. I can't imagine there'll be many other people… or creatures that far out."

"We gonna drive this hunk of junk up in the mountains?" Coop wisecracked.

Kaleb ignored the remark, turned onto West Horizon Ridge Parkway and continued with his idea. "Motorized vehicles aren't allowed past the trail head, but below there are trails for four-wheelers. There's also a place that rents ATVs. Hopefully we can find one."

"And if we don't?"

Kaleb chuckled. "Then we'll be walking. It'll be one hell of a hike, so let's pray we can get a four-wheeler."

"Hmm. Well, I've heard worse ideas."

"From you that's a resounding endorsement."

Kaleb slammed on the brakes, and Coop damn near ate the dashboard.

"Bloody hell, why…."

There was a flock of zombies fifty feet ahead. Most of them were slowly walking toward the van. There was one, a few feet ahead of the others, whose gait was less clunky, more determined than the others. He looked from side to side and when he saw the van, Kaleb could've sworn on a stack of bibles the monster smiled. Fucking grinned! And he walked faster. He was far from Speedy Gonzalez, but he was quick compared to the rest of the lumbering herd.

"Do you see that?" Coop asked. "He smiled! Unbelievable. His brain function must be higher than the others. That doesn't make any sense."

"There's a whole fucking lot here that doesn't make any sense, Coop. Maybe the zombies are more like the ones in 28 Days than The Walking Dead. Or some kind of hybrids."

"Maybe instead of discussing media zombies you should, I don't know, fucking drive!"

The super zombie was closing in, so Kaleb put the truck in drive and floored it, fully intending on slamming into all the creatures as fast as he could. However, when Kaleb was just a few feet from the smart one, the creature dodged to the left and avoided being smashed. Kaleb plowed into the rest, knocking them down like bowling pins. There was a horrible crunching sound as he rode over the creatures.

"Bloody hell."

Kaleb totally agreed.

CHAPTER TEN
COOPER

Coop gripped the edges of his seat, his stomach lurching into his throat. Talk about a bumpy ride. As they rolled over the last of the walking corpses, Coop peered out the window behind them at the pile of flattened, misshapen carcasses. The few left standing ambled toward them, regardless of the fact that the van was quickly putting distance between them. Not so smart, after all.

The single zombie that had dived out of the way stood on the gravel median, its eyes following them, though it made no attempt to move. Coop met its blank gaze and swallowed hard, forcing down the lump forming in his throat. None of the others had even made an attempt to move from their path, so why did that one? Something wasn't quite right about it. It was almost as though the damned thing had thoughts other than sinking its teeth into the nearest living thing. Survival instincts…

"Coop!"

Jerked from his thoughts, he shook his head.

"Dude, were you even listening?" Kaleb asked.

Coop took a deep breath and relaxed back into his seat. "Sorry. I was just thinking."

"Yeah? Care to share?"

"That zombie back there wasn't like the others. What if there's more to this virus than just turning people into flesh-eating, mindless corpses?"

Kaleb raised an eyebrow. "More? Like what?"

"You ever see the first Resident Evil movie? That monster at the end mutated after eating live flesh. It became stronger, faster, and smarter. Maybe these zombies are the same. The more they eat, the more dangerous they become."

"And you just made fun of me for talking about media zombies." Kaleb snickered. The smile on his lips quickly faded, his knuckles going white as he gripped the steering wheel tighter. "You might have a point though. After you left this morning, I bumped into a group of three zombies. Two of them were trying to pull this guy to pieces, when the third one smashed his head in with a rock. He started kicking the crap out of the other two when they tried to get a bite as well. It was like he didn't want to share."

"Never thought zombies would be smart enough to use a rock like that," Coop admitted.

"Just as long as they don't remember how to use guns," Kaleb replied. "Last thing we need is them taking out our kneecaps so we can't run away."

Coop's stomach dropped like a box of lead. It was bad enough he'd been caught halfway round the world when the outbreak happened, but the emergence of these 'super zombies' was something he'd failed to account for in his apocalypse plan. And now the city was already being quarantined. At least the vacation couldn't get much worse.

Before long, they came to a wire fence. The gate had been smashed open and lay across the dry dirt to one side of the road. Behind the ATV rental shack was the Amargosa trail head. The mountains before them were almost barren, wastelands of yellow-brown sand littered with rocks and some occasional scrub brush.

"Looks like we weren't the first here," Kaleb said. He turned the engine off and reached for his Glock, before turning his gaze to Coop. "You know how to shoot?"

Coop snorted. "Of course I do."

"Really? I heard they don't let you have guns in England."

"Shut up and just give me something to shoot with."

"All right," Kaleb replied, motioning to the stored weapons. Coop's eyes widened. "Take your pick."

Fuck, where had he managed to get all those weapons? Was that a shotgun? Sure would do a lot of damage, but it would also be messy. Not a good idea when dealing with a possibly contagious virus. Besides, he'd never fired a shotgun in his life.

Best stick to basics. Something quiet would be a good idea. Loud shots were likely to draw unwanted attention their way.

"Got anything with a silencer?" Coop asked.

"This is the apocalypse, not Splinter Cell," Kaleb wearied. "This should do you. Good ol' Smith and Wesson. Just try not to hit me, okay?"

"Don't tempt me," Coop shot back. He took the gun and aimed it out of the window toward the rental shack to get a feel for it. He lowered it and nodded.

Kaleb stored the weapons back on the floor behind his seat and started up the engine. They drove slowly up the path, their gazes continually flicking left and right until they stopped outside the shack. The place was empty, save for a fenced area out back of the hut with a single ATV in it.

"We'd be a lot safer in an actual car," Coop said. "You know, something with doors and windows, and a roof."

"Ah, come on, it'll be fine. Not like we're gonna run into any zombies in the middle of the desert," Kaleb said, jumping out of the driver's side door.

Coop sighed and stepped out of the van. "I'll grab the stuff," he said. "Why don't you go see if you can find a key?"

Kaleb nodded and walked up to the door of the shack. He tried the handle to no avail. Next he stepped back and gave it a kick, but the door refused to budge.

"Out of the way," Coop said with a sigh. He walked up to the door and with one swift strike it flew inward with a bang, the lock splintering. "That is how you kick a door down."

"That's some power you got there," Kaleb said.

Coop smirked, his arms folded. "Comes with the job."

"Oh, yeah? What'd you do?"

"I play football."

Kaleb arched an eyebrow. "You mean soccer?"

Coop snorted. "No, I mean like real football, where the aim of the game is to actually kick the ball with your feet. Not like that crap you call football."

"So are you famous back in England, then?"

Coop shook his head. "I'm not in a big league club, so no. I always thought that maybe one day... but now tomorrow might never come."

"It was never guaranteed in the first place," Kaleb replied, disappearing inside. Coop walked over to the van and opened the back doors, hauling out his rucksack, the few supplies he'd gathered from the convenience store, and Kaleb's weapons. He set them on the ground and leaned back against the vehicle.

Coop reached for the left pocket of his jeans, and then paused. Two years he'd gone without a smoke, and yet out of nowhere he was reaching for the packet as if it had always been there. Fuck. He chuckled quietly. Maybe the whole thing was getting to him after all. In the middle of nowhere with an annoying redhead for company and the rest of humanity going to hell. Yeah, that would make anyone start craving a few fags.

He tilted his head back, running his hands through his short hair. What if it was too late? How far had the infection spread? Even if by some miracle he managed to find a plane willing to get him home, what were the chances of them being allowed to just fly out of the city?

A storm of emotions raged inside him, rising up from his gut. He had to get home, no matter what. If nothing else, he needed to apologize to Ewan and set things right between them. The tempest within grew larger and faster, desperate to burst outward. God, he could just scream. His mouth opened, and a guttural roar tore through the air.

Coop's heart kicked into overdrive. That cry hadn't come from him. He closed his mouth and pulled the pistol from his waistband, clicking off the safety. He turned on the spot to search around him. Where was Kaleb? They needed to move as quickly as possible.

"Fuck, Kaleb," he muttered.

Coop sprinted into the store as one gunshot sounded, then

another. He burst through the open door, gun aimed in front of him. A pair of bloodshot eyes met his as time slowed to a crawl. The zombie's lips parted into a blood-filled snarl. Coop aimed down the sight, and Kaleb used the distraction to duck to one side of the room and out of the line of fire.

Coop squeezed the trigger, and the bang echoed in his ears. The zombie's head jerked back, its body giving way and crumpling to the floor. Coop inched closer, gun trained on the decaying body sprawled before him. Black goo oozed from the right eye socket where the bullet had entered its skull.

Kaleb joined him at his side. "Nice shot," he cheered. "Killed it in one."

Coop smirked. "Well, now we're even."

CHAPTER ELEVEN
KALEB

"I didn't realize we were keeping score," Kaleb retorted. "Because if we are, I could think of a few things that put me on top." He hadn't meant the words in a sexual way, but that's where his brain went as soon as he spoke them. Kaleb had always laughed at the people in movies who thought about sex in the middle of a life or death situation, but here he was doing that exact thing. Maybe thinking about a good hard fuck kept him from going crazy. Because if he tried to make sense of the situation, he really would go insane.

Coop didn't react to the jibe. Was it possible Coop had been picturing Kaleb physically on top of him as well?

"Any luck with the key?" Coop asked.

Kaleb held up a key ring and with a dozen keys and jangled it. "They were hidden in a drawer. Hopefully, it's one of these. All the other ATVs were probably kept outside and easier to steal. We're damn lucky this one is still here."

They walked out the back door to the ATV. Kaleb straddled the vehicle and began trying the keys.

"I saw a couple of ten gallon gas cans inside. Hopefully, we can get their gas pump to work so we can fill them." The first three keys didn't work, but Kaleb kept trying.

"Can't imagine petrol will be that easy to find once we get up in the hills."

"Blimey no, mate," Kaleb teased in a mock British impersonation. "Petrol will be bloody hard to come by."

"Well, goll-ee, pardner," Coop replied in his best Southern twang. "Why don't you just kiss my ass?"

Despite Coop doing his best to look pissed and deadly serious, the corners of his mouth turned up. They were both laughing when the ATV finally roared to life.

The only way out of the fenced area was a sliding gate with a lock. Kaleb grabbed the two red plastic gas cans while Coop picked up a tire iron, broke the lock on the gate, and slid it open.

Kaleb secured the gas cans to the ATV with bungee cords, then drove to the single gas pump as Coop followed. Kaleb lifted the nozzle and tried it, but nothing happened.

"Damn it."

"Why don't you try one of those keys on the keyhole?" Coop suggested. The second key slipped in and turned. Kaleb squeezed the handle enough to release a squirt of gas. "Awesome!" Kaleb filled up the gas cans, then patted the seat behind him. "Get on." Coop hopped on sideways and when Kaleb took off, he accidentally fell into him. He grabbed the metal bars on the back as Kaleb drove to the van.

The ATV had a large black saddle on the metal rack. It was large but not large enough for everything they had. Kaleb sorted through the weapons and handed Coop a shotgun, a rifle and ammo for all the guns to stuff into the bag.

After adding some food to the saddlebags, Kaleb said, "We aren't gonna have much room for clothes."

"I figured," Coop replied. He opened his luggage and found a clean pair of pants, a shirt and socks and underwear. He had to cram the clothes around the rest of the stuff in the bags.

"You ready?" Kaleb asked. Coop nodded and climbed on, gripping the metal bar behind him.

Kaleb drove down the street then turned onto a dirt trail with a huge sign marked Amargosa Trail. The first section of the trail was fairly flat and they passed the turn-off for the ATV trails and a sign which read No Motorized Vehicles Beyond this Point.

"You drive this fairly well," Coop said loudly over the noise of the machine.

"Pat and I like to come out here and ride when we have extra money."

With an incline ahead, Kaleb dropped a gear and hammered down. The jerk of the machine almost slid Coop off, so he wrapped an arm around Kaleb's waist to hang on.

Kaleb was surprised when he felt Coop grab on to him. Not just because he was sure the man hated having to rely on someone else, but also because it felt good. Kaleb gunned the ATV and smiled when Coop's other hand grabbed his waist. But a second later, both hands were gone. Coop leaned back, reaching awkwardly over the saddlebags in order to grab the metal bars on the back.

"There's going to be some rough terrain ahead," Kaleb said loud enough for Coop to hear over the motor. "You might want to keep a grip just to be safe." Coop's hands returned to Kaleb's waist and when Kaleb's shirt rode up, they were flesh-to-flesh. Coop pulled the fabric down a second later, and Kaleb instantly missed his touch.

Despite the proximity to Vegas, being up in the mountains and hills was like a totally different world. The few trees were scrawny and hardly provided enough shade for an ant. Scrub brush was the most abundant foliage and rocks were everywhere.

They drove higher and higher, and Kaleb wondered how much more daylight they had left. He was sure they wouldn't make it to the airport tonight, not that he'd expected to once they left the freeway. He just needed to find a place to spend the night where they weren't too exposed to the elements or the creatures.

Kaleb drove up a trail onto a wide open piece of flat land, then slammed on the brakes so hard Coop smashed into him. Several hundred feet ahead was a small group of less than half a dozen zombies, milling around the entrance to the canyon where Kaleb needed to go.

"Bloody hell!"

"Check it out."

"No way to avoid them?" Cooper asked.

Kaleb shook his head. "The only place we can stay safe for the night is the old Amargosa townsite. If we turn around, we won't have time to get there tonight. We could be stuck in the open when it gets dark."

"So much for not running into zombies in the middle of the desert." Coop reminded Kaleb of his earlier words.

"Well, excuse the fuck out of me for not thinking of every possible circumstance. They must be tourists who were hiking the trail."

"Calm down, Kaleb. I didn't mean it as a put down. It's a surprise to me as well. I'll admit, going off road was a good idea."

Kaleb was surprised. A compliment. "Any ideas?"

"You any good with that rifle thing of yours?"

"The Remington thirty ought six?"

"The one with the scope."

"Yeah," Kaleb replied. "I'm not as good with it as the Glock, but I can hit something dead on at about four hundred yards."

"Right now they don't know we're here. If you shot one or two now, we'd lose the advantage of surprise."

"I might not be able to take the rest of them out before they caught up to us." Kaleb rubbed his temples.

"Especially if there's one or more of the super zombies."

"Can you shoot the Glock and drive at the same time?"

Kaleb shook his head. "The throttle is on the right hand, so I'd have to shoot left handed. I wouldn't be able to hit the broad side of a barn."

"Damn," Coop muttered.

"The way I see it we have two options. You either do the shooting, or you do the driving. It wouldn't be that difficult. Even if you don't know how to drive, I think you could do it."

"I appreciate the vote of confidence but I don't want to try it in a life or death situation. I'm certain I can handle the shooting. I say we go in with… what's the term? Guns a blazin'?"

"Sounds good to me. You ready?"

"Ready when you are, mate."

"I'm gonna be driving rough and wild," Kaleb said. "You better have a tight grip on something with your free hand so I don't lose you."

Coop reached under Kaleb's shirt and gripped his belt. Kaleb shivered as Coop's knuckles grazed the top of the cleft of his ass.

Kaleb squeezed the throttle, and the ATV took off toward the creatures. The creatures glanced their way and ambled toward them. Thankfully, there didn't appear to be any of the smart zombies.

Cooper shot a female zombie in the shoulder, barely slowing her down. The second shot flew over her head, but the third went through her left eye and she dropped. Coop shot at a male, missing him three times before hitting him in the throat. He fell to the ground, but he was still alive.

Coop pointed the gun at a zombie with long hippy hair and shot, hitting him on the side of the face. His head exploded.

Kaleb swerved to avoid a head-on collision with a zombie. Coop leaned with Kaleb and shot the creature in the stomach. He didn't kill the zombie, but the shot slowed him down enough for them to get by. Kaleb sighed in relief because it appeared they had dispatched all of the creatures.

"Shit!" Coop and Kaleb said in unison as they saw the same thing at the same time. One more monster stood on the trail into the mouth of the canyon where they were headed, and it appeared to be one of the smart ones. It looked directly at them and screamed so loudly, they heard it over the sound of the ATV.

Kaleb braked but was ready to gas it again.

The creature snarled at them and bit at the air but didn't move.

"He's standing right in our way," Kaleb said.

"Damn!" Coop's mouth was right at Kaleb's ear, and the feel of his warm breath made Kaleb shiver again.

"Choices?" Kaleb asked.

"None, mate."

"Guns a blazin'?"

"Yup."

"Ready?"

"Yup."

Kaleb revved the engine as Coop reloaded and reapplied his grip on Kaleb's belt.

Kaleb let the brake go, and the front of the ATV's wheels popped into the air. The wheels settled to the ground as they flew toward the super zombie that didn't appear willing to move.

Coop fired, but the creature moved and took the bullet in the shoulder. It ducked as Coop fired again, and the bullet went over the monster's head.

"Shoot the legs," Kaleb yelled. Coop didn't stop to second guess the order. He fired three times at the zombie's legs, cheering silently as the creature fell to the ground.

"Drive right by it," Coop ordered again. "But not over it."

Kaleb obeyed, driving toward the fallen creature, then swerving to the side. The monster reached out to grab Kaleb, but Coop put a bullet between its eyes as they drove by. The creature's arm fell.

"Way to go, mate!" Coop whooped. "Way to fuckin' go."

Kaleb had never felt so proud of any accomplishment in his life, but he wasn't sure if it was because of what he had done or because of who the praise came from.

Less than an hour later, they arrived at the top of the trail to what had once been Amargosa. There were several houses, one with a wall that had fallen in and one black husk of a house that had burnt down. The one halfway decent building was a classic log cabin whose sign read Amargosa City Hall.

"What the hell is this?" Coop asked. "I thought you said there was a town up here."

1. "Yeah, this is it. The old Amargosa townsite. It's a ghost town,"

"Shit, mate, you didn't say that. I thought it was a real town with supplies."

"Guess I wasn't clear," Kaleb said as he stopped the ATV and climbed off. "But this is the best place to stay for the night. I know we still have a few hours before dark, but if we go further we'll be sleeping outside for the night."

"Where are we going to sleep?" Coop asked.

Kaleb pointed at the city hall. "The city hall was also the home of Eli Amargosa, who was the mayor and sheriff."

Coop read a sign on the side of the building, which confirmed what Kaleb had said. Eli Amargosa had planned a large community, but the population never got higher than a dozen people, including Eli's three wives and four children.

Kaleb busted a padlock off the front door open and walked into the city hall. Up front was a desk and a sitting area. At one point, the home had been open to people as a tourist attraction, but when the economy took a downfall, the BLM could no longer keep it staffed. Prior to that, the building had been maintained as if Eli Amargosa and his wives still lived there.

The door had been locked, so he was sure there weren't any zombies, but he wasn't going to take any chances. A door behind the desk led to a small kitchen with a wood burning stove. Two doors on either side of the kitchen led to bedrooms: a child's bedroom with twin bunk beds and a master bedroom with a king-size bed. Having a real bed for the night was more than he had expected.

Coop followed him in and whistled.

"I call this bed," Coop smiled. "You can have the small kid's bed."

"I don't think so, buddy. We're sharing the bed." Kaleb didn't wait to hear Coop's response as he walked out of the bedroom.

He unhooked the gas cans and the saddlebags from the ATV and carried them inside. He grabbed a bag of Cool Ranch Doritos and sat outside on a bench near the front door.

Coop sat down next to Kaleb with a can of fruit cocktail. He reached in and grabbed a piece of a pear. He looked at Kaleb's chips and shook his head in disgust.

"Christ, Kaleb. Have some of my fruit."

"I don't want to take your food, man."

"We're in this together, Red. You shared your gun with me. I don't see why I shouldn't share the food with you."

For the first time ever, Kaleb didn't mind being called Red. He sat next to Coop, and they quickly devoured the can of fruit and then a can of beans. Cold beans weren't exactly the tastiest food he'd ever had, but Kaleb didn't mind at all.

"We worked pretty well together," Kaleb said.

"Yeah. Ewan and I used to be a rather good team. Before I fucked up."

"You fucked up?" Kaleb asked. "I thought he was the one who cheated on you?"

"That's right. But it was my fault."

"How the hell could it be your fault that he cheated? Did you put a gun to his head and make him fuck someone else?"

"Don't be ridiculous."

"Then how? Explain to me how it could possibly be your goddamn fault the son of a bitch cheated?"

"Forget I said anything," Coop answered. "I don't want to talk about it."

"No," Kaleb replied vehemently. "I will not forget it. Tell me. I swear to God, I am not letting this go. You might as well give in and tell me."

CHAPTER TWELVE
COOPER

Coop clenched his jaw and stood. He took a few steps forward and leaned against the wooden railing as he gazed over the ghost town. Fuck, why did he have to go and open his big mouth? Should have known from experience that the moron was the inquisitive type. Nosey, more like.

"It's nothing," Coop replied. "Just leave it."

"Like hell it's nothing," Kaleb said, his voice getting louder. "If Ewan cheated on you, then it's his own damn fault. Why go beating yourself up for something that bastard did?"

"Shut up," Coop growled, balling his hands into fists. "You don't know anything."

"I know he's a grade-A asshole for going behind your back and fucking someone else."

Coop stared out over the barren desert, a warm breeze ghosting against his skin. Heading out alone would be a stupid move, especially with the sun quickly sinking behind the mountains. The entire place looked the same even in the day, and getting lost wouldn't do much for his chance of survival. He hung his head and let out a long sigh.

"It was my fault," Coop said quietly. Kaleb came up behind him, his feet shuffling against the wooden deck.

"How?"

Coop took a deep breath. "We'd been arguing for months before it happened. He wanted me to come out so we didn't have to keep hiding our relationship. Said he was sick of having to lie to his friends and family about where he was going and who he was seeing."

"Yeah, that must suck," Kaleb said. "Doesn't explain why he'd cheat on you though, or why it's your fault."

"Doesn't it? Every day of our relationship I was putting my

fears and my selfishness ahead of him. It was because I couldn't even face coming out that he had to go find someone else. I drove him to it."

Kaleb snorted. "Bullshit. That sounds like something a cheater would say to try and justify himself. 'Oh, it's your fault for not satisfying me in bed,' or something like that."

Coop turned sharply to face Kaleb, and grated his teeth. He opened his mouth to speak, the words lost in his throat. Just what was Kaleb trying to say?

"Tell me honestly, was it Ewan who fed you all that crap about it being your fault?" Kaleb asked.

"No," Coop snapped. "I mean, yeah, he did say that stuff, but he was right." He walked back to the bench, passing by Kaleb and returning to the spot where he had sat moments ago. "I should have listened to him in the first place."

Kaleb stood in front of Coop and squatted down. "Dude, cheating's wrong, no matter what. Surely you must know that."

"Yeah, but if I hadn't—"

"No. No buts," Kaleb said, placing a hand on Coop's shoulder. "He chose to go behind your back. You didn't make him do shit. If he was really that bothered about you being in the closet, he should have ended the relationship first. End of story."

"So I should just be alone instead? Is that it?"

"Better to be alone than with some guy who'll end up hurting you. You could find someone better than Ewan. Someone who will respect you and wait until you're ready to come out."

Coop huffed. "Yeah, well I didn't exactly get out much and meet other guys, you know? And what are the chances of me finding someone who'd wait around for me?"

"I would," Kaleb replied. "Believe me, I know coming out isn't easy for everyone. Heck, I haven't even told my family yet."

"And how long would it be before you got sick of waiting?" Coop asked.

Kaleb shrugged. "I dunno, but I'd never cheat on you. And I certainly wouldn't guilt trip you into thinking everything is your fault. Ewan's the unfaithful bastard, not you." He paused, his hand squeezing tighter on Coop's shoulder. "Didn't it hurt? To know the man you trusted could betray you like that? How can you just sit there and say it's not his fault?"

"Of course it hurt," Coop replied, lowering his gaze. "I found out from my best friend. She'd seen him at a club making out with some other guy. It felt like I'd been stabbed in the gut and left to bleed out. I wasn't sure what to do at first, so I laid there on my bed, too afraid to confront him about it. It was like I could just pretend it was all a bad dream, and it would go away."

"So did you end up asking him about it, or did he confess?" Kaleb asked.

"I saw him the next day. Found an empty condom wrapper in the bedroom." Coop's fingers curled, nails scratching against the flaking paint of the bench. He drew in a shaky breath. "I asked him about it, and he told me he'd had a posh wank the night before."

Kaleb raised an eyebrow. "A posh wank?"

"Yeah, jerking off with a condom on."

"Oh." Kaleb snickered. "You Brits come up with some weird terms. So he tried to lie to your face too?"

Coop nodded. "I lost it with him. Told him I knew about the other guy. He said it was my fault, and the more he explained it, the more I began to believe him." He clenched his jaw. His blood ran hotter, like fire scorching a path through his veins as the realization seeped in. "I believed him. He cheated on me, and then lied about it. And I fucking believed him when he shoved all the blame onto me. How could I just let him twist things like that?"

"You were scared you wouldn't find anyone else," Kaleb said. "Can't have been easy for you both, keeping the relationship a secret. But no one deserves to be hurt and lied to, Coop."

"Then what do I do?" Coop asked.

"You move on and stop blaming yourself for something that wasn't your fault. Stand up for yourself and say, 'Fuck you,

Ewan.'"

"How? He's halfway around the world...."

Chances of getting back to him were diminishing fast. Every second they waited, the infection could be spreading around the globe. Wouldn't be long before there were no more flights to England. Then what?

"I could think of a few ways," Kaleb replied, his hand trailing down Coop's chest. A finger brushed past Coop's nipple, and he let out a low moan. Damn, the boy had to go straight for his weak spot of all places. He shook his head briefly to regain his senses, and he swatted the hand away.

"This isn't the time or place," Coop said.

"Seems like the perfect time to me," Kaleb replied. "It is the end of the world, after all. Who knows what's going to happen in the next few weeks? And we're in the middle of the desert. Not a zombie in sight."

Coop shrugged. He had a point. "Still, what makes you think you're even my type? You're way too skinny, for starters. And you're like, what? Nineteen or something?"

"I'm twenty-one," Kaleb said. "And so what if there's a little bit of an age difference? It's not like I'm asking you to marry me." He turned his back on Coop, his arms folded.

Coop stood and made his way into the bedroom where they had left the few supplies. He foraged about in one of the plastic bags for a bottle of water. After gulping down a few mouthfuls, he replaced the lid and turned, almost bumping into Kaleb. "Shit, what are you doing?"

CHAPTER THIRTEEN
KALEB

Fisting his hands in Coop's shirt, Kaleb slammed him against the wall. Their faces were just inches apart.

"What is your goddamn problem?" Coop demanded.

"Why can't you see that you deserve more than a cheating dickhead? You act arrogant and conceited but then say shit that makes me think you have a self-esteem issue."

"You don't know what you're talking about." Coop breathed deep.

"I don't pretend to know everything, but I know you deserve someone who treats you right."

"Get your hands off me, asshole."

Kaleb didn't release him, but he stepped closer until their bodies touched. He looked deep into Coop's eyes and refused to look away.

"Listen, Red, I don't know what's going through your head, but you should let me go before I get really pissed."

Kaleb was very aware of the heat between them. He released Coop's shirt but grabbed the sides of Coop's face and pulled him into a kiss. Coop resisted and tried to push away, but Kaleb pressed him harder against the wall. Despite Coop being the larger and stronger of the two men, Kaleb was the one in control. There was no doubt about that. He had to stand on his tip toes to kiss the Brit, but he didn't feel like less of a man.

At first Kaleb was the one doing the kissing and Coop was letting it happen. Then something happened. It was like a switch in Coop's brain had been turned on. He kissed Kaleb back with such a fervor and passion it startled Kaleb for a moment. One hand gripped Kaleb's neck to pull him closer while the other wrapped around Kaleb's waist. Coop opened his lips and let Kaleb's tongue explore his mouth before allowing his own tongue to force its way into Kaleb's mouth. Kaleb wrapped his lips around Coop's tongue and sucked, making Coop moan softly.

Finally pulling away when he needed a breath, Kaleb met Coop's gaze. "You're a sexy man, Brit."

Coop looked away. "You're crazy."

Stepping back, he released Coop. "I'm sorry. I shouldn't have done that." He turned and walked across the room.

"What are you doing?" Coop asked. He didn't answer, so Coop followed him and repeated his question.

"I shouldn't have forced myself on you like that, Coop."

Coop chuckled. "It didn't take much forcing, did it?"

"Did you want to kiss me?" Kaleb asked.

"I hadn't really thought about it until you did, but once you started… yeah, I liked it."

Kaleb smiled, his grin stretching from ear to ear, but he turned around and looked out the window.

Coop walked up behind Kaleb and kissed the back of his neck. "I want you, Kaleb. Just for tonight, I want to be with you."

Spinning around, Kaleb grabbed Coop again and pushed him against the wall. Shoved him so hard, in fact, Coop let out a whoosh of air on impact. It didn't stop Kaleb though. He was hell bent on getting what they both wanted, and there wasn't much short of an earthquake that could stop him. Kaleb kicked at the insides of Coop's ankles, making him spread his feet so his face was a tad lower than Kaleb's

Kaleb wrapped his fingers in Coop's hair and yanked it gently, then pulled him in for another kiss, forcing his tongue past Coop's closed lips. The soft erotic moan Coop gave spurred Kaleb on. He reached under Coop's shirt, pinched his left nipple and twisted slightly.

"Oh, fuck," Coop murmured and slid slightly down the wall. Kaleb released the grip on Coop's hair and wrapped an arm around his waist to keep him upright.

"I'm not done kissing you yet," Kaleb growled. He pushed

Coop firmly against the wall and kissed him as he rubbed his hard crotch against Coop's leg. Coop reached down and palmed Kaleb's dick, drawing some sexy noise out of Kaleb.

Kaleb pulled away. "Damn, you kiss well."

"Let me show you what else I can do with these lips."

Kaleb smiled as Coop slid to his knees and pressed his face against Kaleb's crotch. He traced the outline of Kaleb's cock with his tongue, stopping to blow a deep breath on the head.

Kaleb grabbed Coop's head, pushing it against his crotch.

Coop pushed away, hurriedly opening the zipper of Kaleb's pants. He fished out the thick, heavy cock already leaking precome.

"Christ, kid," Coop said.

Kaleb smiled. His cock was thicker than average, but he wasn't arrogant about it. He wasn't one of those guys who started dates or conversations with the subject of how hung he was. He knew it took more than a big dick to make a good lover. Kaleb liked to figure out what his partner liked and give it to him. In the case of the sexy man on his knees in front of him, Coop seemed to like giving up control when it came to sex. The man was in charge in all other aspects of his life, but when it came to fucking, he had to let go of the power.

Kaleb grabbed both sides of Coop's head and slowly shoved his cock down Coop's throat. Coop gagged, so Kaleb stopped and allowed Coop to swallow so he could deep throat it.

Coop moved back until Kaleb's dick was just halfway in his mouth. With his lips wrapped around the shaft, his tongue massaged the underside. Kaleb reached down into Coop's shirt and roughly tweaked a nipple. Coop's humming grunt reverberated on Kaleb's already throbbing dick.

Kaleb had wanted to make it last as long as possible, but Cooper was just so fucking good at sucking that he was having trouble holding back the orgasm. He tried to push Coop away, but the man wouldn't release his dick. Kaleb was sure Coop knew he was trying to delay the orgasm and wasn't going to let him. Coop swallowed Kaleb's cock to the root and sucked and swallowed while still maneuvering his tongue around.

The desire to come right then was almost irresistible, but he didn't want it to end just yet. Kaleb pulled his shaft out of Coop's mouth, leaned over and kissed him. Lips and tongues still connected, he clenched Coop's shoulders and helped him stand up. Kaleb reached a hand up Coop's shirt, tweaking each nipple in turn and loving the response he received. He reached his second hand behind Coop's lower back and pulled him closer without breaking the mouth-to-mouth contact.

Coop moaned as Kaleb continued the assault on his nipples—tweak, twist and release, tweak, twist and release. He felt the gooseflesh rise on Coop's back, and it turned him on even more. Their erections ground against each other, simulating what Kaleb really wanted to do. The hand he had on Coop's back went south, past the waistband of his pants to the firm, rounded flesh of his ass. He worked a finger between Coop's ass cheeks and pressed against the entrance to his body. Coop groaned and pushed back onto the finger.

Kaleb bit the side of Coop's neck, then his earlobe. "Damn, Coop. I really want to fuck you."

"Same here, Red, but I think we might be missing a few essentials. Rubbers and lube namely."

Kaleb reached into his pants back pocket, opened his wallet, and pulled out a condom. He waved the Trojan at Coop. "Always play safe, even during the zombie apocalypse."

"You've been carrying that around for a while, or do you replace it regularly?"

"I'm not a slut," Kaleb replied. "But I'm not a monk either."

Coop chuckled. "I just want to be sure the rubber isn't past the expiration date. If it's the only one we have, we need to make it worth our while."

Kaleb smiled. "Damn, you're cute."

Coop blushed and looked away.

CHAPTER FOURTEEN
COOPER

"Get on the bed," Kaleb ordered.

Coop's dick stiffened at the order. He climbed onto the mattress on his hands and knees.

Kaleb's low moan thrummed through the room. "I could get used to watching you on your hands and knees with your ass in the air. Maybe that's how we'll do it tonight."

Coop swallowed hard, his dick suddenly straining against the button fly of his jeans. He'd always been a fan of doggie style. Found it strangely erotic having a guy pound his ass from behind. No eye contact, just a good old fucking. Kaleb knelt down behind Coop and grabbed at the waist of his jeans. With a rough yank he pulled Coop's ass back against his hips.

"Is that okay with you?" Kaleb asked, grinding his crotch against Coop, who could only nod and groan.

Kaleb ran the palms of his hands up under the black T-shirt to Coop's stomach, slowly pushing the thin material up and exposing the tanned flesh. His fingers played over the lines of Coop's abs, making their way up to tweak his hardened nipples.

"Oh, God," Coop gasped, now rocking his hips against Kaleb. "Oh, please fuck me."

Kaleb chuckled, rolling the nubs between his fingertips. Coop moaned louder, thrusting his ass back harder. "First time anyone's called me God."

"Shut up and just do it," Coop snapped. That cock needed to be in him yesterday.

"What's the hurry? We've got all night to ourselves," Kaleb replied, kneading the lean muscle of Coop's chest. "I wanna have some fun first."

"Well, hurry up. Before I change my mind."

"You think you will?" Kaleb pinched Coop's nipples again,

pulling harder on them.

Coop opened his mouth to say yes. What was he even doing? About to let some scrawny twink with a huge dick fuck him in the middle of the zombie apocalypse. But damn, if he were to die tomorrow, he wanted to know how that dick felt.

Coop shuddered as Kaleb fumbled with his jeans and jerked the rough denim down over his hips. Kaleb pulled down his own pants, allowing his cock to sit in the crack of Coop's ass.

"Got any lube?" Kaleb asked.

Coop lifted his head to glance over his shoulder at Kaleb. "No. I figured you'd have some."

"Nope."

"Well, shit," Coop replied. So much for that plan. No way was that monster going anywhere soon without lubricant.

"I'll just have to improvise then," Kaleb said, shuffling back and lowering his head.

Coop's heart pounded against his ribs. Was Kaleb really going to…? No one had ever done that to him before. He gripped the blanket beneath him in his hands, tensing as the first swipe of Kaleb's tongue circled his hole. A warm hand wrapped around his dick, and a low moan rose up from his throat. With each lick and stroke, the pressure building low in his gut grew until his cock was so hard it was almost unbearable. God, if this was what he'd been missing out on….

The haze in his mind lifted for a brief moment as Kaleb drew back for breath. He unfurled his fingers from Coop's dick and reached over to place them in front of his mouth instead. Coop sucked them without need for instruction, coating them with saliva.

Kaleb pulled his fingers from between Coop's lips and wasted no time in pressing them up against the tight ring of muscle. The first slipped inside with little trouble. Coop groaned and rocked his ass back and forth, desperate for more. A second finger soon joined the other, and Coop hissed as Kaleb rotated them inside him, stretching his hole further.

"So tight," Kaleb whispered. He inserted a third, pushing against the resistance. Coop bit back a surprised yelp and sucked in his bottom lip. The fingers thrust into him, reaching inside and rubbing against the walls of his ass. Kaleb added some of his own spit before reaching for Coop's dick once more.

Between the invasion of his ass and the hand stroking him, Coop had lost all sense of thought. The pain subsided, lost in the torrent of sensation washing over him. Much more of the torment, and he was going to come right then and there. Kaleb's fist slid down to the base of his cock, exposing the sensitive head to the cool night air. The hand glided over his skin, slick with saliva and precome. His left leg began to twitch uncontrollably.

"Oh fuck, I'm gonna come," Coop moaned. His balls tightened as a shiver raced up his spine. One more stroke and....

"Not yet," Kaleb said, withdrawing his hand.

"Little shit," Coop snapped, panting for breath.

Kaleb laughed and reached for the condom, placing the corner of the foil wrapper between his teeth to tear it open while he continued to ram his fingers into Coop. "I'm gonna make you come while I fuck you. How does that sound?"

"Like you'd better get on with it before I blue ball you."

With a chuckle, Kaleb rolled the latex over his cock. He pulled his fingers out of Coop, who whimpered at the sudden emptiness.

"All right, you asked for it," Kaleb said. He spat into his hand and stroked his cock.

Coop took a deep breath and closed his eyes, willing every muscle in his body to relax. The tip of Kaleb's dick pressed against his ass. He fought the urge to tense up as Kaleb forced his way deeper. Kaleb pulled back until only the head remained inside, before ramming his way back in. A whoosh of air left Coop's mouth from the force of the thrust. His hands balled into fists.

"Shit," he gasped.

Kaleb paused. "Want me to stop?"

Coop shook his head. Kaleb began to rock his hips, slower

this time. He added some more of his saliva to his cock as he slowly drove deeper with each thrust. Coop's hisses and grunts turned into gasps and moans as the pace picked up. His eyes rolled back in his head. Each movement brought him closer to the edge, his dick becoming unbearably hard and dripping with precome.

Kaleb leaned forward, placing an arm around Coop's chest and pulling him up onto just his knees. He reached around to take hold of Coop's cock, jerking him off in time with every push into his ass.

Coop's whole body began to shake as he fought to remain vertical. He moaned louder, the sensation quickly building low in his gut.

"Go on," Kaleb whispered in his ear, fastening his other arm across Coop's chest to keep him upright. Coop gave one sharp cry that echoed off the walls of the bedroom as his orgasm spilled over in several spurts of hot come, each one racking his body with a violent shudder.

Kaleb gripped Coop's hips and impaled him faster and deeper than before. Seconds later, Kaleb was grunting and panting as he gave one last thrust and held it in.

Coop fell forward first, letting out a long moan as Kaleb's dick slipped from his ass. "Fuck," he breathed, rolling over and placing a hand on his chest. His heart pounded against his ribcage.

Kaleb removed the condom, tied it up and threw it to one side. He collapsed next to Coop on the bed. "I second that."

Silence settled in over the cabin as Coop closed his eyes and let his breathing and pulse return to normal. He opened one eye and turned his head to Kaleb, who had rolled onto his side. He reached out one hand and placed it on his shoulder.

"Kaleb?"

There was no reply, save for a soft breathing. Coop sighed and sat up. They might have been in the middle of nowhere, but he couldn't risk zombies wandering upon them by chance. He stood slowly, hoping not to wake Kaleb, and fastened up his jeans. With the Smith & Wesson in one hand, he walked to the window and pulled up a chair. The muscles in his ass throbbed in protest.

"Shit," he muttered. How had he let that happen? He wasn't the kind of guy to go sleeping with a near-stranger, and certainly not with someone like Kaleb. He ran one hand through his hair and drew in a long breath. Couldn't say he didn't enjoy it, though. In a way, it was almost liberating, lifting off the shackles that had been weighing him down since he stepped on the plane to Vegas. Thousands of miles from home, away from any familiar faces and the fear of being outed, he was free to unload and be himself. Now, if he could just find a way to get to England. Back home where Ewan would be waiting. Where he'd have to hide his sexuality or risk ever advancing his career.

Coop glanced back at where Kaleb slept. Almost seemed like it wasn't worth the effort to go back. Almost.

CHAPTER FIFTEEN
KALEB

The transition out of sleep was normally slow for Kaleb, but this time it was a sudden start. He was unsure where he was until he saw Coop standing by the window. He smiled and remembered the incredibly hot sex he'd just had with the man.

He didn't know what had come over him. He wasn't normally that aggressive when it came to sex. He topped most of the time but with aggressive bottoms who pushed him down and took what they wanted. He liked the change up with Cooper. The sex had been mutually explosive, not like some guys who had only wanted Kaleb's dick up their ass and left him to finish himself off once they came.

Wearing just a pair of underwear, Kaleb stood and walked over to Coop.

"Last night was...," Coop started to say.

"Incredible," Kaleb finished.

"I was going to say that was probably a mistake. But yeah, it was pretty good."

"A mistake?" Kaleb shot back. "Way to ruin the afterglow, jackass."

"I've never cheated before."

Kaleb turned his head quickly to the side so he could face Coop. "And you haven't cheated now. You and the creep are broken up, remember? He's the one who stepped out."

"Yeah, but--"

"But nothing, Coop. You're single. I'm single. We didn't do anything wrong. In fact, it was right. Who the fuck knows what's going to happen tomorrow? We could both be dead. Or zombies."

Coop nodded but didn't say anything. Kaleb didn't understand why Coop couldn't see in himself what Kaleb saw. Coop was smart and funny and as sexy as just about any man he'd seen before. Yeah, he was a smart ass and could be aloof and cold, but Kaleb liked that part of him as well. How this Ewan creep could've let Coop slip through his fingers was a mystery. Why anyone would cheat on a boyfriend was unclear, but to do it to a faithful, honorable man like Cooper was totally baffling.

"You're right," Cooper admitted. "It was incredible. Best sex I've had in a long time. Not that I've had sex lately.

"Sorry, I crashed right afterward."

He shrugged. "It's all right. I didn't mind staying up."

"Was it necessary to stand guard?"

"You think zombies sleep at night? You think they all bed down together like a bunch of animals?"

Coop had a point, but did he have to be so goddamn arrogant about it?

"Maybe not sleep, but it is dark." The statement was idiotic, and he prepared himself for a snarky insult.

Coop gave Kaleb a humorous look, and Kaleb felt himself blushing. Coop stretched his arms in the air and yawned.

"Go get some sleep." Kaleb said. "I'll stand guard." He grabbed his clothes and got dressed. He reached under the bed, grabbed the Glock and shotgun and reloaded both.

Coop stood, smiled at Kaleb, walked to the bed and laid down. A few minutes later, Coop's eyes were shut and his mouth moved slightly.

Kaleb had considered asking Cooper to join him at the golf course, but he wasn't sure it would be a good idea. If Cooper wanted to stay, he would have to be the one to ask. Kaleb wasn't going to make the offer. He'd fulfill his promise to get Cooper to the airport, but if the Brit wanted anything different, he would have to speak up.

As dawn broke hours later, Kaleb noticed movement on the trail. He stepped to the side of the window so he could see the zombie but wouldn't be seen himself. A zombie dressed in all camouflage slowly emerged from behind some bushes. Coop was still sleeping. He grabbed a pillow and tossed it at Coop, who quickly sat up.

"What's wrong?" he said, louder than Kaleb wanted him to.

Kaleb pointed outside, and Coop was at his side a second later.

"Is he by himself?" Coop whispered.

"I think so. I don't see… wait. There's one coming from the other way."

The second zombie appeared to be much younger, possibly in his late teens, and wore only torn blue jeans. A few rags of a shirt hung around his shoulders stuck to the dried blood on his rotting skin.

The teen zombie didn't seem to notice the other one, or if he did, it didn't matter. The camo zombie was a different story. He stopped, eyeballed the other one and let out a slight growl.

"The younger one looks weak," Coop pointed out. "He's walking slower than the other."

To Kaleb's astonishment, Camo Zombie looked around on the ground. He found a large branch, picked it up, and walked up to Teen Zombie, who still hadn't noticed he wasn't alone. As the teen walked by, the first monster swung the branch, knocking the youngster to the ground. Camo let out a loud lion-like roar, lifted his foot and brought it down on the other zombie's head. He stomped the skull again and again, then he knelt down and stuck his fingers in the crack. He pulled until the head cracked open like an egg, and he roared again. Camo Zombie reached into the open skull, pulled out a section of brain, and chowed down like he was starving.

"So nasty." Bile rose in the back of Kaleb's throat.

"He's one of those super zombies," Coop said. "Maybe they get smarter by eating brains."

"How the fuck did they figure that out?"

"I'm guessing the virus has different effects on different people. Perhaps some retain a level of intelligence, and they realize they get smarter by eating brains."

"I can't imagine already zombified brains would be as good

for them as fresh ones," Kaleb said.

"Yeah, I'd agree with that. And I think he just found his next meal."

The zombie stared at them as he walked slowly toward them.

Kaleb opened the window, pulled up the shotgun, took aim and fired as Coop yelled. The zombie dropped dead, and he lowered the gun.

"Did you say something?" Kaleb asked as his ears rang from the shotgun blast.

"I was trying to stop you, you dumb son-of-a-bitch!" Coop screamed as he stuck his finger in his ear.

"Why?" Kaleb hollered back.

"Because the noise will…." Coop stopped talking and pointed down the hill. "… attract other zombies in the area."

Only four or five were gathered at the bottom of the hill, but that was enough to prove problematic to their escape.

"We don't have time to get the supplies stored on the ATV and get out of here," Coop said. "I hate having to waste the bullets, but we're gonna have to defend ourselves here."

"You stay here," Kaleb said as he ran out of the bedroom. Coop called out, but he didn't stop.

Kaleb ran out the front door, stood on the ATV and set the Glock and extra ammo on the roof. He then pulled himself up and climbed to the front of the building. Coop took down the nearest zombie with three shots, so Kaleb aimed at the second closest zombie. The bullet skimmed the top of the zombie's head but didn't stop him. Coop finished the job and the monster dropped.

Kaleb took a deep breath and held it in, pointed the Glock at a female zombie with pink capris and shot. The bullet flew through her forehead, and she dropped.

Not taking time to celebrate the crack shot, Kaleb fired at the final two zombies, hitting one in the shoulder and missing one entirely. He slowed down and shot again. Both zombies fell backward and at first Kaleb was confused how one bullet could've taken out both creatures when they were side by side. Coop had killed the second one.

"Good job, Kaleb," Coop shouted.

He couldn't accept the compliment. It was his fault he'd attracted the group. He couldn't believe he didn't even consider the implications of using the shotgun.

"Load everything up and get the ATV ready," Kaleb hollered. "I'll keep watch."

"Okay."

A few minutes later, Coop called out to tell Kaleb he was ready to go.

"Get it started so I can jump on, and we can get out of here."

"You want me to drive?" Coop asked. "I don't think...."

"I know you can do it. No doubt."

Kaleb could just imagine Coop shaking his head and cursing Kaleb under his breath. The machine started up, and Coop sat on it, gripping the handles.

"You sure about this?" Coop asked.

"Yup." Kaleb stuck the Glock in the back of his pants, sat down on the edge of the roof and jumped to the back of the ATV. He wrapped an arm around Coop's waist. "Brake is down on the floorboard. Right hand is the throttle. On the left is the gear shift."

"Throttle?"

"Makes you go forward. Brake slows you down."

"I know what brakes do, smart ass." Coop smiled.

"Watch the speedometer and shift up or down depending on your speed. When the engine revs, it's time to shift. I'll help you with that. Throttle it, and let's get out of here."

Coop gassed it, but the ATV didn't move forward.

"Take your foot off the brake, Coop." Kaleb chuckled.

"Bite me." Coop took his foot off the brake and throttled it. The ATV jerked forward, but Coop quickly got control.

"That way," Kaleb said, pointing to the right. "Follow the trail. It's easy terrain for at least ten miles. When it gets rougher, I can take over."

Coop nodded. He drove up a small incline onto a steep decline. He gunned it too much and almost tipped them over.

"Down shift and go slow," Kaleb instructed. "Follow the trail around the corner at the bottom of the hill."

Coop smoothed the ride and made it safely to the bottom, but they saw two zombies just around the corner.

"Think we can drive right past them?" Coop asked.

Kaleb was about to agree to the plan when he noticed a glint in the eye of a female zombie.

"It's a smart one," Kaleb yelled. "Just drive. I got this bitch." He aimed the Glock at the smart one and hit her in the mouth. She didn't stop, but he was able to shoot off the side of her head. The other zombie was easily taken out, and Coop drove around the twice-dead corpses and headed up the trail.

Neither man spoke for over an hour until Coop leaned back and told Kaleb he needed to pee. Coop stopped in a shrub-filled area and shut off the ATV. Stretching, he walked over to a bush, pulled out his cock and pissed.

Kaleb stepped up to another bush and did the same.

"You afraid of me now?"

"Huh?"

"Why you standing so far away? I've already seen your dick. Had it in my mouth and arse, if you remember."

Kaleb chuckled slightly. "I figured you didn't want me pissing too close to you. Did you want to cross swords?"

"No, mate, I don't go for the water sports. Just wanted to be sure you weren't mad at me."

"Now, why would I be mad at you, Coop?" Kaleb responded as he shook off his dick and stuffed it back in his pants.

"Because I said the sex was only for the night. I thought maybe you hoped for something more."

Kaleb liked Coop enough that he wouldn't have minded something more, but Coop needed to want the same thing.

"That was all I wanted too. I don't think this is the right time to start a relationship. Don't worry, I'm not going to kidnap you, tie you down and make you my sex slave."

Coop shivered and Kaleb smiled. "Though maybe that's what you want me to do."

"Yeah, I like a little bondage," Coop admitted. "Ewan never really enjoyed it, though."

Ewan again. Kaleb held his tongue, but he wanted to ask if Ewan had liked anything about Coop. "I'd better take over driving," Kaleb said. "The trail gets pretty rough."

Kaleb climbed on the front of the four-wheeler, and Coop sat behind him. Coop leaned uncomfortably over the saddlebags grabbing the metal bars on the rear of the ATV. Kaleb didn't mind Coop not touching him. They were getting close to the airport, which meant soon he and Cooper would be going their separate ways, and he could forget he had ever met the man.

For the next fifty miles, the trail wasn't very well maintained, so it was rocky and tricky at times. Slowed down because of the terrain, Kaleb finally made it to a residential area a few hours later. They drove through several blocks of houses, zooming past a few single zombies without incident.

Kaleb turned onto Executive Drive and up ahead was the airport with three large private planes and a handful of tiny puddle jumpers.

"Here you are," Kaleb said, harsher than he'd intended, "the airport you wanted so fucking badly."

"Christ, mate who pissed in your Cheerios? You're not leaving me, are you?"

"I told you I'd get you to the airport, and I did. Did you want anything else?"

"What will I do if there aren't any pilots around?"

"I thought you had that all figured out. You're such a planner after all. You know everything to do in case of a zombie apocalypse." Kaleb wasn't used to talking sarcastically, but he couldn't help himself.

"Fine, I admit I didn't really plan this one out."

Kaleb felt an intense surge of pride at being able to get Coop to confess not knowing everything. But it wasn't enough. If he wanted more help, he was going to have to ask Kaleb.

"Will you help me look around?" he finally asked. "Please don't just abandon me."

"Like you tried to do to me back in Vegas?" Kaleb remarked. "I should leave your ass here."

"Red, I'm sorry about that. It was a rotten thing to do, and I regret it." Coop grabbed Kaleb's shoulder and squeezed.

Damn it! Kaleb hated being such a soft touch sometimes. "Hold on." He gassed the ATV and drove onto the tarmac up to the main building, which wasn't very large. The airport was mainly for private and business use, so a large terminal wasn't necessary. The front doors weren't locked, so Kaleb and Coop walked in with their guns ready.

One by one, they checked each room and found no signs of life or undead.

"What next?" Kaleb asked.

"The planes I guess," Coop responded.

The puddle jumpers were easy enough to check, but the private planes were all locked with no way to break in. Using one of the wheeled staircases, Kaleb was looking in the windows of one of the planes when he saw movement.

"There's a guy in here," Kaleb shouted to Coop who was down on the ground.

Coop bounded up the stairs and knocked on the window.

"Open up," he yelled a few times. "I need your help."

A few minutes later, the door cracked open. "How do I know you're not zombies?" he asked timidly.

"Would zombies knock on the windows and ask for help?" Kaleb asked.

The guy chuckled. "I guess not." He opened the door the rest of the way, allowed Cooper and Kaleb to step in, then shut it behind them.

Coop and Kaleb introduced themselves to the man, whose name was Johnny.

"You a pilot, mate?" Cooper asked.

"Yeah. I was supposed to be flying my boss out yesterday. I was here, but he never showed. I was about to go home when I saw all these… creatures outside. A couple attacked one of the airport staff and tore her to shreds. I've been locked in since then. It's airtight in here, so I knew I was safe. I've been trying to decide where to go."

"I need to get to England." Coop said. "Can you get me there?"

"It'd take several stops to re-fuel and each time we stop, that puts us in danger, correct?"

"We might be able to outrun the virus," Coop offered. "We don't know how far spread it is."

"That's a mighty big if," Johnny said.

"I can make it worth your while if you get me all the way. I have money and not the useless paper kind. I have gold bars stashed."

"How do I know you're telling the truth?" Johnny asked. "What if we get there, and you're full of shit?"

"You think you'll survive forever locked in an airplane?" Kaleb asked. "At least there's a chance things are better in England." If Coop wanted to leave, he could do so. Kaleb just wanted to get the fuck out of there and go find his brother.

The pilot nodded at Kaleb's comments. "Okay, you got a deal. Let's make like birds and get the flock out of here."

"That's my cue to leave," Kaleb said.

"You ain't joining us?" the pilot asked.

"No, this is his trip. Not mine."

Johnny nodded and walked to the cockpit.

"I guess this is good-bye." Kaleb extended his hand. Coop grabbed it and pulled him into a hug.

"See ya, Red. It was a pleasure knowing you."

"Same here, Cooper. Good luck. I hope you find what you're looking for."

Kaleb stepped out the door and walked down the steps to the ATV. Without looking back he drove off. As he was about to leave the tarmac, he spun the machine around to face the plane.

Coop stood at the airplane door and waved. Kaleb did the same before turning around and leaving.

CHAPTER SIXTEEN
COOPER

Coop stepped inside the plane and turned to gaze out over the runways. Kaleb was some distance away now, though he had stopped the ATV to look back toward the plane. It stung a little inside to know it was the last time he'd see the redhead, but Kaleb had his brother to go to, and Coop needed to get back home. He waved his arms. Kaleb waved back, and then spun the ATV around to drive off into the distance. Coop lowered his arm and let out a long breath. Hopefully, Kaleb would be okay, and his brother too.

"You all set to go?" the pilot asked.

Coop nodded and made his way to the passenger area where he strapped himself in one of the seats. Before long, the engines started, and they were traversing the runway. He watched out of the window as the plane took off, the desert below growing farther away until it was nothing more than an endless sea of yellow and brown. As the plane leveled out, Coop unfastened his seatbelt and paced the length of the cabin. At least there weren't any screaming babies this time.

He found a few books stowed away in a small compartment and, having nothing better to do, opened one of them up. Anything to take his mind off the flight. Several sentences in and the words began to swim on the page. He shut the book and threw it to one side with a groan, before standing and making his way to the cockpit.

"Can I come in?" he asked, peering inside the curtain.

"Sure," the pilot replied. "Take a seat. Honestly, I think I could do with the company right about now."

"Yeah, me too," Coop said, parking himself in the co-pilot seat.

"So, you really think things'll be better in England?"

"Hope so. News gets around fast. Maybe they were able to stop the infection from reaching them."

The pilot shrugged. "There's been plenty of people coming and going from Vegas these last few days. Who's to say the infected didn't slip by before the shit hit the fan?"

Of course that was something he'd considered. Still, there was a chance they'd have better luck over there. At the very least, he'd be able to get his hands on his supplies and weapons, allowing him to outlast the virus for a while. And then what? He certainly wasn't getting back with Ewan. In fact, he'd take great pleasure in putting a crossbow bolt between the bastard's eyes if he happened to become one of the walking dead. Thank God for Kaleb making him see sense.

Kaleb.

What was his plan after he found his brother? The smart move would be to hold down the golf club for as long as possible. A place like that ought to have a good stock of food and water. They could survive for a while there, providing they were sensible about keeping guard and barricading themselves in.

"Penny for your thoughts?" Johnny asked.

Coop shook his head. "It's nothing. I just need a distraction."

"You and me both. I've been going out of my mind these past two days. Tried listening to the radio for a while, but most stations stopped broadcasting last night."

"Shit. Things are that bad? What about air traffic control?"

Johnny shook his head. "Lost contact with control about twenty-four hours ago. Seems like they abandoned the airports almost instantly. No surprise really."

"What do you mean?"

Johnny's body tensed, his fingers tightening around the wheel. "When the infection broke out, where do you think everyone tried to go first?"

"As far away as possible," Coop replied. Which meant the local airports. The faster and further they could go, the better.

"They didn't care if they might be infected or not. They just wanted out, and fast. That many people in one place... It spread like wildfire. It was a bloodbath."

"You were there?" Coop asked.

"Only long enough to refuel, but I saw enough. Got out of there as soon as I was able. Been waiting at Henderson ever since for my boss to arrive, but he never showed."

"Damn." Good job he'd decided not to head to McCarran or another airport. Of course he'd known the airports would be dangerous, but how else was he supposed to get back home?

Coop slumped back in his seat and stretched his arms as he let out a long yawn. Staying up most of the night to watch guard meant he'd only had a few hours sleep before he was up and moving again.

"You look like you could use a good rest," Johnny said. "There are some bedrooms at the back of the plane. You can use them to get yourself cleaned up and rested if you like."

"Thanks," Coop replied. He did as suggested and had a quick shower before pulling on a clean set of clothes and stretching out across the bed. Sleep sounded like a great idea, though he'd never been one for falling asleep while on the move without some chemical assistance. He yawned once more and closed his eyes. Within moments, he was asleep.

A rough jerk from the plane brought Coop back into the land of the living. He bolted upright, the plane still shaking to and fro, and managed to make his way down the cabin.

"What's going on?" he shouted.

"Just some bad turbulence," Johnny replied. "Nothing to worry about."

Coop sat himself down and gripped the arms of the chair until his knuckles turned white. "Easy for you to say. So how long have we been in the air?"

"Almost an hour."

"Shit. Is that it?" Coop sighed heavily. So much for his nap.

"Yup. 'Fraid so."

"Any news yet?"

Johnny shook his head. "I've been listening out for any radio signals, but it's mostly silent. Did get one message, though I'm not sure how they managed to tune into this frequency. Group of people holed up somewhere crying for help back in Henderson. Must've listened to them screaming for a good ten or fifteen minutes before I had to turn the radio off. Fuck, I've never been so conflicted in my life."

"You wanted to go help them?"

"Of course I did."

"Then why not?"

"Because," he said with an exasperated sigh, "I have the fuel to think of. Turning back now means we'd have wasted two hours worth of fuel. Besides, what if one of them was infected? How would I know who I could trust?"

"You made the right decision," Coop assured him. Yes, it was heartless, but anyone could be infected. Even Johnny. Maybe even Coop himself. The less people involved, the better.

"Yeah, I know. I just can't stop thinking about those poor souls up at Black Mountain. From the sounds of it, they've been surrounded by zombies."

Coop's heart stopped dead in his chest as all heat seemed to leave his body. "Did you say Black Mountain?"

"Yeah, the country club up in Henderson. You know the place?"

"We have to go back right now," Coop demanded. If the country club was under attack from zombies, then Kaleb was walking right into a death trap.

"But what about the fuel? Like I said, if we turn back now we might not have enough to outrun the virus."

"Fuck that," Coop snapped. "I'm not leaving him to march to his death."

Home may have had weapons and supplies and a safe place to hide up in for a while, but that was it really. Every day he had lied to his friends, to his family, to himself. Even if he survived the apocalypse, what would be left for him in England? Jack shit. In Vegas, he had little in the way of supplies. His future there would be more uncertain, but maybe that was a good thing.

Johnny raised an eyebrow, but turned the wheel. "All right. But don't say I didn't warn you."

CHAPTER SEVENTEEN
KALEB

Kaleb wasn't sure what he'd expected—maybe for Coop to jump out of the plane and tell him he wanted to stay. Kaleb wanted Coop to stay, but hadn't said anything because it had to be Coop's decision. He had spun the ATV around before Coop closed the door, not needing to see the plane leave to know Cooper was gone. He'd never see the Brit again.

Getting from the airport to the golf course was a tricky ride. It entailed getting back into the populated areas and crossing a major highway. It should've taken him less than an hour to get there, but it took longer because he had to avoid zombies and make it through the mazes of stalled cars and dead bodies.

He slowed as he entered the first neighborhood, just one of the many upper class communities in Henderson, full of million dollar homes that were now worthless. He hated that he not only had to watch out for zombies, but he also had to be careful of the smart ones. The walking dead wasn't enough; there had to be zombies who could learn and adapt and get smarter.

Three blocks later, he turned a corner and saw two ambling monsters headed his way. They growled at him but didn't speed up. Assuming neither one was a smart zombie and not wanting to waste any more bullets, Kaleb decided to drive between them since they were on opposite sides of a narrow street.

He gassed the ATV, but as he passed between them, the zombie on the left suddenly leapt toward Kaleb. The creature missed Kaleb's arm, but he did grab onto the rack on the back of the machine.

"Jesus Fucking Christ!" Kaleb cursed as he tried to keep in control of the ATV while shaking the zombie. He purposely drove up on the sidewalk and made a sharp right turn, the back end of the ATV just inches from smacking into a metal fence. The zombie's lower body hit the chain link, and he lost his grip. Kaleb throttled the ATV without looking back to see what happened to the creature.

He drove down an alley and pulled into an open garage. Needing a few minutes of quiet, he closed the door by pressing a button on the wall. The incident had shaken him up, and he suddenly wished Coop was still there. Even if the guy was insulting him, at least he wouldn't be alone.

"Fucking zombies can act now," Kaleb muttered. How smart could these monsters be? He walked around the garage looking for something that could be used as a weapon so he could save bullets. He grabbed a hammer and put it in the side bag of the ATV. He was thrilled when he found a cordless nail gun. The battery would die before too long, but until then it would be a damn fine defense. He practiced shooting with his left hand since he would need his right hand for the ATV's throttle.

Securing the nail gun with him on the ATV so he had it handy, he opened the garage door and took off. The first corner he turned, he nearly collided with a zombie in a pair of pink hot pants. He swerved and clipped the creature with the back end of the four-wheeler, knocking it to the ground.

Kaleb kept the machine gunned as he finished the last few blocks of residential neighborhood before the highway he would have to cross. There were a few lone zombies and a couple groups of two or three. He only had to use the nail gun twice, but he pulled to a stop when a horde of at least half-a-dozen undead came into view.

Trying to decide the safest way to proceed, he weighed his options for a moment. He couldn't avoid that many, but he didn't want to get close enough to use the nail gun and end up having to do battle with one, or more, of the smart ones. He needed a way to differentiate the normal, dumbass creatures from the others.

Kaleb pulled out the rifle, used the scope to aim at an obviously normal creature and shot him in the head. As the monster fell, the other zombies turned to Kaleb and marched toward him. Two of the zombies stepped out of the pack and ran in Kaleb's direction.

"Bingo!"

Putting the rifle away, he got the nail gun ready, revved the ATV and took off. Less than ten feet from the duo, he fired a nail into the head of one of the Super Zombies. Driving by the other beast, he shot a nail through him as well. He took out four of the remaining zombies, avoided the other two and finally drove out of the residential area.

He stopped when he got to the highway. It was jammed in some sort of weird motionless traffic jam. He didn't see any movement but knew that didn't mean anything. He drove down the side of the road for a bit, trying to find a spot where the four-wheeler would fit since most of the cars were bumper to bumper.

Half a mile down, he found a gap where a Geo Metro had been smashed by a Cadillac. Judging by the police motorcycle, the cops had cordoned off the area around the accident. He could squeeze the four-wheeler into one side, but not the other. However, he found room to drive down the middle of the road between the cars.

Kaleb had to go slow to avoid the rearview mirrors and open doors of the abandoned cars. He began to get claustrophobic and was about to abandon the ATV and scramble over the tops of the vehicles to get out of the jam when he found a gap wide enough to fit through. The ATV scraped against the bumpers, but made it through to the other side.

Once he had cleared the cars, Kaleb stopped to take a breath. A loud growl from behind startled him, and he gunned the ATV, then spun it around with the nail gun ready.

This zombie didn't pose any danger to Kaleb. It was a small boy, probably no older than eight. He was still several feet from Kaleb and moving slowly. Kaleb aimed the nail gun then dropped it. Could he really kill a kid? An odd thought popped into his head. What would Coop do? Coop would tell him the kid was just another zombie. Whatever humanity had once been in the body was now gone.

But Kaleb still had his humanity, and he wasn't sure he could handle ending the life of someone so young—killer zombie or not. Then Kaleb put himself in the boy's situation. If he had turned, he wouldn't want to live as a zombie. He would want someone to put him out of his misery for good. If Kaleb was humane, he had to put the kid down. He lifted the nail gun and fired without hesitation. The boy dropped, and Kaleb sped off before he could think about what he had done.

The ATV had served its purpose. He needed a better vehicle, preferably something like an SUV that offered him better protection. He drove down several streets passing up choices he discarded for one reason or another until he saw a red 2013 FJ Cruiser, one of the most expensive SUVs on the market.

Kaleb parked next to the cruiser, pulled out the Glock, made sure the clip was full and checked the door of the SUV. It was locked, so he peeked in the window but didn't see anything. "Guess I'll check out the house," he murmured.

Looking around for any sign of undead, he walked to the front door of the house and tried the knob. The door opened. Kaleb checked the living room for a set of car keys but found none there or in the kitchen. He checked two smaller bedrooms, then the master bedroom. There weren't any keys, but Kaleb noticed the sliding glass door to the back yard was open.

A female body lay face down in the grass outside. He inched forward slowly and nudged the body with his toe. She had a huge hole in the back of her head, and her brains were gone. Kaleb knelt and patted the woman's pockets, feeling like he was a pervert frisking a dead woman. He felt a set of keys in the front pants pockets so he rolled her over and fished them out. Kaleb hoped the key fob was for the FJ Cruiser.

A rustling sound caught Kaleb's attention. He didn't see anything but could sense something was watching him. He backed up to the sliding glass door and closed it. A zombie jumped out from behind several trash cans in a corner of the yard and ran at Kaleb. On instinct, Kaleb stepped back with the Glock out, not realizing there was a cedar chest at the foot of the bed. He sat forcefully on the chest as the zombie approached. Without aiming, he fired four times, sure he would connect at least once.

The glass shattered, and he squeezed his eyes shut. When he opened his eyes, Kaleb saw the zombie on its back still outside.

Making sure he still had the car keys in his hand, Kaleb hurried outside and cheered silently when he pressed the unlock button on the key fob and the vehicle's lights flashed. Kaleb loaded his stuff into the back of the cruiser and sped off, leaving a strip of rubber behind him.

Kaleb breathed a sigh of relief when he pulled onto Greenway Road, which was less than half a mile from Black Mountain Country Club. He stopped at the beginning of the circular driveway leading onto the course. The clubhouse sat in the distance, but he could still see movement outside. He pulled out the rifle and peered down the scope.

"What the fuck?" The clubhouse was surrounded by dozens of zombies. There were several of the dumbass ones but also a fair number of the Super Zombies. The smart ones were trying the doorknobs and hitting windows. If Pat was in there, he and anybody else were trapped. Kaleb was sure Pat had weapons, but he would've needed more than a couple people with guns to take down all the zombies.

Continuing on Greenway Drive, Kaleb scoped out the building from almost every angle. There wasn't an inch of the outer wall not covered by zombies. He drove onto the green looking for an area he could take a stand.

Kaleb had no idea what he was going to do. He had to try and save his brother even if he risked his own life to do so. Pat was the only family he had left, and he didn't want to lose him. He estimated he could take a few out with his rifle and draw some of the intelligent ones away. That might buy Pat enough time to eliminate a few of the creatures around the building. Kaleb wasn't sure how many of the Super Zombies he could get before they got to him, but it was the only idea he had.

He raised the rifle and was about to pull the trigger when the roar of engines overhead distracted him. An airplane flew by, which would've been commonplace two days before but was now a unique sight. It passed by, then turned.

The plane was familiar, but Kaleb was sure it was just his imagination. It couldn't be the plane Coop got on, could it? He should be on his way to see his beloved cheating boyfriend.

Kaleb was floored as the plane started its descent onto the golf course. The pilot had plenty of room to land on the wide open green but Kaleb wondered how much more difficult it would be than landing on tarmac. Apparently, the pilot thought he could do it.

The rough landing was anything but graceful, and Kaleb was glad he wasn't in the plane. As soon as it stopped, Kaleb drove the SUV to it and the door opened. He was sure it was the same plane Coop had left on, but he didn't want to get his hopes up. The intensity of his desire surprised him.

The door opened, and there stood Coop with the biggest shit-eating grin. "Hey, Red. Miss me?"

"Like a bad rash, you evil bastard. What the hell are you doing here?" Kaleb drove the Landcruiser closer to the plane, opened the door and reached out so he could help Coop down. When their hands touched, a spark of electricity ran through Kaleb's entire body.

"Johnny heard voices on the radio asking for help. He said it was the golf course, so I knew your brother was in danger. I didn't want you walking into a disaster."

"You came to save me?" Kaleb asked.

"Don't get all sentimental on me. You saved my arse, I figured I should repay the favor—again."

"What about Ewan and going home?"

"Ewan is a cheating son of a bitch. He doesn't deserve me. As for home, I don't have much there. Nothing wrong with starting over, especially with a friend."

"Just a friend?" Kaleb asked teasingly.

"I don't let just friends do what you did to me, but don't be going all mushy on me or anything."

Kaleb raised his hands in mock surrender. "Not pushing. Just wanted to let you know I like you and yes, I did miss you."

"Nice ride," Coop said, gesturing to the SUV.

"Thanks. I wanted something with a little more kick than the ATV."

"You guys gonna fuck or should we kick some zombie ass?" Johnny asked.

"You joining us?" Kaleb asked.

Johnny shrugged. "Figured there's no use hiding. And if I'm gonna survive this fucking zombie apocalypse, I better learn how to protect myself." He stepped back and into the cockpit, returning quickly. We got a bunch of 'em headed our way. You guys ready?"

"Hell, yeah!" Coop shouted. He tossed the shotgun up to Johnny along with extra shells. "Stay up there. Shoot the ones that come up to you. Don't let them get too close. There are some smart ones who might be able to climb aboard. Close the doors if you need to, and we'll come back for you."

"Smart zombies? I thought this was Night of the Living Dead, I guess it's more like Resident Evil," Johnny sighed.

"Again with the movie references." Coop shook his head as he got into the passenger side of the cruiser.

Kaleb drove to the other side of the airplane to prepare for the zombie onslaught. Kaleb aimed the rifle out his window and took down several zombies from a distance. Coop opened the passenger window and sat half in and half out as he fired the Smith and Wesson, managing to kill several monsters.

"Get in," Kaleb shouted. "I'm gonna do some fancy driving."

Coop climbed back in the vehicle, reloaded his pistol and kept it aimed out the window

Kaleb drove to the left of the herd as Coop shot as many as possible. A Super Zombie leapt at the passenger side of the door, latching onto Coop's arm. The creature roared and leaned forward to take a bite, but Coop put the pistol to its forehead and pulled the trigger. The monster released Coop, fell under the vehicle, and the back wheels crunched its bones.

After taking down the last few creatures in the immediate

proximity, Kaleb pulled to a stop a couple hundred feet from the main building.

"What's next?"

CHAPTER EIGHTEEN
COOPER

Zombies clawed at the brick walls and pounded their fists against the metal shutters boarding the windows and doors. Must have been twelve, at least. They seemed sure their next meal was waiting for them inside, though how long they'd been trying to get in was anyone's guess. Definitely not the smart variety.

"Well, it looks like the survivors are safe for now," Coop said, nodding in the direction of the clubhouse. "Doesn't look like any of those corpses'll be getting in any time soon. So how do you wanna do this?"

"Too many to take head on. I can drop a few from a distance, but I'll need to get closer."

"Then what? We have no idea how many more there might be lurking around the place."

Kaleb narrowed his eyes at Coop. "My brother might be in there. I'm not waiting for him to get eaten alive."

Coop placed his hands on Kaleb's shoulders, squeezing them firmly. "There's no need to be hasty. If your brother's in there, he's safe for now. Let's just think about this for a moment before one of us ends up becoming zombie chow."

"Okay," Kaleb said, his body relaxing. He scratched his chin with one hand, tilting his head slightly, "What about a distraction? Maybe if they see some fresh meat, they'll follow that instead."

"It could work," Coop replied, folding his arms. "I dunno about splitting up though. And how would we decide who gets to be the bait?"

"I will," Kaleb said with a smirk. "I can drive the SUV, but you can't."

Coop furrowed his brows. "Bastard. You realize this means I'll be the one finding your brother. If there's any sign he's infected, I'll shoot him then and there."

Kaleb's head drooped, the grin fading from his face. "I trust you. If he's... He wouldn't want to live like that. And I don't know if I could...."

"What's your brother's name?"

"Pat."

"I'll keep an eye out for him," Coop said. He opened the passenger door when Kaleb grabbed his wrist. Coop paused and turned back to face him, one eyebrow raised. Kaleb reached into the back of the SUV and grabbed a spare clip, which he held out to Coop.

"Last one, so be careful," Kaleb warned. "You only have ten bullets in that clip."

"Thanks," Coop replied, taking the clip and shoving it into the pocket of his jeans. Only two clips, and he'd already fired at least five shots from the current clip. Hopefully it would be enough. "Wish I had my crossbow with me."

"Seriously? You have a crossbow?" Kaleb asked.

"What's wrong with that? They're silent, deadly, and if you're careful you can reuse the ammo. You can even fire them underwater if the need arises. Guns are too unreliable, and you'd run out of bullets eventually. Plus one gunshot could bring a whole horde of zombies knocking on your doorstep."

"It's scary how much you seem to have thought all this through ahead of time."

Coop chuckled. "Everyone thought I was crazy, you know? Stockpiling tins of food, building a zombie-proof shelter out in my back yard—"

"You actually built a bunker? Dude, what else did you prepare for?"

"Just the usual."

Kaleb arched an eyebrow. "There is nothing usual about this. Come on, honestly, what other world-ending scenarios did you plan for?"

Coop scratched at the back of his neck. "Just this, mainly. Always knew science was gonna be our downfall one day. Oh, and nuclear war, I guess. Aliens, just in case. I mean, I don't actually believe in them, but you can never be too careful. That thing I said about Diana was a joke, by the way."

"Wow. Anything else?"

"No, that's it. Oh, actually, I've got another one. Economic collapse. With the way the world was going, it was only gonna be a matter of time before full-scale riots broke out and everything went to hell. And hackers, too. Everything's controlled by computers, right? Imagine if one day someone managed to bring down all those systems. We'd be screwed."

Kaleb blinked once, and then twice. "Coop, you are certifiably crazy. And I'm glad you are. At least one of us was prepared for this whole mess."

Coop laughed. "Being nuts paid off for once, eh? Well, shall we get started? You draw the zombies away and kill as many as you can. I'll sneak up to the clubhouse and take out the stragglers before taking care of the survivors. Okay?"

"Gotcha. We'll meet back up at the plane."

Coop climbed out of the SUV and closed the door behind him. He started off into the trees where he could remain hidden from sight. The SUV's engine revved and Coop paused, glancing over his shoulder. "Kaleb."

"Yeah?"

"Promise me you'll be careful."

Kaleb smirked. "You gonna go all emotional on me now?"

"I came back to save your arse. Least you can do is stay alive, okay?"

"Don't worry about me. I can handle myself," Kaleb replied. "And don't you be dying on me either. I still owe you some payback for being a complete dick earlier."

Coop lowered his head, gazing at his mud-caked sneakers. "I thought maybe it would make things easier for us if...."

"You can explain later," Kaleb interrupted. "Now let's go off some zombies."

"Right."

Coop gripped the gun tighter in his hand and made his way into the thick of the trees. He walked slowly, his eyes scanning all around him as he stepped over tree trunks and avoided crunching any twigs underfoot. Under the dark canopy of leaves, everything was silent save for the pounding of blood in his ears and his hushed breaths. Not even a bird chirping. He came to the edge of the trees, about a hundred feet from the building, waiting for his opportunity.

The zombies pounded against the clubhouse, groaning as they tried to gain access. A bang echoed through the air, followed by one of the walking corpses collapsing to the ground with a hole through his skull and blood streaking down the brick wall. They turned almost in unison and let out a collective growl, ambling onto the green as a second gunshot tore through the cacophonous mob and struck one of them in the shoulder. It jerked back before continuing as though the bullet was merely an insect bite. Several more fell as the dumb creatures walked straight toward Kaleb and his rifle without any regard for their own survival.

Coop stepped out from his hiding place, quickly sprinting across the open ground to the clubhouse. He kept close to the wall and moved around the perimeter. At the back entrance, two zombies were trying to clamber onto a dumpster where a small window was unprotected. He stopped and shook his head. Damn things weren't even smart enough to figure out they were too large to get through the gap.

He inched closer and took aim, shooting the first one in the head. He dropped to the concrete with a crack as his skull leaked red and black goo. His friend, a short middle-aged woman, turned and opened her mouth to scream. Coop squeezed the trigger again, the bullet flying wide. He fired twice more, her head snapping back as the bullets pierced her throat with ease. With one final shot, she slumped against the dumpster. Only after a few seconds did he lower the gun, satisfied that the monster wasn't going to be moving again. After reloading, he continued his sweep around the building. Ten bullets left. Such a nuisance.

"Psst. Hey," a male voice whispered.

Coop paused in his tracks and spun around.

"Hey. Yeah, you."

"Who's there?" Coop asked.

"Over here, by the window."

Coop moved closer to the dumpster, making sure to keep some distance between him and the lifeless bodies. Being extra careful couldn't hurt where the undead are concerned.

"Heard the gunshots. Can't say how glad I am to see someone who's still alive. Figured we were done for."

"How many of you are in there?" Coop asked.

"Four of us."

"Anyone been sick recently? Coughing. Fever. Anything like that?"

"No."

Coop breathed a sigh of relief. "Okay, good. We need to get you guys out of here and fast."

"And go where?"

"We've got a jet at the bottom of the green with enough space to get us all out of here. But we have to go now, before any more zombies show up."

For a moment, there was silence. "Okay. I'll go let the others know. Meet me round the side entrance. I'll open the shutters for you."

"Thanks," Coop replied.

He made his way round, dispatching a lone zombie who had stumbled out from the car park. A lock clicked from inside.

"Is it safe?" the man asked.

"For now," Coop replied.

Metal screeched as the shutters rose up part way. Coop scanned the area around him one last time before ducking under and into the clubhouse. He entered into a small bar where a man with short brown hair speckled with grey at the temples greeted him. At one of the booths sat an elderly woman, an empty tumbler on the table in front of her. And over at the counter were a young man and woman. The male must have been in his mid-twenties with shaggy brown hair and some stubble adorning his chin.

"Name's Brian. You have no idea how grateful we are that you came," said the man, extending his hand.

"Coop." He hesitated for a moment, before cautiously accepting the handshake. Seemed like everyone was okay at least. No sign of any infection. He walked across the room to the other man. "Are you Pat?"

"Yeah. Do I know you?" he asked.

"No, but I know your brother."

"Kaleb? Is he here?"

"Yeah, he's at the plane waiting for us all," Coop replied. "Speaking of which, we should get going as quickly as possible. Won't be long until more zombies show up. Grab whatever supplies you can: food, water, and anything you can use to defend yourself."

"Oh, what's the point?" the old woman asked. "This world's already doomed."

"Come now, Ethel. You don't know that for sure," Brian said. "There's still a chance the virus hasn't spread too far."

"You saw it yourself on that's kid's whatyamacallit phone...."

"Smartphone," Pat said.

"What's that?" Coop asked.

Pat jumped up from his chair and fished about in his pocket for his phone. "The internet here is still working from time to time. Managed to find this article on the infection," he said, holding the screen up for Coop to see. "There were major outbreaks in Denver yesterday, and a few reported cases as far east as Mississippi."

"Then the infected could be everywhere already," Coop replied. "Did it say anything about England?"

"There have been a couple of reports from around the world,"

Pat said. "At least a few in England, but I didn't have time to get any of the details before the signal died again. Seems like we got hit the hardest, though. Not surprising since they say the virus came from Area 51."

"Well, shit," Coop said. From the sounds of it, nowhere would be safe. At least, not for long.

"What are our options?" Brian asked.

Coop shrugged. "Canada, maybe? Alaska."

"You're joking, right? It's freezing up there," Pat said. Coop glared at him. "You're serious?"

"Could all just shoot ourselves now," Ethel said. "Be a helluva lot less painful."

"Ethel," Brian snapped. "You're free to stay if you wish, but I'm getting as far away from here as possible. How about you, Julia?" he asked, nodding to the younger woman.

"Count me in," she replied, grabbing a golf club that had been leaning against the bar. "

"Last chance, Ethel. Come with us or stay here," Coop said.

She groaned and slowly stood. "Oh, have it your way then."

"Right," Coop said, standing before the rest of them. It was very much like the times he'd stood in front of his team back home as their captain. Made him feel safe and in control again. "Grab what you can carry without slowing you down. We still don't know how many more zombies are out there. Pat, stay close to Ethel. Brian. Julia. I want you to keep an eye on our flanks and rear. I'll take point and lead you to the plane. Understood?"

"Quit your yappin,' and let's go before I change my mind," Ethel grumbled.

Coop let out a long breath. At least the others were in agreement with his plan. He set off outside first, ducking under the shutter and turning on the spot to survey the area. No zombies so far. He signaled for the rest to follow him out, and they walked hurriedly across the lawn to the trees, each sticking to their assignment.

As they reached the trees, there was a slight rustling noise from ahead. Coop froze, motioning for the others to be silent. The wind? It came again, louder this time. He raised the gun and aimed, watching for any signs of movement. A deep groan sounded as a tall, pale frame ambled out from behind one of the large trunks. Coop fired instinctively, the first shot grazing the bark of the tree. He cursed under his breath.

The zombie groaned again as it lurched forward. Coop held his breath, waiting for the lumbering corpse to draw closer. He fired once, hitting the zombie square in the forehead. It landed with a dull thud, and then there was a scream. Coop went to turn when something heavy collided with him, knocking him to the ground. He lost his grip on the Smith and Wesson, sending it spinning out of reach. His shoulder hit the grass, sending a jolt of pain throughout his arm. He rolled to one side and jumped to his feet, coming face-to-face with his attacker. The zombie smirked, flashing its blackened teeth. Its right eye socket was merely a crater of hardened black goo.

"You!" Coop gasped. "I killed you when we got the ATV."

Its rotten lips parted further. "Possum," it spoke, in a raspy, almost breathless tone.

Coop took a step back, his heart threatening to burst through his rib cage. The damn thing could speak? "No fucking way."

Behind One-Eye, Julia had snuck closer, her golf club already raised to strike.

"Stay back!" Coop yelled.

She froze, and the zombie turned in her direction, its arms already reaching out. Coop rushed forward and kicked out at its legs. It stumbled and fell forward, barely missing Julia's feet. She jumped back and re-joined the group. Coop glanced around his feet for the gun, but found no sign of it.

"Catch," Brian shouted, throwing one of the clubs his way. He caught it and brought it up over his head. One-Eye jumped to its feet, barely dodging the swing as it hit the grass with a thud.

Coop swung sideways, aiming for its neck. The zombie stepped back out of reach and let out what could only be described as a wheezing chuckle.

"You're fast for a dead guy," Coop said.

One-Eye took a step forward, and then stopped. The rumbling of an engine grew louder until Pat shouted at the top of his voice. "Kaleb!"

CHAPTER NINETEEN
KALEB

Kaleb gassed the SUV toward the group of people a hundred feet away. He could see Coop trying unsuccessfully to take out a creature. Both the rifle and Glock were out of ammo. He reached behind him to grab a different weapon, but the only thing he could find was the nail gun. He wasn't sure if there was any battery life left, but it was his only chance.

"Get out of the way!" he yelled. Coop stepped back as Kaleb yanked the wheel, slammed the brake, skidded to a stop and looked into the eyes of the creature. It stared back at him and roared.

He aimed the nail gun and pulled the trigger, hoping it had enough battery power. The nail shot out, but it went over the monster's right shoulder. It growled, and he swore the damn thing smiled. It turned to Coop and stepped forward.

"Fuck off and die, monster!" Kaleb screamed and repeatedly pulled the trigger. Nails flew in and out of the creature's chest and left arm. It stopped and turned back to Kaleb, letting out another snarl. Kaleb pulled the trigger again but nothing happened. "Damn battery."

The zombie grinned and stepped toward Coop again. Coop glanced behind him then raised his hands and motioned to the monster. "Come on! Bring it on!"

"What the hell?" Kaleb swore. He was about to get out of the vehicle when he noticed Coop looking at him.

"Come on! Over here! Right this way!"

Coop wasn't just speaking to the beast; he was also talking to Kaleb. Backing the car up, then pointing it in the direction of Coop and the monster, Kaleb revved the engines.

"Yeah! That's right!" Coop yelled. "Right this way."

Kaleb put the car in gear and slammed his foot down on

the gas pedal. Just before impact, the creature turned to see the vehicle, and Coop jumped to the side. Kaleb felt tires roll over the zombie, and he applied the brakes. Opening the door, he looked down and back. The monster's legs had been crushed, but his head was intact and he still had the use of an arm. Kaleb backed up until the creature's head was exactly in line with the front driver's side tire. He then gassed the vehicle and drove over the skull. There was a loud pop as the skull cracked, signaling the second end of the monster's life.

As soon as Kaleb hopped out of the Landcruiser, Coop was there, pulling him into a quick embrace and kissing him quickly on the lips.

He stepped back. "Sorry, Red."

Kaleb didn't mind the unexpected PDA but wasn't sure what their audience would think of it, specifically Pat. He'd never told anyone in his family he was gay.

Kaleb turned to face his brother, who had a shocked look on his face. Kaleb couldn't tell if there was anger or disgust as well. "Everybody in," Kaleb called out hoping to use the distraction to delay the conversation with Pat.

Once everyone was in the vehicle, Kaleb drove back to the plane, tracking over the numerous bodies of the dead undead. He pulled up to the airplane door, where Johnny stood with the shotgun ready.

"Calm down. No zombies here." Kaleb motioned to everyone.

"Well, climb on in," the pilot said, extending his arm. Cooper and Kaleb got in first then helped everybody else. It took Pat and Brian both to get Ethel in.

Ethel plopped into one of the airplane seats and leaned back. "Ehh, not bad. I never flown first class before."

Pat reached out and pulled Kaleb into a tight, warm embrace.

"First of all, little brother," Pat said as he stepped back from the hug. He pointed at the zombie and the SUV. "That thing with the nail gun and the zombie was fucking a-ma-zing. Second, I am so happy to see you. I was so worried. Didn't think you'd make it."

"I had some help." Kaleb pointed to Cooper who didn't say anything.

"Okay." Pat sighed. "So you're gay?"

Kaleb nodded. "Is that a problem?"

Pat looked at him. "A problem? Fuck no, why would it be? Just a surprise is all. Makes a lot of sense now. Never saw you with no chicks ever. Guess I should've seen it. But, no. Ain't no problem at all."

Kaleb sighed in relief. "Pat, this is Cooper Lockwood. He's an arrogant British bastard, but he's not so bad when you get to know him. He's saved me more than once."

"Thanks for saving my brother's ass," Pat said as he shook hands with Coop.

"It's such a cute arse, it'd be a shame to waste it." Cooper grinned.

Pat was silent for a moment, then smiled as well. "You and the Brit are pretty good at this survival thing. I don't mind us all hanging together. As long as you and your boyfriend don't make out in front of us."

"We're not a couple," Kaleb and Coop said at the same time.

Ethel stared at both of them and shook her head. "Young people can be so dumb sometimes."

"Where's Chelsea?" Kaleb looked around.

Pat's face fell. "Chelsea was attacked just after I called you from the hospital. I went home even though you said I shouldn't. I wanted to save you or Mama if I could. Brian here gave me a ride."

"Shit," Kaleb responded. "I saw her just as she turned. I ran off after you. I didn't know what the hell was going on."

"Brian here took care of her." Pat motioned to the man and woman who were holding hands.

Kaleb gave Brian a nod of appreciation.

"Now that we've had this lovely little family reunion and

introduction to the happy queer couple, you think we can get this show on the road?" Ethel asked.

"I agree. What's the plan, folks?" Johnny asked. "I'm up for whatever you guys decide."

"You got enough gas to make it to Alaska?" Coop wondered.

Johnny nodded.

"Why Alaska?" Pat asked.

"I did some research a couple of years ago," Coop said, ignoring the bemused look on Kaleb's face. "One of the popular theories was that zombies wouldn't be able to handle the cold."

"You did research on zombies?" Pat asked.

Kaleb touched his brother's shoulder giving him a don't ask look.

Coop continued. "They don't have circulation, so they can't keep warm. Chances are they'd just freeze solid. Even if someone was sick and turned, they wouldn't survive out in the open."

"Sounds good to me," Kaleb said. "What does everybody else think? Alaska or bust?"

Everybody nodded except Ethel, who was already asleep and snoring lightly.

"Let's make like a bird and get the flock outta here," Johnny cracked. "Everybody needs to buckle up. There's a private room in the back, small bed all made up. My boss was always renewing his membership in the Mile High Club."

"I call the bed!" Coop said loudly.

Pat laughed. "You gonna join him, K? Even though you're not a couple or anything."

Kaleb shrugged. Of course, he wanted to go with Coop, but it wasn't like he'd been invited. Coop walked to the back of the cabin, stepped into the room and shut the door. His gut dropped, but maybe it was for the best. He didn't want to get too attached to Coop if the man wasn't interested. He ignored the sad stares of Pat, Brian, and Julia and was about to sit down when the bedroom door opened.

"Hey, Red! Get your arse in here."

He smiled and practically ran to the back of the plane, tackling Coop to the bed and kicking the door shut.

"You're an evil bastard." Kaleb held Coop down and bit his neck softly.

"Then we're a pair, aren't we? A couple of evil bastards."

"Oh, so we're a couple now?" Kaleb teased. Kaleb felt Coop stiffen nervously. "I didn't mean it like that, Coop. I'm not asking for a ring and a commitment ceremony or a promise of monogamy."

"Monogamy wouldn't be that hard, considering the group we're with."

Kaleb laughed. "What I'm saying is that I like you. I'd like to keep doing this. If you're interested, that is."

Coop's hands traveled down Kaleb's back and under his shirt. "Yeah, I don't mind doing this some more."

Kaleb would've preferred Coop to say he liked him, too, but he would take what he could get. Being emotionally open wasn't the man's best quality.

"Get naked," Kaleb ordered, "but do it slowly so I can watch."

Coop got up and began stripping. As commanded, he did it slowly, watching Kaleb's face. Shoes, socks and then his shirt. Coop stood half naked, Kaleb's erection making an obvious outline in his pants. He rubbed it as Coop put on his show.

Coop ran his hand across his stomach and tweaked his nipples. Kaleb let out a low murmur in response. Satisfied he was getting the reaction he wanted, Coop smiled and resumed stripping. He unzipped his pants leisurely, turning around when he dropped them to his ankles so he could wiggle his ass in Kaleb's direction.

"Sexy mother fucker," Kaleb moaned. He reached into his pants, stroking his cock, but not pulling it out.

Coop faced Kaleb again, his own erection straining against the fabric of his boxer briefs. Coop squeezed his dick and a wet spot formed on the cotton.

"Take them off." Kaleb's voice was so quiet Coop almost didn't hear him.

Coop grinned and slowly removed his underwear, his dick slapping his stomach when it was released. He wrapped his fingers around his shaft and slowly stroked it, pushing the foreskin over the flared head. He tugged gently on his ball sack, unable to stifle his own hum of pleasure.

Kaleb's eyes were still glued to Coop's gorgeous body, but he had taken his cock out and was tenderly playing with it.

Slowly turning around, Coop bent slightly forward with his ass jutted out. He reached back with both hands, gripped his ass cheeks and spread them.

"Mother fucker!" In less than a few seconds, Kaleb was off the bed and on his knees with his face buried in Coop's ass.

"Uhhh." Coop leaned his head against the wall to balance himself and still keep his cheeks spread while Kaleb continued his literal tongue lashing. Kaleb licked up and down the sides of Coop's ass then thrust his tongue into the tight hole.

Without warning, Kaleb spun Coop around and pushed him on the bed.

"Christ, Red." He tried to sound at least somewhat angry, but the grin on his face showed the truth.

Kaleb said nothing as he examined Coop's shaft. He pulled the skin down so it stretched tight then slowly stroked back up so the foreskin was wrapped around the head.

"It's amazing." He tugged down and then back up and precome oozed out over the skin.

With the flesh pulled down, Kaleb leaned forward and sucked half of Coop's cock into his mouth. Coop grunted, arching his hips up, but Kaleb pushed him back down with one hand. He stroked upward with the other hand, keeping his lips wrapped around the erection. His tongue snaked in between the foreskin and the head, tasting the sweet liquid and lapping up as much as he could.

"Oh my god," he exclaimed when he pulled back. "You taste

so good. I've never been with a guy who had so much precome."

"Having the foreskin creates a natural lubricant," Coop said. "Never did understand why you Americans insist on removing something nature gave us."

"It's fucking awesome." Kaleb leaned down and swiped his tongue around the inside of the skin, before pulling it down and swallowing Coop's dick to the root. This time when Coop pushed his hips up, Kaleb allowed it, breathing in so he wouldn't gag.

Kaleb sucked and licked Coop's shaft, alternating between being gentle and rough. Coop seemed to like either way, so Kaleb kept switching it up. Flipping around so they could suck each other's cocks at the same time, Kaleb slowly pushed his dick into Coop's warm mouth. Moaning as Coop's tongue licked at his length, Kaleb fought the urge to ram it down the Brit's mouth.

Lifting Coop's legs, he buried his face between the cheeks again. He licked at the hole before pushing his tongue inside.

"Kaleb," Coop whispered. "I'm gonna come if you don't stop."

"Would that be a bad thing?"

Coop moaned. "I wanna come while you fuck me."

He climbed off. "You want me to fuck you again?"

He nodded. "You don't want to?"

"Hell, yeah I want to fuck you. Trouble is, I don't have any condoms."

"Bloody hell."

"Hold on." Kaleb pulled on his pants stepped to the door and opened it.

"Pat! Come here."

"What's up, Kaleb?"

"You got a condom?"

CHAPTER TWENTY
COOPER

Coop's eyes widened. Did Kaleb seriously just ask his brother for a condom? He shook his head and rolled over on the bed, opening up one of the drawers in the bedside table. Empty.

"What did you say?" Pat shouted down the hallway.

"I said, do you have a condom?" Kaleb yelled back.

"Eww, Kaleb! Too much information, bro. Bad enough knowing you're sleeping in the same bed. I don't need to know that you're actually gonna be doing it."

Coop chuckled and climbed off the bed. He walked into the bathroom and opened up one of the cupboards. Sure enough, he found an unopened pack of rubbers on the top shelf. "Got some," he said, taking the box back into the bedroom along with a few travel packets of lube. "Guess Johnny wasn't lying when he said his boss liked to frequent the mile-high club."

Kaleb shut the door and grinned. "Guess not. It'll be my first time. How about you?"

"Same here."

Coop threw the condoms and lube onto the bed, and wrapped his arms around Kaleb's waist as he drew their bodies together. He leaned down slightly to capture Kaleb's mouth in his own, his tongue pressing into the warm opening. His hard dick ground against the smaller man's stomach, the head still slick with precome. He grunted into the kiss, almost losing himself as his hips continued to rock.

Kaleb pulled back first, shoving Coop onto the bed. He landed with a gasp as Kaleb quickly removed his pants, climbed over him and straddled his chest. The monster dick hung limply above Coop's mouth. Kaleb wrapped his forefinger and thumb around the base and stroked it with his other hand.

Coop lifted his head and rolled his tongue around Kaleb's

sack. He drew one of his balls into his mouth, sucking hard. Kaleb moaned loudly, stroking faster as his dick hardened.

"Fuck it," Kaleb gasped. "Open up. I wanna fuck your mouth."

Kaleb leaned forward and Coop opened wide. The thick cock slipped past his lips, filling his mouth. The tip pressed against the back of his throat, and he fought against the tightening of his stomach muscles. Kaleb pulled all the way out, leaving Coop to gasp for breath before quickly ramming it back in. He thrust his hips, driving his dick as far as it could go before Coop's body tensed.

Coop jerked himself off as the already huge appendage seemed to grow larger still inside him. His jaw strained to take it all, and his hands balled into fists, gripping the bed covers as Kaleb continued to fuck the wet hole. He drove his cock in one last time before pulling out slowly. Coop closed his mouth and wiped it with the back of his hand, cleaning off the spit that had dribbled down his cheek.

Kaleb reached for the box of condoms and tore into it. He opened up one of the foil packets and rolled the latex over his cock down to the base. Next he ripped open a packet of lube and squeezed some out onto the tips of his fingers. Coop tensed as the cold gel brushed against his ass. Kaleb pushed two fingers in side by side. He moaned and arched his back.

"Yeah," he breathed. "Fuck me."

Kaleb smirked and withdrew his fingers. He lifted Coop's legs over his shoulders and lined his cock up against Coop's hole. "Ready?"

Coop gripped tighter onto the covers and nodded. Lubed or not, it was still going to hurt like a bitch at first. He took a deep breath, relaxing his body as his hole was slowly stretched until Kaleb's cock slipped inside.

"Shit," Coop yelled, his body jerking in pain. He placed his hands against Kaleb's hips, preventing him from going any deeper as he took short, shallow breaths. When the pain had mostly subsided, he dropped his hands and Kaleb took that as a signal to continue. He drew out slowly at first before pushing back against the muscles clamping down around him.

"Damn you're tight," Kaleb said.

Coop snorted. "It's not me, you're just huge."

Kaleb shrugged and rammed his dick back in, drawing a long moan from Coop's throat. He picked up the pace and soon the room was filled with the sounds of flesh slapping and heavy breathing. Kaleb took hold of Coop's cock and jerked him off with a rhythm as furious as the pounding he was giving Coop's ass. Coop wrapped his hands around the back of Kaleb's thighs, holding on as though he might get washed away in the sensations building inside of him. And with one particularly forceful thrust, he threw his head back and cried out, the pleasure spilling over and onto his stomach.

"Oh, fuck," Coop gasped, Kaleb's hand still tight around his cock, stroking him past the edge of the orgasm. He squirmed from every little touch as Kaleb's fingers passed over the sensitive head, the gentle touch suddenly much more intense, like thousands of tiny lightning bolts against his skin.

Kaleb grunted, his rhythm faltering. He drove himself inside faster and deeper, finally letting go of Coop's softening cock to push against the backs of his knees, lifting his ass higher into the air. The change in angle had Coop whimpering and groaning, clawing at the mattress. Kaleb gave one last thrust, holding it deep inside. He leaned down, taking advantage of Coop's parted lips. Their tongues danced between them, each panting for breath until Kaleb pulled back.

Coop groaned as the cock slipped out of him inch by inch, leaving him with a feeling of emptiness. "Wow," he said, pressing one palm against his chest. His heart thudded beneath his ribs, barely contained by the wall of flesh, muscle, and bone.

Kaleb smiled and slipped the condom off, tying it into a knot before disappearing into the bathroom. He was back seconds later with a towel, which he threw to Coop.

"So, I guess we're both members now, huh?" Kaleb said, lying down next to him.

"Uh-huh," Coop replied, still trying to calm his body and mind. He wiped down his stomach and then sighed, every muscle seeming to melt into the bed.

Kaleb snuggled up to him, placing one arm over his chest and melding their bodies together. "I wonder what'll happen now," he said quietly.

Coop paused wiping himself down and lifted his head to turn and meet Kaleb's eyes. "Anything could happen. That's the beauty of it."

"Yeah, but doesn't it scare you? Being so far away from home, in a strange place with people you barely know."

"Course it does. Back in England, I had everything. At least, I thought I did." He slumped back down onto the bed, gazing up at the white ceiling. "I had everything prepared. Food, weapons, shelter. But the one thing I didn't have was someone I could just be honest with."

"Even Ewan?" Kaleb asked.

"Not even him. Sometimes he'd want to go on nights out together, and I'd make up stupid lies just because I was afraid of being caught out in public with him. Here though, I have you. And I know we didn't meet that long ago, but I feel so much happier knowing you're around. I can tell you anything, and I don't have to be afraid anymore. It's kinda liberating."

Silence settled in over the cabin, save for the roaring of the jet engines outside. The future was uncertain, that was for sure, but Coop really did have everything he needed. Except a crossbow. Damn guns were too noisy. The plane was perfect as a shelter, and there was no shortage of weapons with the mini-arsenal Kaleb had brought with him, although there wasn't much left of the ammo. They had sufficient food to last at least a couple of weeks. Hunting would have to become a priority before long, though. Maybe if they found somewhere near a lake to camp up. And now he had companionship too, someone to share the experience of post-apocalyptic life with and keep him sane. The odd fuck wouldn't hurt either. At least, not in a bad way.

"What about you?" Coop asked, breaking the silence between

them.

"Hmm?"

"Well, it can't be easy for you. I heard what your brother said about your mom."

"Oh, that," Kaleb replied. "I never really had time to stop and think about it before, you know? When I came home from work, she was already one of them, and I ran. I just couldn't bring myself to pull the trigger."

Coop hummed in agreement, though he couldn't even begin to imagine how it must have felt.

"I didn't even understand what was happening at the time," he continued. "I knew she was gone, but it didn't make any sense. I'm glad at least I know what happened to her. I don't have to wonder if she's still out there wandering the streets. I think the not knowing would have hurt more."

Kaleb's breath hitched. Coop wrapped his arms around Kaleb tighter as the younger man sobbed against his chest. A knife seemed to stab deep into his chest, old memories of his own losses being dragged to the surface. He swallowed hard, forcing them back to focus on the present.

It was only when Kaleb had quieted that he finally spoke again. "If it's any consolation, it really does get easier with time. You just have to keep putting one foot forward."

Kaleb sniffled and wiped at his eyes. He pulled away from Coop's embrace and sat up, picking up his pants that lay at the foot of the bed. "You hungry?" he asked. "I'm starving."

Coop pushed himself up onto his elbows, arching an eyebrow at Kaleb. "Yeah, famished. You sure you're okay?"

Kaleb hesitated before nodding. "I think I just needed a moment to let it all out. So, thank you for being there for me."

"You're welcome," Coop replied. "You thought about what you're going to do next? I mean, once we land, it's probably gonna be back to living in a horror movie."

"I figure I'll just take your advice," Kaleb said, smiling. "One foot forward, taking each day as it comes and trying to survive.

Besides, I bet you've already figured out what we're going to do about food and everything already."

Coop smirked and held up his hands. "Guilty."

Kaleb snickered and shook his head. "You're fucking crazy, Coop. Please don't ever change that. Now, come on, let's go eat before I decide to go all zombie and eat you instead."

THE END

GHOUL'S GYM

ZOMBIE BOYZ

TJ KLUNE
ERIC ARVIN

Z

ULY

Damn! It's a pristine morning on Euclid Avenue. Makes a fella happy to be alive, don't it? The grass is glistening wet in the sun from the oscillating lawn sprinklers. The trees are filled with a chorus of birds who take up the same verse every day. Neighbors' dogs play and bark, and the children dress up their cats in pirate outfits, for every day in suburbia is Halloween.

The two story homes on Euclid are, every one, a model of taste, each looking as if it was the winner of some extreme home makeover program where the host carries around a megaphone and shouts "Get 'er done!" like an overcompensating football coach. That's not far from the truth, actually. We all compete with each other, I'll admit that. Everything in life is a competition. It's instinctual, or primal, something like that. Except now, instead of fighting over who gets the biggest piece of meat, we fight over who has the nicest car, biggest house, most perfect body. It's the twenty-first century, and this is what matters.

This is our two-story Tudor home with a large pool and a two car garage. We're pretty lucky, I think. I had a smile on my face as big as the gosh darn moon the day Jake and me signed our lives away for it a few months ago. It's usually a quiet neighborhood, too, but not this morning. No, sir. And that's our fault. We're upstairs fucking so hard we're gonna wake the dead.

Jake Howell, that's my man. He's a lanky looker, and he commands my attention whenever he walks into a room. And me? I'm the gym bunny with his ankles in the air. My name is Ulysses Florence Hoak. I kid you not. I was named after a family war hero, blah, blah, blah.

Most folks just call me Uly.

I know how to get Jakey going. He's watching the news in bed this morning. I'm feeling a bit more rambunctious, so, as usual when this occurs, I get up and parade around, picking up dirty clothes and the like from the floor while dressed in nothing but my sexiest undies. I make sure to bend over a lot. Jake is on me like a squirrel on nuts. I work out that derriere just for him, so it's good to see he appreciates it.

The whole room is shaking as Jake plows into me. And man, does he plow! So deep I can feel it in my tummy. Most of the yelling is coming from me, but it's what I asked for after all.

This morning, though…damn! He's skewering me with his dick. And there's this look on his face like he's still listening to the news. Like I'm there but I'm not there. Don't get me wrong. It's still hot in its own way, but Jake seems distracted.

In between thrusts and kisses, in between my groaning and his grunting, I hear bits and pieces of the news: a strange outbreak of violence here, a startling new virus there. Everyday stuff. And Jake keeps stabbing me, like he's fucking me to death. There's definite passion in each thrust, but it feels more like anger than lust. And when he comes, he grabs my hair like he's going to bash my face in. When he's finished, he rolls off me and mumbles something about the fitness center where I work.

I, my friends, am feeling like a Twinkie—cream-filled and rejected.

Jake makes his way to the shower as if we hadn't just had Richter scale sex. I try to hold my tongue. I try not to say a damn thing. But I've never been very good at that. I can hold hundreds of pounds in my hands securely, but my tongue is another matter altogether. I am still naked on the bed, and I ask him ever so polite-like, "What the fuck is wrong with you?"

Z
JAKE

What the fuck is wrong with me?

Shit.

What the fuck isn't wrong with me?

I try and school my face. Relax my shoulders. Not seem so combative. It's not working. I clench my fists. Grit my teeth. My dick is still half hard, like it's mocking me, still slick with lube and come. Go down, I tell it. Just fucking go down.

"I asked you a question," Uly says from behind me. He's trying to use what he calls his redneck polite voice, but we've been together a year now. Lived with each other half that time. I know he's pissed. At me. Not that I blame him. I just fucked him within an inch of his life and couldn't be bothered to make sure he enjoyed it. Uly doesn't take shit like that lying down. Well, not figuratively.

"I heard you," I tell him, keeping my voice low. The bathroom door is only feet away, and I have to resist the urge to go through it and close the door behind me. Lock it all out. Including him. Goddammit.

"Well?" His patience is wearing thin.

"Can we not do this now?" Or ever. That would be awesome too.

"Oh? Then when do you wanna do it? Seems to me the only time we talk now is when you tell me if you want me on my back or on my knees."

I try not to shrink back at the bitterness in his words. He's right, of course. How could I have let this get so bad? But then that fucker Stephen pops back into my head, and I see red again. I swear to fucking Christ I could tear him apart with my hands if I ever have to see him again. Twinkie, he calls me. Uly's little princess. The Prince and the pea.

Yeah, Uly's a big fucker, muscles piled on top of muscles.

Some people might think it's gross how jacked he is, but not me. There's something about the way his veins look so pronounced that gets my cock hard. The cut and defined lines of his arms and thighs. The massive chest. Everything about him is big. Every single part of him. Personality, body, mind. Everything.

Except for me.

He says he doesn't care. He says he doesn't care that I'm a third his size, that he outweighs me by a good hundred pounds. He says he doesn't care that I'm not cut, or ripped, or jacked. He says he doesn't care that next to him, I'm just a shadow. I see you just fine, he told me once. I don't need you big like me. I just need you to be you.

Yeah. I'm a thirty-year old homo with body issues. I don't get bigger, no matter how hard I work out. No matter what I eat. No matter what I do. I stay the same. The fact that I'm a walking cliché isn't lost on me.

And now, it's starting to affect us both.

But it's really because of him.

Stephen Fucking Dorian. Uly's boss at the gym. He's made it no secret how he thinks Uly would be better off sitting on his cock rather than mine. Stephen Fucking Dorian isn't exactly an expert in subtlety. He's like a fat kid, and Uly's his cake. All frosted and ready to be plowed into.

I've seen the snide little looks I get from him, the hushed whispers to the other gym bunnies, the laughs in my direction anytime I go with Uly to the gym. Oh look, he says every time he sees me. Here comes Uly's princess. How is the sweet pea these days? Fucker. If I was a little bit bigger, I'd rip his fucking dick off and—

"Jake?" Uly says. Goddammit. Lost in my own head. Again.

"What?" I snap. I don't mean to. I hear him move off the bed and stand behind me. He doesn't touch me.

"You got something to say?" he asks. The redneck politeness is gone. Good ol' boy has come out to play.

Yes. "No."

"Then treat me with some goddamn respect."

My spine stiffens. Anything I say now is going to make it worse. I'm pissed off. Not really at him, but it'll come out that way. When we fight, rare as it is, it's always epic. You can't put someone like Uly and me together without us clawing at each other every now and then.

"Christ," he mutters. "Look, I don't know what's going on in that head of yours, but sure as shit, it ain't right. Fix it, Jake. Tell me what's wrong or do something about it. But for fuck's sake, fix it. It's like I'm dating a stranger. I want Jake back."

"It's not…" I start. Then stop. What am I supposed to say? It's not that simple? It's not you, it's me? It's not what you think?

It's not something I can fix on my own?

No. It's not that at all.

It's how all your friends are bigger than me. It's how you don't really do anything to shoot Stephen Fucking Dorian down. It's how he smiles at you, stands too close to you, and you say it's just how he is. He's your boss, after all. What harm could he do? It's not you I don't trust. It's everyone else. It's myself. It's how I wish I could—

"I'm going to be late," he mumbles, pushing past me. He goes into the bathroom and shuts the door behind him. We never shut doors. Not even if we're taking a shit. We've never had a reason to.

Fuck. He's really pissed.

I sit on the bed and look at my hands. I'm still sitting there minutes later when he opens the door in a swirl of steam. I can't think of anything to say aside from the truth. I want to be bigger. Stronger. Better. I know it doesn't matter to him, but it matters to me.

I glance up and for a moment, I take in his reddened skin, the way the water drips down his chest, beading on his stomach. The set of his jaw, the tenseness of his shoulders. He doesn't say anything as he drops the towel and dresses quickly. Sleeveless gym shirt, showing off the arms. Tight shorts, molded around his thighs. He rubs the towel over his head once more and hangs it from a hook on the closet.

I look at the bedside clock and see it's earlier than I thought. He usually doesn't go in until later on the Saturdays he works. "Don't you still have a couple of hours?" I ask him quietly.

He shakes his head as he packs his gym bag, and it's like he deflates slightly. "Stephen asked me to come in early today. Needs me to help him with some new equipment we're getting since that shit got stolen from the last break in."

"Yeah," I say with a scowl. "I bet he does."

He ignores this. "Besides, we could use the extra money. Italy isn't going to come to us, Jake. We want to get there someday. We need the cash."

"Yeah." Italy. A dream. A hope. A little villa we can call our own. Just me and him and all the wine we can drink. It's been a dream almost since the beginning. Everything we do is saving for it. We want it sooner rather than later.

"Hey." He crouches in front of me, his big hands on my naked thighs. I look down at my lap, but he leans forward and presses his forehead against mine. His eyes are so close that I can't help but meet them with my own. I know what he wants. I'll give it to him because he deserves it.

"Even if we're mad at each other," he prompts. "Even if it's bad between us."

"We don't leave it that way," I tell him. "We say good-bye like we mean it."

It's something ingrained in him since he was a kid. He and his dad fought over something small, insignificant. He left for work the next day, a stony silence between them. The next time Uly saw him was at his viewing in the back room of a funeral home that smelled like rotting flowers. T-boned on his way to the office. Died instantly. One of those things, I guess. Now, we don't leave each other without saying good-bye. Even if I'm being a dick, he always says good-bye.

He watches me for a moment. "You gonna tell me what's going on in that head of yours?"

I shrug like an asshole.

He lets it go. For now. "You coming into the gym later?"

I nod. Might as well.

He grins wickedly. "Wear those little red shorts I got you."

I snort, and he knows he's cracked my flimsy barrier.

"Pervert," I say fondly. "Those things are obscene. You can tell I'm circumcised."

"And such a pretty circumcision it is," he says, reaching out to squeeze my dick, still sticky from our fuck.

"Ass."

He pulls away and looks at me again. "You know I love you, right?"

"Yeah." Because I do.

"Good. Gotta go." He kisses the top of my head and grabs his bag, heading out the door.

"Tell Stephen Fucking Dorian I said hello!" I call after him.

"And then he should fall into a volcano?" he says back.

I smile. Big bastard knows me too well. "With lava and everything."

"Gotcha, baby. I'll have Griff throw him in for you."

The front door opens and closes. I hear his car start up. And then he's gone.

I sit for a minute, making stupid decisions because that's what you do when you want to be better than everyone else. I mean, I can't really be considering this now, can I? I'm not that shallow, am I?

I guess I can. And I am.

I walk past the TV and barely register the local newsman saying something about something that can be passed by saliva as I reach my phone on the dresser. I find the number I'm looking for and put the phone up to my ear. It only rings once. He's reliable, but then drug dealers usually are.

"Yeah?"

"Dusty? It's Jake."

"My man! How the fuck are you?"

"Good. Hey, you remember what we talked about a few months ago?"

"Sure, sure. I remember. I also seem to remember you shot me down. 'Go fuck yourself,' you said."

Yeah, I remember that. "I meant it in the nicest way possible."

I think.

"Uly know you calling me? I don't want no shit from him. He's a scary fucker."

I laugh. "You're almost as big as he is."

"Yeah, but when it comes to you, the big guy doesn't fuck around."

"No. He doesn't know."

"Well, then? What?"

I look at my reflection in the mirror, as insubstantial as it appears at the moment. "I've changed my mind. I'm in."

ZULY

Pretty pretty pretty day. Yessir. It's a gorgeous day. You just keep telling yourself how beautiful everything is, and you don't have to think about what the hell just happened back at the homestead.

I'm on my way to work in my fancy green Alero. This car is so not me, but Jake and I decided that we both needed to be more "frugal." I think that was the word. Frugality meant I had to get rid of my Jeep, and Jake had to trade in his pretty red Corvette. We both now drive Aleros. His is black. I feel like a clown behind the wheel of mine. Like a big muscley clown in a tiny, green clown car. If we are judged by the cars we drive, I lose.

Ah, Jake. What the fuck was that? He seems so damn lost lately. Rips my ass apart, but he seems miles away while doing it. Like a politician. Like a gosh darned politician. I've got to get hold of him today when he comes into Art of Man – that's the name of the fitness center I be employed with. I can sneak away from my clients for a bit. If we can't get this figured out early on, I'm gonna be thinking about this all day long, and it's gonna hurt my tummy. Then I'll get grouchy, and the day will be plumb ruined.

Yessir. Pretty pretty pretty day.

Man, there sure are a lot of cops on the road this morning. People must be extra dangerous today, wild hairs up their butts or a full moon tonight. I've seen three wrecks already. People on cell phones, I'll wager. You gotta listen to Oprah, people. Get off your cell phones when you're driving. They're turning the country into a bunch of zombies, these cell companies. Even at the gym all I see are people squawking on their fancy schmancy new phones.

Well, looky here! Somebody's done accosted a police officer! And so close to the gym too. Too close to the gym with all the juicing that takes place there. Damn! That cop is going to town on that poor fella, though. There's gonna be an investigation for sure. Probably a suspension. I see blood. Ol' trooper is right pissed off. That's some crazy shit.

Inside Art of Man, and it's as busy as a hive of hornets already. Every morning is pretty busy. There ain't a machine that's not in use. The place throbs with music, especially in the free weight area—all bass and drums, heavy stuff that's supposed to get you going and keep you going. I'll be honest, though, the older I get, the less inclined I am to hear that as "music."

The weight area is massive and it's the first thing that greets you on entering. Farther on back is a set of stairs going up to racquetball courts, tanning rooms, a multipurpose area, and the like. On the ground floor are aerobics and biking rooms. At the very back of the fitness center is an Olympic-sized swimming pool and a big ol' glass office for our fearless leader, Stephen Dorian. No ladies ever come to Art of Man. I mean, they can if they want, but they don't want. This is pretty much a gay muscle gym.

"Uly!" I hear a chorus of big burly voices near the dumbbells shouting at me.

And there are my guys, the ones who show up every day, no matter what, more loyal than the United States Postal Service. Six in all and wearing as little as possible so they can show off as much as possible. It's like their muscle fibers are eating their textile fibers. They spend hours here, pumping and posing in front of the mirrors, joking and lusting, flirting, and fucking when nobody's watching.

The biggest guy is named Griff. He's so juiced-up, he's like one giant pharmaceutical with roadmaps. They're gonna need to come up with another clothing size just for him. Tobey is a priest—I kid you not—and he takes that "body is a temple" thing to heart, adding "for the Lord" after every rep. I trust him more than anybody I know, aside from Jake. Chris and Johnny are former Abercrombie models who have bulked up to a decent size and are now dating each other. Casey is the resident know-it-all who comes close to being kicked out of the group every day. He thinks he's at least five times prettier than he actually is, bless his heart. And Thad is the level-headed one in the group. The superhero. He's the one who gets the most dates. He's also got the biggest set of glutes I've ever seen. Seriously. The man has a huge ass. An intrepid explorer could get lost in that rump canyon if Thad would allow it. Total top, though. I don't think he's even been finger-banged before.

"Hey, fellas," I say with a grin.

"How do we look this morning?" asks Thad, giving his ass a good flex that causes ripples in time and space.

"Ah, the sin of pride on display here!" says a faux-shocked Father Tobey. "But while you're doling out compliments…" And he flexes a massive bicep.

"Looking good, fellas. Bringing some meat to the table, I see."

"Don't need to tell us," says Griff in his deep, sleepy voice. "You going to drop by and chat with us later?"

"You know it. How could I avoid my favorite meatheads in the gym? Why, my day isn't complete without conversing with you guys."

"Be careful," Casey sneers. "Jake might get jealous."

I let it slide and walk to the office. Fucking Casey. But he's not wrong. Poor Jake gets so damn jealous. Sometimes I think he'd prefer I was a kept man, waiting on him like June Cleaver. I guess I've always known this.

It was his loneliness, his dejected puppy expression, at a bar one night that drew me to him anyway. I thought it was just going to be a one-night thing, but then something happened. We clicked, and I don't click romantically with too many people. By the end of that night, we were laughing like we were school buddies. By the end of that week, we were the main subjects of each other's conversations with friends.

My mind is wandering again. Focus, Uly. Focus.

I'm still trying to figure out this new method of signing into work that Stephen's concocted. It's one of those electronic pen do-dads, but it don't ever seem to work with me. Me and technology haven't ever been true friends, but sometimes it's like this building's got a mind of its own since the new security system was installed.

I feel a tight grab on my ass and a wandering finger up my hole.

"Dammit, Stephen," I say, swatting his paw off me. "That is sexual harassment. I'm not one of your newbies who likes that sort of thing."

Stephen Dorian rolls his eyes. "They mean nothing to me, baby."

"Well, I'm sure their little gay hearts are broken to pieces by that. You're such a damn catch and all." I get away with talking to him like this because he honestly believes he's gonna be taking a trip up Hoak Alley.

"I am a catch. I own my own fitness center, and it's going to be a chain soon. Play your cards right, and there could be something in it for you."

I know this guy. "Stephen, there is only one type of chain you have ever imagined me in, and it's not anything to do with corporate. It's more of the floral variety." I pick up my clip board and head off for the morning equipment check. Stephen, of course, follows me, most likely staring at my ass in these tiny shorts he chose. This uniform is gosh-darn ridiculous.

"How's the princess?" he chortles.

"Jake is just fine," I say as I grit my teeth.

"When you going to leave him, baby? Your fine body needs to be appreciated by someone with a body equally as fine. Someone like me."

"Thanks for clarifying," I say, picking a stray weight up off the floor, expecting to be goosed for it.

"Sweet Jesus, I would treat you so good. You'd be my queen. You could have all of this," he gestures to the gym, "and all of this," he gestures to himself. His smile makes me want to take a shower. It's like someone just spilled their slut juice all over me.

I am about to tell him to go fuck himself when Tobey, the preacher man, calls me over to the free weights. I have never been a religious man, but I need to remember to give the big guy a little shout of praise tonight. He saved me today. I am saved.

"What's up, Tobey?"

"We are having a bit of an argument, sir," Tobey explains, his arms folded across his torso so that his gold crucifix has disappeared between his chesticles. "We're wondering who of the six of us has the lowest body fat. Do you think we might be able to use the underwater scale so you can measure us?"

"Well, I can give you the key, but you'll need to do the measuring yourself."

"Bless you, my boy."

My boy. As if he's more than two years older than me. If I had a priest that looked like him, I might have been more god-fearing, I'll tell you what.

"My money's on you, Father," I say, handing him the key.

"Bullshit," says Casey. "It's me. Just look at us in the mirror. I'm shredded."

"In the head," says Johnny. "You've got the worst case of body dysmorphia I've ever seen."

"Yeah," Chris agrees. "Objects in your mirror...AREN'T THERE."

"Well, it certainly isn't me," says Thad, with a pleasant smile. "I'll weigh myself, but I'm all ass and I know it." He gets some hoots and hollers and a couple of loud smacks on that cartoonish derriere for that, and then the group heads off for the scale. They're already removing their clothes before they're even in the room. That is a lot of ass.

One door over, I see our newest employee, a young twinkish thing, stumble nervously into the locker room. And, of course, Stephen Dorian trails him with a wolfy grin on his face. The fucker may as well have his dick out already. That poor kid ain't got a chance.

JAKE

"You know," Dusty says, when I arrive at his house, "as all fucking anti-this shit you were last time, I'm surprised you called me. Well, maybe not exactly surprised. Couldn't stay away from me, could you?" He winks at me over his shoulder.

"Things change," I mutter as I follow him down the hall, trying to ignore his overt flirting by distracting myself with my surroundings. I don't know what I expected the home of a drug dealer to look like, but I'm pretty sure I saw a tea set complete with a crocheted tea cozy sitting on the table in the kitchen we passed. Somehow, a big man like Dusty doesn't scream tea cozy.

To be fair though, Dusty isn't your normal drug dealer. Not that I have much experience in the matter.

"I don't handle crank or meth or any of that other fucking shit," he told me in low tones when we met at the gym months back. "That shit fucks you up. Ruins your body. My body is a fucking temple, and I worship the shit out of it."

And he did. Not a day that went by at the gym that didn't have Dusty admiring his physique in the mirror as he hefted weights heavier than me.

"Then what do you handle?" I asked.

He grinned at me. "Think of it as… body enhancers. I can make out here," he said, running his hands up my chest, "match what you think it should look like in here." He tapped my forehead. He took a step closer, brushing what felt like his considerable package against my groin. "And, hey, if you want to blow me in the sauna, I can hook you up for free. Think of it as my gift to you for letting me fuck that pretty mouth of yours."

I politely declined and pointed to Uly, who was bench-pressing what had to be at least four hundred pounds. Dusty never asked again, though I could feel his eyes on me whenever our paths crossed. Uly was not a man to be fucked with, but that didn't stop Dusty from looking.

Turns out he has a twink fetish. Don't know how I feel about that.

"Oh?" he asks now, as he reaches a closed door at the end of the hall. "What's changed?"

"Does it matter?"

"Of course it does." He looks at me as if I'm stupid. "Are you doing this for you or for someone else?"

"Are you for real?"

Dusty shrugs. "If you're changing who you are because of what you think others expect, then you'll never be fucking happy."

Oh, great. A dealer with a heart of gold. Fantastic.

"Let's just get this over with," I say with a scowl. "I didn't come here to be analyzed."

He smiles at me. "That's the only reason people come here," he says, sure of himself.

Whatever the fuck that means.

He opens the door and starts down a lit stairway. As soon as I cross the threshold, I hear sounds of sex rising up to greet us: the slap of skin, low grunts, a long moan. Dusty glances over his shoulder at me, a wicked smile on his face.

"My boys have started without me," he says, as if this should explain everything. And maybe it does. There's always at least two or three muscled twinks following Dusty around at the gym like he's some kind of god. I always thought they were just admirers, but he was rumored to be fucking at least one, if not all of them. They all look interchangeable—blonde and bronzed, tight shirts, tight shorts. I'm pretty sure I heard him fucking one of them in the showers one day, but I didn't stick around to find out. Not my scene.

But holy fucking shit. It's like I've walked into a porno.

I enter the basement behind Dusty, almost crashing into him as he stops to admire what's spread out before him. Three of his muscle twinks are in various stages of undress, rutting in a heart-shaped bed in the middle of the room that can't possibly be the real thing, but is. I almost expect there to be piles of cocaine and gold bars sitting on a table nearby, but I hear Dusty in my head reminding me he's not that kind of drug dealer.

One of the twinks lowers his head and bites the nipple of another, stretching it out to an almost impossible length. The biter growls in the back of his throat almost menacingly while the owner of the nipple lets out a guttural groan, raking his fingers over the biter's back, leaving red trails. The third twink gags on both their cocks shoved in his mouth, spit dribbling down his chin, lips spread obscenely. Tears stream down his face at the effort, but he's pulling them closer, not pushing them away. They can't be more than twenty years old.

"My babies," Dusty says, the fondness in his voice so out of character that I look at him in surprise. He's squeezing and pulling his cock through his shorts. His other hand is on his tits, tweaking his own nipples.

"You know," he says, without looking at me, his voice going a bit deeper. "You could always get on the bed with them. I'm sure you could teach 'em a thing or two. I've seen that body of yours, Jake. You may not think it's good enough, but take it from me—I'd fuck the shit out of you."

I snort. "What makes you think it'd be you doing the fucking?"

He looks over at me, a single eyebrow raised, still jerking himself off. "Yeah? Huh. Didn't figure Uly to be the fuckee." He shrugs and tortures his nipples a little more. Talented multi-tasker, that one is. "Well, whatever works. I haven't been fucked in a while. You'll have to go slow with me. Start with your fingers. And your tongue."

"I'm not going to fuck you, Dusty." I watch as the boys on the bed start fingering one another all at once, as if they can hear each other's thoughts. Surreal doesn't even begin to describe this moment.

"Uly would never have to know. It'd be our little secret."

"He'd find out. Besides, it looks like you have plenty there already." I cock my head as one of the blond twinks—but they are all blond, so, the blonder one—bends at an impossible angle and two sets of balls rest on his face, his tongue darting out and wetting the sacks.

"You can never have too much of a good thing," he tells me.

I fight against rolling my eyes. It's a battle I do not win. "Gluttony."

He laughs quietly, the twinks still oblivious to our presence. "Only said to be a sin because those who wanted couldn't have."

Great, now we're getting philosophical. Why the fuck can't I know just a regular dealer? Go in, get the shit, pay, get out.

"Three seems like a bit much," I say. "Even for you."

Dusty shrugs, his dick now completely exposed. He grunts as the men on the bed collapse on each other in a flurry of arms and legs and saliva. I think he's going to come in his shorts when he stops. He drops his hands and frowns.

"Three," he says, but it's to himself. "Huh." He looks around the room but doesn't seem to find what he's looking for. He looks back to the bed as if cataloguing each of the men, and even I can start to see the subtle differences between them. For one, their cocks are different. But beyond that, their hair is different shades, different lengths. Their skin is bronzed the same, but there are little imperfections, a mole here, a freckle there. I don't think that even Dusty is as twisted as to be involved with triplets, but I wouldn't put it past him. The three guys fucking could almost be brothers.

"Babies," he calls out, and they immediately stop their ministrations and focus on us. Their eyes dart over me, and I am completely and thoroughly eye-fucked. Tongues come out and wet their lips as they glance between the two of us.

"Is he for us?" one asks, his hand going to his dick and tugging.

"He's a little small," the second says, pouting.

"We could make him bigger," the third replies before licking the second's neck.

"We could hold him down."

"And eat him," the second says, his voice going into a snarl that almost seems inhuman.

"Eat him up," the third agrees, his mouth stretching into a feral grin. For a moment, his eyes flash with something animalistic, but I can't quite place it. I don't know if I want to.

"Horny little fuckers," Dusty says like he's the proudest man in the world. He glances over at me. "They've been like this all morning. I mean, normally we're all over each other, but this has been non-stop. They just had to try the new shit before anyone else. I mean, yeah, I did too, but they've been fucking for hours now."

"New shit?" I ask.

"You'll see," he says. He turns back to the twinks, who have started rubbing on each other again, growling as they bite flesh. Their eyes roll back in their heads, and they look like they almost bite down hard enough to break the skin. If I didn't know any better, I'd think they were all as high as can be. Poppers, ecstasy, something. But from what Dusty says, he doesn't allow that shit in his house.

He walks over to the heart bed and stands in front of them. They ignore him in favor of each other.

"Babies," he says. "Listen to Daddy. Listen, now."

They stop, mewling and growling.

"Where's A?" Dusty asks them.

"A?" I repeat.

He points at each of the men in turn. "B. C. D."

"You call them letters?"

His eyes narrow. "In my house, things are done a bit differently," he says. "Just because you and Uly live a certain way, doesn't mean everyone else does. Here, they don't have their names. They go by what I call them. I'm their Daddy."

"Is he going to be E?" D asks, a look of disdain on his face.

"I bet he bleeds," B growls.

"Bleeds a lot," C agrees with a nasty curl of his lip. "Make him bleed a lot." He gnashes his teeth together.

I take a step back. "Uh, if you could pull your guard dogs back, that'd be great."

Good job, Jake. Another awesome situation you've put yourself in. Stop being a fucking idiot and get the fuck out of here.

Dusty frowns at the men. "You feeling okay?" he asks them. He reaches out and touches each of them in turn. They push into his hand like cats, and I almost expect them to start purring, except I see the way their lips twitch like they're getting ready to bite him. For a second, I expect them to snap out and bite the finger off he's trailing along their cheeks, but they don't. "Maybe we should have waited to try the new stuff until everything else was out of your systems. Where's A?"

"He isn't feeling well," D says, starting to jerk off again. "I want to come."

The other two follow suit, spitting into their hands and fisting their dicks.

Dusty slaps each of their hands away. They glare at him but say nothing.

"You're being impertinent boys," Dusty says. "No coming until Daddy says."

Their fingers spasm at their sides. One of them is growling in low tones, but I can't tell which one it is. The hairs on the back of my neck stand on end.

"Where is A?" Dusty asks again.

All three raise their hands and point to a door in the corner.

"What's wrong with him?"

"Said his stomach hurt," B says.

"Said his brain hurt," C says.

"Said he was breaking," D says.

"Are they always like this?" I ask Dusty.

All three snap their gazes to me. And smile. It's terrible. Feral. C sniffs the air in my direction. B and D tilt their heads and watch me. I don't think they blink.

"There's nothing wrong with them," Dusty says, though he doesn't sound like he quite believes his own words. "Boys, why didn't you tell me A was sick?"

"Sorry, Daddy," B and D say.

They don't sound sorry at all.

"I want to bite him," C says, still looking directly at me.

"Maybe later," Dusty replies, sounding distracted.

"Uh, no thank you," I tell them all. "Look, I think I'm going to go—"

A low moan comes from the closed door in the corner. Goose bumps prickle along my arms. The muscle twinks turn their heads slowly as one and stare at the door. Dusty takes a step toward it and then stops. Something seems to cross his face, and the closest thing I can equate it to is rage. For just a second, Dusty's face twists into something horrific, almost animalistic. His hands clench at his sides, and he takes another step forward, dragging his foot along the ground, in a lumbering, shuffling step. He stops again. He shakes his head, and the extraordinary fury on his face disappears. His shoulders tremble.

Another low groan comes from the closed door.

Neither Dusty nor the muscle twinks move toward the door.

"For fuck's sake," I mutter. I ignore the staccato beat of my heart as I push past Dusty. I am walking by the bed when C snaps his arm out, gripping my bicep.

"You should get into bed with us," he growls at me. "Make you feel good."

"Not gonna happen."

He jerks me closer, his fingers digging in to my arm. My hand inadvertently brushes against his erect cock, and he growls again. Suddenly, there are two more sets of hands on me, rubbing against my arms, my chest. Lips against my neck and the scrape of teeth against my carotid artery. It's almost enough to make my eyes flutter close on their own, but this isn't me. This isn't who I am.

I jerk away from them and take a step back as another sound

comes from behind the closed door. I turn to tell Dusty to get his fuck toys under control, but his hand is at his dick again, fisting his impressive erection as he watches me.

"Jesus Christ," I groan. "You are the weirdest fucking people."

"Maybe he can be A," C says as he pants. One of his arms is wrapped behind him, jerking up and down as he fingers himself. "Bite him and he can be A. Or E. Or… or…" His face scrunches up as his hand moves faster. A moment later, he comes with a grunt. B and C laugh—a deep, raucous sound—as they run their fingers through the spilled spunk before licking their hands clean.

It would be hot if it wasn't so goddamn creepy.

Dusty moans quietly from behind me. He sounds like he's gargling gravel. "Maybe," he says. "Maybe he'll be A."

Something scrapes on the other side of the door.

Without thinking, I take the remaining few steps toward the door.

"There's nothing there," I say quietly to myself.

I put my hand on the doorknob. It's cold against my skin.

"There's nothing there."

Another sound from the other side. The door vibrates slightly in its frame.

"There's nothing there."

I pull it open.

There's something there.

My eyes take a moment to adjust. The light in the room is darker than the basement behind me. Even before I can see clearly, I know that there's someone in the room with me, standing almost right next to me. I can hear the wheezing intake of breath, the low rattling in the throat as it exhales. It doesn't sound human.

My vision adjusts as I hear Dusty and the twinks crowd in behind me, hands brushing against my ass, a hardened dick poking my hip. I'm almost able to ignore them completely as I see a fourth blond muscle boy in front of us, sitting on the edge of a small cot, his arms wrapped around his middle as he rocks back and forth. Apparently, none of them own clothing as he's bare-assed naked as well. His fat cock lies flaccid against his thigh.

"A?" Dusty asks from behind me. "You okay?"

"Sick," B says.

"Broken," D intones. "Broken, broken, broken."

"You can be A," C says to me, his lips trailing along my ear.

"A?" Dusty says again.

A stops rocking. His hands drop to his sides. He sniffs the air, just like the others did. He immediately zeroes in on me. For a moment, he looks wild, the same rage adorning his face that was on Dusty's. His skin looks alive as it rolls and twitches, and his feet press harder into the ground, as if he's coiling up and getting ready to spring and attack. I take a step back and hit a solid wall of men behind me.

"I feel better now," the man on the bed says. It comes out as a snarl.

Dusty almost knocks me over as he moves around me, cooing at A, telling him he's a good boy, Daddy's boy, and didn't he know how much Daddy was worried? Daddy was so very worried, and A is never to do that again. He takes A into his arms, rubbing his hands all over every inch of exposed bronze skin. A's response is to rumble at the back of his throat and rub his face against Dusty's chest.

"So, he's not sick?" I ask him.

"No, he's fine. Aren't you, baby?"

"Yes, Daddy. I'm fine." He bites into Dusty's chest. Dusty chuckles even though it looks like from the tense of A's jaw that his bite is hard enough to bruise.

"Look, I think I'm gonna go," I say.

Dusty tears his gaze away from the man in his arms and looks at me, and that feral wildness is back in his eyes for a split second before it disappears again.

"Nonsense," he says, and I can't help but notice his voice is a bit deeper than before. "We'll discuss why you came over here to begin with. Now that the little family drama is over. Everything is once again right in the world."

"I wouldn't go that far," I mutter. "Dusty, it's been real. But I've changed my mind. Okay? I'll figure something else out." I turn to leave, but three naked muscle twinks block my way out. C leans against the door, trailing his fingers over his cut stomach, tracing a pronounced vein near his hip bone.

"Dusty," I say, a warning in my voice.

"Babies, come to Daddy," he says from behind me. "Let Jake go."

For a moment, I think they'll ignore him and instead advance on me. The looks they're giving me border between hunger and anger. Just as I start to sweat, they part, leaving the doorway open. They move around me until they are all curled up against Dusty, licking and biting his neck and shoulders. I turn to leave. I've only taken a step when Dusty speaks again.

"After all," he says, "Jake doesn't know what we know, does he, babies?"

"No, Daddy," they all moan to him. It sounds like wind blowing through dead leaves. "He doesn't know."

I'm smarter than this. I'm better than this. Don't. Don't fall for this.

"What don't I know?" I ask quietly without turning around.

"Hmm?" he says. "Oh, nothing much, I'm sure. Just something I overheard Uly saying."

Just go.

"When he was at the gym."

Just leave.

"Talking with Stephen."

Motherfucker.

"What did he say?" I ask through gritted teeth.

The sounds of skin against skin come from behind me.

"Not much, I suppose," Dusty says. "Just that he wished you

could be… you know. Bigger."

Lies. He's lying.

"Uly wouldn't…"

"Wouldn't what, Jake? Wish for things that could never be?" He laughs, and it turns into a groan. "I think we all do that at some point. It's human nature."

"But—"

"You came here for a reason, Jake. You want help. I have the means to help you."

"I…"

"Don't you want me to help you?"

"I don't know," I whisper.

He laughs again. "That means you do, and you just don't want to say it. It's not much, Jake. Just a little nudge in the right direction. Why wouldn't you? Give Uly what he wants. Give you what you want. Like my babies wanted."

"Okay," I say before I can stop myself.

A hand drops on my shoulder. "I knew you'd see it my way," he says near my ear.

And it's those words that play in my mind minutes later when I'm lying on the bed, pants half-way off my ass, exposing skin. A finger brushes against my hip.

"Very nice," Dusty murmurs quietly. "Just a little…nudge. That's all you need." All four of the muscle twinks are lined up around the bed. Thankfully, Dusty had them put on shorts, even though they hang precariously off their hips.

"You said this was new shit," I tell him, trying to keep from cringing. "What did you mean?"

"Military grade," he says. "Meant to make Uncle Sam's boys bigger, better, faster killing machines. It's a fucking rush, let me tell you. When this stuff hits, man, it hits."

"Where'd you get it?"

He chuckles. "I never reveal my sources. But I'm not the only one using, trust me. This is going to revolutionize what we can do with our bodies. Limits that seemed impossible before will become nothing to us."

Something cool brushed against my skin.

"What are you doing?"

"Disinfecting the injection site," Dusty says. "Wouldn't want you to get infected or anything."

I start to panic. "Infected? Maybe—"

"Hush, baby," he says. "I know what I'm doing. Trust me. I did the same for my boys, and they all look fine, don't they?"

The muscle twinks grin down at me like sharks, all teeth. B holds a clear vial in his hand. D has the needle and draws the steroid up into the syringe. Once it's full, he taps it with his fingers once, twice. A little pearl of liquid catches at the end of the needle, reflecting in the light.

"Yeah, I think I'm gonna—"

"It'll burn," he says, overriding me, "as it's injected. It's minimal, but you'll still feel it. Just a little pain, and then you'll be on your way."

"Bigger," B says. "And you can stay here. With us."

C's fingers spasm at his sides. "And you can bite stuff with us." He clicks his teeth together again and again.

D hands the syringe over my head to Dusty, seated behind me.

No one seems to notice how A is grimacing, his face going white as his lips curl up into a sneer.

"What's wrong with him?" I say loudly.

"He's fine," Dusty coos. "Isn't he?"

"Fine," A barks.

He doesn't sound fine.

"Just a pinch," Dusty says. "And a little burn. And you'll be on your way."

I start to move off the bed. "Look, Dusty, I appreciate—"

A needle dimples my skin.

"Wait!" I shout.

He waits.

I try not to move so the needle doesn't prick me.

"I've changed my mind," I say. "Please, just let me up. I'm sorry. I shouldn't have come here. Uly wouldn't say those things. You must have misheard. He's not like that."

The pressure on the needle increases, and I can feel the sting of it.

"Are you sure?" Dusty asks quietly.

"Yes. Yes, oh God, yes. I'm sure." And I am. I don't need this shit.

The needle moves away from my skin.

"No," A snaps as he lunges forward impossibly fast.

I turn my head and before I can react further, before I can even think, he grabs the needle from Dusty and slams it down into my ass. There's instant pain as the needle pierces my skin and then a burning like I'm covered in fire as he injects the steroid into me. I cry out and try to roll away, but it's too late. He pulls the empty syringe out of me and tosses it against the wall where the plastic breaks with such a tiny sound.

"You fucking asshole!" I shout at him, standing up and buttoning my jeans. I take a step toward him, not exactly sure what I'm going to do as he outweighs me by a good thirty pounds. All I know is that I'm on fire, and I want to break him into pieces. I never should have come here. I never should have been this stupid. And all I want to do is—

bite

—hurt him. I want to hurt him bad.

But I only get one step toward him when A groans again, wrapping his arms around his stomach. He bends over, his mouth stretched open wide. He gags, a thin line of drool hanging from his mouth. His shoulders convulse, and there's a growl coming from the back of his throat, getting louder.

"A?" Dusty asks from behind me.

A vomits a mass that looks to be tinged with blood. It splatters onto the floor as he jerks forward. He vomits again. And then again.

"Jesus fucking Christ!" Dusty shouts.

A jerks up, his eyes wide and bloodshot. He's trembling, almost seizing, growling louder and louder. He stretches his jaw impossibly wide, displaying teeth tinged with bile. Blood hanging from his lips. The sound in his throat grows louder. His hands are like claws.

He takes a shuffling step forward, his head cocked to the side, his eyes on me.

Bite, I think, though I don't know why. Tear. Kill.

I don't move, even as he gets closer. No one steps between us.

He stops right in front of me, inches separating us.

His eyes are getting redder, even as I watch. His mouth hangs open, the stench unbearable, like he's rotting from the inside out. I shudder as he rubs his nose against my cheek, inhaling deeply, that rumble in his throat vibrating along my skin. His lips spread, and I can feel his teeth along my pulse point. They close around it briefly, pinching the skin… and then withdraw.

He pulls away.

Looks me in the eye.

And speaks.

"Help. M-m-me."

Then he seizes, falling back onto the bed. His body shakes and contorts. It goes on only for a moment until he takes in a gasping breath which rattles on its way out.

Then he stills.

I pull out my phone, dialing 911, and I'm about to hit send when Dusty grabs my cell from my hand.

"What the fuck is wrong with you!" I shout at him. "He needs help!"

"You can't!" Dusty roars back. "No cops. No hospital!"

"Dusty, give me the fucking phone!"

"No, you can't! He's full of steroids. You'll get us all arrested." He takes a step back.

"He could die. Fuck getting arrested!"

"He's only seventeen!" Dusty shouts at me. "They'll take him away!"

"Oh you fucking bastard," I whisper.

"It's not… it's not what you think."

"What about them?" I ask, pointing at the other three who stand around us, each looking extremely agitated. C gnashes his teeth at me as I meet his gaze.

"Legal," Dusty tells me. His voice is deeper. The veins on his arms are sticking out as if he's just gone through a long work out. "I haven't hurt him. I swear. I couldn't. I can't. I love him. I love them all."

"He's hurt right now!"

He looks up at me. "That's it. We've got to take him back. He can help us. He gave me this shit. He knows. He can help us."

"Who?"

He pushes past me, dropping the phone into my hands before standing above A. He leans over, tenderly brushing a lock of blond hair off the boy's forehead. Dusty lifts him up in his arms, A's head lolls back, and he exhales another of those rattling breaths. Dusty turns to me again. "You'll have to drive. We gotta go to him. He can fix this. We just gotta get to the gym." His words are pleading, but the delivery is guttural. The muscle twinks move and stand behind him. Their eyes. All of their eyes are getting redder. So many teeth.

"Who, Dusty? Who gave you the steroids? Who the fuck did this?"

"Stephen Dorian," he says.

No.

Uly.

"Let's go," I say, turning and heading for the stairs.

It's on our way to the gym that I call Uly.

He doesn't answer. I call again. Nothing. I don't leave a message as all I can think of is finding Stephen Fucking Dorian and tearing him apart piece by piece until there is nothing left but a pile of flesh. A mound of bones.

His blood, dripping from my hands.

ULY

Somebody find Morgan Freeman. We got ourselves an outbreak.

Three clients and one of our trainers are sick as dogs, and I can't make hide nor hair of it. They've gone all white and clammy, smelling as sour as a fraternity head, and moaning something awful as they double over and rock back and forth.

I can't really do much for them but try and be some kind of comfort, maybe offer some water. But even when I do that, they growl at me like sick dogs not wanting to be touched, and then they look around the gym as if they're some rabid trapped critter in some big snare.

Is this some type of flu, I wonder? Maybe food poisoning? Whatever it is, it sure looks rough. Two of them have already vomited blood. I need to find Stephen right now and get his permission to call 911. He has rules about calling ambulances or cops to Art of Man, and with good reason, I suppose. Half the people who work or workout here are on some illegal muscle enhancer. The only way Stephen hasn't been raided before is because some of the cops ain't so clean. There's a reason why our city has the best-selling hot cop calendar in the country.

Our intrepid leader is still in the locker room with that new twink trainer (wish I knew his name), so I make my way back there to pay them a visit. I see that Jake has called on my cell phone while all this has been happening.

Sorry, baby. It looks like work is going to be killer today.

I would love to hear Jake's voice, but he rarely leaves messages. He hates the sound of his own voice. I don't understand that. It soothes my nerves.

I hear my boys having fun with the water scale in the next room over from the lockers.

"Get your balloonish self in there, Griff!" demands Casey in that fed-up manner we know so well. His hands are most likely placed firmly on his hips. "This is a competition, dammit!"

"I don't feel good, guys," Griff says, his voice as mopey and deep as my momma's molasses. "I need to go sit down."

Shit. I hope he isn't getting sick too.

I head quickly into the locker room. Trying to walk with any speed in these shorts is painful. Stephen made certain I got the tightest pair. My balls have found themselves in such a position this morning that they are going through separation anxiety.

Stephen is always in the very last shower with his victims and conquests. I find him easily enough, with his back against the wall and poor little Wish-I-Knew-His-Name on his knees in front of him. Both are still fully clothed and, strangely enough, it's the twink who seems to be enjoying himself more. He's all grunting and carrying on as if he's in a pig daddy porno.

Stephen, on the other hand, has his eyes closed and looks downright sick. Like he's gonna blow chunks all over Wish-I-Knew-His-Name. End of scene. Stephen's pale face is beaded with sweat, but not the sexy kind. Rather the kind that balls up bigger than tears and just sits there, waiting to be wiped away.

He sees me standing there watching and, regardless of how awful he must feel, this revs his engine. He starts pounding this kid's mouth like he's trying to find treasure at the back of it. Stephen's grinning at me like a jack o' lantern and shouting expletives and things like, "How do you like my protein shake, bitch?" I'm trying to get his attention, trying to tell him that we have an outbreak of some type going down, and he needs to pull out and come up front, but he ain't listening. His dick don't have ears. Only a big head.

But he grimaces. It's slight, interrupting his show a mere second, but it's definitely noticeable. He grimaces a second time, though, and it brings everything to a stop. He smacks the twink's head roughly.

"Hey!" he shouts. "No biting!"

The kid don't seem to be listening, though. He keeps his lips tight around Stephen's cock and growls even more fiercely. His fingers are now claws pressing into Stephen's thighs. It's no longer a sexy growl coming from Wish-I-Knew-His-Name. The sound is something far more ferocious, primal even.

For a brief moment, as Stephen is holding the twink's head, trying to pull his dick away, he looks at me. There's fear in his eyes. Motherfuckin' terror. He screams, and blood is gushing from the twink's mouth. Not just gushing, but spurting out. Stephen has finally pulled himself away from the twink, but… I am frozen. My jaw has dropped, my eyes are twitching.

Am I seeing this? Am I truly seeing this?

Stephen is now on the floor in a pool of blood, screaming as he clutches at his groin, at what used to be there. Wish-I-Knew-His-Name kneels above him, his hands like claws, a sickly hungry growl filling the shower room. He's no longer sucking Stephen's dick. He's eating the damn thing. The whole thing is in his mouth, and he's chewing, chewing on it, as if it were country fried steak or something. Stephen, shaking and whimpering, tries to climb to the shower bench, but the ravenous twink lunges for his balls.

"Fuck me!" I scream.

This is a mistake. I have just surmised this. The twink's attention leaves the coach's bloody balls and is now squarely on my beefy chesticles. One look into those blood-red eyes, and I'm running.

I'm thinking it's every man for himself in a situation like this. These tight little shorts are nearly doing for me what Wish-I-Knew-His-Name is doing to Stephen, but I ain't stopping to adjust myself. I can still hear Stephen screaming behind me. My mind is racing. What the fuck am I supposed to do? Is this for reals? Is this for goddamn reals? This was not in the employee's manual.

The music in the fitness center is so damn loud, no one can hear the screaming from the locker room. Fuck the rules. I need to call the cops, and the hospital, and freaking Van Helsing while I'm at it. I think Stephen would be okay with this decision. You lose a dick and you gain perspective. But the air of the gym is charged. Almost panicked. Like everybody knows something big and terrifying is about to happen, but no one can say what it is.

"Uly," says Thad, as he, Casey, and Tobey come running at me, bouncing, naked and wet, from the water scale room. They tackle me as I'm running out of the locker room. "Uly. Something's wrong with Griff."

"What?" I say, out of breath. "What's happened?"

Tobey puts a hand on my shoulder. "You okay, boy? You look like you just saw Lucifer the Devil in all his sexy glory."

"Something close to it, sure thing," I say. "I need to call an ambulance…or three. Fuck! We need to get the police here immediately."

"Make it four ambulances," says Casey. "I've never seen Griff look so gross and swollen."

I frantically draw the gate across the locker room entrance and lock it, expecting any minute to see a hungry twink on the other side, and then I hurriedly follow my naked companions into the water scale room. There, seated by himself on a bench that bends as if it's begging for mercy, is the big beast of a man we call Griff. Chris and Johnny are standing a ways back from him, watching him with concern.

Griff is shaking like San Francisco 1906, and he looks as whitewashed as Stephen did in the locker room. Beads of sweat have accumulated on his skin and, if possible, he looks even more enormous than he did this morning. His entire body is pulsing, pumping like a heart. It's the darnedest thing. Well, it would be if I hadn't just seen the darnedest thing.

"Griff," I say, approaching him carefully. "Griff? What's going on? Are you sick?"

Griff grumbles. "I'm real sick, Uly. I've never been sicker in my life."

He looks like a gay muscle cartoon. Like one of those superheroes who has more muscle than clothes and fights crime with his cock. His vascularity is brilliant blue, rising from his flesh as thick as fingers.

"Don't you worry, big guy. We're gonna get an ambulance right over here, okay." I nod to Tobey, who dials for help. "Griff, do you remember eating anything? Taking anything different? Any new supplements?"

"No," says the giant. "Only…yeah…only that new muscle juice Stephen gave me. Said it was crazy monster-making stuff. Said I'd be the biggest…" He grabs his stomach in pain and cries out like a precious baby. "…said I might finally be worth something…So I took lots of it, maybe too much…"

"That asshole," I say. Should I feel bad about that? Because I don't. Stephen may have lost his penis, but he's still a dick.

"The ambulance is on the way," says Tobey. "Hang in there, brother."

"Father Tobey," Griff cries. The pain is clearly unbearable. He's starting to pulse more quickly, it's like his heart is gonna explode.

"What do you need, big buddy?"

"I need my last rites read. Can you do that? I'm no Catholic. Shit. I'm…I'm not even religious, but a person shouldn't… shouldn't die without making amends first."

"Griff," Tobey says, kneeling naked in front of the mass of quivering, pulsating muscle. "You're not going to die. The ambulance…"

"Father!" yells the big man. "I'm not going to make it out of the gym today."

The bench he's seated on breaks and Griff falls to the floor.

JAKE

In the ten minutes it takes to get to the gym from Dusty's house, A goes from yowling loudly to growling softly, his head in Dusty's lap as the dealer whispers words to him I can't quite make out. The others take up A's noises as their own, and the car sounds like it's filled with animals. It isn't until I pull into the parking lot of the gym that I notice Dusty has stopped speaking too, his voice a deeper growl then the rest.

I glance in the rearview mirror and find all eyes staring back at me. The Alphabet Twinks, as I've started thinking of them, look almost ferocious. They'd all climbed into the back of the SUV, seeming to want to stick close to each other. I convince myself it's a trick of the light when C's eyes flash red. It has to be. He grins at me with that shark's smile. I try not to shudder.

But then none of that matters anymore because I see Uly's car—the beloved piece of shit that it is—and the relief that washes over me is palpable. So much so that I can almost taste it. Uly's here. He can help. He'll make things okay. He'll—

bite tear kill

—know what to do. He has to.

The parking lot to the gym is full, and I can't help but think I'd like to murder the owners of the vehicles parked next to Uly's. It would be easy, wouldn't it? I'd just have to wait for them to come out of the gym to their cars. Once they started to unlock the doors, I could come up from behind them. Put my hands around their necks. Dig my fingers into their skin. I would be able to feel the blood coursing through the carotid artery. The beat of the pulse as the heart pumps. I could squeeze, like a vise. My fingers would break through the skin, and the blood would spurt out all over me, and I could grip the tendons in the neck and pull until they stretched out the side of the neck, and I would lean forward and snap my teeth, and it would taste so fucking good, and I could kill. Kill them. I could—

There's another growling in the car, louder than all the rest. I look up in the mirror again. My eyes are narrowed. Teeth bared. It's coming from me. The sound. It's me. I want to bite everyone. I want to—

I shake my head, trying to clear these thoughts. These horrible thoughts that no one should have. It's not normal. It's not right. Forget them. I'm okay. Uly's here. Everything will be fine.

"We can bite them," C whispers near my ear, and I tremble because it's like he can hear my thoughts. "Bite them. Make them bleed. All of them."

"No," I say, shaking my head again, trying to get his words out of my thoughts. I find an empty parking space and pull in. "We're here to find Uly."

"And Stephen," Dusty snarls.

I turn off the car and twist in my seat. All of them watch me, even A who has sat up from Dusty's lap.

"How is he?" I ask Dusty.

"Find Stephen," A says.

"Hunt him," B says.

"Touch his insides," C says.

"Touch them a lot," D says.

"He did this," Dusty says.

"Yeah, maybe you guys should just wait in the car," I tell them.

They stare at me. I can no longer ignore the flashes of red in their eyes, the way their skin is sallow. I should have said fuck Dusty and taken us to the hospital. It's too late now. We're already here, and the call within me to find Uly is now a roar. I need to find him so I can chew his skin.

No. That's not right. No. I want to find him so he can fix this. I don't want to hurt him. I don't. I can't. I love him. I do. He tastes so good. So good.

"Wait here," I tell them, my voice rough.

They don't say anything back.

"Fuck this," I mutter to myself as I get out of the car. I start walking toward the gym entrance when I hear footsteps behind me. I glance back and stop in my tracks when I see the Alphabet twinks—still clad only in those low-slung shorts—and Dusty shuffling after me. "I told you guys to stay here and wait for me."

Nothing but obscene smiles and all those teeth. Even A, who I've only known for an hour, seems to have changed. His eyes have no spark in them. They're flat, like an animal's.

I don't have time for this. I have to find Uly.

I turn back toward the gym. They follow after me.

When I push through the front doors, it's like the world rights itself slightly when the comforting, normal sounds of the gym wash over me. Blaring music. Shouts. Laughter. Machines. The sharp metallic sound of weights hitting each other. It'll be okay. I can breathe easier now.

There's no one at the front desk, which is good because I don't have my pass. Though everyone here should know me by now. I walk through the lobby and onto the main floor of the gym. So many people. So many men. I stop. The twinks and Dusty crowd behind me, pressing against my back. My sides.

So many men here. So much skin. Veins bulging. Sweat dripping. The shift of muscle. The grunts of exertion. The inhalation of breath. Gritted teeth. Tongues moistening lips.

"So good," C sighs.

"So many," B whispers in my ear.

"All of them," D snaps.

A just growls. Loudly.

"Find Stephen," Dusty says. "Fix this."

"Uly first," I say, closing my eyes. In the dark, then, in my head, there is only violence. My fingers itch at my sides to reach out and touch. To caress. To invade. To destroy.

"Uly first," they all say around me.

"Bite him?" D asks hopefully.

Yes. That sounds good.

"No," I say hoarsely. "We don't bite him."

"Jake?"

I open my eyes. A man stands before me. I recognize him. From here. At the gym. His name? Carson. Carey? Carl? I can't remember. It's lost in the dark.

"You okay?" he asks me, concern in his voice. "You look a little… off."

Off. I feel off.

"I'm okay," I grunt. He takes a step back away from me, and I know it's because those around me have started growling again. Carson/Carey/Carl widens his eyes.

"You seen Uly?" I ask him, staring at the cords in his neck.

He nods, taking another step back. "Yeah. He was in the locker room when I got here. He was just coming on shift, I think. Griff and Tobey were there too. You know, the usual crowd."

"Stephen?" I bite out.

"Yeah, Jake. He was there too. Look, I gotta get going, okay? Gonna cut my workout short today, I think." Carson/Carey/Carl looks scared.

"You could stay," C says.

"With us," B says.

"Or we could go with you," D says. "All of us."

"At the same time," Dusty says.

A snaps his teeth together.

"I'm good," Carson/Carey/Carl says. He takes another step back and glances around. No one is paying any attention to us. It would only take a second, I know, to reach out and grab him by the front of his tank top, to pull him toward us and descend upon him at once. It would only take a second. But somehow, my hands stay at my sides.

"Need to find Uly," I say again.

"Jake," Carson/Carey/Carl says. "Are you sure you're okay?" He glances over my shoulder quickly. "I've never seen you hang with this crowd before."

I am so far from fine I can't even remember what fine feels like.

"I'm fine," I say.

"Fuck, man?" I hear someone complain. "Who the fuck locked the gate on the locker rooms? All my shit's in there!"

Locker room. That's where Carson/Carey/Carl said Uly was. With Stephen Fucking Dorian who probably locked the gate to keep Uly in there with him. He thinks he owns Uly. That Uly is his. That Uly belongs to him. He doesn't. Uly is mine, and I have to find him. He has to fix this. And if Stephen is with him, I'll let the Alphabet Twinks have him. They can do whatever the fuck they want to as long as we get the answers we need.

My head clears again. Carson/Carey/Carl is gone. I have to get into the gate. Keys. I need keys. They keep a spare set behind the desk in the lobby. I push back through the Alphabet Twinks and Dusty, ignoring their hands that reach out and claw at my skin. All I can think about is—

bite tear kill

—getting to Uly. I reach the desk and dig through the drawers. It's not there. It's not there. Where the fuck is it? Where the fuck—

BITE and TEAR and KILL

goddamn key to goddamn gate? I'll break it down if I have to. I'll break down the gate with my bare hands so I can—

Found it. I grab the key and turn back toward the gym. The Alphabet Twinks and Dusty are where I've left them and are attracting attention. I see the way people glance at them, the slight narrowing of their eyes. The way the whispers start up. It doesn't help that they've all started growling and rubbing up on each other again. Both B and D are sporting erections that their shorts do nothing to hide. They try and grab at me as I push by them, but I'm able to pull away before I can get pulled back in.

All I can think of is Uly. I have to get to Uly.

I don't know if they follow me. I don't care. I don't care what they do now because I'm here. Uly's here somewhere. If Stephen

Fucking Dorian has done anything to him, it'll be the last thing he does. I won't let the Alphabet Twinks have him. He's mine. And I won't stop until he's in pieces.

I hit the gate.

"Uly?" I call out.

Nothing.

Then:

A low snarl from back in the locker room.

Goose bumps prickle along my skin.

"Uly? It's Jake."

The sound comes again, like a cornered animal about to attack.

I put the key in the lock.

I start to twist it.

A scream from behind me.

I turn and step back around the corner.

And descend into hell.

Dusty, A, and C stand where I left them, their heads cocked as they stare at the middle of the gym floor. I follow their gazes until all I can see is red, splashed along the floor, along the machines. A twitching foot on the ground attached to a twitching leg. The rest of the body is blocked by B and D, bent over the man on the floor. I look up the subtle ridges of their spines to their bowed heads.

D jerks back up and even above the music, even beyond the shouts that are filling the gym floor, I can hear the tear and snap of skin as he uses his teeth to pull the shredded flesh off the stomach of the man on the floor. Blood and gristle coat a yoga mat.

The man stops twitching.

B and D rise. And turn.

Blood and pieces of flesh drip from their mouths. Their eyes are red. Their hands are like claws at their sides, covered in gore. They take a shuffling step forward, their growls getting louder.

People run toward the exits. But even before they can reach the exits, an alarm shrieks and metal gates fall across the doors that lead to the parking lot. The windows are shuttered. The overhead lights flash and dim.

The gym is locking down.

I look back to the man on the floor. B and D are gone, lost in the crowd. Dusty, A, and C are making their way to me. A and C look like they are about to follow the other two. Dusty's eyes are wide and for the moment, seem clear. He has a hand wrapped around each of their necks as he pushes them toward me, though his eyes seem to follow almost everyone that rushes past them, dodging A and C's outstretched hands.

From behind me, farther into the darkened locker room, the growl comes again.

Uly.

I turn, grab the key, and—

bite tear kill

—unlock the gate. It rises in front of me.

And from deep in the locker room, I can hear the shuffle of feet dragging along the floor.

I step inside.

ULY

So, here I am. A fitness center supervisor in a uniform as tight as a Jimmy Dean sausage casing, with five wet, naked bodybuilders trying to convince a sixth wet, naked bodybuilder not to freak out and die before an ambulance can arrive and try to fit him in the damn vehicle.

I never thought I'd say this – it's sacrilege to a bodybuilder – but I can now see there is such a thing as too big. Especially when someone's body makes an ambulance look like a clown car. Poor Griff is expanding by the minute and, damn, it looks and sounds painful. I've known him a year now, and there ain't a sweeter fella on the planet.

"Where's the damn ambulance?" shouts Casey, pacing back and forth.

Tobey is on his knees in front of Griff, holding the big guy's hand and praying. It's a nice thought, but clearly that's all it is. If God's up there, he's the hands-off type.

Thad pulls me aside. "What do you think is going on here?" he asks. Thad's like the big brother everyone wishes they had. Movie star good looks, a compassionate heart, and, oh yeah, that rockin' ass. "You think he got hold of some bad juice?"

"What else could it be?" I say, still frazzled from what I saw earlier in the locker room. "Look at him. He's a dang mess, Thad. We can see every vein in his body. He's freakish and not in a good way. It's gotta be the stuff he said Stephen sold him."

"That man is a fucking villain."

I grab Thad's forearm. "He ain't so much a man anymore, and I think that may be his own doing. Something tells me this day is just gonna get stranger as it goes."

"Fuck me!" Thad says. "Where is that ambulance?"

I really hope Jake holds a grudge today and stays away from the gym. I'm gonna call him and tell him so when I get a moment. I'll be all Now, Jake, listen. There's some bad shit going down.

Cock hungry twinks, morphing muscle beasts, you name it. Just stay home, baby.

What the holy fuck is going on, anyway?

Tobey rises and comes toward me and Thad with a look of true apprehension wearing him down. I can't help but notice he's got a smaller cock than the other guys. But then, that's what years of disuse will get you, I guess. "I give my cock to the Lord," he had told me once. He's a filthy bastard. It's nice and shaved, though. He stands with me and Thad and looks at the big guy. Griff is rocking back and forth and whimpering on the floor, grinding the heels of his hands into his eyes. His whimpers occasionally seem to have a deeper, more menacing edge to them—like a cornered puppy.

"The ambulance may not be here for a while, boys," Tobey says. "Apparently, we picked the wrong day to have an outbreak at the Art of Man. The world is a dangerous place, my brothers."

"Do you think –" But I'm not able to finish the question. That's never good.

"Uly!" shout Johnny and Chris.

They and Casey are standing back from Griff as the big guy is moaning and groaning and struggling to his feet. His hands are on his head now, and he's dancing around in circles like a crazy person. Every muscle in his body is visible through his flushed skin, every vein pulses. His cock is hard and red, with an ugly jagged vein leading from cockhead to abs.

And, oh shit, he starts to split open, fissures in his flesh from cock to forehead exposing moist pink muscle. He screams, and none of us knows what to do. What the fuck can we do? His muscles are spilling from his body, stretching his skin at first like wet clothes, and then like stretched cheese. The muscles are pushing up, bubbling out, not able to be contained by his skin, and he convulses as blood pours from each new wound. His screams are deafening, and I realize he ain't the only one screaming.

That's me screaming, "What the fuck! What the fuck!"

That's Tobey praying for an end to Griff's suffering.

That's Casey's high-pitched cry of terror.

And suddenly, there is an explosion. Bits of Griff go all over the room, filling the water scale, turning it red and painting us all sickening colors of human debris. Oh, sweet baby Jesus, if you're real, find me a mop!

We're all quiet. Disbelieving. Who knows the right words to say after their friend has just detonated all over them, right? But I just have to bellow out, "What the fuck, man?"

Now, I know my vociferous vocals are not loud enough to garner any alarm-worthy attention, but the new security system Stephen has installed is blaring like it's the end of the world. I'm thinking it wasn't my shouts, after all, but the sound of a human being exploding that might be the culprit. I can hear the gym lock itself down with great heavy bangs as bars slide over windows. The lights dim, the music shuts off, and the clients are…screaming?

I race out of the room, frantically wiping Griff off me. My five naked friends follow, some retching as they go. The fitness center is in utter chaos. I don't understand what's happening. The siren screams, and I see people rushing for windows, doing their darnedest to break them, to get out. But Stephen got the best security system he could find. That glass ain't gonna break. People are panicking, rushing by me as if something is after them…and holy Marie Laveau, now I see something is after them!

The first sign – and it's a doozy – is a poor power lifter on the leg press machine who is now supper for the three clients who first came to me claiming they were sick. He's screaming as one is having some leg, another some breast, and the third some face. At this point, I'm pretty certain we got us some zombies.

"Guys," Thad says in hushed and rushed tone, "we need to get the hell out of here."

"Hell, yeah," I say. "You five look like the main course at a Thanksgiving dinner."

"My beautiful cock!" says Casey. "Don't let them eat my

beautiful cock!"

All I want to do is break out into another chorus of What the fuck, man, but I keep my head. The only way is up. Or at least, that seems the safest choice at the moment. I know if this were a horror movie that wouldn't be the smartest choice, but fuck Wes Craven. That's where we're heading.

The second level has no classes this early, so if there's any place in the building to hide out and wait for Superman or Zombie Jesus, it's there. In situations like this – you know, when zombies attack a locked down fitness center – you gotta take care of your own, and with Jake not here, these guys are my own. I try to block out the screams of agony and terror all around me as I lead the guys up the stairs.

I'm stopped in my tracks near the top. I hear Johnny screaming below me. Chris gets pulled back down the steps, and he is obliterated in seconds by two of Dusty Doyle's harem boys. Johnny is frozen and screaming as the two boys rip Chris apart, legs and arms being pulled out of joints and flying through the air as they feast on the young model. Chris's face is one of shock the entire time. He never knew what was coming, and he isn't making a sound.

Casey and me pull Johnny up the stairs, even as he struggles to free himself, screaming for his boyfriend who is now long past saving. Tobey and Thad spring from behind us wielding heavy silver barbells. Thad doesn't hesitate. With one strike he knocks a harem boy's head round on his neck like Linda Blair. Tobey takes a bit longer, praying just a little bit, it seems, to make certain this flesh-eating zombie is beyond redemption.

When this harem boy looks up at Tobey and lunges, he shouts, "Holy demon of hell!" and strikes the infected fucker's head with such force the whole thing explodes, and the lifeless body falls down the steps.

"Get your asses up here!" I shout at them as I survey the destruction and gore going on below. It's a fucking George Romero movie down there. For us anyway. I suppose for them zombies, it's a damn buffet. Who knew being sexy could be so deadly?

“Where to?” Thad asks breathlessly. He is caked in blood. It almost don’t look real.

“There’s a utility closet,” I say. “We can hide in there and figure out what to do next. I still got my cell phone. We can call out, get some info.”

Johnny is shaking in shock. He ain’t going nowhere by himself. Thad picks him up, and the five of us head off to find some safety.

JAKE

Even above the chaos behind me, there's a distinct quiet in the locker room ahead. Most every part of me is screaming to turn around, to run as fast as I possibly can. To find a way out. To go home. To climb back in bed and pull the covers over my head and pretend today hasn't happened, that I haven't seen the things I have, that I haven't thought the things in my head that are telling me to bite and tear and kill.

Most every part of me doesn't want any part of this.

But there is another part—above the noise behind me, above the storm in my head—that whispers to me. It says Uly. It says I have to find Uly. It says that I need to make sure he's okay. That he's safe. That even though it's bad, even though we might be angry, we never leave it that way.

Uly, it whispers.

I take another step. Screams from behind me. An alarm ringing. Lights flashing overhead. Voices shouting "Please, don't!" and "What the fuck is happening?" They sound frightened. Horrified. It makes me angry. They are all so concerned with themselves. They don't care about others. They don't care that Uly is in the dark. They don't care he's trapped in the locker room with God knows what. I want to turn around now. Every part of me. Find the voices. Make them bleed. Make them scream. Make them—

A hand drops on my shoulder.

"Jake," a rough voice says.

I turn and look up into inhuman eyes in sunken sockets. The whites are almost gone, lost in red, like he's exploded from the inside. There's a terrible curve to his lips, teeth bared. His gums are inflamed, leaking blood. His teeth are coated in it. His skin is bone white. Dusty doesn't look like Dusty anymore.

But then neither do the muscle twinks at his side. A and C. They look like they're completely gone. They watch me with those animal eyes.

"My babies," Dusty snarls. "Gone. I need them."

B and D. They'd been eating that man.

"I have to find Uly," I tell him. My voice is rough. Deeper.

"I have to find them," Dusty says. "They're sick. Have to find Stephen. He'll fix this. He has to fix this."

I hope he's right. I refuse to think of the alternative. It's not a possibility. This can be fixed. It will be fixed. Stephen Fucking Dorian will fix this.

And if he doesn't….no. He will. There's no other choice. But that has to wait.

"I need to find Uly first."

"A and C will stay with you," Dusty says, pushing them toward me. They drag their feet along the ground like they can't remember the act of walking clearly. They stand on either side of me, facing Dusty. I can hear them now, both of them. They sound like they're growling from the backs of their throats. I try not to flinch when they reach out and grab my hands, clutching my fingers tightly in their own. Their skin feels hot, like their entire bodies are burning with fever. It's only then that I notice my own skin feels warmer than normal. But none of us sweat.

"They will stay here," Dusty says. "You watch them. I will go get my babies and come back here. Then we'll find Stephen."

"Dusty—"

"Daddy loves you," he says, ignoring me completely. He bends down and kisses A first, and then C. C grins as their lips touch, and he immediately bites down on Dusty. Dusty's eyes flutter closed, and he does nothing to pull away, even as C's teeth pierce his skin. Blood flows, dripping down their chins. C's hand squeezes mine harder, and I don't look away. C pulls his head back, stretching out Dusty's bottom lip, and I wonder if it will rip. I wonder if it will tear. I wonder what it tastes like, the red. The lip. The skin. I wonder what it would taste like on my tongue. I bet it would taste like strength and life. And it would go into me, and I would be the one taking it. I could take it all.

Just when I think Dusty's lip can't take any more before it has to tear, C lets go. Blood coats his mouth and chin. I can't look away. I don't, even when Dusty says, "You keep them safe, or I'll kill you." I don't look away, even when he leaves.

C doesn't look away either. I don't know how long we stare at each other, him watching me. Me watching a bead of blood drip from his chin to the floor. I don't know how much time passes before he raises our joined hands, smearing the blood along my knuckles. He then brings our hands to my face.

"Good," he says. "Tastes good."

I lick my lips. Dart out my tongue. It's so close. I just need to tilt my head forward a little more. That's all it would take. Just a little bit more and—

"No," I whisper. "No."

He pushes our hands against my face. The blood smears against my lips.

"Tastes good," he says again, those red eyes on my lips. "Try."

I twist my head and brush my face against my shoulder. The blood smears against my shirt. C starts growling again, but he doesn't let go of my hand. I try to pull away from both of them, but they won't let go.

"Have to find Uly," I tell them.

They say nothing.

I turn us all back toward the locker room. He has to be here. He has to be here and safe and sound, and he'll make the monsters go away.

"Even if I'm the monster," I whisper, hyperaware of the blood on C's face, the blood on my shirt. "He'll make it all okay."

As if in response, a low groan comes from the locker room.

"Uly?" I call out, above the alarm, above the terrified cries from the gym behind us. "Uly, you in here?"

I walk forward and for a moment, C and A don't move. I pull them along behind me, their shoes scraping along the floor. We round the corner. Rows of lockers along the left. The benches are empty. Steam pours into the room from the right, where the showers are. I can hear water running. Uly can't still be in the showers, can he? He wouldn't stay there, not with all the noise coming from the gym.

Unless he's hurt, I think. Unless he's hurt and bleeding all over the floor, and it's covering the tiles and he's bite, he's tear, he's kill. Kill. He's—

"Uly?" I say again, leading us toward the shower. It's hard to make out anything through the choking steam. It swirls up around us and soaks our skin. A and C growl their displeasure and try to pull me back, but I don't let them. If he's here, I have to find him. I won't let A and C stop me.

I take another step, and the steam parts as if a breeze has blown through it. The tile in front of me is soaked in red, splashed brightly against the bone white tile. There's so much of it. It seems to be everywhere.

And then, even as I look back up, the steam parts again, and two men stand against the far wall of the showers. One faces the wall, banging his head against the tile. He's naked, his ass clenching and unclenching. Clenching and unclenching. Blood drips down between his legs and pools below him. His feet and legs are soaked in it. What looks like the shredded remains of his clothes are plastered on the floor.

The other looks like a kid. He would look so much younger if his face wasn't covered in gore, if he didn't look as if he was chewing flesh. He's clothed and crouched near the floor, splashing in the red water as he chews.

He stops chewing as he sees me.

The other man continues to beat his head against the wall. Bam. Bam. Bam.

The kid rises.

Bam. Bam. Bam.

He cocks his head at us as the other groans and shudders.

The kid moves toward me, the steam of the showers twisting around him. His bare feet drag in the blood water.

Bam.

His eyes are red. His mouth hangs open. His tongue is covered in bits of flesh. He moans. His fingers twitch at his sides. He's been infected. He's like the others. Like Dusty. The Alphabet Twinks.

Like me.

Bam.

He stands in front of me, ignoring A and C. He leans forward, and I turn my head away from him, trying not to gag at the stench pouring from his mouth. A and C squeeze my hands so hard I'm sure my fingers will break.

Bam.

He drags his nose along my cheek, inhaling. His teeth scrape my jaw bone. He growls against my ear.

Bam.

Another scream from behind us, out in the gym.

The kid jerks away from me, his eyes going over my shoulder. He snarls again and then shuffles around us, toward the cries of the others.

Bam.

The guy against the far wall continues to hit his head. It's not Uly. I know that now. He's big, but he's not Uly. I would know Uly anywhere. And that's not him. He's not in here. Which means he's out there somewhere in the middle of the chaos. I have to find him.

"Let's go," I tell A and C. I turn us all and walk out of the showers

Bam. Bam. Bam.

And then silence.

I stop. Something shuffles behind us.

"Jake," a voice says from behind me. "That you, Jake? That you?"

A and C let go of my hands. I turn back toward the man.

Stephen Fucking Dorian stands against the far wall. He looks as if he's seen better days. His hands are like claws at his sides, his skin gray. He looks like the rest of them, though maybe not as far gone. Not yet. But even with all of this, even through fighting to keep from launching myself across the room to tear him apart because this is all his fault, my eyes go to the disaster that is his groin, or what is left of it. His dick is gone, and suddenly I realize what the kid had been chewing on. His testicles hang low, spilled from the torn sack.

Remarkably, horrifyingly, I laugh. Somehow, I laugh.

"Jake," he says again, starting to tremble.

"Dickless," I gasp. "You're fucking dickless. You did this to us, and you're fucking dickless."

"Jake," he says as the shaking gets worse.

"Where is he?" I ask, taking a step forward. "Where the fuck is Uly?"

He groans and bends forward, clutching his stomach.

"Where is he, you fucking dickless asshole? Where is he?"

He starts to seize.

"Where is he!"

Bite. Tear. Kill.

Dickless Stephen Fucking Dorian vomits onto the floor—dark, red, and vile. A rancid smell fills the showers, carried by the steam. It smells rotten, like an animal on the side of the road, bloated by the sun. He vomits again. It splashes onto his feet.

"What the fuck have you done? Where is Uly!"

He moans. A thin strand of bile hangs from his lips. "Uly," he says. "Uly."

"Yes, Uly. Uly! Did you give him the juice? Did you infect him too?"

He stands up straight. His eyes have gone completely red. "Uly," he says again.

And quicker than I've ever seen anyone move, he rushes forward. I have no time to react before he crashes into me, knocking me off my feet. My head raps against the floor, red water splashing up around my face and for a moment, all I can see are stars, bright and shining across the world. And even in these stars, I wait for my throat to be torn out by teeth. But it never comes.

I hear Dickless say "Uly," again, but it sounds far away. The slap of his feet against the tile fades.

It's only a moment later that my vision clears. A and C stand above me, looking down. They're smiling again, like they're amused at me on the floor. But the emotion doesn't reach their eyes.

"Stephen?" I ask them in a croak.

They don't respond.

I push myself up off the floor. As soon as I'm standing, the Alphabet Twinks take hold of my hands again.

"We gotta find Stephen," I tell them. The last word I heard him say was Uly, and I have no doubt about where he's headed. "We gotta go after him."

A and C don't reply.

I start to pull them out of the showers when someone blocks the entrance.

It's Carson/Carey/Carl. And he's holding a long silver barbell in his hands.

"What the fuck is going on?" he cries at us, his voice high and strained. "Was that Stephen?"

"Move," I tell him.

"Jesus fucking Christ! What's happening here? We've got to find a way to get the fuck out of here!"

"Move," I growl at him.

His eyes grow wider. "You," he whispers, glancing at A and C. "You're…no. Oh, please no."

"Move," I snarl at him and think bite.

"Tear," C says.

"Kill," A whispers.

Carson/Carey/Carl waves the barbell at us. "Not you too,"

he says.

"Move now."

"No," he says. "I can't let you leave here. I'm sorry, Jake. But I can't let you hurt anyone. You're sick."

A sheen of red falls over my eyes and for a moment, I think it's my extraordinary rage manifesting itself. But by the look on Carson/Carey/Carl's face, it's much more than that and much darker. He brandishes the barbell.

"You have to stay here," he says, his voice cracking. "Please. You have to."

"Last chance," I tell him because this is a man, a stupid man, a foolish man standing between me and what's mine. He's keeping me from Uly, and there is nothing I won't do to get to him. Even bite. Even tear.

Even kill.

A and C are at my side one moment and flying at him the next. He's able to cry out once as he tries to backpedal, but his feet slip on the water. He reaches out and grabs the wall to keep from falling.

A and C aren't as lucky. Their feet slide out from under them, and they go down hard, snarling and snapping their teeth together. They grab for Carson/Carey/Carl, their fingers brushing against his legs. C is able to wrap his hand around his ankle and pulls as hard as he can, the muscles in his arm tensing. Somehow, Carson/Carey/Carl is not only able to break free but keeps his balance. He jumps over A and C, toward me into the shower. He's already spinning, even as he lands, the barbell raised high above his head.

I'm moving without thought. One moment I'm frozen and the next, I'm standing directly behind Carson/Carey/Carl. The barbell clatters to the floor as my teeth sink into his neck. He screams as I bite. The blood sprays as I tear. The red descends as I kill.

A and C join in a moment later.

ULY

We are all back in the closet – the utility closet, that is. Yes, sir. We are five slabs of all-American prime beef hiding from the butchers in the dark. I will never eat a hamburger again. I swear it.

The utility closet is in a hallway on the second level of the fitness center where we keep all the defunct machines that need some work – the treadmills upended so the repairman can get to the undercarriages and fix them, and the cable machines pulled all to hell and as wiry as Medusa. There ain't no lock on the closet door, so we're all hoping and praying that zombies don't know how to turn door knobs. All we can do is hold tight to it. Tobey and Thad have their barbells in hand just in case.

But damn, it's crowded in here. My closet back home is bigger than this, and I'm no clothes whore. The five of us are packed tight, tit to tit, cock to cock, face to face, covered in Griff and sweat in the dark, while I try to figure out what the hell is going on with the internet on my cell phone. The sheer adrenaline-inducing power of the moment has caused more than one of us to sprout boners, and as pretty as that flesh bouquet is, I keep thinking of Stephen getting his wiener gnawed off, and I want to throw up. I'm also glad I'm not naked like my poor friends here.

Johnny shakes like a tweaked out club kid as Tobey tries to comfort him. I really don't know what good it's doing.

Casey sneezes, a chunk of Griff flying off the top of his head and hitting me in the forehead. "It's too damn crowded in here," he complains. "Anyone want to be a sacrifice for the greater good? Johnny? How about you?"

"Hush your fucking face, Casey," Tobey says. Tobey's a man of the cloth, but he ain't wearing any cloth at the moment so I guess he can cuss all he wants.

"Oh, come on," says Casey. "Everyone here can see the guy's a freaking redshirt. I don't want to be around when those zombies get him. Do you, preacher man?"

"Pay no attention to him, Johnny," Tobey says. "You're going to make it through this just fine. I'll see to that. God will see to that."

"I could use some comforting, Father Tobey," Casey says, sex ever on his mind.

"Get your finger out of my ass, Casey," Tobey says.

"Why? It feels even holier than the rest of you." He snickers. "Get it? Holy."

"You're an ass, Casey," Thad chimes in. "Shut the fuck up."

"Maybe we should sacrifice you, Superman?" says Casey, his face drawn and serious. "I love a good hero-in-peril story. Besides, your ass is taking up most of the room in here. Why don't you lay off the squats? Unless you want to do them on my face."

"Nothing belonging to you or any other man will ever make it in my ass, Casey," says Thad, unperturbed. "Total top. Though someone needs to explain that to this mop handle behind me."

"Lucky mop," mumbles Casey.

"I can't get through to Jake," I say, interrupting the banter. "It's ringing, but he won't pick up the dang thing. Maybe he's got it on airplane mode."

"Is he on an airplane?" asks Thad.

"No." I don't get what that has to do with anything.

I scroll through the newsfeeds on the Internet. The reception in the closet is weak, so my cell is taking its sweet time in bringing up any information. What is coming through, though, is taking me aback. I feel like I'm suddenly in a crappy Bruce LaBruce film with zombies and bodybuilders but minus the camp and ketchup.

"Holy shit," I swear, maybe too loud. "Is this for real?"

"What is it?" asks Thad. "What's going on out there?"

"The AP is saying we're in an honest to Jesus zombie apocalypse! You know, like they have on the TV. It's crazy out there. People are chowing down on one another at Denny's, at baseball games, on fashion runways. They're still trying to figure out what's going on."

"We're ahead of them there," says Tobey.

We all go silent. I know what's happening in their heads. We're thinking about our families and friends, our loved ones, our grandparents and baby nieces and nephews. We're all hoping against hope that somehow they're all okay.

My heart quickens. Oh, Jesus. Jake. Stay safe. Lock yourself in the house.

A slight scuffling catches our attention above the far-off cries of terror still coming from the weight room. Someone is outside the door, stumbling through the minefield of broken machinery, bumping into things carelessly. We're all trying to be as quiet as we can, but Johnny is shaking so bad, he reverberates like a muscle quake. We hold our breath and I hold the door knob, as if that's gonna do any good at all against a horde of bodybuilder zombies. I look to Thad and Tobey. They are ready with their barbells, clutching them tightly, but I'm still hoping maybe we won't need them. Maybe whoever it is, whatever it is, will simply pass us by. Maybe I'm right, and zombies can't open doors.

I'm wrong.

The door knob gets torn from my grasp and Casey – the fucking three year old – lets out a squeal that a pig would laugh at. A kinda familiar face stares at us. Dusty Doyle stands in front of us, breathing heavy, looking dangerous.

I give him a nervous smile.

"Dusty Doyle!"

This guy is a zombie.

"You look good!"

I don't think he believes in my insincere sincerity. He looks at us, eyes spreading over us like we are butter on toast.

"Why?" he sputters out, his voice cracking with emotion but underlined with menace. He has blood in his saliva, and his face is wet with tears. "Why'd you do it?"

I try to calm him. He is definitely in what one would call

an agitated state. Aside from the whole zombification thing, he looks like a spurned lover.

"Just calm down, Dusty," I say, stepping out of the closet with Thad and Tobey close behind. I hope they have those barbells ready, because I think we're gonna need them. "What did we do?"

"My boys!" he shouts, his voice breaking. "You killed my boys. I found their beautiful bodies on the stairs. Why'd you kill my boys?"

His voice is attracting attention. There's a moaning coming from the corner behind a busted cable machine. I have never been a fan of moans coming from dark corners.

"Your boys?" Then I remember the two zombies that got Chris, dragging him back down the steps and flaying him as they went. "Dusty, they were making lunch of our friend."

This, apparently, is not the right thing to say. His face changes then, from something slightly recognizable as human to something absolutely I'm gonna eat your lips off terrifying.

"They were hungry," he growls, drooling and spitting and gritting his teeth. "They were growing boys!"

And now, coming out of the shadows behind Dusty, I see Stephen. Or what was once Stephen. I hear Thad whisper Holy shit behind me. And as my two protectors are distracted by the dickless boogeyman, Dusty charges at me.

It's all happening so quick, I have no time to react. He pushes me back into the utility closet, pinning Johnny and Casey in there as well. Dusty's mouth is wide open and chomping, trying to snatch any morsel off me he can get between his teeth, and he's drooling something awful. His eyes are demon red. Casey is screaming and Johnny is shaking, both of them no help at all. I'm fighting off Dusty as best I can, but his strength and ferocity, powered by rage, is brutal. He tears my shirt and nearly rips off a nipple with his crazy zombie hands. I can't say I blame him, though. I've got beautiful nipples.

I look past my attacker to Thad and Tobey for help, but they got their hands full with Stephen. In movies, zombies don't move nearly as fast as these motherfuckers do. But Thad and Tobey are using their barbells, fighting like Jedi masters against the ugliest Sith lord this side of Palpatine.

Finally, some help comes from behind me. Casey stops screaming long enough to grab a can of Pledge and sprays it directly into Dusty's face. Dusty stumbles off of me, tearing at his face with his claws, still growling in rage. I kick the bastard away, but he lunges for me again, his hands still ripping at his eyes. Casey throws the mop at my feet, and I pick it up and swat Dusty as hard as I can across the jaw. The mop breaks, and he howls and bangs backward against an upended treadmill, then falls to the floor.

This is my chance, maybe the only one I'll get. As Dusty struggles to rise to his feet again, I stand behind the treadmill and, with all my strength, I push the thing off balance to the floor. It lands on Dusty with a loud pop and a crunch, and I can see by the blood oozing out from beneath the machine that his head is flattened. He jerks for a bit, nerves screaming, and his synapses firing their final impulses, then he lies still. And that's a shame. He was a nice guy. The nicest drug dealer I ever met, in fact. But he was a damn ugly zombie.

Thad and Tobey have Stephen cornered behind the cable wires, but they can't get to him. The cables are so tangled and so numerous, they can't do any true damage to the dickless asshole. If anyone deserves a gruesome end here, it's this guy. No matter. We have got to get out of here before more zombies appear.

"The main office!" I shout to everyone. It's as good a plan as any. "We need to get to the main office downstairs by the pool. We can override the security system from there and get the hell out of Dodge Ram."

I hope.

Tobey goes back to the utility closet to get Johnny, and we're off again. Stephen is still snarling and jumbled up in the cables. He reaches out for us we pass him, an angry zombie trapped in the mess he made. He leers at me. He knows who I am somewhere deep inside. The glint in his eye makes me extremely uneasy. I don't like the idea of leaving that thing alive, but nobody has any cable cutters on them and this ain't This Ole Big Gay Fitness Center, dammit. Ain't nobody got time for that shit.

JAKE

All I see is red.

All I taste is flesh.

The man whose name I can't remember has fallen silent. And still. And in pieces, along the floor.

A and C rise in front of me. Their faces are covered in gore.

They reach out to take my hands again. I feel the raging heat of their skin. The tightness of their grip and—

my name's Uly

—I squeeze their hands back because they are mine. They belong to me. They are like me, and we are the same and—

what's your name

—what is that? What is that voice I hear? It's like teeth biting against my brain, fingers curled into my mind and shredding all that's left. It sounds so familiar, but it's in the back, underneath the red. In the dark. I try to take a step forward but—

I love you

—there's a flash in the rage. Movement. It comes forward. I see a face that causes my bones to ache, though I know not why. It bursts through the bite, and the tear, and the kill and even though it's red, it's there, and I can hear him. He's there with me.

A and C pull on my hands, and I hear the screams ahead of us. I look down at what remains of the man on the floor. Blood swirls in the water. My shoes are soaked in it. Bits of flesh dot the tiles. A piece falls from my lips and lands in the water. It splashes up red.

I don't step over the man. I step in him and drag my feet along the floor, spreading him around further. A and C laugh in low, guttural tones. One kicks a severed arm littered with bite marks, a shiny, white knob of bone poking through the shredded skin. The other runs his tongue along his lips and closes his eyes, groaning as he sucks bits of flesh from his teeth.

Part of me wants to kill them, rip them apart just to see what their insides would look like on the outside. How pretty the coils of their intestines would look as they slipped through my fingers. How red it would look against the white. I grip their hands tighter and know it wouldn't take much more for their bones to splinter and pierce the flesh and stand out in stark relief, and they would howl and shriek as I bend down and suck the marrow out.

They watch me, heads tilted.

Part of me wants to destroy them and bathe in what remains.

Another part says they're mine. That I have to protect them. Keep them safe. I was told to keep them safe. It seems so long ago. It's lost in my head. But I promised. Didn't I? It's lost in the red and hidden behind his face. He who tells me his name is Uly. He who tells me he loves me.

It seems their insides will stay inside.

For now.

I let them pull me away, away, away. We descend into chaos. People are screaming around us. Lights are flashing. Alarms are shrieking. There is blood on the floor. On the walls. The ceiling. Through the red, I see people catching sight of us. Their eyes widen. Their faces drain of color. They turn and run. It smells of them. Reeks. It smells like fear and flesh. Bone and terror. I can taste it on my tongue. I want it down my throat.

One comes rushing at us, roaring as he raises a heavy weight above his head, meaning to smash it down on us. A and C tense at my sides, snarling in unison. The face hidden in the dark recesses of my mind comes forward again, and he tells me My name is Uly. What's yours? I love you. I say goodbye.

But it doesn't happen. I don't leave this place. Instead, the man is attacked by one of the infected who crawls along the floor, his shattered legs dragging behind him. Teeth embed themselves in fat calf muscle, and our would-be attacker shrieks in agony as skin and tendons are shredded. His hands slip, and his howl of pain is cut off when the weight drops on his upturned face. There's a loud crack as his skull splits, as his face is flattened in on itself. The weight slides off his face and drops on the infected's head, smashing his skull. The man gurgles once as the infected seizes on the floor, still attached to his leg. A thin spray of blood erupts from the man's head as broken teeth fall from his mouth. He falls face first to the floor. He jerks once along with the infected. Twice. A third time. And then he's still.

A and C pull me along.

Everyone runs from us now. No one tries to attack. Some hide, but I can hear them. Smell them. I could find them, if I wanted. I could find their hiding places and taste them. But the face in my head, the one rising up from the red and dark, says my name over and over, and my body trembles. I know him.

We stop as I tremble, cramp up, and I bend over and vomit onto the floor. A and C stand limply at my sides, staring off into nothing. There's a finger in the stinking bile at my feet. Almost intact. The fingernail is manicured almost perfectly. Carson. Or Carey. Carl. It belongs to him.

My name's Uly, the face says. What's your name?

I don't know.

My name's Uly, he asks again. What's your name?

I don't know. I don't—

"J-Juh," I moan, a line of spit hanging from my mouth. "J… Jay—Juh. Juh. Jay. Jake. Jake. Jake."

Jake, huh? I do believe it's my pleasure to meet you, Jake.

"Jake," I whisper. "Jake. I'm. Juh. Jay. Jah! Jake! I'm Jake!"

I pull myself up. A and C pull me along. The face in my head becomes sharper, clearer. It's strong, that face. It's beautiful. It's home. It's like so much home, and I hear more screams as we round a corner. "Please!" they cry. "Please don't hurt us! Oh, Christ, is that Jake?"

"Juh," I tell them. "I'm Juh. Jake. I'm Jake."

They scream again, then they're gone.

Time passes. We reach a door. A presses against it, grunting as it doesn't move, his face pressing against the door. He pulls back, and there's an imprint of his face against the wood. It's red.

It drips, and it looks like he's crying in the wood. He snarls and presses against the door again.

I let go of his hand and grasp the handle. Turn it. It opens.

Tanning beds, stretch out in front of us. The tanning room. It looks empty. The face in my head isn't in here. It's not—

Movement from one of the beds. A hand drops down and scrapes along the floor. The arm is dark. And alive. It pulls back up into the tanning bed. A and C shuffle ahead, cocking their heads as they approach the bed. I wait behind because the face is clear now. So clear.

A and C raise the lid of the bed. There's another man there. Eyes covered. Earbuds in his ears. He doesn't know. He hasn't heard. A and C look back at me. Those red eyes. I stay where I'm at because of the face. They turn back to the man. And descend.

As he screams, the face breaks through the red and his name is Uly. His name is Uly, and he's mine, and I remember.

The first time we meet. Jake, I tell him. I'm Jake.

Jake, huh? I do believe it's my pleasure to meet you, Jake. And then he smiles.

A tears a long stretch of skin off the man's stomach as he tries to fight them off.

Our first date. I'm a bit nervous, he says.

I'm surprised. Why?

Because I have a feeling you're amazing, and I ain't got that much to offer.

I reach out and take his hand in mine.

C tears off the man's ear with his teeth. The man shrieks.

The first time he told me. You've been acting weird all day, I tell him. What's wrong?

You always know, don't you? he says with a sheepish laugh, a dark blush to his face.

I know you, I say. Because I do.

It's just… I just.

Uly! What is it?

He looks at me, and he's not all red. He's breaking through. I just… love you. You know? It's too soon. I'm sorry. No. No, I'm not. I don't care. I love you.

I can't stop the sunshine that explodes in my chest. Yeah?

Yeah, he says, a smile forming on his face. Yeah.

The man chokes on his own blood as C buries his face into his neck and bites.

Are you sure about this? I ask him. This is what you want?

He laughs at me. Why wouldn't I? It's a house, Jake. A house for us! Of course I want it. Don't you?

I do. I want it so bad. But I worry. What if it doesn't work out? I ask, my voice quiet.

He leans down and kisses me sweetly. He presses his forehead against mine. It'll work, he whispers. You and me? This is it, Jakey. This is all I ever wanted.

I laugh, and he picks me up, tossing me over his shoulder, carrying me into the house.

The man doesn't make much noise anymore. Just gurgles. The tanning bed is soaked in blood. A and C snarl as they bite. Snap as they chew.

You awake? he asks me, late into the night.

Yeah.

Can't sleep?

I dunno.

He pulls me over to him, and I lay my head on his chest. You think too much, he tells me.

I laugh quietly. Yeah?

It ain't right for a man to think as much you do. I can hear the smile in his voice.

It's got me this far.

He jostles me a little. It's got us this far.

Yeah. Uly?

Hmm?

Tell me again.

The man doesn't move. The only sounds that come from him are the sounds A and C make as they eat him.

It'll be on the coast, I think. Along the Mediterranean. There's nothing like seeing the sunrise over the water. It's something that I can't even find the words to describe. We'll find a little town. You'll learn Italian and have a little shop and make bread. I'll work in the fields with the grapes. And at night, every night, we'll come home to our little villa, our little piece of the world, and it'll be ours. It'll be for us, and no one can take that away from us. No one can tell us what to do. It'll be us, Jake. There, in that little town. In our little place. I promise you, it'll be us.

A and C stand before me, covered almost completely in the man from the tanning bed. Uly's face is clear in my mind. I know what I have to do. I can beat this. I can survive this. If only I can get to him, this will all be okay. I know it. I know it and one day, so far in the future, we'll look back on this and barely remember what happened. But it won't matter, because we'll have our little villa. And no one can take that away from us.

"Uly," I tell them. "I have to find Uly."

They say nothing.

I hold out my hands.

They look down at them but don't move. Seconds go by. Finally, after what feels like ages, they raise their arms as one and grab my hands. My hands are instantly coated in blood and pieces of skin.

"Uly will fix this," I whisper to them.

To myself.

Nothing. No response. They're gone now.

I turn and lead them back out into the gym. The screams pick up almost immediately.

ULY

We're in the multipurpose room on the second level of this state of the art fitness center. It's dark as all get out in here, and every shadow is teasing us, terrifying us. Every time my shoes squeak on the floor, I jump. We're all breathing as shallow as we can, but asking a bodybuilder to breathe shallow is like asking a zombie to fast.

The back stairs are just over there, if we can get to them. They'll lead us down to the pool and then to Stephen's big ol' glass-walled office where I can hopefully override the security controls. Leave it to Stephen to put his office in the pool area, the filthy bastard. He loves – er, loved to see that water polo team workout. I wouldn't be surprised if he had underwater cameras installed for his own personal use, if you catch my meaning.

We're on guard, each of us in some defensive posture, eyes peeled for zombies. Zombies. It's still a word I want to smirk at as if it belongs in a Laurel and Hardy film and not in real life. The other guys may be naked, but I'm just as vulnerable as they are here in the dark. And these zombies are feisty when they see fresh meat.

There was something like lust in Dusty Doyle's eyes before he died. Food and sex. No two things can make a man more primitive if he's deprived of them long enough. For a zombie, especially a horned-up zombie with crazy-ass spiked testosterone coursing through his system, a minute without gorging himself must be an eternity.

The multipurpose room can be used for anything from volleyball to basketball to tumbling. Somebody was definitely using the room this morning. There's a hollowed-out corpse taking a rest over by the rolled up rubber mats. I shudder. I think I see it move, but if it did, there ain't enough body left for it to be much of a bother. My teeth are rattling, my eyes are playing tricks on me, and I'm hearing things.

Thad motions to me to get against the wall. Turns out I ain't hearing things after all. Something is coming. Fuck.

Tobey and Thad have their barbells. Me and Casey reach for whatever is nearest to us, which ain't much but bags and racks of balls. Johnny's still in no shape to do anything. He stands with us, his hands over his privates like a terrified frat boy during pledge week.

We wait.

Every breath counts out the seconds. We hear a shuffling. It's getting louder and the room seems to get a little bit darker. My vision tunnels so that all I can see is the doorway. I'm a healthy boy, but dammit if it don't feel like my heart is gonna explode. Somebody needs to tell a joke. Somebody needs to break the tension.

Then we see them. They sniffed us right out. I don't need to see their eyes to know they got the blood lust.

"Grab your balls, boys!" Thad says.

We do, and we let them fly. It's like playing the most vicious game of dodgeball ever. It's ultimate dodgeball, only we're playing against a team that doesn't care for the rules. Me and Tobey are wailing these zombies in the head one after another. Even in the dark, my aim is good. I was the king of dodgeball in school. I do it with grit and a grin.

I have to admit the sound of a ball hitting these zombie heads is satisfying stuff. SMACK. POP. THWACK. I'm hearing a few cracks, and it's good to know I've still got my throwing arm. My goal is to break a neck. It could happen.

I haven't played a game like this in a while. The last time was with Jake. We played one-on-one volleyball. Dammit if this memory don't make me smile as I'm throwing. He gets so competitive, one of us usually walks away pissed. By "one of us," of course, I mean Jake. But goddamn, it's cute to see him pout. We'll have to play again soon.

Johnny is standing against the wall, still holding his crotch and shivering. He's emitting a low whining sound. The boy is cracking.

Thad is using his barbell as a baseball bat, tossing a volleyball up in the air, giving it a great whack, and making it sail across the room where it temporarily flattens a zombie. He's enjoying this game. Baseball. That's where that ass comes from.

Casey's at the bat…kinda. He has maybe the best idea. He's found the pitching machine used to throw balls during batting practice and is aiming it at the infected. One of them is hit so hard in the noggin, the damn thing caves in, showering the gym floor with bone and blood. Another goes down and doesn't come up. Casey is cackling like crazy ass Bill Paxton in that alien movie.

But most of the zombies are on their feet again after being hit. There's more infected folk coming, too, and our balls are dwindling in size and number. We've got a major "oh, shit" moment on our hands, and we all know it.

"Johnny," Casey shouts as he continues firing the baseballs. "If you don't stop that whining, I'll aim this machine at your face. Now, shut up!"

This does not help matters. Johnny only gets louder and more full-voiced.

Tobey wails Casey in the side with a dodge ball. "Lay off the boy, heathen!" the Bible man says.

But now I'm getting a bit annoyed with Johnny's brand of crazy, too. His voice is echoing through the multipurpose room, bouncing off the walls and the rubber floor, and making everything that much more chaotic. Here we are, like the last survivors of some naked Spartan army, and one of our own is the biggest distraction. He's worse than the alarm still blaring overhead.

Before I can even think about doing anything, though, Johnny shakes his head like he's got fleas, and he gets this real determined—even possessed—look on his face. He's looking right at these zombies, and he starts to shout some sort of battle cry, only I can't make out the words. It's all "ooga booga" and "niiiii."

I half expect him to glance toward us and say "For Frodo," because I know what's coming. The boy's gonna run. Suddenly, he's off, racing at the hungry bastards who we've spent the day trying to get away from. His Abercrombie model booty is obscured from our sights as the demons are losing interest in us and clambering after him. He's still alive, though. He's a wiry fella. Might as well be oiled down, he got in between those zombies so fast. We can still hear his battle cry echo as he's pursued down the way we just came, headed for the weight room. Father Tobey tries to go after Johnny, but me and Thad pull him back.

"We can't do anything for him," says Thad. "He's gone, buddy. He's made his choice."

"He just saved our asses," I say. "Let's get down to the office before those zombies come on back. Maybe Johnny will be safe. Did you see how slick he was, dodging them and rolling out of their clutches? Maybe he'll find a place to hide out."

Casey sticks his one cent in, too. "I told you he was a redshirt."

JAKE

I try to ask everyone if they've seen Uly. I ask them, though the words are hard. I ask them because I can't find him. All I want is Uly and all I need is Uly and all I hear in my head is Uly, Uly, Uly, and it's like a chant.

But no one answers me. No one tells me where Uly is. They all run from me. They try and hide from me. They scream at me. No! they cry. Don't hurt me! I don't want to die. Jake, please don't!

It makes me angry that no one wants to help me. It makes me want to bite. And tear. And kill. I want to kill them and make them bleed all over the ground so I can lick it up from the floor.

But I don't. I can't. I won't, I think to myself, even though I run my tongue over my teeth and gums, chasing the copper tang that was Carson/Carey/Carl.

"Uly?" I ask a man who cowers away from me in the corner. He can't get away from us, and he has nowhere to hide. He can tell me now. He screams and holds his hands up toward me, as if to ward me off. His face is wet. Snot drips out of his nose onto his chin. His eyes are wide and bright as he shouts at me incoherently. I recognize him. Somehow. I can't remember his name. I've seen him before. I've talked to him before. So has Uly. Friends? Are they friends? I don't know. It doesn't matter. He's scared, but that doesn't matter either. "You seen Uly?" I say as he takes a shuddering breath.

"Please don't hurt me!" he moans. "No, Jake, please don't. Oh, why? Why? What is happening? I just want to go home! Please let me go home."

A and C growl at him, that low sound in the back of their throats. They start forward, trying to pull from my grasp, but I hold on tight, even as the blood slides over our hands, making us slippery.

"No," I tell them.

They snarl at me.

It gives me ideas.

"Uly?" I ask the cowering man again. "Where is he?"

"I just want to go home," he says, starting to cry. "Home. It's all I want, I don't care. I just want to go home."

"They'll eat you," I tell him, holding up A and C's hands. "They eat people now. They're hungry."

A and C snap their teeth at him.

The man sobs.

"Slippery," I tell him. "They're slippery. Can't hold them for long. Where is Uly?"

"Please! Don't."

"Oops," I tell him, trying to sound regretful. "I'm slipping." A and C jerk forward, their other hands outstretched toward the man. "They eat people," I tell him again, in case he's forgotten.

I smile, but I must have Carson/Carey/Carl in my teeth still because he starts to scream again. It's so loud, and it hurts my head. All this noise is starting to hurt my head, and I want to eat it and swallow it down until it's gone and nothing can hurt me. I want to eat it to make it go away.

"I get hungry too," I say, as he tries to shrink into the corner. "Slipping. I'm slipping."

And I am. I am slipping, and I need to find Uly. I need to fucking find Uly right fucking now so he can get rid of this red that is in my mind, this rage that is in my heart. "Where is Uly?" I growl at him, snapping my teeth. "If you don't tell me, we'll eat your skin. And your eyes."

"Upstairs," he gasps. "I saw him head upstairs. With others. He was with others."

"Who?"

"Casey. Johnny. That big Jesus freak. Please! I don't know any more! Don't eat me. Please don't eat me!

"Tobey. Jesus freak is Tobey."

His eyes are so wide and wet. They look like they'd pop in

between my teeth. "Yes! Tobey! Yes!"

"Upstairs," I say to A and C. "We have to go upstairs."

They snarl in protest. They want to eat this helpful man with the big eyes.

"Not now," I tell them. "We need to find Uly." I look back at the man. "We won't eat you. Your eyes. We won't eat your eyes. Even though… no. Not today. You helped me."

And he did. He's a good person. He's a person. He's meat and blood and bone that I could chew, and I could bite him until it—

"No," I whisper. "No. Uly."

A and C tilt their heads as they watch me.

I pull them away from the cowering man. I hear him cry out in relief. It's only a moment later when it turns into a scream of agony. I look back. Someone else is eating him. The infected is big, and he bites into the helpful man's neck, his teeth tearing into the tendons. The helpful man doesn't scream for long. His blood is everywhere. The walls. The floor.

I feel bad.

More people run away from us as I lead A and C toward the stairs. That's okay. Uly's upstairs, and I'll get to him. I don't need their help anymore.

I step around people getting eaten. I step over people eating. A man lurches forward, holding his intestines in his hands like he's offering them to us. Or trying to hold them in his stomach. I almost take his offering because of how shiny the coils look, but then he falls to his knees, and his nose is chewed off by a smaller man. His intestines fall to the floor and lay on the ground as his face is gnawed on. I don't think I want to eat floor intestines.

I see the stairs, but there is a man in front of them. He's big, and he looks very angry.

"Move, please," I tell him politely.

"Fuck you, you fucking monster," he says. "I'll fucking kill all of you right here."

"That was mean," I say. I let go of A and C. They eat him.

"You should have moved," I tell him as he screams, and I float on the red, on the rage and think of Uly.

A and C finish and take their places back at my side. A offers a piece of the man. I can't tell what it is. His ear? Maybe. I shake my head. "Not now." A eats it himself.

We head up the stairs. We're not even at the top before I see two bodies on the ground I recognize. The other two Alphabet Twinks. B and D. They are dead.

"I'm sorry," I tell A and C as they stare down at their friends. I wait, giving them a moment, in case some part of them knows what has happened. They watch B and D for a minute, and then, as one, they bend over. I let them go. A touches B's flayed cheek. C rubs D's arm. They stand back up. And take my hands again.

And only a moment later, it happens again when we see a familiar arm sticking out from underneath an upended treadmill. Dusty. The drug dealer with a heart of gold. Dusty, who loved his boys. A and C howl. They scream. They snarl at each other. They snap their teeth and bite their own lips clean through. Both rub their faces on Dusty's arm, leaving trails of blood and gore. They know. Regardless of what they are—what we are, the red reminds me—they still know. They still feel. They know.

And now they are angry.

"We'll find who did this," I promise them.

They look up at me.

I hold out my hands.

They turn to each other, and without words, they speak. It's in their eyes. Their red, harsh eyes.

They come to their decision and take my hands. I pull them up and hold them close.

"I'll take care of you," I whisper. "Both of you. I promise."

They rub their heads on my shoulder.

A growl comes from behind us.

All three of us turn and look.

Through the chaos, the destruction, the horror, we see him.

Stephen Fucking Dorian. Dickless. He lurches down the hall, away from us. Toward the multipurpose room. Uly, he'd said. Uly.

Uly.

If Dickless is going that way, then Uly has to be there too.

"We'll follow him," I tell A and C. "We'll follow him, and we'll find Uly and he'll make everything okay."

A and C say nothing. I don't think they have words anymore.

We head down the hall, leaving Dusty behind.

My boys never look back. Maybe they know we'll find Uly. Maybe they know we'll stop Dickless. Or maybe they know I meant it when I said I'd take care of them. Regardless of what they know, they are doing what I tell them. I let them eat a man who tries to hurt us as my way of saying how proud I am of them.

So very proud.

ULY

The pool area, large and unending in the dark, is so humid it's uncomfortable. The heaters are humming and drumming around us, a chant of whispers, like we're in one of them human sacrifice scenes from an old Dario Argento film. In the end, the heaters say, this will all be blood.

Only the red glow from the pool lights beneath the water lets us see where we're going. That is anything but a relief, though, let me tell ya. I'd almost rather it be pitch black in here. Aside from what or who may be hiding in the shadows, we're all postulatin' on what's in that hellish water. We hear it lapping gently along the sides of the pool. That's normally a comforting sound, right? Yet I'm guessing bits of gym patrons are floating around in the water. Everybody loses their trunks in the pool at some point in their life, but they usually remember to take their ass with them.

It's just the four of us now. Me, Father Tobey, Thad the stud, and Casey the weasel. The office is just ahead.

"Let's just break the glass," Casey says as if we're all a bunch of morons. "Why do we need to unlock the damn door? Just break it. It's a glass office, for fuck's sake!"

I breathe a slight sigh of relief when I get there. I've got the keys in my hand and I'm shaking, scared as an itty bitty baby leaf in a hurricane. I can't see which key is which. They're all silver and labeled with a tiny piece of white paper that can't be read in the dark. You'd a thunk Stephen would've gone more high tech with the keys like he did with everything else and made them those slidey cards like hotels use or eyeball scanners. But then, keys have more weight, more heft than a slidey card, and Stephen is a big proponent of heft.

"We're trying to create a bit of a barrier between us and them," says Thad. He's keeping an eye out, as are Tobey and Casey. There are noises all around us, any one of which could be the devil himself. "The glass might slow them down a little. We need it not to be in shards."

Fuckin' keys! They all look the same. I notice even in my head my curses are whispered.

I keep my eyes open on what's happening around me. Tobey is clutching his crucifix necklace with one hand and his barbell with the other. He's the nearest to me. God ain't never had a warrior his size before. I guarantee that. Casey is looking for a place to hide in case we're attacked before we get into the office. Thad is by the pool's edge, he of the comic book superhero physique, looking in and around it. He's still holding his barbell too, but I'm hoping he won't need to use it. I've had my fill of these juiced-up zombies. They're in better shape than we are, dammit.

"Hurry the fuck up, man!" says Casey. He's not keeping his voice down. "They're coming! I can hear them coming!"

"Shut it, Casey," says Tobey. "You're not helping matters by stressing him out. Now, stop freaking out."

Thad turns to face us. "I think we're okay for now. The room looks clear. There's no movement in the shadows." He spots something on the floor between his feet and crouches down to investigate, his big ass hanging over the pool's edge. He picks it up and folds it over in his hand, putting the barbell down beside him. "Were the water polo guys in this morning?"

We all look at him at the same moment, our mouths dropping. He knows he's too near the pool. Now. Now he knows this.

Behind him, several heads are rising out of the water. He's got no chance! He isn't even able to turn around before one, the biggest one, grabs Thad's dangling dick and pulls him backward into the pool. Casey is screaming. Tobey is yelling for Thad. There's a struggle in the pool, but it already looks red from the lights, so if there's blood.... We can't tell what's happening, but, Jesus, we know.

"The door!" Casey screams, backing farther and farther away from me and Tobey. "Unlock the door!"

"I'm trying!" I'm fumbling in the dark. Shit. Shit, shit, shit.

But with a big ol' howl and explosion of water, Thad is rising again from the pool. Wailing, he shoots straight up like a star.

And he has help. The big man is being hoisted like some juiced-up Ethel Merman, fisted into the air, an arm buried elbow-deep in his beautiful virgin ass and sinking in deeper. He's bitten and torn, one nipple already hanging loose. His legs are spread wide and shaking. His eyes are rolling back in his head, and, holy shit, as he's screaming he's coming like a motherfucker. He's coming like the damn Trevi Fountain, his dick as hard as it's likely to have ever been.

He's still got mind enough to try and get away, though, and so he rocks back and forth on the zombie's arm even as it slips deeper inside of him. There's so much going on in the water around him. He's become sport for the other zombies. It's the most macabre game of water polo ever played, an obscene Olympic sport without the sportsmanship. They charge with unbelievable speed at the holder just as Thad makes a giant rocking motion forward. With a sickening crack, the zombie's arm is ripped clean off his shoulder as Thad rocks one way, and the players force the holder to go another.

Thad goes under for a bit, then resurfaces. Struggling, he somehow pulls himself up out of the pool, but we can all see he's close to gone. Not even Tobey dares approach the water to help. The water polo player's large arm is still lodged in Thad's ass, and the poor bastard is still coming. He's moaning and looking at us as he crawls, all glazed and incredulous. This can't be. Heroes ain't supposed to die like this. The water polo team is on him in two shakes of a lamb's tail. He screams – he screams – as teeth and fingers sink into his ass, tearing and ripping chunks of it away. He claws at the floor, eyes now wide with realization and terror, as he's dragged once again beneath the water. I never thought I'd witness the death of a superhero. Superman is dead.

We can't mourn Thad right now. The hullabaloo from the pool has attracted others wanting to turn us into meat kabobs as well. Tobey is keeping them off me. He's whacking zombies this way and that with the barbell. He abhors violence, being a man of God and all, so he sends the infected off as nicely as he can. "God bless you, motherfucker!" he yells with each zombie head dislodged.

Casey is no good. Casey is a dead man. He has wandered too far from us, from the office, from any hope of protection. I hear him bellowing, "No! Stay away! I'm not a redshirt! I'm not a redshirt!" And he screams, but I don't look. I can't. I focus on the keys. I don't want to see what my own death is gonna look like. And I don't hear Casey anymore.

"Found it!" I yell, as if it's gonna make a difference now. We're all dead. I know that. Me and Tobey are still alive, but we're all dead.

I wanna see Jake. I need to see him. Damn tears in my eyes. Just open the door and die in there. Make sure your last thoughts are of Jake.

Behind me I hear another voice, hollering and carrying on. It's Johnny. He's not dead after all. In fact, he's laying waste to the zombies with a deadly discus and a mean-looking javelin. My heart skips a beat. Crazy might be just the thing to get us out of here, and, damn, Johnny looks crazy as all get out. I may be dipskittles, but there's a spark of hope in that lunatic. He's with us now, and Tobey has a second wind and a big ol' grin.

And I got the door open.

We get inside the office and lock ourselves in there. These zombies are crafty. It won't be long before they're able to break the glass, but until then it might afford me enough time to unlock the fitness center. Then the three of us can get the hell out of here. With the newfound adrenaline Johnny has brought, I think we might be able to fight our way through the hordes.

Yeah. I'm definitely dipskittles. But, fuck me, I'm smiling.

I find the controls and flip a switch. Easy as that. Easy as pie. So easy it's annoying. Johnny jumps up naked on Stephen's desk and roars in victory at the zombies outside the office as the lights of the fitness center come back on. There is devastation all around the pool area and lots of hungry fitness fanatics eyeing us like we're the biggest lobsters in the tank, but I'm laughing. I'm smiling. I'm feeling good!

But wait.

How did he get in here? How did….? Oh, Christ, no!

Jake.

JAKE

I shouldn't have stopped to let A and C eat that man. Even though he deserved it. He got in my way. Our way. But I shouldn't have stalled. I've lost sight of Dickless. He's supposed to lead me to Uly. I have to find them both before they find each other.

Through the multipurpose room. Bodies litter the floor. They look like they are the infected. Some of them still twitch along the ground, as if their bodies have yet to catch up with the fact that they're dead. Violently, messily dead. Who did this? Who killed them? I shouldn't feel remorse like I do. I shouldn't feel bad. They are monsters. Or, were monsters, rather. They hurt people. They attacked. They killed. Like A. And C.

Like me.

There's a kinship there, whether I want it or not. They are like me. They are me. Uly can fix this. He can make this better. But until then, until that moment when my mind is free and clear of the red sheen and the bite, the tear, the kill, I understand. I know what they are. I know why they did what they did. It's not our fault. It's this thing inside of us, this rage that wants to slash apart all that are not like us. Those that shriek in fear. All we want to do is swallow that fear down and let it fill us.

I understand them. I understand them all.

A and C stare blankly at the infected dead along the floor. They shuffle their feet, dragging them through entrails and limbs. We step over an infected whose mouth is open, teeth bared, and I remember a time that Uly came to my work out of the blue. We hadn't been dating long, maybe a few months, and I was still a bit skittish around him. I was unsure what to make of him. But there he was, as large as life, that smile on his face, carefree and wonderful.

"I'm here to take you out to lunch," he said, as if he did it every day. "No need to be cooped up in a cubicle when the sun is shining."

I smiled at him, unsure of what to say.

He held out his hand.

I watched it for a moment and then leaned forward and bit his fingers off. He screamed as the tendons and skin tore, as the bone shattered under my teeth. I jerked my head back. Blood sprayed my face as I chewed, and it was in my eyes, and all I could see is red and all I can see is red—

I stop. That's not… that's not how it happened. I didn't do that. I didn't hurt him. I couldn't hurt him. He's mine. I don't hurt what's mine. I think back again, but all I can remember is biting his fingers off and feeling the warmth drip down my face.

Other memories. When we first met. He told me his name was Uly. I bit through his carotid artery.

Our first date. He grinned at me. I ate his tongue from his mouth.

I love you, he said. I put my hands inside his abdomen and pulled out his spleen.

Our house. Our little house. He's stretched out along the kitchen table, body flayed open and there is so much red that I can't do anything but howl and scream. Groan and snarl. Because this is our house and these are my memories and they are all filled with death. And blood. And bone.

"Ahhh," I moan, my stomach cramping. A and C don't let go of my hands as I bend over and vomit dark red chunks onto the floor. It's hot when it splashes up against my legs. "N-no. My. Nuh. Name." I vomit again. I don't know how there's anything left in me. Unless it was the man I ate. "Muh. My n-n-name. Jake. I'm. Juh. Jake. I'm. Jake. I'm Jake. I'm Jake. I'm Jake!" I'm screaming. I'm screaming because it's all red now. My past. Everything is red, and his face is in the red. It's there, but it's falling and fading and I don't know how much time is left.

"Fast," I tell A and C as I pull myself upright. "Move fast."

They watch me with red eyes.

And we move. We move quickly now. Even as we move, I try and find something, anything, in the recesses of my mind, something that isn't buried in rage, something that can still be my own. Something that happened the way I remembered it happening. Something about me and him. I push through all the memories, but I can't find anything free. Anything clear.

Nothing.

Stairs, on the other end of the multipurpose room. Do I take them back down? Or keep going? Where would Uly have gone? Where would Dickless have gone?

Think. Think.

I do. Uly bought me flowers once. I ripped his head from his shoulders.

He laughed in the low way that he does, and I put my thumbs through his eyes.

He lay below me as I thrust into him. He arched his back and sighed my name, and I pulled his ribs up through his chest one by one and sucked on their shiny tips.

Th-think. Thuh. Think. Think!

"Downside," I say as my stomach cramps again. No. Not right. "Downstairs. It's downstairs. It's there. Office. It's downside. Down. Go down."

And we do. We descend back into madness. Into chaos. I hear people scream. My name is called, but I don't stop because nothing in my head is free and clear. Not anymore. It's all red and rage, and all I can think about is how many times I've killed him. Every day since I've known him I've killed him. His screams fill my head like a hurricane, and I'm all twisted up inside him and I love it, because no one feels like he does on the inside. No one makes me rage as much as him.

I vomit one last time, but it doesn't matter. It's a thin, red bile, and it's nothing because I know. I know where he is, and I'm going to find him.

I reach the doors to the pool and the crescendo in my head builds to an almost unbearable roar. I drop A and C's hands and bring my own to cover my ears. I don't think I can take another step. I don't think I can go any further. I should just sink into all that is inside me and let it consume me. Let it take me over. Let it be finished.

Let this be the end.

I'm sorry, Uly. I'm so sorry.

It'll be on the coast, I think, he whispers through the storm.

He sounds free. Clear. Like home.

Along the Mediterranean. There's nothing like seeing the sunrise over the water. It's something that I can't even find the words to describe. We'll find a little town. You'll learn Italian and have a little shop and make bread. I'll work in the fields with the grapes. And at night, every night, we'll come home to our little villa, our little piece of the world, and it'll be ours. It'll be for us, and no one can take that away from us. No one can tell us what to do. It'll be us, Jake. There, in that little town. In our little place. I promise you, it'll be us.

It will be us. It's enough.

I push the pool doors open.

"I'm not a redshirt!" a man I know screams. His name is lost, but I know him. I do nothing as infected descend on him. He's not my concern. A and C start forward, wanting to join in. I grab their hands. I have to protect them. They're mine now. They growl at me but don't try to pull away. They understand.

It's dark, except for the lights from the pool. The water is red. Screams from the other end, near the office. A door slams shut.

The man who is not a redshirt gurgles as he dies. The tile floor is wet with him and water. The infected who eat him do not look up as we pass.

More are in the water, splashing around what remains of another man. They look like circling sharks. The man in the water does not move.

And even more in front of the office ahead. They rub their hands along the glass. They groan angrily.

From up above, the lights switch on. They are harsh. They burn my eyes. Pierce my skull. All of us, all of the infected, groan as one.

The ones in front of the window to the office hear my coming from behind them. They turn their heads. And, as if they know, they step back. They part in front of me.

And there he is. Him. My Uly.

He has a smile on his face. The man of God stands behind him. There's another man. Can't remember his name, but it doesn't matter. Uly's here. And he's smiling.

He sees me. His gaze drifts over me…and passes. But then he stops. The smile freezes on his face. Then it melts. He looks back at me. His lips part and even though I can't hear his whisper through the glass, I see the word: Jake.

Silence descends in the pool. It seems that everyone and everything waits for us.

A and C don't protest when I let them go. I move toward the glass divider, and I can see it in his eyes, the fear. The anger. The horror. The love. For a moment, I see my reflection in the glass, and it's obscene. Foul. What reflects back at me is a monster. I am a monster.

I stand in front of my man. I look up at him, past the monster in the reflection. He has gone pale. The other two men with him stare at me over his shoulder, their jaws dropped.

"Jake?" Uly says. He's muffled, but I can hear him through the glass. "Oh, Christ. Jake?"

Yes. I'm Jake. "I'm Juh," I tell him. "I'm Juh-ake. Jake. I'm Jake! I'm Jake!"

"No," he moans, his shoulders hunching over. The other two try and pull him away. They try to pull him back, but he struggles against them. He's big. He's so big, and he breaks loose and comes back to the glass. That's good. That's okay. If they tried to take him away, I'd kill them. He's mine.

"Jake."

Yes. I'm Jake.

A tear falls from his left eye. "Oh, baby," he says. "Oh, Jake. No. Please."

Yes. I'm sorry. I don't know what happened. I'm sorry.

"We'll fix this, okay? We'll fix this. I promise you."

Yes. I found you. I found you so you could fix this.

He turns away and looks over his shoulder. "Open the door," he barks at the naked man and the man of God.

"Uly," the God man says. "You know we can't do that. He's one of them."

"You can't," the naked man says. "I'm sorry, but you just can't. We need to stay here until help comes."

Uly starts for the door, but they block him. He screams at them, but they don't move. He threatens them, but they don't move. They yell at each other, but the God man and the other naked man say no, no, no. They're all quiet when a sharp sound echoes into the pool, bouncing off the tiles. It sounds like an explosion. It's followed by small pops.

"Gunfire," the God man says. "Praise Mary, mother of God, that's gunfire."

"Jake!"

I look back at Uly. He's pressing himself up against the glass. "I'm Jake," I tell him.

He chokes back a sob. "Yeah, you're Jake. Good. Listen to me. You can't stay out there. You hear me? You can't stay out there. Find a place to hide. They're coming!"

A and C rumble deep in their throats. The other infected snarl.

"You have to hide!" he screams at me.

"Uly," I grind out. "I'm Jake. I… I'm. Love. You."

He presses a big hand against the glass.

I raise my hand and press mine to his. It leaves a gory smear. "I know, baby," he cries. "I know! I love—"

I only see it at the last second. I was so distracted, I forgot about the other one. The one who hurt us all. I'd found Uly and forgotten.

But Dickless hasn't forgotten.

Stephen Fucking Dorian smashes into the opposite side of

the office, the glass shattering in on the three inside. The shards skewer his flesh, but he doesn't seem to notice, his full attention on Uly. The God man and the other naked man are knocked to the floor as Dickless drags himself over the partition.

"Uly," Dickless says, blood dripping from his mouth.

The sounds of gunfire grow louder even as the infected around me begin to move. It's chaos, and my only thoughts are of Uly. The infected press up against the office, shattering the glass on all sides. The door is knocked down. I hear God man and other naked man cry out as they are pulled out of the office, kicking and swinging.

I'm over the divide even before the last pieces of glass fall. Shards stick out of my hands and arms. Glass tears at my hips and knees. None of that matters. What matters is that I move faster than Dickless. Before he's over the partition completely, I'm standing in between him and Uly. Dickless pulls himself up and stands before me. His body looks completely destroyed. He's leaking from everywhere. And still he moves.

Stephen Dorian lurches forward, his arms outstretched, ignoring me completely. He's seen Uly, and that's all he wants. Uly tries to pull me away, but I snap my teeth at him over my shoulder and he stops. I ignore the terror I see in his eyes.

I turn back to Dickless and kick the hole where his dick used to be. My foot catches inside of him on bone, and I push as hard as I can. Dickless shrieks as he falls back. He hits the far partition and as he slumps over, I pick up a large shard of glass from the floor. I walk over to him and fist his hair, pulling his head back. I look down into his red eyes, knowing mine look the same.

"Uly," he mewls at me.

"Mine," I snarl before I slam the shard of glass up through the bottom of his jaw, slicing into his mouth and into his brain. His eyes bulge, and he thrashes along the floor, his body convulsing as his brain fires from its death throes. It's only a moment before he stills.

"Jake," a voice says from behind me. I hear it through the red. The rage.

I turn.

He stands there. My man. He's there, and he's watching me. Even as God man and other naked man battle behind him, even as the sound of gunfire grows louder, he watches me. I see the carnage stretched out along the pool. Two figures I know lie face down in the water. Two boys I promised to protect. I can't remember their names now. Only the way their hands felt in mine. They're dead. They don't move. They don't....

"Jake?" the man says, taking a step toward me.

I growl, and he stops.

Bite.

My man. He's... his name. What...?

I can't see in all this red. I can't see.

Tear.

It's in me now. Can't stop this. I want to break him. I want to hurt him. I want to destroy him until I can bathe in his skin.

"You," I tell him. My voice is a rasp. "You have..."

Kill.

"Jake," he says, his voice breaking. "Please."

Bite.

"You..." An image in my head of splitting his face.

Tear.

"You have to..." Peeling the skin from his back with my teeth.

Kill. Yes. Kill. Kill the man whose name I can't remember.

"I promise you, I'll fix this," he says and in my head, I hear him say I promise you, it'll be us.

I think it's too late for that. No time.

"You have to kuh," I croak. "You have to kuh-ill me. Kill."

He shakes his head wildly. His hands come up to touch me, but I gnash my teeth and he recoils.

"Can't stop," I manage to get out. "Gonna...hurt you. Can't stop it. Anger. Rage. Please." Because I don't want to hurt him, even though I do. And that part of me, the part holding back, is almost gone.

"I can't!" he cries at me. "Oh, Jesus, Jake, I can't do that to you! I can't!"

"Please," I mutter as another red wave washes over me. "Hurry."

"They're getting close!" the God man screams. "Help's almost here!"

Other naked man yells out incoherently. He sounds like he's in pain.

"You," I say to the man in front of me. "Please. You. They'll. Has to be. You."

"No, I won't," he cries. "I won't. There has to be some other way!" But he doesn't look like he believes it. Not anymore.

And I remember something about him. Something to tell him. It will take all I have. Once done, I'll be gone. I can't hold on much longer.

"Even if," I snarl at him. "Even if… we're mad. At each other." I start to shake. "Even if it's bad. Between us." I take a step toward him. Hands out. Like claws. "We don't. Leave it. That way." Bite him. Tear him. Kill him.

"We say goodbye," he whispers. "Like we mean it."

I remember now. Him.

My heart. My soul.

My Uly.

And then I descend into the red. It obliterates all I see.

ULY Z

If I was in the world's deepest, darkest cave, things could not be more confusing. Or more terrifying. Or more hopeless. I hear echoes of pop pop pop, but I can't say where they're coming from. I think maybe that's the sound of my mind coming apart, every synapse, every thread and fiber, ripping away from one another. I hear the shattering of glass, and I think it's my own heart breaking.

My hands are around Jake's head. It's an involuntary thing. My body has taken over in an act of self-preservation leaving me, Ulysses, a viewer to my own awful reality show. I can't comprehend what's happening here. This is my boyfriend, this is my Jake.

But it's not. This is Jake on Halloween. This is Jake with red contact lenses in his eyes and fake blood and flesh in his teeth to scare the neighborhood children.

Wake up, Jake. Be okay.

Even as my body fights with him, holding him away, all I really want to do is caress his head. I want to bring it to my chest and laugh, and say, "Damn, boy! You had me going there, you joker."

But Jake has never been much of a joker.

Pop pop pop. My neurons are firing at each other. Shooting each other dead.

Tobey and Johnny are yelling at me from some place far away. I can't make out what they're saying. It doesn't matter. Me and my baby are dancing. He hates this dance. I can tell. He's snarling. He doesn't want to be here. Not like this. Me neither, baby.

Still, I'm holding on tight. Holding his face back so I can look at him for just a little longer, because there's this awful sense of the inevitable. I want to hold onto him this tight forever.

Wake up, Jake.

POP POP POP.

The synapses fire again. Jake hears it too and jerks his head to the side, but my hands stay stationary, and SNAP.

Did you do that, Jake, or did I?

Suddenly there's a change that comes over him. His face loses its contortion, and he resembles something of himself again. Something of the lanky and lonely fella I fell in love with. He looks into my eyes as he goes limp, and I collapse to the floor with him.

The cave is bereft of light, and it is only me and Jake. He is in my arms, and I hear his last breath leave his body, and, with it, too, my will to live.

JAKE

Through the red, I see white.

It's so bright. And warm.

It blinds me, and I close my eyes.

For just a moment, it grows brighter. Then it fades.

I open my eyes.

I'm on a dirt road. The white light is the sun. The sky is blue. It's a beautiful day.

I'm surrounded by fields. Deep purple grapes hang heavy from dark vines. I can smell them, ripe and wild.

I walk down the road. I don't rush. Somehow, I know there's time.

The red tries to follow me as I walk. It tries to pull at my legs. My hands. My skin. It tells me that I need to bite. And tear. And kill.

I tell it no. It screams at me, but then it's lost in the fields. I don't look back.

Eventually, I see it. A stone house. A little villa, rising up at the end of the road.

A man stands in front. He sees me and raises his hand in greeting. The smile that splits his face blazes brighter than the sun.

"Hey," he calls out. "I've been waiting for you."

"I got held up," I tell him. A tear tracks its way down my cheek. I brush it away.

"Oh? That right?"

"Yes."

"The red?"

"Yes."

"Ain't that somethin'."

"Yeah."

He shakes his head. “It won’t get you here, Jake. It’ll be just us.”

“You promise?” Please promise. Please.

Uly takes my hand. It’s a calloused grip. Familiar. Like home.

“I promise, baby,” he says. “You ready?”

And I smile because it’s him. Because I’m ready. Because all I see is white.

Free. And clear.

ULY

"I promise."

I hear myself say these words, and it's as lucid as I've been in days. Months? Years? Who knows how long I've been out. There's light pouring in from an official looking window, and I'm on an official-feeling bed. And in front of the window sits Jake. Behind him is a field of golden barley and a big blue sky.

He's smiling at me, and it's beautiful.

But now this reality yanks the string, and a curtain is pulled over these things. Jake disappears as if he weren't never there, and my heart breaks again. Only this time I have to feel it. This time my body don't shut down. This time I'm all raw nerves. Everything hurts. There ain't even a window there anymore. It's just an off-white cinder block wall that makes me nauseous.

I feel a comforting hand being placed on my leg. At the end of the bed, in a hospital gown that barely fits him, sits Father Tobey. He lets me sob. The room is silent but for the machines around me droning on as if my world hasn't ended. The fluorescent bulbs overhead are harsh. The air has the taste of antiseptic. It's hard air. Too purified. Where's the character here?

"Where am I?" I ask. My voice is cracked and strained. The bed is not my own.

Tobey's face does not wear concern well. He's the most honest man I've ever known. I can totally tell, even in my tore up state, that something ain't right. There's a hardness and a hurt to his eyes I ain't seen before. Like he's been lied to.

"We're in a hospital," he says quietly. "I don't know which one. They won't tell any of us where we've been brought."

My head is slowly clearing. "We're prisoners?"

"They won't say as much, but…" He shrugs. He looks to the room door. There's a man there, a guard, it looks like, just outside. "They say it's for our own good. For the country's own good. They say they want to make certain we're not contaminated or infected. They got Johnny and a bunch others locked up in the psych ward. He was bitten, and they say they're keeping an eye on him. I think they're doing much more than that."

There's that look again, only now there's a hint of real anger.

"They say we might be infected," he repeats in a whisper more to himself than to me.

"By the red." I remember something from a dream.

"That's a word for it. Yeah." He leans forward, all hushed like, his bulk casting shadows. "But now you need to listen to me, Ulysses. You need to hear some things, and they aren't going to be easy. God in heaven knows they weren't easy for me. And when I'm through telling you everything, then we can decide what to do. Either way, if you're with me or no, I've got a lot of souls to save."

I swallow. If only uneasiness were that simply gotten rid of. Swallow it down and it's gone. It may taste like bile, but it's gone.

"After you passed out, after Jake died," (Ah, Jesus) "the SWAT team came and killed most of the other infected. Those they didn't kill, they captured. I'm guessing for study. Me and Johnny and the others in the gym who weren't dead were gassed and brought here. I woke up still naked, strapped to a table, every inch of me being inspected by probing fingers. Eventually, they let me up. I've spent the last week trying to get information on what happened, on what caused all this. Most folk are pretty tight-lipped, but there are a few still left with souls..."

"I thought it was rotten 'roids that were the cause," I say. "The ones Stephen Dorian was pushing."

"That's what we were all are meant to believe, but there's more to it. Much more."

"Shit, Tobey. You're making this sound like some Oliver Stone conspiracy."

He takes a deep breath and his grip on my leg tightens. "Uly, there are people in this world who hate us, who still hate our kind."

"Bodybuilders?"

"Homosexuals. Gay men and women. LGBT. The sexually fluid. Whatever you want to call us. These people, some of them in the highest echelons of government, driven by some misguided religious zeal, will go to any lengths to wipe us out once and for all."

He hushes for a moment as a nurse walks by the room. The guard is still there, unmoving.

He continues. "Stereotypically, gay men are known fitness junkies. Many of them, like you and me, have sought out chemical aids to help us achieve that unattainable physical perfection. These people in the government secretly released a toxin into some of these supplements, supplements popular among gay men, in hopes that it would start an epidemic. It worked."

I try to laugh. "Tobey, that's just silly. We're here. You and me. We ain't been infected."

"No. But we also haven't been released, and I don't think we will be anytime soon." He pauses like he's about to tell me I've got cancer. "Uly, there was a cure. There was a cure all along. The populace is being inoculated now, from what I've been told. The higher-ups thought that once the outbreak had occurred, and everyone infected had been rounded up or killed, once the public saw it was caused by homosexuals and had at last turned against all gay-kind, they could simply roll out the cure and everything would be hunky dory. But the infection – the red – spread much faster than they thought possible. Add to that, one of their own went ballistic and put the stuff in baby formulas and soft drinks and who knows what else. What we got on our hands is the end of the world."

My mind is unraveling again. I feel it snapping and popping. I see colors, most of them shades of red.

"This was an attempted genocide? They had a cure?" I can't believe it. "Jake," I whisper. I'm staring off into my own thoughts, and every one of them is centered around Jake.

"Apparently, the cure was released even as we were holed up in the gym. The apocalypse-makers realized then that things had gotten out of hand."

"Jake."

The word falls from my lips like a broken tooth. I'm clenching my jaws, my fists. My body is tight, every muscle ready to fight. I hear the heart monitor spike. I'm seeing all red now, but mine is a deeper shade than the infection. It's still filled with a hunger, only my hunger ain't for flesh.

"What do you want to do, Uly?" asks Tobey. I see his crucifix necklace is missing. They must have taken it from him when they brought him here. "Because I want to set things right, and I'm going to need help in doing that. I want to track the people down who did this, the people who lit humanity's spiritual road on fire, and I want to make them look deep into that fire. What do you want?"

I am shaking with a kind of rage I've never known before. These people, they've taken the most precious thing in the world from me.

What do I want?

Wants don't matter anymore. It's all about need now. I feel this is a brand new world, and this antiseptic air can do nothing to quell the acid I'm gonna spew all over it. I'm grinding my teeth and already preparing myself for one hell of a battle.

"I want Jake."

"Sorry, buddy. That can't happen."

"Then I want these apocalypse-makers to pay."

"Be ready then," Tobey says. "I'm getting us out of here. Me, you, and Johnny, and anyone else who wants to come along with us, and we're going to cause all kinds of trouble. God as my witness."

"We don't need no witnesses, Tobey," I say. "What we're gonna do best not be seen by anyone."

And I mean that. God? He's gonna piss his pants when he sees what I have planned. Me and Jake always went to bed with clear heads. Never go to bed angry at each other, that was our motto.

But what about angry for each other?

Because, Jake, from this point on, I ain't never going to be anything but angry. And it's all for you, baby. It's all for you.

THE END

Trademarks Acknowledgment

The author acknowledges the trademark status and trademark owners of the following places and items mentioned in this work of fiction.

Jockeys: Jockey International, Inc.
BMW: Bayerische Motoren Werke Aktiengesellschaft
Facebook: Facebook, Inc.
Tumblr: Tumblr, Inc.
Loony Tunes: Times Warner Entertainment Company, L.P.
Birkenstock: Birkenstock Orthopaedie GmbH & Co. KG
The National Enquirer: American Media Operations, Inc.
Glee: Twentieth Century Fox Film Corporation
The Walking Dead: AMC Film Holdings
Say Yes to the Dress: Discovery Communications, LLC
Lost: Disney-ABC Television Group
Jason and the Argonauts: SCI Games Limited
YouTube: Google, Inc.
Fluffernutters: Durkee-Mower
Dumpster: Dempster Systems, Inc.
MSNBC: MSNBC Cable LLC
CNN: Cable News Network, Inc.
The Discovery Channel: Cable Educational Network, Inc.
Oscar Mayer: Kraft Foods Group Brands LLC

Trademarks Acknowledgment

The author acknowledges the trademark status and trademark owners of the following places and items mentioned in this work of fiction:

7-Eleven: 7-Eleven, Inc.

Glock: Glock, Inc.

World of Warcraft: Blizzard Entertainment, Inc.

Stay-Puft Marshmallow Man: Hasbro, Inc.

Jack Daniel's: Jack Daniel's Properties, Inc.

Superman: DC Comics

Transformers: Hasbro, Inc.

RAV4: Toyota Jidosha Kabushiki Kaisha Speedy Gonzales: Warner Bros. Entertainment Inc.

Splinter Cell: Ubisoft, Inc.

Smith & Wesson: Smith & Wesson Corp.

Remington: RA Brands, L.L.C.

Trojan Latex Condoms: Carter-Wallace, Inc.

Cheerios: General Mills IP Holdings I, L.L.C.

FJ Cruiser: Toyota Jidosha Kabushiki Kaisha

GEOFFREY KNIGHT

From palace-hopping across the Rajasthan Desert to sleeping in train stations in Bulgaria, from spinning prayer-wheels in Kathmandu to exploring the skull-gated graveyards of the indigenous Balinese tribes, Geoffrey Knight has been a traveller ever since he could scrape together enough money to buy a plane ticket. Born in Melbourne but raised and educated in countless cities and towns across Australia, Geoffrey was a nomadic boy who grew into a nomadic gay writer. When he's not travelling the world, Geoffrey is travelling the world of his imagination—where the adventures, thrills and romance are limitless.

He currently owns his own advertising and design agency which he runs from his island home on the Great Barrier Reef, and can't wait to buy his next plane ticket—whether it's real or imaginary.

ALSO BY GEOFFREY KNIGHT

To Catch a Fox
The Pearl
The Boy from Brighton
Miami Moon: Vampire's Lair Book One
Cairo Curse: Vampire's Lair Book Two
The Cross of Sins
The Riddle of the Sands
The Curse of the Dragon God
Drive Shaft
Scott Sapphire and the Emerald Orchid
The Gentlemen's Parlor: Room of Chains
Hotel Pens
Harm's Way
On the Overgrown Path
Paperboy: Boys of Perfection
Boy Scout: Boys of Perfection
Under the Bridge
The Declaration
Together in Electric Dreams
Video Store Valentine
Nude Surfing
Why Straight Women Love Gay Romance

ETHAN DAY

I am a gay man living in Missouri...I can hear the gasps already!! How very un-chic of me, yes I know. It was here I was born and here I have stayed. The youngest of four children and the only boy, I've always suffered from an extravagant fantasy life. When I played with my Star Wars action figures as a child, I liked to make up my own stories. Naturally, Luke Skywalker and Han Solo were totally meant for each other, and Princess Leia made a bitchin' wise-cracking Fag Hag.

I managed to survive high school living in a small, racist town in Southeast Missouri and emerged unscathed, realizing life was too short to pretend to be anything other than who I was. It was very Lifetime Movie Network meets After School Special, I assure you.

After several stints in college, I signed up for a Creative Writing course, choosing the class because there were no tests. For once my scholastic laziness paid off, and I found an outlet for all the fantasies running amuck inside my head. It was love at first write, and I've been doing it off and on ever since.

ALSO BY ETHAN DAY

At Piper's Point
Self Preservation
To Catch A Fox
Dreaming of You
As You Are
Sno Ho
Life in Fusion
A Summit City Christmas
Anything for You
Second Time Lucky
A Token of Time
Love in La Terraza

ETHAN STONE

Ethan Stone has recently returned to Oregon after 12 years in Nevada and is working on re-growing his webbed feet. He has been obsessed with two things in his life: books and all things gay. After spending years trying to ignore the voices in his head, he finally decided to sit down and listen to them. What he discovered was a perfect union of his two obsessions.

ALSO BY ETHAN STONE

Past Tense
In The Flesh
Flesh & Blood
Blood and Tears
Wolf Moon
Being Taught
Starting Over
Bartender, PI
Subject 13

DANIEL A KAINE

Daniel was born and raised in the Land of Rain, more commonly known as England. Originally trained as a biology teacher, he was always unsure what to do with his life. That is, until he chanced upon a fanfiction site and began jotting down stories between his favourite anime characters. To this day, he still cringes at the mere memory of all that cheese.

In 2010, Daniel came across the NaNoWriMo boards and started work on his first original piece of fiction. Since then, his fingers have been unable to keep up with all the ideas and characters his brain keeps throwing at him.

ALSO BY DANIEL A KAINE

Dawn of Darkness (Daeva, #1)
Origin of Darkness (Daeva, #2)
Jacinto's Voyage

TJ KLUNE

When TJ Klune was eight, he picked up a pen and paper and began to write his first story (which turned out to be his own sweeping epic version of the video game Super Metroid—he didn't think the game ended very well and wanted to offer his own take on it. He never heard back from the video game company, much to his chagrin). Now, two decades later, the cast of characters in his head have only gotten louder, wondering why he has to go to work as a claims examiner for an insurance company during the day when he could just stay home and write.

He lives with a neurotic cat in the middle of the Sonoran Desert. It's hot there, but he doesn't mind. He dreams about one day standing at Stonehenge, just so he can say he did.

ALSO BY TJ KLUNE

Crack the Darkest Sky Wide Open

Bear, Otter, and the Kid

Who We Are

Elementally Evolved Book I: Burn

Tell Me It's Real

Into This River I Drown

John & Jackie

ERIC ARVIN

Eric Arvin resides in the same sleepy Indiana river town where he grew up. He graduated from Hanover College with a Bachelors in History. He has lived, for brief periods, in Italy and Australia. He has survived brain surgery and his own loud-mouthed personal demons. Eric is the author of Woke Up In A Strange Place, Subsurdity, Simple Men, Galley Proof, and various other sundry and not-so-sundry writings. He intends to live the rest of his days with tongue in cheek and eyes set to roam.

ALSO BY ERIC ARVIN

The Mingled Destinies Of Crocodiles & Men
Azrael and the Light Bringer
Crack the Darkest Sky Wide Open
SubSurdity: Vignettes from Jasper Lane
Suburbilicious: Vignettes from Jasper Lane
Simple Men
Another Enchanted April
Woke Up in a Strange Place
Galley Proof
SuburbaNights
Kid Christmas Rides Again
Man Falls Down
She's Come Undone
Miss Locks
Roids, Rumps & Revenge

Anthologies:
Slight Details & Random Events
Mr. Right Now
Uniform Appeal
Erotica Exotica: Tales of Sex, Magic, & the Supernatural

Comic Books:
The Blackbeard Legacy

CPSIA information can be obtained
at www.ICGtesting.com
Printed in the USA
FFOW02n2058031013
1953FF

9 781925 031423